P9-DVI-348

NEW YORK TIMES BESTSELLING AUTHOR

RaeAnne
Thayne

The Christmas
Ranch

&

A Cold Creek Holiday

HARLEQUIN® SPECIAL EDITION®

If you purchased this book without a cover you should be aware
that this book is stolen property. It was reported as "unsold and
destroyed" to the publisher, and neither the author nor the
publisher has received any payment for this "stripped book."

ISBN-13: 978-0-373-83806-6

The Christmas Ranch & A Cold Creek Holiday

Copyright © 2014 by Harlequin Books S.A.

The publisher acknowledges the copyright holder
of the individual works as follows:

The Christmas Ranch
Copyright © 2014 by RaeAnne Thayne

A Cold Creek Holiday
Copyright © 2009 by RaeAnne Thayne

Recycling programs
for this product may
not exist in your area.

All rights reserved. Except for use in any review, the reproduction
or utilization of this work in whole or in part in any form by any
electronic, mechanical or other means, now known or hereinafter
invented, including xerography, photocopying and recording, or in
any information storage or retrieval system, is forbidden without
the written permission of the publisher, Harlequin Enterprises Limited,
225 Duncan Mill Road, Don Mills, Ontario M3B 3K9, Canada.

This is a work of fiction. Names, characters, places and incidents are
either the product of the author's imagination or are used fictitiously, and
any resemblance to actual persons, living or dead, business establishments,
events or locales is entirely coincidental.

This edition published by arrangement with Harlequin Books S.A.

For questions and comments about the quality of this book, please contact us
at CustomerService@Harlequin.com.

® and TM are trademarks of Harlequin Enterprises Limited or its corporate
affiliates. Trademarks indicated with ® are registered in the United States Patent
and Trademark Office, the Canadian Intellectual Property Office and in other
countries.

Printed in U.S.A.

www.Harlequin.com

CONTENTS

THE CHRISTMAS RANCH   9

A COLD CREEK HOLIDAY   217

To my wonderful readers,
for sharing this amazing journey with me.
I consider myself extraordinarily blessed that
I can spend my days spinning stories with
happy endings, while hoping that my words might
make someone's day a little brighter. Thank you!

Dear Reader,

Those of you who have followed my Cowboys of Cold Creek series surely know how very much I love this time of year. Of the eleven Cold Creek books to date that span several different miniseries, six stories take place during the holiday season.

The Christmas Ranch is the first in an all-new Cowboys of Cold Creek trilogy featuring the Nichols sisters, Faith, Hope and Celeste. This time, all three stories will be centered around this most magical of seasons. The Nichols sisters have faced some tough times in their lives and are desperately in need of a few Christmas miracles...and a little holiday spirit along the way.

Wishing you and yours the happiest of holidays, filled with laughter, joy, family and books, of course.

All my very best,

RaeAnne

THE CHRISTMAS RANCH

Chapter 1

Though Thanksgiving was still a week and a half away, Christmas apparently had already rolled into Pine Gulch, Idaho, in all its snowy glory.

Hope Nichols looked through the windshield of the crappy old Ford pickup truck she had picked up for a cool thousand dollars at the edge of a Walmart parking lot in Salt Lake City. On a late afternoon in November the storefronts of the small but vibrant downtown area were alive with Christmas displays—trees, lights, toy soldiers, the occasional Nativity scene.

As she drove through more residential areas on her way to Cold Creek Canyon, she saw the holiday spirit extended here. Nearly every house had decorations of some sort, from inflatable snowmen to a full-fledged Santa and reindeer display.

She didn't mind even the kitschiest of decorations,

even though to some it might seem early in the season. Considering she hadn't spent the holidays at home for the past five years—or even in the country—she couldn't wait to embrace the whole Christmas thing this year.

She supposed that was a good thing, since her family's ranch was the holiday epicenter around here.

This area of eastern Idaho already had a few inches of snow—not much, but enough to cover everything in a lovely blanket of white and add a bit of seasonal charm to the town she remembered with such warmth and affection.

While Pine Gulch wasn't exactly her hometown, it was close enough. Hope and her sisters had lived here through most of their formative teen years, and she loved every inch of it, from the distant view of the west slope of the Tetons to the unassuming storefronts to the kind people who waved at her even now, though they couldn't possibly recognize her *or* the old blue pickup truck with the primer on the side.

She had come to be pretty fond of the old Ford. It didn't exactly drive like a dream, but it had four-wheel drive and all its working parts. Buying it had been an impulsive decision—she had intended to rent a car in Salt Lake City to drive home after she flew in from northern Africa, but had suddenly realized she would need transportation permanently now. This truck would get her through the gnarly winter season until she figured out what she would do next. After a decade of wandering, she was ready to stay put for a while.

Nerves in her stomach danced a little, as they had been doing throughout the five-hour drive from Salt

Lake, while she tried to anticipate the reaction she would find at the Star N Ranch when she showed up out of the blue with her duffel bag.

Aunt Mary would probably cry, her older sister, Faith, would be shocked and her younger sister, Celeste, would smile in that quiet way of hers.

The children would at least be happy to see her, though she knew Louisa and Barrett—and everyone else, for that matter—were still reeling from the death of their father. Travis, Faith's husband and childhood sweetheart, had died four months earlier in a tragic accident. Hope had come back for his funeral, of course, but her correspondence and video chats with her family since then had mostly been superficial.

It was time to come home. Past time. Since Travis's death, she couldn't shake the feeling that her family needed her, despite their protests that all was fine. The holiday season was insane at The Christmas Ranch and all hands were necessary, even when those hands belonged to the wanderer in the fam—

Whack!

With a noise as loud as a gunshot, something hit the passenger-side window of her truck, jerking her thoughts back to the present. In the space of a heartbeat, the window shattered as Hope slammed on the brakes, ducked and instinctively yelled a curse word her mostly Berber students taught her.

What the…?

Who would be shooting at her? For a crazy moment, she was a terrified, desperate thirteen-year-old girl again, heart pounding, adrenaline pulsing. She didn't have flashbacks very often, but when she did, they could roll over her like a bulldozer.

She drew in a breath, forcing away the panic. This was Pine Gulch. There were no snipers here, no rebel factions. Nobody would be shooting at her. She glanced at the window. Because the truck was older, it didn't have tempered glass and the entire window had shattered. All she found was a melting pile of snow amid the shattered glass—and a healthy-sized rock.

Not a gunshot, then. A dirty trick. Tentatively, she raised her head to look around. At first, she didn't see anything, until a flurry of movement on that side of the vehicle caught her gaze.

A young boy stood just off the road looking shocked and not a little guilty.

Hope pulled over to the side of the road then jumped out of the driver's side and headed for him.

The kid stared at her, eyes wide. He froze for only a moment as she approached, then whirled around and took off at top speed across the snow-covered lawn just as a man walked around the side of the house with a couple of snow shovels in hand.

"You're in luck, kid," he called. "I found shovels for each of us."

The man's voice trailed off as the boy raced behind him, using what were quite impressive muscles as a shield, as if he thought Hope was going to start hurling snowball-covered rocks right back at him.

"Hey. Come back here. Where do you think you're going, young man?" she demanded sternly in her best don't-mess-with-me teacher's voice.

The big man frowned and set the snow shovels blade-down on the sidewalk. "Excuse me, lady. What the he— er, heck is your problem?"

She told herself her heart was racing only from adrenaline at her window suddenly shattering. It had nothing to do with this large, muscled, *gorgeous* man with short dark hair and remarkable hazel eyes. Somehow he seemed even bigger as he bristled at her, overpowering and male.

She, however, had gone against bullies far worse than some small-town cowboy with a juvenile delinquent and an attitude.

She pointed to the pickup truck, engine still running, and the shattered passenger window.

"Your son here is the problem—or more accurately, the rock he just tossed through my window. I could have been seriously hurt. It's a miracle I didn't run off the road."

"I'm not his son," the kid snapped. He looked angry and belligerent at the very idea.

She supposed it was only natural her mind immediately went to kidnapping, especially after the sudden flashback.

"You're not?"

"I'm his uncle," Sexy Dude said, with a frustrated look at the boy. "Did you see him throw it? I'm sure you must be mistaken. Joey is not the kind of kid who would throw a rock at a moving vehicle—especially a *stranger's* moving vehicle."

Was he trying to convince her or himself? His words rang a little hollow, making her wonder if Joey was *exactly* the kind of kid who would vandalize a vehicle, whether he knew the owners or not.

"Then explain to me why my window is shattered and why he took off the moment I stopped my truck to talk to him about it."

The guy frowned. "Joe. Tell the nice lady you didn't throw a rock at her window."

The boy lifted his chin obstinately but after meeting her gaze for just a moment, he looked down at his snowboots. "I didn't throw a rock," he insisted, then added in a muffled sort of aside, "It was a snowball."

"A snowball with a rock inside it," she retorted.

He looked up and gave his uncle an imploring look. "It was a accident. I didn't mean to, Uncle Rafe. I swear."

"Joey." The uncle said the single name with a defeated kind of frustration, making her wonder what the situation was between the two of them. Where were the boy's parents?

"It was a accident," he repeated. Whether it was genuine or an act, Joey now sounded like he was going to cry.

"*An* accident," she corrected.

"Whatever," the boy said.

"Using proper English is important when you wish to convey your point." Yes, she sounded prim but six years of combined experience in the Peace Corps and teaching English across the globe had ingrained habits that were probably going to be tough to break.

"Okay. It was *an* accident," he spoke with such dramatic exaggeration that she almost smiled, until she remembered the crisis at hand.

"That's better, but I'm still not sure I believe you. I think you were aiming right at my truck."

"I didn't mean to break the window. I wasn't even trying to hit the window, I was trying to hit the hubcap. My friend Samantha and me are playing a game and we get five points for every hubcap."

"My friend Samantha and I," she said. She couldn't seem to help herself, even though she noticed the correction only made the uncle glower harder, making him look big and rough-edged and even more dangerous.

She suddenly felt small and not nearly as tough as she liked to think.

"Can we deep-six the English lessons, lady, and focus on your window?"

She was nervous, she suddenly realized. Was it because of his military haircut or the muscles or because he was so great-looking? She pushed away the uneasiness and forced herself to concentrate on the real issue.

"Sorry. Reflex. I'll stop now. I've been teaching English in northern Africa the past few years and was in the Peace Corps before that. I'm just returning to Pine Gulch to visit my family. They live in Cold Creek Canyon and…"

Her voice trailed off. He didn't care about that. She cleared her throat. "Right. My window. It was a very dangerous thing you did, young man. Tell your friend Samantha it's a bad idea to throw snowballs at cars, whether the snowballs have rocks in them or not. You could distract the driver and someone could easily get hurt—maybe even you."

The boy gave her a pugnacious sort of look but said nothing until his uncle nudged him.

"Tell the nice lady you're sorry."

"I don't think she's very nice," he grumbled.

Again, Hope almost smiled, until she met the man's gaze and found him looking extremely unamused by the entire situation.

Humorless jerk.

"Too bad." The boy's uncle—Rafe, was it?—frowned at him. "Tell her you're sorry anyway."

Joey looked down at the snow-covered ground again and then finally met her gaze. "I'm sorry I hit your window and not your hubcap. We don't get any points for hitting windows."

As apologies went, it was a little weak but she would still take it. She was suddenly weary of the whole situation and wanted to continue on toward the Star N and her family.

"In your defense, that window had a crack in it anyway. It probably wouldn't have shattered if it hadn't been for that."

"You're not going to be throwing any snowballs at cars again," the boy's uncle said sternly. "And you're going to tell Samantha not to do it either, right?"

"But I was winning the contest! She was gonna give me her new Darth Vader LEGO minifig if I won and I was gonna give her my Green Ninja minifig if *she* won."

"Too bad. The lady is right. It's dangerous. Look at the trouble you've already caused!"

The boy didn't look happy about it but he finally shrugged. "Fine."

"We'll pay for the window replacement, of course. If you get an estimate, you can have them send the bill to me here. Rafe Santiago. I'll warn you that I'm only going to be in town for another few weeks, though."

The name seemed to strike a chord deep in her subconscious. Had they met before? Something about his hazel eyes—striking against his burnished skin—reminded her of someone but she couldn't seem to pin down who or where.

She didn't remember any Santiagos living in this little house before. From what she remembered of Hope's Crossing, this had always been a rental house, often used short-term for seasonal workers and such.

"I will do that." She held out her hand, deciding there was no reason they couldn't leave on good terms. "I'm Hope Nichols. You can find me at The Christmas Ranch, in Cold Creek Canyon."

At her words, something sparked in those hazel eyes but she couldn't identify it.

"Nichols?" he said sharply.

"Yes."

Perhaps he knew her sisters, though Faith went by her married name now, Dustin, and she couldn't imagine quiet, introverted Celeste having much to do with a roughand-tumble man like him. Maybe Joey had caused trouble at the library where Celeste worked. She could believe that—though, okay, that might be a snap judgment.

"Can I go inside?" Joey asked. "Snow got in my boots and now my feet are *freezing*. I need to dump it out."

"Yeah. Go ahead. Dump the snow off on the porch, not inside."

Joey raced off and after a moment, Rafe Santiago— *why* was that name so familiar?—turned back to her.

"I'm sorry about my nephew," he said, rather stiffly. "He's had a...rough time of it the past few weeks."

She wondered what had happened, but when he didn't volunteer any further details, she accepted it was none of her business. "I'm sorry if I came down too hard."

"I didn't say you did. Whatever he's been through isn't an excuse anyway. I'll talk to him about this stupid contest and make sure he and his friend both realize it's not a good idea."

He gave her another searching look and she had the strangest feeling he wanted to say something else. When the silence stretched between them, a little too long to be comfortable, she decided she couldn't wait around for him to speak.

"I should go. My family is waiting for me. I'll be in touch, Mr. Santiago."

"Rafe," he said gruffly. Was that his normal speaking voice or did she just bring out the rough edges? she wondered.

"Rafe. Nice to meet you, even under the circumstances."

She hurried back to her pickup truck and continued on toward home, though she couldn't shake the odd feeling that something momentous had just happened.

Rafe watched the taillights recede into the early evening gloom until she turned a corner and disappeared. Even then, he couldn't seem to make himself move, still reeling from the random encounter.

Hope Nichols.

Son of a bi…gun.

He checked the epithet. He was trying not to swear, even in his head. Joey didn't need any more bad habits. If Rafe didn't *think* the words, he wouldn't *speak* them. It was a logical theory but after twenty years in the navy, seventeen of those as a SEAL, cleaning up his language for the sake of a seven-year-old boy with an enormous chip on his shoulder was harder than he ever would have imagined.

He didn't have a choice. Like it or not—and he sure as he—er, heck, *didn't*—Joey was his responsibility now.

Hope Nichols. What were the odds?

He knew she and her sisters had come to live in Pine Gulch, Idaho, *after*. He might have been a green-as-alfalfa rookie who had never been on an actual mission before that tense December day seventeen years ago, but keeping track of the Nichols girls had been a point of honor.

They had an aunt and uncle here who had taken them in. He remembered being grateful for that, at least that they had *someone*. He had received a letter from the oldest, he remembered, a few months afterward…

The girl couldn't have been more than fourteen or fifteen but she had written to him like a polite old lady. He had memorized the damn—er, darn—thing.

Dear Special Warfare Operator Santiago,
Thank you for participating in rescuing us from Juan Pablo and his rebel group. You and the other men in your navy SEAL platoon risked your lives to save us. If not for you, we might still be in that awful camp. You are true American heroes. My sisters and I will never forget what you have done for us.
Sincerely, Faith Marie Nichols
PS: It is nobody's fault that our father died. We don't blame anyone and know you tried your best to save us all.

The carefully written letter had been sweetly horrible and he had carried it around in his wallet for years to remind him that navy SEALs couldn't afford even the smallest error in judgment.

Hope—the annoying grammarian with the ancient pickup truck—had been the middle daughter, he remembered, all tangled blond hair and big, frightened blue eyes. She had screamed when her father had been shot, and the echo of that terrified, despairing scream had haunted him for a long, long time.

He let out a breath. And now she was here, just a few miles away from him, and he would have to interact with her at least one more time.

Had she recognized him today? He couldn't be sure. She had given him a strange look a few times, as if she thought she knew him, but she hadn't said anything.

Why hadn't he identified himself and explained their old history?

He wasn't sure—maybe because the opportunity hadn't really come up. How does a guy say, *Hey, I know this is a strange coincidence but I was there the day your family was rescued from terrorists nearly two decades ago. Oh, and by the way, my inexperience contributed to your father's death. Sorry about that and your broken window, too.*

He let out a breath, marveling again at the strange, twisting corkscrews of fate that had brought him to Pine Gulch, in such proximity to the Nichols sisters. When Cami called him in tears and explained that she had been arrested and that Joey had gone into emergency foster care, he had known immediately he had to help his nephew, whatever it took.

The fact that his path would bring him to Pine Gulch, where the Nichols sisters had landed after the tragedy of that Christmas day so long ago, hadn't really hit home until he drove into the city limits two weeks ago.

In the midst of trying to settle into a routine with his nephew, he had wondered during those two weeks whether they were still in town and if he should try to contact any of them—and now that decision had been taken out of his hands by Hope.

That seemed to be a common theme to his life the past month—being in a position that left him few choices.

His life had changed dramatically in the past month. He had left the only career he had ever known in order to take on the responsibility for a troubled seven-year-old who wanted nothing to do with him.

He was determined to do his best for Joey. The poor kid hadn't been given very many breaks in life.

Rafe still couldn't quite believe how far his sister had fallen, from an honor student in high school to being tangled up with a man who had seduced her into coming to Idaho and had then dragged her into a life of drugs and crime.

He had done his best for his sister, had joined the navy the day he turned eighteen so he could support her and had sent money for her care to their aunt, who had taken her in—but apparently that effort hadn't been enough to provide the future he always wanted for her.

He had failed with Cami. Now he had to see if he could do a better job with her son.

He opened the door to the short-term rental he had found in Pine Gulch after Cami begged him to let Joey stay here until she was sentenced, which at this point was only a few weeks away.

Joey was sitting on the bench in the foyer with his

boots and coat still on, as if he were bracing himself for the punishment he fully expected.

Rafe's heart, grizzled and tough from years of combat, couldn't help but soften just a little at his forlorn posture and expression.

"I didn't mean to break the mean lady's window," his nephew said again, his voice small.

The kid needed consequences in order to learn how his choices could have impact in others' lives. Rafe knew that, but sometimes this parenting thing sucked big-time when what he really wanted was to gather him close and tell him everything would be okay.

"You might not have meant to cause harm, but you saw what happened. You messed up, kid."

The irony of those words seemed to reach out and grab him by the throat. Joey's actions might have cost Hope Nichols a car window, something that easily could be replaced.

His actions toward her and her sisters had far more long-reaching consequences.

If his reflexes had been half a second faster, he could have taken out that jacked-up, trigger-happy rebel before the bastard squeezed off the shot that took her father forever.

"Will I have to pay for the window?" Joey asked. "I have eight dollars in my piggy bank. Will it be more than that?"

"We'll figure it out. Maybe I'll pay her and then you can work to pay me back."

The boy looked out the window. "I can shovel the snow."

"Hate to break it to you, but I was going to make you do that anyway. That's going to be one of your regular chores, helping me with that. We'll have to figure out how to pay back Ms. Nichols some other way."

As for the debt *he* owed her, Rafe knew there was no way he could repay her or her sisters.

Chapter 2

Something was very, very wrong.

Hope wanted to think she was only upset from the encounter with Rafe Santiago and his very cute but troublesome nephew. Perhaps she was overwrought as a natural by-product from first having her window shattered in such a shocking manner and then coming face-to-face with a big, dangerous-looking man.

But as she approached the Star N and especially The Christmas Ranch—her family's holiday-themed attraction that covered fifteen acres of the cattle ranch—she couldn't seem to shake the edgy, unsettled feeling.

Where was everyone? As she approached, she could see the parking lot in front of the charming and rustic St. Nicholas Lodge and it was completely empty, which made absolutely no sense.

There should at least be a maintenance crew getting

ready for the season. It usually took several weeks before opening day—which traditionally happened with a grand lighting ceremony at dusk on the Friday after Thanksgiving—to spruce things up, touch up the paint, repair any damage done throughout the summer.

Instead, the place looked like a ghost town. All it needed were a few tumbleweeds blowing through to complete the picture.

Maybe everybody had simply gone home for the day, but she suddenly realized the reindeer enclosure was missing slats *and* reindeer, nor did it look like any of the colored lights had been hung on the fence or in the shrubs lining the road.

She drove farther down the road with cold air whistling in from the shattered window. As she approached the parking lot entrance, her stomach suddenly dropped and she hit the brakes.

A banner obscured the sign that usually read Welcome to The Christmas Ranch, where your holiday dreams come true.

In huge red letters on a white background, it read simply, Closed Indefinitely.

Closed. Indefinitely.

Shock rocketed through her faster than a speeding sleigh. Impossible! She couldn't believe it. Surely her sisters wouldn't have closed down The Christmas Ranch without telling her! This was a tradition, a gift from the Nichols family to the rest of Pine Gulch and this entire area of southeastern Idaho.

Families came from miles around to partake of the holiday spirit. All of it. The horse-drawn sleigh rides. The sledding hill. Visits with Santa Claus. The reindeer herd in the petting zoo and the gift shop filled with local handicrafts and the huge collection of Nativities, many of which had been sent from around the world by her parents as they traveled around as missionaries.

Even the cheesy little animatronic Christmas village was a family favorite.

It was a place of magic and wonder, a little piece of holiday spirit for the entire community to enjoy.

How could her sisters and Auntie Mary close it, indefinitely or otherwise?

And how many shocks in the space of an hour could one woman endure? Her hands shook on the steering wheel as she drove the remaining three hundred feet to the driveway leading to the ranch house.

She drove up the winding road with her heart pounding. At the house—a rambling white two-story farmhouse with a wide front porch—she parked and stomped up the steps.

Though she was tempted to dramatically storm inside—she had spent all her teen years in this house, after all, and still considered it her own—she forced herself to stop at the front door and knock.

Though Aunt Mary still lived here with Faith, it was really her sister's house now and Hope didn't feel she had the right to just barge in. Living in other cultures most of her life, barring the years she spent here, had given her a healthy respect for others' personal space.

Nobody answered for a few moments. She was about to pound harder when the door suddenly opened. Instead of Faith or Auntie Mary, her nephew, Barrett, stood on the other side of the door.

At the sight of her, his darling face lit up with a joy that seemed to soothe all the ragged, battered edges of her spirit and made the whole long journey worthwhile.

"Aunt Hope! What are you doing here? I didn't even know you were coming!"

"I'm sure it will be a big surprise to everybody," she answered, a little grimly.

"The best, best, *best* kind," her sweetly loyal nephew claimed as he wrapped his arms around her waist. She hugged him, feeling better already—even as she thought of the last little boy she had encountered, who hadn't been nearly so enthusiastic about her presence.

"Oh, I missed you," he exclaimed.

"I missed you, too, potato bug."

Barrett was seven and most of their relationship had developed via email and the occasional video chat when the vast time zone conflicts could be worked out.

She hadn't received nearly enough of these hugs in her lifetime, she suddenly decided, with an almost painful aching for family and home.

"Who's at the door, Barrett?" she heard her sister call from the kitchen.

"Don't tell her," Hope said, managing a grin even though some part of her was still annoyed with her sister.

"Um, nobody," he answered back, obviously not good at coming up with fibs on the fly.

"How can it be nobody?" her older sister said, and Hope could almost hear the frown in her voice.

Holding a finger to her mouth for Barrett, she headed down the hall toward the kitchen where her sister's voice originated.

In the doorway, she caught a glimpse of Faith at the work island in the center of what was really command central of the house. Her sister's dark hair was held back in a messy ponytail and she looked tired, with deep circles under her eyes and lines of strain bracketing her mouth.

More of Hope's half-formed displeasure at her sister slipped away. Her sister had lost so much—everything!—and Hope hadn't been here for her.

"Seriously, Barrett. Who was at the door? Was it UPS again, delivering something for Auntie Mary?"

The boy giggled, a sweet, pure sound that drew Faith's attention from the vegetables she was cutting at the island. She looked up and her jaw sagged.

"Hope! What in the world?"

Hope mustered a smile. "Surprise."

Her sister wiped her hands on a dish towel and came toward her. Faith had lost weight. Hope was struck again by how fragile and slight she seemed, as if a sharp gust of wind from a December storm would blow her clear out to the barn.

Those lines around her mouth had been etched by pain, she suddenly realized. Her sister had lost the love her life, her childhood sweetheart, a mere four months earlier in a tragic accident and had barely had time to grieve. She would be reeling from the loss of her husband for a long time.

Travis Dustin had been killed after he had rolled an all-terrain vehicle while rounding up cattle in the mountains. He hadn't been wearing a helmet and had been killed instantly, leaving behind Faith and their two children.

Hope still couldn't believe he was gone. If she closed her eyes, she could almost picture him the last time she saw him alive, nearly two years earlier when she had been able to come home briefly between assignments in time for New Year's Eve. He had been a dear friend as well as a beloved brother-in-law and his loss had hit her hard.

She had been here four months earlier for his funeral but had only been able to stay a few days. It hadn't been long enough.

Hope crossed to her sister and hugged her hard, wishing she could absorb some of her pain.

They were extremely close to each other and to Celeste, their sibling relationship forged through their unorthodox upbringing and the tragedy that had changed all of them so long ago.

Faith rested her cheek against Hope's. "Oh, what a wonderful surprise. I thought you were going on to Nepal after you finished your teaching stint in Morocco."

"That was the plan, but I decided to take a break for a few months to figure things out. I thought maybe, I don't know, I could take a rest from traveling. Maybe stay and help you out around here for a while."

"Oh. It will be so wonderful to have you here longer than a few days!"

"I thought I could stay through the holidays, if you'll have me."

While Faith smiled at her with apparent delight, Hope didn't miss the sudden wariness in her gaze. "This is your home, too. You're always welcome here, you know that."

She paused and gave Hope a searching look. "I guess you must have seen the sign at the Ranch on the way in."

Hope tried to summon a little of the anger that had accompanied her on the short drive to the ranchhouse but it was impossible to dredge up more than a little kernel at this sister she had always loved and admired for her courage, her sweetness, her practicality—all the things Hope didn't have.

Her sister had suffered great pain and somehow continued to trudge on, though Hope had no idea how she was managing it.

"I saw the sign. I don't understand what it means."

"It means we're not opening The Christmas Ranch this year," Barrett announced, sounding just as disgruntled as Hope had been when she first spotted the empty parking lot.

She placed a hand on his shoulder. "That's what I suspected when I saw the sign. I still can't quite believe it. Why didn't you tell me?"

Faith's mouth compressed into a tight line. "I would have told you eventually, if you had asked how things were going with The Christmas Ranch, but I didn't see any point in stirring the pot when you weren't here anyway."

She couldn't blame her sister for that, she supposed. Her family had no reason to believe this year would be any different from the last handful, when she hadn't been able to manage coming home for longer than a day or two for a quick visit, if that.

"What gives, though? Why are we 'Closed Indefinitely'?"

Her sister pounded a little harder on the dough she was working on the table. "Auntie Mary and I decided to take a break this year while we figure things out."

She gave a meaningful look to her son. "And speaking of Mary—Barrett, go find her. I think she went into her room earlier to do some knitting."

"You mean to take a nap," he said with a grin as he headed out of the room.

"A nap?" she asked as soon as her nephew was out of earshot. The idea of her vibrant aunt taking a nap was as foreign to her as she imagined Couscous Friday—a Moroccan cultural tradition—would be to her family.

"She takes a nap just about every afternoon. She starts in with watching a television show and usually dozes off in the middle of it for a few minutes. Don't forget, she's in her seventies and not as energetic as she used to be, especially since Uncle Claude died."

Hope hated thinking of her aunt slowing down. Mary was her aunt by marriage, wed to the girls' father's oldest brother. She and her husband had become the only thing they had to parents after their parents' tragic deaths only a few months apart.

"You're telling me she wants to close the ranch, too?"

"Celeste voted, too. It was a mutual decision. We didn't have much of a choice."

"But people around here love it. It's as much a tradition as the giant Christmas tree in the town square and the ice rink on the tennis courts behind city hall."

"You think I don't know how much people love the place? I completely get it. This is my home, remember? You haven't been around since you graduated from high school and left for your study abroad in Europe."

Though she didn't think her sister meant the words as a barb, they stuck sharply anyway.

"But the Ranch is hemorrhaging money, sis. Money we just don't have. Last year it was the stupid motor on the rope tow that had to be replaced, the year before that the roof on St. Nicholas lodge. The liability insurance alone is killing us."

Hope frowned. "But Travis loved it. You know he did. Uncle Claude loved it! It was his life's work. He loved everything about Christmas and found the greatest delight in his life by helping everyone else celebrate the holidays. How can you just close the door on all that tradition?"

"Uncle Claude is gone now. So is *Tr-Travis*." Her voice wobbled a little on her husband's name and Hope felt small and selfish for pushing her about The Christmas Ranch.

"It's just me, Mary and Celeste—and Mary isn't as young as she used to be and Celeste works fifty-hours a week at the library in town. That leaves mostly me and it's all I can do to keep the cattle part of the Star N functioning without Travis. We wouldn't have survived harvest and round-up if Chase Brannon hadn't stepped in to help us and sent a couple of his guys on semipermanent loan, but he's got his own ranch to run."

"I'm here now. I can help. I *want* to help."

"For how long this time?"

The question was a legitimate one. Hope didn't know how to answer. She had finished her teaching obligation in Morocco and had been actively looking around for another one, but at this point her plans were nebulous at best.

"I don't have anything scheduled. I can stay through the holidays. Let me run The Christmas Ranch. You can focus on the cattle side of things at the Star N and I'll take care of everything on the holiday side."

If she thought her sister would jump at the chance for the help, she would have been disappointed. Faith only shook her head. "You don't know what you're saying. It's more than just wearing an elf costume and taking tickets. You haven't been here during the season in years, not since Claude expanded the operations. You've got no experience."

"Except for the five years I spent helping out when I was a kid, when we all pitched in. Those were magical times, Faith."

Her sister's expression indicated she didn't particularly agree. Faith had never much liked the Christmas village, Hope suddenly remembered.

When they had come to Cold Creek Canyon and the Star N to live with Mary and Claude so long ago, they had all been traumatized and heartbroken. Three lost young girls.

Their father had died on Christmas day. The next year, Claude had put them all to work in the concessions stand at what was then only the reindeer petting zoo and the Christmas village with the moving figures. Her older sister had been reluctant to help, and never really wanted much of anything to do with it. She had only agreed after Claude had continued to hint how much he needed her help, in that gentle way of his.

No wonder she had been so quick to close the attraction at the first opportunity.

"Well, *I* thought they were magical times. I love The Christmas Ranch. I can make a success of it, I swear."

"You have no idea what you're talking about. Thanksgiving is next week. There's simply no time to get everything ready in a week and a half!"

She didn't know why this was so important to her but she couldn't bear the idea of no Christmas Ranch. Only at this very moment did she realize how much she had been looking forward to it this year.

She opened her mouth to say so but a flurry of movement in the doorway distracted her. Her aunt appeared, with Barrett close behind.

Her heart squeezed when she saw that it did, indeed, look as if Mary had been napping. The graying, old-fashioned bun she always wore was lopsided and her eyes were still a little bleary. Still, they lit up when they saw her.

"Oh, Hope, my darling! What a wonderful surprise!"

Mary opened her plump arms and Hope sagged into them. This. She hadn't realized how very much she needed the steady love of her family until right this moment.

She could smell the flowery, powdery scent of her aunt's White Shoulders perfume and it brought back a flood of memories.

"Why didn't you call us, my dear?" Mary asked. "Someone could have driven to the airport to pick you up. Even one of Chase's ranch hands. Did you fly into Jackson Hole or Idaho Falls?"

"I actually flew into Salt Lake City last night and bought a pickup truck near a hotel by the airport. I figured I would need some kind of four-wheel-drive transportation while I was here anyway and I didn't know if you had any extra vehicles around the ranch."

"We could have found something for you, I'm sure. But what's done is done."

Hope didn't mention the noisy engine or the fact that it now was missing most of the passenger-side window.

She made a mental note to find some plastic she could tape up to keep the elements out until she could take it somewhere in town to have the window replaced.

"How long are you staying?"

"I haven't decided yet. Fae and I were just talking

about that. What would you say if I told you I would like to run The Christmas Ranch this year?"

For just an instant, shock and delight flashed in her aunt's warm brown eyes, then Mary glanced at Faith. Her expression quickly shifted. "Oh. Oh, my. I'm not sure that's a good idea. I don't think you have any idea how much work it is, honey."

She had lived on her own all over the world. She could do hard things—and maybe it was time her family accepted that.

"I know it will be, but I can handle it, I promise. You won't even have to lift a finger. I'll do all of it."

"But, my dear. The reindeer. The sleigh rides. It's too much work for you."

The reality *was* daunting. A tiny little voice of doubt whispered that she didn't have the first idea what she was getting into but Hope pressed it down. This was suddenly of vital importance to her. She *had* to open the ranch. It was a matter of family pride—and belief in herself, too.

"I'll figure something out. I might not be able to do everything, but even a limited opening is better than nothing. Please. Just let me do this. It's important to me. I have such wonderful memories of The Christmas Ranch, just like everyone in town who has been coming here for years."

Aunt Mary was plainly wavering—and in the long run, the Star N was still her ranch and she ought to have final say. Her aunt glanced at Faith, who was pounding the pizza dough so hard it would be a miracle if she didn't pummel all the gluten right out of it.

"The decision to cancel the whole season *was* a huge disappointment, and not just to me," Mary admitted.

"You wouldn't believe the comments I've been getting in town."

Hope decided to press her advantage. "It's our civic duty to keep it open this year, don't you agree? Why, it wouldn't be the holidays in Pine Gulch without The Christmas Ranch."

"Don't go overboard," Faith muttered.

"Please. Just give me the chance. I won't let you down."

She could see her sister was wavering. Faith let out a deep sigh just as her niece Louisa skipped into the kitchen.

"Mom, there's a strange pickup in the driveway. It's kind of junky," she said, then stopped when she spotted Hope.

"Aunt Hope! Hi!"

"That's my junky pickup in the driveway. I'll move it."

"What are you doing here?" her niece asked as she gave her a big hug.

"Guess what? She's going to run The Christmas Ranch!" Barrett exclaimed. "We're going to open after all!"

"Really?" Louisa exclaimed. "Oh, that would be wonderful!"

"We haven't decided that yet," Faith said firmly. "Children, go wash up for dinner and then you can set the table. I'm about to throw the pizza in. Aunt Celeste will be home any minute and we can eat."

"I'm so glad you're home," Louisa said with another hug.

At least a *few* members of her family were happy to see her. Celeste wasn't here yet but she and her younger sister had always been close—of course, she thought she and *Faith* were close, yet her older sister fairly radiated disapproval and frustration.

As soon as the children left the room, Hope suddenly realized her sister wasn't just frustrated. She was angry.

Hope again felt small and selfish. If she were in Faith's shoes, she would be furious, too. Her sister was doing her best to keep the family together. She was managing the ranch, taking care of her children, trying to keep everything running while still reeling from her husband's death.

Now Hope came in and expected to shake everything up and do things her way.

"There is no money, Hope. Do you not get that? You'll have virtually *no* operating budget. You'll barely make enough to pay the salaries for Santa Claus and anybody you hire to work in the gift shop."

Oh. Right. How was she going to find people to help her in only nine days?

Mary could help line her up with the seasonal employees who had worked at the Ranch in previous years. Surely a few of them might still be looking for work.

"You said it's been hemorrhaging money. Is it really that bad?"

"People just aren't coming to holiday attractions like this one much anymore. The only reason we kept it going was because Uncle Claude loved it so and Travis wanted to honor his memory."

Her sister's words were sobering.

"You've always been enthusiastic about things, Hope. It's one of the best things about you. You jump right in and try to fix things. But you can't fix this. The Christmas Ranch is a losing proposition. We just can't afford it anymore. There's no money. We're holding on by our fingernails as it is. If things don't pick up, we're going to have to sell off part of the cattle herd and possibly some of the pasture land along the creek. Wade Dalton made us a more than fair offer and Mary and I are seriously considering it."

"Oh, Faith. I'm sorry. I didn't know."

"I didn't know the whole picture either, until after Travis died. He was very good at putting on a cheerful face."

Faith was quiet for a moment, then walked around the island. "I should probably tell you, I had a very respectable offer for the reindeer. A guy with a petting zoo in Pocatello. We've talked about it and were planning to take that, too. He was interested in taking them before the holidays."

The small herd of reindeer had been part of the ranch as long as she had lived here. They were part of the family, as far as Hope was concerned.

"Sell the reindeer?"

"I know," Mary piped in. "It breaks my heart too."

"Did you sign any papers?"

"No, but..."

"Don't. Please, Faith. Wait until after Christmas. Give me this season to prove I can turn things around. I know I can do it. I am going to make money with The Christmas Ranch this year, enough to tide the Star N over the rest of the year. You'll see."

Her sister sighed. "You have no idea what you're up against."

"Maybe not, but that could be a good thing, right? Ignorance is bliss, and all that."

"Oh, Hope. You always could talk me into anything."

Mary gave a short laugh. "That's my girls!"

Relief and excitement and no small amount of nerves washed over Hope like an avalanche. "You won't be sorry. This is going to be our best year ever, I promise."

She had no idea how she would keep that promise but she intended to try.

Chapter 3

He was so not cut out for this.

Rafe tried to scrape up the burned bits of the red sauce from the bottom of the saucepan with a wooden spoon but that only mixed the blackened remains into the rest of the mix.

Apparently he would now have to open a bottle of store-bought spaghetti sauce, which is what he should have done in the first place instead of hunting down ingredients then measuring, pouring and mixing for the past fifteen minutes.

Joey wouldn't care if his spaghetti sauce came from a jar. He probably wouldn't even be able to taste the difference.

Rafe headed to the sink and poured the concoction down the sink. There went twenty minutes of his life he wouldn't get back.

Rafe didn't mind cooking. He really didn't. Okay, he didn't mind *grilling*. Apparently there was a difference between throwing a couple of steaks on the old Char-Broil and concocting something nutritious that a seven-year-old kid would actually eat.

He had decided they couldn't live on brats, burgers and take-out alone so had decided to try his hand at a few other things—including spaghetti, which Joey had admitted was one of his favorites.

Now his nephew was due home from his playdate in a half hour and Rafe would have to start over.

Playdates were yet another activity that seemed completely out of his understanding. Give him a terrorist cell and a clear-cut objective to take them out and he could kick some serious ass but apparently he wasn't capable of navigating the complicated politics of playdates—who was allowed to play where, whose turn it was to host, which friends weren't allowed to come over on certain days of the week and which couldn't play at all until their homework was finished.

Truth to tell, the whole parenting thing from soup to nuts scared the he—er, *heck* out of him. What did he know about seven-year-old boys? He could barely remember even *being* one.

He would just have to figure things out. His nephew needed him and he couldn't let him down like he had Cami.

He couldn't let the kid go into foster care. He and his sister had gone the rounds with that, being bounced around between their grandmother, their aunt and finally foster care after their mother's death.

Sure, there were really good foster families out there. They had been lucky enough to have placement with a few, but he wasn't willing to roll the dice with his nephew's well-being.

Right now, though, he couldn't help but wonder if the boy might be better off taking his chances in the system. Joey might think so. They weren't exactly hitting it off. Rafe never expected to come in like some kind of white knight and save the day but he thought Joey at least might be a *little* grateful to be living with family instead of strangers.

In truth, Rafe was connected by blood to the boy but that was about it. They had lived separately. He had usually been stationed far away from where Cami lived in her wandering life and his relationship with the boy had been mostly through phone calls and emails and the occasional visit.

He supposed he shouldn't be that surprised that trying to establish a normal parental-type relationship with him would be a struggle.

He wasn't sure why the past few weeks had seemed so tough—maybe because he felt out of his element here in this community where he didn't know anybody and didn't have anything else to focus on. Perhaps things would go more smoothly after they returned to California and he figured out what he was going to do now that his whole life wasn't defined by being a navy SEAL.

On the surface, he and Joey should be tight. He had been in the kid's situation when he was young, lost and afraid with no safe harbor. The only difference was that Rafe had had a little sister to worry about, too.

He could completely relate to his nephew's stress and uncertainty that resulted in behavior issues.

His mother had been wild and troubled—giving

birth to two children from two different men, neither of whom had stayed in the picture long.

She would clean up her act and regain custody of them for a few months and then something would happen—an unexpected bill, a bad date, even somebody making an offhand comment in the grocery store—and she would fall off the wagon again. All her hard work toward sobriety would disintegrate and they would end up with their elderly grandmother or their aunt, who had been busy with her own family and a husband who hadn't wanted the burden of two more mouths to feed.

A boy should never have to deal with the burden of his mother letting him down, time after time.

More than anything, he wished he could spare Joey that. Since it wasn't possible, he would do his best to provide the kid a stable home environment while his sister was in prison—and if that meant trying to figure out how to provide nutritious meals without burning them, he would do it.

He opened the cupboard and was looking for the bottle of spaghetti sauce he knew he had purchased earlier in the week when the doorbell suddenly rang.

Oh, yay. Maybe when he wasn't paying attention, his subconscious had called for pizza delivery.

He headed to the kitchen and opened the door, only to find someone else unexpected.

It was *her*. The blond and lovely Hope Nichols, who dredged up all kinds of disastrous memories he had buried a long time ago—and who made him feel even more lousy at this whole parenting thing than he already did.

She beamed at him, disconcertingly chipper. "Hi. It's Rafe, right?"

He felt big and stupid and awkward next to all her

soft and delicate prettiness. "That's right. Rafe Santiago."

She was probably here to give him the bill for the broken window. What other reason would she have for showing up at his doorstep on a Tuesday evening?

"May I come in? It's freezing out here. My body still hasn't acclimated from the desert."

"Oh. Yeah. Of course. Come in."

He held the door open, kicking aside the backpack Joey had dropped after school that afternoon.

She sniffed and blinked a few times. "Wow. That's… strong."

The house—which was clean and warm but not very homey otherwise—smelled like charred red sauce, he suddenly realized with chagrin.

"Kitchen mishap," he said, embarrassed. "I was making spaghetti sauce and forgot to stir. I just tossed it out but I'm afraid the smell tends to linger."

She gave him a sympathetic look. "Been there, more times than I can count. I'm a lousy cook."

"We could start a club."

She grinned. "Except we'll be very clear that our members are *not* to bring refreshments to meetings."

He couldn't help smiling back. "Definitely. We'll put it in the bylaws."

She paused, then tilted her head. "Do you need a little help? Maybe it's like grammar, you know? Two negatives making a positive. Maybe with two lousy cooks working together, we can come up with something a little more than halfway decent."

"English and math in one paragraph. You must be a teacher."

"Well, I have dual degrees in art history and education. I should also add that while I couldn't bake a decent chocolate cake if cannibals were waiting to nibble off my arms if I didn't deliver the goods, I do make a kick-ass red sauce."

Was she really offering to help him fix dinner? Okay, that was unexpected...and a little surreal.

He ought to politely thank her for the offer and send her on her way. He really wasn't in the mood for the messy conversation about her parents he knew they needed to have—but he had also spent the past few weeks with very little adult interaction and he was a little desperate to talk about something besides Star Wars and Ninjago.

"Couldn't hurt. Between the two of us, maybe we could come up with something Joey might actually eat. So far, my efforts in that direction have fallen pretty flat."

"Excellent. Let's do it." She reached to untwist her multicolored scarf then unbuttoned her red wool peacoat. Beneath, she wore a bright blue sweater that matched her eyes. She looked bright and fresh and just about the prettiest thing he had ever seen.

After an awkward moment, he reached to help her out of it, with manners he had forced himself to learn after he joined the military.

Up close, she smelled delicious, some kind of exotic scent of cinnamon and almonds, and she was warm and enticing.

He told himself that little kick in his gut was only hunger.

He took the coat and hung it on the rack then led the way into the kitchen. "Where do we start?" he asked.

She paused in the middle of the kitchen. "First things

first. If you don't mind, I'll just rinse out the rest of
this saucepan before the fumes singe away more of my
nasal lining."

"Go ahead."

She headed to the sink and ran water in the sink to
flush it down then started opening cupboards and pulling things out. "So where is the little snowball-throw-
ing champion?"

"Next door. Playdate with his partner in crime."

"Is this the infamous Samantha?"

"The very same. Last night we had a talk with her
and her parents about the dangers of throwing snowballs at cars. It should now be safe to drive through the
neighborhood."

"Whew. That's a relief." She started mixing things
in the now-clean saucepan. "So what's the story here, if
you don't mind me asking? Where are Joey's parents?
I would love to hear they're on an extended cruise to
the Bahamas and you're just substituting in the parental department for a few days."

His mouth tightened. "I wish it were that straightforward."

It really wasn't her business but the truth was, he
didn't have anybody else to talk to about the situation
and found he wanted to explain to her.

"Joe's dad took off before he was born, from what I
understand. I don't know the details. I was overseas."

"Military?"

"How did you know?"

"The haircut sort of gives it away. Let me guess.
Marines."

"Close. Navy."

For reasons he didn't want to look at too closely, he

didn't mention he had been a SEAL. It was a snap decision—similar to allowing her into his house and his kitchen. If he mentioned it, she might more easily make the connection between him and that rebel camp in Colombia and he couldn't see any good reason to dredge up the painful past they shared while they seemed to be getting along so well.

"Ah. A sailor." She seemed to accept that with equanimity. "So Joey's dad isn't in the picture. What about his mom?"

He pulled a large pot out to boil water for the pasta. Again, he debated what to tell her and then decided to be straightforward about this, at least. "It's a rough situation. My sister is in trouble with the law. She's in jail."

"Oh, no!"

He could have left it at that but he was compelled to explain further. "Last week she pleaded guilty to a multitude of drug charges, including distribution to a minor. Multiple minors, actually. Right now she is in the county jail in Pine Gulch while she awaits sentencing."

"I'm so sorry."

"It's a mess," he agreed.

"So you stepped up to help with Joey."

"Somebody had to. We don't have any other family."

She mulled that as she opened a can of tomatoes and poured the contents into the saucepan. "Are you on leave, then?"

"I had my twenty years in so I retired."

It had been the toughest decision of his life, too, but he didn't add that.

"You gave up your career to take care of your nephew?"

He shifted, uncomfortable. "I'm not quite that noble.

I'd been thinking about leaving for a while." That was somewhat true. As he headed into the tail end of his thirties, he had started to wonder if he still had the chops for what was basically a younger man's game. He had started to wonder what else might be out there, but he hadn't been ready to walk away quite yet and had all but committed to re-up for another four years, at least. Everything changed after that phone call from Cami.

"So what will you do now? Are you sticking around Pine Gulch?"

"Only until my sister's sentencing. I'd like to go back to the San Diego area where I have a condo and a couple of job offers, but she begged me to stay until she is sentenced so she can see her son once or twice. I figured it wouldn't hurt to let Joey finish school here since he has friends and seems to be doing okay."

"San Diego is nice. Pretty beaches, great weather. An excellent place to raise children."

He let out a breath, more uneasy at her words than he should be. He was now raising a child. How the he—er, heck was he supposed to do that? The past few weeks had been tough enough. Looking ahead at months and possibly years of being responsible for a boy who wanted little to do with him was more daunting than his first few weeks of BUD/S training.

He would get through this new challenge like he did that hellish experience, by keeping his gaze focused only on the next minute and then the one after that and the one after that.

Right now, the next minute was filled with a beautiful woman in his kitchen, moving from counter to stove to refrigerator with a graceful economy of movement he found extremely appealing. He liked having her here in the kitchen, entirely too much.

Something about her delicate features, the pretty blue eyes and those wild blond curls held back in a ponytail, made his mouth water more than the delicious aromas now wafting from the saucepan she was stirring on the stove.

He wasn't sure he liked this edgy feeling. As a rule, he tended to favor control, order.

His turbulent childhood probably had something to do with his need for calm. He had a feeling Hope was part of it, too—after the way he had screwed up on his very first mission as a SEAL, he had channeled all his guilt and regret into becoming a highly trained, totally focused, hard-as-titanium special warfare operator.

His platoon members called him *Frío*, the Spanish word for cold. Not because he was unfriendly or unfeeling but because he generally turned to ice under pressure.

Come to think of it, that need for order might be one of the reasons he and Joey were struggling to find their way together. Seven-year-old boys—especially troubled, unhappy seven-year-old boys—tended to generate chaos in their wake.

He'd need to find a little of that ice water in his veins pronto and remember he had enough to deal with right now without this unexpected and unwelcome attraction to someone who would likely hate him if she knew who he truly was.

She hadn't been lying when she said she wasn't much of a cook, but maybe she had exaggerated a little.

She wasn't *terrible* exactly, she just generally didn't

have the patience or time for it. There was something quite satisfying about having one specialty, though, and she could say without false modesty that her red sauce was something truly remarkable.

Rafe Santiago and his nephew were in for a treat—if she could relax enough to finish the job while the man glowered at her from his position leaning against the counter next to the sink.

Why did he seem so familiar? She wished she could place him. It could just be that she had encountered more than her share of big, tough military types.

Usually they turned her off. She tended to gravitate toward scholars and artists, not big hulking dudes with biceps the size of basketballs.

The truth was, Rafe Santiago made her nervous and it was a feeling she was completely unaccustomed to.

She forced away the feeling and focused instead on the red sauce. She gave the pot a stir and then grabbed a clean spoon so she could taste it.

"Mmm. Needs more oregano." She shook in a little more and stirred a few more times then grabbed another clean spoon to taste again. "There it is. Perfect. See for yourself."

"I trust you."

"Come on. Try it." She held out yet another spoon for him. After a moment, he rolled his eyes then leaned in and wrapped that very sexy mouth around the spoon.

"Right?" she pushed.

He gave a small laugh that held no small amount of appreciation. "Wow. That is much better than anything I could have come up with."

"Again, to be clear, a good red sauce is literally one of my very few skills in the kitchen. My aunt Mary de-

spaired of me ever learning to even scramble an egg.
I have conquered a halfway decent omelet and the red
sauce, but that's about it. Oh, and couscous. I just spent
three years in Morocco and you can't leave the country
without at least trying to make tagines and couscous."

"In the space of five minutes, you've gone from starting a club for people who are helpless in the kitchen to
spouting culinary words I barely even know."

"A tagine is both a cooking implement and a dish.
Sort of like the word *casserole*. It's a pot that comes
with a domed lid. Tagines are also very delicious meat
and vegetable dishes, kind of like a stew. I make a really
delicious one with honeyed lemons and lamb."

"Sounds delicious."

"Maybe I'll make it for you sometime."

As soon as the words escaped her mouth, she wanted
to yank them back. Why on earth would she say that?
She wasn't going to be cooking for the man again. She
shouldn't be here now. She had a million other things
to do at the moment and none of them had anything to
do with fixing a red sauce for Rafe Santiago, even if
she was incredibly drawn to the man.

How could she help it, when he talked about giving
up his military career to rescue his nephew? It was a
wonder she hadn't melted into a mushy pile of hormones
on his kitchen floor.

"So what time will Joey be back?"

He glanced at the clock on the microwave.

"Hard to say. I told him five-thirty. So far obeying
the rules doesn't seem to be one of his strengths."

She smiled a little at his disgruntled tone. "Well,
you'll want to give the red sauce about fifteen minutes
more than that, stirring every few minutes. Don't for-

get to stir. Seriously. Don't forget! I always set a timer to remind me every two or three minutes. If you start your pasta water boiling now, you can add it just as Joey gets back."

"That's it? You come in, throw together dinner and then just take off? You could at least stay and eat it with us."

Oh, she was tempted. If circumstances had been different, she would have jumped at the chance. But, again, she had a million things to do and she couldn't afford any distractions. Rafe Santiago was the very definition of the word *distraction*.

"Sorry, but I can't."

He gave her a challenging sort of look. "Why not? That would at least give you a chance to finally bring up the reason you came here in the first place."

She laughed. "Ulterior motive? Me? Why, you suspicious man. You mean I can't convince you I stopped by just to save you from certain culinary disaster?"

"Yeah, sorry. Not buying it, though I won't complain about the pleasant secondary outcome."

Oh, she liked this man. Entirely too much. Again, she thought how familiar he seemed and was vexed that she couldn't place him.

"All right. You caught me. The truth is, I found an excellent way for Joey to work off the cost of replacing my truck window."

"I suspected as much."

"Okay, here's the skinny. I know you're not from Pine Gulch but are you at all familiar with The Christmas Ranch?"

"Don't think so."

"Well, let me just tell you, sailor, it's a magical place

near the mouth of Cold Creek Canyon. My uncle and aunt started it years ago, shortly after they were married. Christmas is kind of a big deal in my family. My family name, Nichols, used to be Nicholas. As in St. Nicholas. You know, the big guy in the red suit with the beard. It was shortened when my ancestors migrated to America several generations ago. Despite that, my uncle Claude and aunt Mary always took the whole holiday thing very seriously."

"Makes sense."

"In spring, summer and fall, the Star N is like any other working cattle ranch, with a pretty small herd but enough to get by. But from Thanksgiving to just after the New Year, an entire section of the ranch is set aside to celebrate Christmas. We have a huge holiday light display, sleigh rides, a sledding hill, even a reindeer petting zoo."

He raised a dark eyebrow. "With real reindeer?"

"You guessed it. We have a herd of ten."

He looked puzzled. "Ten? I thought there were only eight who pulled the big guy's sleigh. Oh, right. You can't forget Rudolph. But then who's the other one?"

"We do have a Rudolph, only we call him Rudy and he doesn't have a red nose except when we stick one on him, which he hates. We've got a bunch more. Glacier and Floe, Aurora and Borealis—we call him Boris for short—Brooks and Kenai and Moraine. Oh, and I can't forget Twinkle and of course Sparkle. He's kind of our favorite. He's the smallest one in the herd and also the sweetest."

"Okay. And you're telling me all this why?"

"It's kind of a long story. Stir the sauce while I tell you."

He made a small, amused sound at her deliberately bossy tone but headed for the stove anyway and picked up the spoon. She tried not to notice how gorgeous he looked doing it.

"My oldest sister and her husband had been running the Star N for the past few years—that's the cattle operation—along with The Christmas Ranch, but Travis was killed in a ranch accident this summer."

"Oh. I'm sorry."

She accepted his condolences with a nod, feeling a sharp ache in her chest all over again. Travis had been her friend and she had loved him from the time he came to live with Mary and Claude to help them run the ranch. She would always miss him but she grieved most that her sister had lost her husband and Barrett and Louisa their father.

"Faith—my sister—is understandably overwhelmed. She's hardly had time to grieve and so she and my aunt Mary and my sister Celeste all decided to take a break from operating the holiday side of things. Since I'm here now and don't have anything going, I offered to take over and run The Christmas Ranch this year. As you can imagine, I have a gazillion things to do if we're going to open in little more than a week. That's where I need Joey's help."

"I hate to break it to you, but I don't think he knows anything about reindeer."

She made a face. "He won't need to deal with the reindeer unless he wants to. But I could really use him after school helping me get everything ready in time for our traditional opening the day after Thanksgiving."

Ten days. She had no idea how she would accomplish the tiniest fraction of what she had to do but she had to start somewhere.

"If Joey can help me every day after school for a few hours that should make us square on the three hundred dollars it's going to take to replace my truck window."

"It would be far easier for me to just pay you the three hundred dollars now and be done with it."

She made a face. "You're absolutely right. But raising boys into men isn't about the easy. It's about consequences and accountability. What lesson would he learn if you stepped in to fix his problem for him?"

"Yeah, yeah. I know. Fine. I'll bring him out tomorrow after school. You said it's in Cold Creek Canyon?"

"Yes. You know where that is?"

"Yes."

"Great. I'll see you tomorrow afternoon, then. Thanks. Have him wear boots and warm clothes. And don't worry. I'll find something fun for him to do."

"Sure you don't want to stay for dinner? Seems only fair, after you did all the work."

She was extraordinarily tempted. She liked the man, entirely too much, but the hard reality was, she didn't have a minute to spare. Even the fifteen minutes she had spent here already was too much.

"I appreciate the invitation and I really wish I could, but I'm afraid I'm going to have to pass."

"I think you're just chicken your sauce won't be edible after all, for all your big talk."

She gave a short laugh. "Wait and see, sailor. Wait and see. Bring that cute nephew of yours over after school, whenever he's done with homework. We're on the north side of the road, about three miles up the canyon. You can't miss it. There's a sign over the driveway that says The Christmas Ranch."

"I'll figure it out."

"Great. See you then."

He started to walk her to the door but she shook her head. "I can find my way out. You need to stay and stir that sauce."

And she needed to do her best to figure out how she was going to keep from losing her head over a man with hazel eyes, a sweet smile and shoulders made for taking on a woman's cares.

Chapter 4

By the time she finally made it back to the Star N, spaghetti with Rafe Santiago and his nephew sounded like the most delicious thing she could imagine, even if the man somehow ended up burning the sauce again.

She was exhausted and starving and trying not to feel completely defeated at the magnitude of the task ahead of her.

Nothing seemed to be going the way she planned. Of their six regular temp employees in years past, three were unavailable or had already found other positions for the season and one had moved away. Only two of their regulars were available to help this year—Mac Palmer, who had been their Santa Claus for years, and Linda Smithson, who helped out in the gift shop.

She was glad to find workers where she could, at least, but she would definitely need to find extra help—

in a town she hadn't lived in with any regularity in a decade. It was an overwhelming undertaking.

She was most concerned after her last conversation with Dale Williams. The retired schoolteacher had been their general handyman for a decade and also stepped in to play Santa Claus sometimes, trading off with Mac when needed. But he had had bypass surgery just three weeks earlier and wouldn't be in any shape to help her this year.

She faced the most uphill of uphill battles. A truly epic vertical slope.

While she was tempted to throw in the towel now, before she even started, she absolutely refused.

This might not be the most memorable holiday season The Christmas Ranch had ever enjoyed but she was going to make darn certain it was still a good one.

She repeated the mantra that helped her through the jitters she always had when taking a new teaching job. She could handle this. Heaven knows, she had faced tougher obstacles before.

She and her sisters had survived being kidnapped with their parents by leftist rebels in a foreign country—being held for several weeks in very tiny rooms with no running water and a bucket for a toilet, watching her mother growing increasingly sicker from the cancer ravaging her body while they were helpless to get her the medical help she needed, watching her father die in front of her just when they all thought they would be rescued, then losing her grief-stricken mother just a few months later.

She was a survivor, just like Faith and Celeste. They had found a home here, a true haven after their wandering childhood, and The Christmas Ranch was a big part of that.

She intended to carry on the proud tradition of the ranch and refused to admit defeat simply because she encountered a few obstacles.

She pulled into the circular driveway of the Star N, with its big front porch and the river rock fireplace climbing the side.

She loved this place. No matter where she wandered, from her tiny apartment overlooking the unearthly blue-painted medina in Chefchauan to the tent in the Sahara where she had taught English to Berber tribesmen for a few months to the raised hut on the beach where she lived in Thailand during her Peace Corps time, this was the home of her heart.

Where would she and her sisters have been without Uncle Claude and Aunt Mary to take them in, to wipe their tears and help them back into a routine and put them to work?

They had been extraordinarily lucky to find a place here. Maybe that's why the idea of Rafe Santiago walking away from his naval career to rescue his nephew touched a chord deep inside her.

The living room was dark when she walked inside and she thought for a moment maybe no one was home, until she heard the low murmur of voices coming from the kitchen. She followed the sound and as she approached, she realized it was her younger sister, Celeste. She was reading a children's story and after only a few words, Hope was enthralled.

"It wasn't anywhere close to the magical Christmas Eve Sparkle had dreamed about during the long spring, summer and fall while his antlers turned velvety and soft. It was so much better. The End."

Silence descended for a few seconds when Celeste finished speaking in her melodious, captivating voice— as if the listeners needed time to absorb and reflect— and then both children cheered and begged to hear the story again.

Hope wanted to cheer, too. She walked the rest of the way into the kitchen and found her younger sister at the table with a computer printout in front of her. "Oh, that was a wonderful story!"

Louisa beamed at her. "I know! It's the best one *ever.* I thought nothing could beat the story last year, when Sparkle saved the Elves' Christmas dinner but this one was even *better.*"

"Aunt Celeste wrote it," Barrett exclaimed. "Can you believe it?"

She looked at her younger sister, whose cheeks were pink with embarrassment. Celeste was so pretty but hid her loveliness with long bangs, a pony tail, little makeup and no jewelry.

"I can believe it. Celeste has always been the *best* at telling stories."

"I love all the Sparkle stories. She writes a new one every year but I think this one is my very favorite," Louisa said.

Barrett giggled. "Yes. He's so funny, always getting into trouble. In the stories, Sparkle is the smallest reindeer, too, but he's always the one who saves the day."

She had no idea Celeste was a writer but she shouldn't have been surprised. Her youngest sister had always loved books. During their wandering childhood, Faith had always been happiest if she could find a baby to hold or play with, Hope had always been out playing ball or going on adventures and Celeste was perfectly happy reading and rereading the small collection of books their mother had dragged from village to village.

She suddenly had a random memory she must have suppressed, of Celeste and their father trying to keep their spirits up during those dark days of their captivity—when none of them were certain they would survive and their mother was growing increasingly ill—by taking turns spinning stories about heroes and heroines, talking dragons and playful little mice.

They had been wonderful stories, delightful and captivating. Had Celeste been writing stories in her head all this time?

She suddenly felt as if she barely knew her sister. She had thrown so much energy and time into trying to fill some emptiness inside herself by wandering the world and her family had gone on without her.

"I only heard the last few moments but it's lovely. Charming and sweet, Celeste."

"Thanks," her sister murmured. "I have fun coming up with them."

"Do you read them to the children at the library?"

Celeste was the children's librarian in Pine Gulch—the perfect job for her, Hope had always thought.

"Oh, no. Only to Barrett and Louisa."

"They're our special Christmas tradition," Louisa said. "Every year, we have a new one. Aunt Celeste said some day she might put them all in a book so I can read them when I have children."

Hope suddenly had an idea. A perfectly wonderful idea that made her toes tingle and made her arms beneath her sweater sleeves break out in goose bumps.

"Is that the story?" she asked, gesturing to the computer printout on the table.

"Yes," Celeste said warily. "Why?"

"Do you mind if I borrow it?"

"You want to borrow *Sparkle and the Magic Snowball*."

"Yes. I'd like to read it when I'm not starving to death and can appreciate it better. You've really got a lovely way with prose—take it from someone who has been teaching the basics of the English language for the past four years."

Celeste looked as if she were trying to decide whether to be flattered or suspicious. She must have decided on the former. "You can keep it. I have the digital file on my computer."

"Thanks." She picked up the story, her mind already whirling with ideas. She saw pictures in her mind, probably not surprising since she was an artist at heart, despite the past few years spent teaching English.

"Go ahead and find something to eat. There's some chicken noodle soup in the refrigerator you can warm up and some of Mary's buttermilk breadsticks there on the counter."

Her stomach growled rather loudly and embarrassingly. Barrett snickered while Louisa tried to hide her smile behind her hand.

"You weren't kidding when you said you were starving to death."

"Apparently not. Where are Faith and Mary?"

"They had a shareholders meeting at the irrigation company. I offered to babysit and was just about to tuck these two into bed."

"I can do it," she offered. She had months and years of bedtimes she had missed to make up for.

Celeste shook her head. "You'd better eat before you fall over. I've got this one. I'm sure you'll have plenty of chances to tuck them in before you leave again. Come on, kids."

The children gave her tight hugs then followed Celeste out of the kitchen.

Hope quickly found the soup, thick and rich and brimming with homemade noodles, and warmed a bowl of it in the microwave. She did her best to reheat the breadsticks in the toaster oven then slid down at the table with dinner and her sister's story.

The second time through was even more enchanting. Possibilities danced through her mind and she sketched a few ideas on the edges of the paper. She was still there, her soup now finished, when Celeste came in sometime later.

"You are a fantastic storyteller," she told her sister.

Celeste looked pleased as she started drying dishes in the rack by the sink and putting them away. "Thanks. I guess it's part of the job description when you're the children's librarian."

"You know what we need? A children's storytime at the St. Nicholas Lodge. You would be perfect! You could dress up as Mrs. Claus instead of Aunt Mary doing it and could tell stories to the children. We could call it Christmas Tales with Mrs. Claus! I love this."

Celeste fumbled a plate but caught it before it could hit the ground and shatter. "I'm glad *you* love it."

"How could you not love it? It's a brilliant idea, if I do say so myself. When you were reading to the children, I completely missed the first part of the story but it didn't matter. The way you told it, I was still enthralled. You have a gift and should share it with the rest of the town."

Celeste's mouth tightened into a line and in that moment she looked remarkably like their older sister. After a moment, she set the dish and the towel on the counter and came over to the table and slid into a chair across from Hope. "You know I love you, darling, but this just has to be said. You're not going to be able to pull this off in time. You know that, don't you? The ranch is supposed to open in only ten days and nothing is ready."

The panic threatened to flow over her like lava pouring down the mountainside but she pushed it back. "Why do you think I can't pull it off?"

"You have no business experience. You don't know the first thing about what goes in to making The Christmas Ranch come together each season."

"Uncle Claude wasn't exactly the world's greatest businessman, either," she pointed out.

"Which is one reason the Star N and The Christmas Ranch are operating in the red."

"I'm going to turn things around. You'll see."

"How? You're so good at chasing dreams, Hope. I admire that about you, I do. But when the season is over, you're just going to take off again, leaving all of us to clean up after you. That's assuming you even last through the season."

Was that how her family saw her? As some flighty, irresponsible gadfly, always chasing after the next thing? Dreams, jobs, opportunities. Boyfriends. She hadn't stuck with much of anything for very long.

"You haven't been here the past few months," Celeste went on before she could respond. "You have no idea how tough things have been on all of us. Travis might have been Faith's husband, the children's father, but he was like a brother to me and Mary considered him like a son."

"I know that. I loved him, too, Celeste."

"Losing him hit us all so hard. Everyone is still reeling. I think Faith has probably cried herself to sleep every night since the accident and the kids try to be so brave but I can tell their little hearts are still shattered."

"Poor things," she murmured.

Coming home for the holidays had been the right decision, she thought. Her family needed her, whether any of them wanted to admit it or not.

"None of us has an ounce of holiday spirit this year. How can we? That's the main reason we decided not to open The Christmas Ranch this year. How are we supposed to help other people feel the magic of Christmas when we aren't feeling it ourselves?"

"You know what Mom and Dad always used to say. When your heart is broken, the best way to heal it is to first mend someone else's."

Celeste gave her a hard look. "And Mom and Dad were so smart, they both ended up dead after dragging their daughters from one godforsaken corner of the world to another."

Hope caught her breath, shocked at the bitterness in Celeste's words. How could she argue, though? It was certainly true enough, just not the entire picture.

"That's one way of looking at it," she said quietly. "I prefer to think that they gave their lives doing something they cared about passionately while trying to make the world a little better place."

"We might have to agree to disagree on that one,"

Celeste said. "I don't have quite your rosy view of what happened to us. The past isn't the issue here, though. The fact remains that I honestly don't understand how Faith and Mary could agree to let you go forward with this harebrained scheme to open the Ranch after we all decided to take this year off while we figure things out."

"I guess they have a little more faith in me than you do," she retorted.

Her sister's expression softened. "I have faith in you. I love you. You know that. And I admire you more than I can say. I love that you go out into the world to explore and dream and *live*."

"But?"

Celeste sighed. "No buts. I know there's no way I can convince you this is a lousy idea. You always did have to charge into things and figure them out on your own."

It was as close as she was likely to get to her sister's approval and she decided to take it. "Thanks, CeCe." She held up the paper. "By the way, I really did love the story. Would you mind if I worked up a few illustrations to go along with it? I have a friend who owns a printing company in Seattle and I was thinking maybe I could talk to her about putting a rush order on printing a few copies and then we could sell them in the bookstore."

Celeste looked alarmed. "Sell them? No! Absolutely not!"

"Why not?"

"Because I was just messing around, trying to come up with something to make Louisa and Barrett smile."

"You did. It's a wonderful story."

"Not wonderful enough to be in a book!"

"Oh, stop. It's a delightful story. You've a gift, my dear. Louisa said you talked about printing up your stories so she could have them to read to her children eventually, right?"

"Well, yes."

"You're going to have children of your own someday. Think of what a wonderful tradition it would be to read a story to them you wrote yourself."

"That would be lovely," Celeste said. She was obviously wavering as she considered the possibilities, so Hope pushed her advantage.

"I have to see if I can come up with some illustrations first. My art skills are a little rusty so I might not be able to—and then I have to check with my friends who own the printing company."

"So it might not happen?"

Oh, she was determined to make it happen. This story was too adorable not to send out into the world.

"Look at it this way. If we don't sell any in the bookstore, you can always give them to Barrett and Louisa for Christmas."

"I guess that's true."

"Do I have your permission, then?"

Celeste—lucky enough not to be named Charity, thus sparing the sisters that triumvirate of virtues for names—finally nodded.

"Sure. Go ahead. I can always use a few more Christmas presents."

"Excellent. Perfect. This is going to be wonderful, CeCe. You'll see."

Her sister didn't look particularly convinced but Hope didn't mind. Her sister would be thrilled with the finished product. She intended to make sure of it.

Chapter 5

Rafe had survived plenty of miserable places during his twenty years in the military. He had hunted through caves in Afghanistan, parachuted into deep, all-but-impenetrable jungles in Laos and had lived off bugs and snakes for two weeks when his platoon had been cut off from radio contact during a mission in Iraq.

Few of those places had struck him as depressing as this small county jail in Nowhere, Idaho, on a late November day.

It didn't help that he sat in front of his sister, wondering again how in the world she had let things go this far. She used to be so pretty, a little round, with big cheeks and dimples. She was always smiling, he remembered, even when their own family situation hadn't been the greatest.

Now she was thin to the point of gauntness, with

huge circles under her eyes and a three-inch scar down her cheek that was new since he'd seen her eight months ago. She looked hard, worn down by the miles she had walked on tough, thorny roads.

"My attorney is really excellent," she was saying now. "Her name is Rebecca Bowman. She's been very kind. She was the one who told me bluntly that the case against me was so clear-cut, my best chance was a plea deal. Because I agreed to testify against Big Mike, I might be able to get a sentence of two to three years, out in eighteen months. That's better than five to ten, right?"

"Sure."

He didn't add that eighteen months was forever in the mind of a seven-year-old. Cami hadn't been thinking of her son in any of this—not when she hooked up with the son of a bitch bar owner slash drug dealer she had met online.

He hated these visits. Not only did they dredge up tough memories of their mother—who had been in and out of jail when they were kids and had spent her last two years on earth behind bars on drug charges before she died of a brain aneurysm—but they also provided stark evidence of his own failures.

He had tried his best for his sister. He had joined the navy as soon as he could and sent almost every penny back to his aunt, who had reluctantly agreed to take Cami into her home.

Cami had been terribly unhappy there and had gone from a laughing, smiling, rosy-cheeked girl to a quiet, sullen teenager. She told him she didn't like living with their aunt and begged him to get out of the military and come back to find a job closer to home. He had tried to explain to her that he didn't have many options to make an honest living, with no training and no college education. He was an eighteen-year-old kid who could barely take care of himself, forget about his sister.

The military had seemed the best option to build a better future for both of them, and he consoled himself that the money he was sending back each month had to be making her life a little more comfortable.

He had no idea until Cami told him years later that his aunt's husband had been abusing her in just about every possible way.

He *should* have known. He should have done whatever was necessary to protect her and he had failed— now here she was in jail because another son of a bitch had used her and abused her trust.

"Time's almost up," the guard in the corner announced, and Rafe tried not to feel another layer of guilt at his relief.

"How's my little guy?" Cami asked. "Is he doing his schoolwork and staying out of trouble?"

"He's doing okay on the schoolwork front," he said. After a moment's internal debate, he decided to tell her the rest of it. "He broke a window of a pickup truck the other day by throwing snowballs. He was having some kind of contest with one of his friends to see who could hit the most cars and decided to put a rock in one."

"Oh, no. I hope nobody was hurt."

She hadn't seemed too concerned about hurting innocent people when she dragged her son across the country so she and her low-life boyfriend could deal drugs out of the back room of his bar.

"Nobody was hurt. It just scared the truck owner. A woman by the name of Hope Nichols. After school lets out today, we're going to her place to help her with a little work and repay the debt."

"Joey will probably hate that."

"Too bad," he said. "He made a poor choice and now he has to do what he can to make amends."

It was a message more about her than about her son and both of them knew it. After a moment, Cami nodded. "You're a good uncle and a good man, Rafael."

He wished he could agree. He saw mostly his mistakes and his weaknesses. He saw a man who had been out saving the world when he should have been home helping his sister keep her life on track.

A man whose error in judgment had ended up in the death of a man he was trying to rescue.

"I wish I could have found a man like you instead of a jerk like Michael Lawrence. I don't know what I was thinking."

He could have answered that she was thinking she wanted some kind of safety and security. Mike Lawrence had been a business owner, running a tavern in Pine Gulch, when they met online. After they had been chatting for a few months, he had somehow sweet-talked her into coming to Idaho to "help him out" at the tavern.

Helping him out had meant selling illegal prescription drugs out of the back room of the bar.

Why his sister hadn't picked up her son and gone back to California the minute she figured out what was going on was something he would never understand.

"Time's up," the deputy intoned. "Back to your cell."

Cami stood up, looking small and vulnerable. He hated thinking of her behind bars. He just had to hope she had the strength of spirit to accept the consequences of her own choices better than their mother had.

"Thank you for coming to see me. I know you hate it."

"I hate it," he acknowledged. "But I love you, which makes it a little easier."

Her eyes softened and filled with tears. He wished he could reach out and hug her but physical contact was forbidden.

"Thanks for everything. Give Joey my love, okay?"

He nodded and watched her being led back to her cell, his emotions in tumult. He wanted to pound something. A tree, a concrete wall. He didn't care what.

He walked out of the jail into the pale sunshine, wondering what the hell he was going to do now. Joey wouldn't be home from school for another three hours and he sure as hell didn't feel like going back to that crummy rental house and watching daytime TV.

He climbed into his SUV, tempted to drive to the *other* tavern in town, the Bandito, and have two or three—or ten—beers. Since he made it a point never to drink when he was upset, instead he headed on impulse toward Cold Creek Canyon.

He told himself he was only scoping out the place, doing a little recon to make sure he could find The Christmas Ranch when Joey's school let out.

That didn't quite explain why, when he saw the sign for The Christmas Ranch, where your holiday dreams come true—and a smaller one that read Closed Indefinitely—he found himself turning into the parking lot.

No harm in looking around, he told himself, seeing what might need to be done.

The place looked pretty vacant. He saw a boarded-up lodgelike building with big river-rock chimneys on either end and an empty pen next to it with a barn that must be the home for Rudy, Sparkle, Whosywhatsit and the other reindeer.

The place had a certain charm, he had to admit, but he could see it needed some basic maintenance work. As he climbed out of the SUV, he could see a few sagging shutters, a rain gutter that had come loose, a big hole in the fence.

If she was going to whip this place into shape, she needed some serious help.

He walked around the building, casing the situation like he would gather advance intel for a mission.

The weather had turned warmer, melting off what remained of the few inches of snow they'd had over the weekend. It wasn't quite strip-off-your-coat weather, but the wind didn't have that bitter bite of a few days earlier.

For a moment, he lifted his face to the pale November sun and breathed in air scented with pine and sage. A guy could get used to this, definitely.

He headed around the building, taking note of a few other repairs that needed to be finished. When he returned to his vehicle, he found a familiar old blue pickup truck parked next to his SUV—and a beautiful woman climbing out.

Something in his chest gave a quiet little sigh when he spotted her. He decided not to let that bother him. So he was happy to see her. There was no crime in that.

"Hi! What are you doing here?"

He suddenly found himself wanting to tell her the whole ugly business. About Cami and the ass-hat she got messed up with, about her sentencing—and, further back, about their mother and her complete lack of nurturing.

He pushed away the demons. "I was in the neighborhood," he lied, then decided there was no point in it, since nobody drove into the out-of-the-way box canyon of Cold Creek unless they had a reason to be here.

"Okay, I wasn't in the neighborhood. I drove here on purpose. Call it a recon mission. I wanted to make sure I could find the place later when I need to bring Joey. And since I was already here, I decided to take a look around. Looks like you've got your work cut out for you."

"Funny, sailor. By the looks of you, I never would have guessed you're a master of understatement."

He smiled, his mood suddenly much brighter. She headed around the back of the pickup truck and pulled down the tailgate then reached to tug a ladder out of the bed.

Rafe followed her and took the weight of the ladder from her. "I've got this."

"You don't have to help me. I can handle it."

"You're doing me a favor. I was looking for something physical to do. This fits the bill nicely. Where are we heading with it?"

"Over there." She pointed to the sign above the entrance to the parking lot. "I need to take down the closed sign and let people know we are no longer *closed indefinitely*."

She pulled another sign out of the pickup bed, a huge painted white sign that read Opening the day after Thanksgiving, and below that, Better than Ever.

In light of all the obstacles she faced, he found her

optimism refreshing, a bright spot in an otherwise miserable day.

He carried the ladder back to the entrance and set it up under the other sign.

"Thanks. Thanks a lot." She headed to the bottom of the ladder and set one foot on the first rung from the ground.

"Can you hand me the sign when I go up a few more rungs?" she asked. Her hands suddenly gripped the side of the ladder for dear life and a sudden fine sheen of perspiration had appeared on her top lip. Her hands were shaking, he realized. Despite the obvious signs, it took him a minute to put everything together.

"You don't like heights much, do you?"

She set her foot back on the ground. "How did you guess?"

He wasn't sure she would appreciate knowing her pale face and pinched lips sort of gave things away. Instead, he only smiled again. He had only great admiration for people who were afraid of things but confronted them head-on anyway.

"I must be psychic. Hand over the hammer and the nails. I've got this."

"Oh, but…"

He shook his head. "No worries. I've got no problem with heights. I'm used to jumping out of airplanes or helicopters or boats for that matter."

"No. You don't have to. I can do this."

Yeah, he respected the heck out of that determination in her voice. "So can I. Were you planning on using that hammer in your pocket to adhere the sign? Hand it over, then, and whatever nails you want me to use."

She looked at him and then up at the sign again.

Apparently she decided there was no shame in accepting help.

"Fine. Here you go. Knock yourself out."

She reached into the pocket of her jeans and pulled out a handful of nails, still warm from being so close to her body heat, then handed over the hammer. Their hands brushed as she dropped the nails into his palm and he was aware of a little quiver of awareness in his gut.

"So why don't you like heights?" he asked, mostly to distract himself from an attraction he didn't want to feel and wouldn't do anything about anyway.

She shrugged. "I just don't. Never have."

Did it have anything to do with that frantic helicopter ride in Colombia, when she had fought and screamed and tried to jump back out to race toward her father, who was obviously beyond saving at that point?

He could help her, more than just hanging this sign.

As he climbed the ladder and started taking down the other sign, he realized he wanted to try. Helping her get this big worn-down mess ready for the holidays would give him something to fill his days and maybe, in some small way, would help him feel like he had at least tried to make things up to her.

He couldn't do anything for his sister right now, except take care of Joey. But he could take a little burden off the shoulders of Hope Nichols by helping her make this place ready for the season.

He pulled the Closed sign off. "Watch it," he called down before he dropped it to the ground.

"You ready for the new one?" she asked.

"Yes."

He stepped down a few rungs and took the sign she

handed up to him. One side was easy. He lined it up in the same holes as the other had been but the new sign was much longer than the other one had been so he had to climb down, move the ladder over to within reach, then climb back up.

He glanced down at her. "Tell me when it's straight."

She tilted her head, looking bright and lovely in the afternoon sun. "A little higher. No, now down just half a hair."

"How's that?" he asked around the nails in his mouth. "Is it straight?"

"Oh, perfect. Absolutely perfect."

He decided to take her word for it as he hammered the nails in then climbed down the ladder.

"There you go."

"Thank you. I'm sorry to be such a big baby. About the height thing, I mean."

He raised an eyebrow. "Did I say you were a baby? From what I saw, you didn't want to climb that ladder but you were ready to do it anyway. That's the exact opposite of cowardice."

His words obviously surprised her. Head tilted, she studied him much the same way she had the sign, trying to figure out his angle.

He didn't want her looking too closely, wondering at his motives for helping her. "What else can I do? I've got two hours before I need to pick up Joey from school and nothing on my agenda but finding something to fill the time. I noticed a couple shutters loose on the lodge. I'll start there."

"You're not serious."

"Completely. I want to help. You want the truth, I need something to do or I'm going to go crazy. I'm at loose ends right now while Joey is in school, until Cami's sentencing. We won't be here long enough for me to look for a job somewhere and I'm not very good at sitting around watching daytime television. I'm grateful to have something to do—and by the looks of it, you have enough work to keep a dozen of me busy."

"At least," she muttered.

"So what's keeping you from letting me help? I worked in construction here and there while I was in high school and the summer before I joined the navy. I'm not a master carpenter but I can make a straight cut and drive a nail."

She looked at him suspiciously. "I don't understand. Why do you want to help me? If you think you're going to get a huge paycheck, I'm afraid that's not happening. I can pay you, but not much more than minimum wage."

He wanted to tell her she didn't need to pay him anything but he knew that would only make her more suspicious. He couldn't tell her *why* he owed her so he only shook his head.

"I'll help pay off Joey's window debt. After that, you can take the money you would have paid me and donate it to your favorite charity. A school for girls in Afghanistan. Clean drinking water in Guatemala. I've got a buddy who works at a recreational therapy program for injured war veterans outside of Hope's Crossing, Colorado. I can hook you up with him, if you want, and you could donate it there."

He suddenly remembered her family situation. "Or just give it to your sister. You said she lost her husband a few months back. Maybe she can throw a little extra Christmas cheer in her kids' stockings this year."

It was apparently the right thing to say. Her eyes

softened and the smile she gave him was as sweet as a summer evening. "Oh. You are a very good man, Rafe Santiago."

This was the second woman who had said that to him in the past hour. He wanted to tell her he was far from good but he wasn't willing to explain all the reasons why.

Instead, he shoved the hammer into the pocket of his jacket and folded up the ladder.

"Show me where to start."

If she had an ounce of sense, she would tell him to move along, that she didn't need his help.

Yes, it would be a lie. She needed his help rather desperately but she didn't *want* to need his help.

This man was dangerous. She didn't mean that in a physical sense. Though he radiated a sense of implacable strength and barely leashed violence—he had probably done very well for himself in the military— she sensed he wouldn't hurt her. Or anyone else in her family, for that matter.

She was incredibly drawn to him and she didn't want to be. For one thing, the timing was horrible with all the other plates she had spinning. For another, he was just too big, too tough, too *male* for her to be at all comfortable entertaining this unwilling attraction.

"I did mention I've only got a few hours before I have to pick up Joey, right?"

With a start, she realized he had asked her a question and was waiting for an answer. How long had she been standing there staring at him?

"Yes. Sorry. My mind, er, wandered." Into areas she had absolutely no intention of sharing with him.

"Any idea where you'd like me to start?" he asked again.

Hope drew in a breath. This was stupid. If she wanted to prove to her sisters she could handle the responsibility for running The Christmas Ranch, she needed to use her brain. She couldn't afford to turn away an offer of help simply because she was too attracted to the man making the offer—especially when he didn't want to take a salary for his work and insisted she donate it to a needy cause instead. How much more perfect could he get?

"If you're sure, the fence around the petting zoo has a few slats that need to be replaced. Once you finish that, we can bring the reindeer over from the other pasture and get them settled in."

She eyed him up and down, trying not to notice the breadth of his shoulders or the way his jacket hugged narrow hips. "You're not really dressed for kneeling in the dirt," she pointed out. "It might be muddy, especially after the uncertain weather of the past few weeks."

"Don't worry about me. I'll be fine," he assured her. "Everything is washable. I even have work gloves in my SUV, believe it or not."

"I appreciate a man who is prepared. I just came back from a trip to the lumberyard and you should find plenty of supplies in the back of my truck. I can drive closer to the pasture to unload it."

"Sounds good."

She climbed back into her truck, grateful again for whatever crazy impulse had prompted her to buy the pickup in Salt Lake City just a few days earlier instead of renting a small compact car for her stay.

Had it really only been a few days since she had

landed from Africa? She couldn't believe her life had changed so much in such a short amount of time.

He met her at the pasture after she backed the truck up as close as she could manage, then started unloading the lumber she had purchased to replace the damaged section.

Rafe immediately started tearing off the broken, weather-rotted slats, as if he had done this sort of thing before.

"How does your typical Idaho cattle rancher end up dipping his toes into the reindeer business?" he asked while he worked.

She smiled a little. "I told you how much my uncle Claude loved Christmas. He had a friend in Montana who got a couple of reindeer and talked him into trying it."

She remembered how much her uncle had loved introducing children to the usually docile creatures—starting with his nieces. "My sister wants to sell the reindeer. I don't know how she can. They're like family now."

She felt guilty all over again that she hadn't been here these past few years since Claude died to help with the Star N and The Christmas Ranch. She didn't know whether she could have made any difference in the balance books but she would have liked to try.

"Neither of my sisters wanted me to open the ranch this year. Safe to say, they are both quite opposed to it. I thought we all had wonderful memories of working here, but apparently I was the only one who really enjoyed it. Funny, how individuals can remember the same events very differently, isn't it?"

"I suppose it's all about point of view. We all filter

our situations through our own unique lens, which is shaped by our history, personality, experiences."

She nodded at the insight. "Exactly."

"Six guys on the same mission can tell very different stories in the debrief. It's an interesting phenomenon."

She wondered about his background. If he had been in the military for twenty years, she could only imagine the stories he might tell.

She found Rafe an incredibly fascinating man—and not only because she liked how he looked and the way he moved. She couldn't help being intrigued with a man who would give all that up to take care of a seven-year-old kid.

"When you showed up, you said you needed something physical," she said. "Forgive me if I'm jumping to conclusions, but you seemed upset. Is everything okay?"

His hands tightened on the hammer and he may have pounded just a little harder than before but other than that he showed no emotion. "Not really. I just came from the jail, visiting my sister. I try to go a couple times a week."

"Oh, that must be tough. I'm sorry. How is she doing?"

Surprise flickered in his gaze for just a moment, as if he hadn't expected the question.

"She's holding up okay. She knows she's in this mess because of her own choices and that she can't get out of prison time. It's just a matter of how long she'll be in, at this point, and that's entirely up to the judge."

"That must be tough, especially when she has a cute little boy who needs his mom."

"Maybe she should have thought about that before

she made a string of really stupid choices that led her where she is."

She might have thought his words cold and unfeeling, if not for the shadows in his gaze and the thread of pain she heard twisting through his tone.

"Your plan is to stick around until her sentencing?"

He hammered a little harder. "Yeah. I can't say I'm thrilled about it but it makes the most sense. Joey has been doing well in school this year, which is something of a miracle, judging by his past record. The school counselor and principal met with me last week and both suggested it might be best not to start him at a new school until after the Christmas break. Since that coincides with Cami's sentencing a few days before Christmas, I guess that's the plan."

He was silent for a moment. "I haven't really been there for her over the years. I guess the least I can do is stick around right now when she needs a little moral support."

Oh. She could really lose her head over a man like him.

Not that she intended to let herself. On a strictly emotional level, he made her nervous. She liked being in control of most situations, which was probably why she typically dated rather passive men who let her take the lead in their relationships.

She had a feeling Rafe wasn't much of a follower.

Not that she intended to put that theory to the test. She could accept she needed him to help out here at The Christmas Ranch but she simply had no time for a relationship—and certainly not with a man whose personal life was even more tangled than hers right now.

They were done far earlier than she would have expected. "That was quick. You do good work. Maybe you should think about becoming a builder now that you've left your seafaring ways behind."

A muscle worked in his jaw, and she couldn't tell if he wanted to smile or frown at her.

"I've still got an hour before I need to pick up Joey from school and bring him back here. Is there something else I can do in that amount of time?"

"My checklist is longer than Santa's right now. Everything needs attention. This morning, I was thinking the top priority should be probably be the main building. We call it the St. Nicholas Lodge. This is where you'll find the ticket office, the gift shop, the concession stand where we sell hot chocolate and roasted chestnuts, that sort of thing. It used to be an old barn until Uncle Claude fixed it up. That was years ago, right after we came to live on the Star N."

His expression seemed tense suddenly, though she couldn't begin to guess why.

"Things are starting to fall apart inside the building," she went on. "I noticed a few of the tables were wobbly and some of the chairs have lost their legs. The whole place just needs basic attention."

"I picked up the same thing outside when I was walking around earlier. Why don't I do a quick inventory to see what needs to be done inside? Since I'm heading back into town anyway to pick up Joe, we can stop by the hardware store and pick up any other supplies I might need before we head back here."

She smiled, grateful all over again for his help. Having him on her side helped make the whole undertaking seem a little less daunting. "Excellent. I like a man with a plan."

Something hot and intense flashed in his gaze for only a moment then was gone. Still, just seeing it there sent heat rushing to her cheeks. She knew she must be blushing, the curse of her fair skin.

She turned away, hoping he would think her rising color was from the cool wind that had just picked up and was playing with a stray lock of hair that had fallen from her ponytail. "Come take a look inside. When you see how much work needs to be done in only nine days from now, you might be sorry you ever offered to help."

Chapter 6

Rafe followed Hope, trying not to notice how well she filled out the soft pair of old blue jeans she wore or the enticing swing of her ponytail that made him want to pull all that wavy tangle of blond hair free and wind it around his fingers.

He needed to remember the reason he was here. He had an obligation to this woman and her sisters dating back seventeen years—an obligation that firmly superceded any inclination he might have to ogle her lush curves.

He followed her into the building, which seemed dark and musty and cold.

She flipped a switch and a couple of big light fixtures made up of entwined elk antlers illuminated and warmed the cavernous space divided into a ticket counter, a small area with display cases that looked like it held old holiday paraphernalia, another area with empty shelves that likely held a gift shop, a large thronelike chair in one corner that was probably Santa's domain and two huge river-rock fireplaces that dominated each wall. A massive spruce tree had been set up in one corner but was currently undecorated.

"It's impossible to keep this place warm enough, as you might have guessed. We run both fireplaces during the season and it's still drafty in here, unless the place is packed. The rest of the time, we try to get by with the industrial-size space heaters, which seem to do okay."

Though the space was large, it was quite comfortable and he imagined that children and adults would probably find it very appealing.

"This is nice."

"Thanks. Everything could use a coat of new paint but we don't have time for that. Maybe next year."

Would she still be here the next year? From all she had said about her history, she seemed to like to wander.

"You said the tables are a little wobbly?"

"Yes, and we've got a couple of chairs that somehow lost their legs while they were stored over the summer. Oh, and I noticed the armrest on Santa's chair has come loose."

If someone had told him a month ago that he would find himself in a place called St. Nicholas Lodge in rural Idaho, repairing Santa's chair, he would have called them crazy. His life had taken some really crazy twists and turns over the years but this had to be one of the craziest.

"I'll take a look."

"Great. Thank you. Do you need something to write down what you need in the way of supplies?"

"That wouldn't hurt."

She disappeared for a moment through a door behind the ticket counter and emerged with a pad and pencil. "Here you go. When you're done, find me in the office back there. I'm still in the middle of taking inventory of the gift shop stock left over from last year so I can see what else we need to order."

"Got it."

She disappeared into the office and he wandered through the building, taking note of what needed to be fixed, prioritizing things as he went into columns under *urgent, important* and *long-term.*

When he finished, the list was longer than he expected but most items were things that could wait. He made his way behind the ticket counter and paused for a moment in the doorway, watching her.

Even though they had only been separated for fifteen or twenty minutes, he was taken by surprise all over again by how lovely she was, rather wild and untamed-looking with her stunning blue eyes and that mane of blond curls. He could only imagine what an exotic creature she must have appeared in her travels in Morocco and Thailand.

She was looking at something on the desk and he could tell by the furrows in her forehead and the tension in her shoulders that it upset her.

As far as he could tell, she wasn't crying but she still looked sad. He should leave her alone. She wouldn't appreciate being spied on in a moment of distress. He was about to turn away and head back outside but she sensed his presence and turned before he could escape.

"Oh," she said, her voice a soft exclamation. "Hi."

He cleared his throat. "Everything okay?"

"Yes. Sorry. I just found a picture in a drawer while I was looking for a receipt. It brought back a lot of memories."

He moved closer to stand beside the desk and found an old snapshot of three girls. She and her sisters, he realized. They looked very much like he remembered from that botched rescue. Maybe a little older but not much. They were standing around an older couple, the man in a Santa suit and the woman dressed as Mrs. Santa.

"Cute."

"That's Uncle Claude in the Santa suit and Aunt Mary as Mrs. Santa." She smiled a little. "That was about a year after we came here, when The Christmas Ranch started becoming what it is today. I've never been so busy. I think Claude and Mary purposely gave us a million things to do on the ranch that Christmas so we wouldn't have time to brood. Genius, really."

"Brood about what?" he asked, even though he obviously knew the answer.

"Oh, you know. The first Christmas without our parents. Our dad was killed on Christmas the year before that picture and our mom died of cancer just a few months later."

He should tell her.

The inner voice prompted him loudly that now would be the perfect time but he pushed it away. She didn't need to know he had been there. If she did, she might not let him help and he suddenly found he wanted to, more than he would have believed possible a few hours earlier.

"That's tough," he said in a noncommittal sort of way.

She shrugged. "It could have been worse, believe me.

We were okay here and, most important, we were all to-gether. Claude and Mary loved us and did the best they could to show us that. We were lucky, really."

"That doesn't make it any easier."

"No. It doesn't. But nobody's life is perfect, right?" She smiled a little and he was fiercely drawn to her. He gazed down at her, thinking how easy it would be to lean in a little more or, better yet, pull her out of the chair and into his arms.

He drew in a breath, his heartbeat loud in his ears.

At the very last minute, before he would have acted on the insane impulse, he tossed the list in front of her and forced himself to ease away from the desk and from her. "This is what I found that needs to be fixed. It's a pretty long list but many of the things on there aren't necessarily urgent. I figured I would focus on the most important and see how far I get."

"Let's see." She picked up the list. While she perused it, she absently licked her bottom lip and he almost threw his good intentions out the window and kissed her anyway.

"You're right. It's a big list."

"I figure I can knock off many of those things in a few hours of work today or in the morning, especially if I can pick up the supplies now."

She looked worried, suddenly. "Look, I've been thinking. I appreciate your help but I can't take advantage of you like that."

Go ahead. Take advantage of me, any way you want.

He shook his head. "We've covered this. I've got nothing to do right now. In truth, you're doing me a favor by giving me something to do, so just let it go. Please. And speaking of going, I need to. Joey will be out of school in a few minutes. I'll take him home to change into work clothes and then we'll run to the hardware store before we come back here. I'll see you in an hour or so."

She looked as if she still wanted to argue but he didn't give her a chance; he simply picked up the list from the desk and headed out the door, before he did something really stupid.

Hope waited until he walked out of the office and she heard the outside door to the lodge close before she sank back down into Uncle Claude's chair.

She pressed a hand to her stomach, where an entire ballet troupe of butterflies seemed to be performing the *Nutcracker Suite*.

Had Sexy Navy Man really just almost kissed her? Maybe she had misread the signs—that slight flaring of his pupils, the way he suddenly couldn't seem to take his gaze off her mouth.

Maybe he hadn't wanted to kiss her. Maybe she had a piece of lettuce stuck in her teeth or something.

She wanted to believe that explanation. It would be simpler—though, of course, more embarrassing—than trying to accept the idea that a gorgeous guy like Rafe Santiago might be interested in her.

She drew in a shaky breath, trying to remind herself he wasn't her type. *At. All.*

The few casual boyfriends she had allowed herself over the years in college and then through her time in the Peace Corps and while she was teaching English had been the lean, erudite, scholarly types. Guys who would rather stay up all night discussing philosophy or politics or art than making love.

Something told her Rafe Santiago would *not* be that sort of man.

Not that she had any intentions of finding out. Neither of them had time for this sort of distraction right now. If this happened again, she would have to just be blunt with him and explain she had too much on her plate right now to worry about a sexy sailor with hazel eyes and a broad chest that made a woman think he could bear all her troubles without even blinking...

She drew in a sharp breath and placed her hands on the desk. What was the point in angsting about it for another instant? Good grief, the man hadn't even kissed her. If he had even been considering it, he obviously came to his senses. She would focus on that and be grateful one of them, at least, was thinking clearly.

She turned back to the inventory list just as she heard the outside door to the lodge open.

"Hope? Are you here?" she heard Faith call.

"Yes," she answered. "In the office."

A moment later, her sister poked her head in the doorway. She was wearing a ranch coat, boots and jeans—and a concerned frown.

"Who was that guy I just saw driving away?" she asked. "I didn't recognize the vehicle."

Only the most fascinating man she had met in a long, long time.

"Do you remember I told you about the boy who knocked out my window the day I arrived? He is going to work off his debt to me by helping out around here, since I'm in desperate need. His uncle was just checking out the situation before he brings his nephew out after school. He's offered to help with some of the basic maintenance while we try to whip this place into shape."

Faith gave her a sharp look. "While *you* try, you mean. Keep the rest of us out of this, if you please."

While her sister might have reluctantly agreed to let her open The Christmas Ranch, she had obviously not reconciled herself to the idea completely. She wasn't openly hostile but every time the subject came up, Faith was quick to point out that the struggling cattle side of the ranch took precedence.

Hope adored her older sister and always had, even before the tragic events of that long-ago December. Faith was the strongest person she knew, with a tough resilience that was tempered by soft compassion.

When they moved from place to place as girls as their parents took new missionary assignments, Faith had always been the one to make friends first and to help her younger sisters find their way.

That shared trauma had forged a stronger-than-usual bond between all three of the sisters and Hope regretted this conflict between them.

She held out the old picture from Claude's desk. "Look what I found while I was cleaning today."

Faith moved closer to take a look. "Seems like a lifetime ago," she said. "Look at my hair. What was I thinking, with those huge bangs?"

"I know. I'm the brace-face there. We had fun that season, didn't we? Do you remember how Uncle Claude made us dress up in little elf costumes while we sold concessions and handed out candy canes to the children?"

Faith shuddered. "I remember being so humiliated when friends from school would come out to the Ranch that I would try to hide in the bathroom so they wouldn't see me."

"I remember my friends acting like they were too cool to have fun when they came here but they were always the first ones to go all goo-goo-eyed over the reindeer and always fought each other to be the first one to sit on Santa's lap," Hope said.

She paused. "We were so busy that first Christmas, we didn't really have time to grieve. Don't you think it was good for us to have something to occupy our time and energy when otherwise we might have been sitting home brooding on the anniversary?"

Faith gave her a long, measured look. "Do you really think I don't know where you're going with this? The answer is no."

She leaned back in the chair. "Hmm. Can you be more specific? I don't know what question you thought I was going to ask."

"You want Louisa and Barrett to help you out here."

Faith had always been entirely too perceptive. Hope could never fool her.

"Nothing too strenuous," she assured her. "I thought they could help me with a few fun jobs like setting up the Christmas village and decorating the tree in here."

"They have enough to do after school with schoolwork and their chores."

Faith was their mother, Hope reminded herself. She knew best. Still…

"Uncle Claude was a genius. I don't think I fully realized it until today, looking at that picture. Do you really think he wanted to expand The Christmas Ranch that year for his own sake? Or did he do it to keep three grieving girls busy during that first Christmas without our parents?"

"Distraction isn't always the best policy."

"In this case, it worked, didn't it? Think of how lost we would have been without those silly elf costumes, the sleigh rides, the reindeer."

"We were much older than Louisa and Barrett are," she pointed out.

"Yes," Hope acknowledged. "And we had already had nearly a year to go through the grieving process, while they are still only a few months out of losing their father. I know. The situations aren't the same. I just thought helping out here might give them something to look forward to in the afternoons. I'll pay them, of course, and they can use the money for Christmas presents for you and Auntie Mary and Celeste."

Faith didn't look convinced. Perhaps she ought to let it drop. She didn't want to argue with her sister or have one more point of contention between them. Yet when she looked at the picture still in her sister's hand, she couldn't help remembering all the good times they'd had here.

In many ways, working at The Christmas Ranch had shaped their childhood as much as those early years as the children of earnest wandering medical missionaries. It had reinforced to her the magic of Christmas and the joy that could be found in bringing that to others.

"Please, Fae. It will be good for them and I'll make sure they have fun."

Her sister let out a heavy sigh. "Fine. I'll talk to them. If—and only *if*—they want to help after their homework and regular chores, I won't stand in the way."

She beamed and stood up to give Faith an impulsive hug. "Thanks! You know you're the best older sister ever, right?"

Faith snorted but hugged her back. "Cut it out. I already said I would let them help you. You don't have to lay it on any thicker."

Maybe Rafe had changed his mind and decided not to come.

Hope frowned at her watch. It was nearly four-thirty. He had been gone for two hours. Perhaps he had decided he didn't want to become entangled with her crazy plans after all, that she was too much trouble.

No. She couldn't believe that. He had promised and she sensed he was a man of his word. He must have encountered a problem.

Louisa and Barrett hadn't come down from the main house either, but she hadn't expected them yet, with their homework and chores. Meanwhile, it would be full dark by six-thirty, which gave them very little time to accomplish what she had hoped for the evening.

Since the afternoon was moderately warm for November—jacket weather, not parka—she had decided to focus on some of the outside jobs while they had the chance.

Snow was forecast for later in the week and she and the children could decorate the Christmas tree when they were stuck inside. She carried another box and set it on the flatbed wheeled wagon and had just turned to go back into the storage room off the back of the lodge when she heard a vehicle in the parking lot.

A moment later, she saw Rafe climb out of his SUV and open the door to the backseat. Joey hopped out and followed him over to Hope, though she couldn't help notice he was dragging his feet.

"Hi," Rafe said in a harried sort of voice. "Sorry

we're late. We had some issues after school with another kid."

Joey lifted his head and she blinked at the truly impressive shiner he had going.

"Oh, honey. What happened?"

"Nothing," the boy muttered. He was so full of pain. It seemed to radiate off him in waves and her heart ached for him. He must be so frightened to be without his mother.

She hated seeing anybody hurting and she wanted to help him, but how could she? She wasn't a counselor or a social worker. She was a stranger brought into his life by accident, who would only be there for a few weeks.

"I'm so glad you're here," she said suddenly. "I really need some help and I think only you can do it."

"Me?" He still looked sullen but she could see a trace of curiosity in his expression, as well.

"Yes. Come on over here, please."

She led the way to the reindeer pen, where she had just finished moving the herd.

He gaped at the animals inside the pen. "Are those real reindeer?"

"They are indeed."

"Are they babies? I thought they would be bigger."

"Lots of people do. Reindeer are actually often smaller than mule deer. Our herd is from a particularly small strain."

"Can they hurt me?"

"They're very gentle, since we have raised them all from very young. They're more like pets. But you don't have to go close to them if you don't want and you should never go near them unless an adult is there, too. Now wait right here and you can help me."

He leaned against the fence Rafe had just fixed while she slipped between the slats and headed for Sparkle, the smallest of the lot. He came to her readily, always friendly and up for fun, and she attached a leadline to the bridle she had already put on him and led him over to where Rafe and Joey watched. She held the line out to him.

"I need you to hold this for me while I go find a friend to help us."

"Me?"

"Yes. Do you think you can do it?"

He looked at Rafe as if for permission. His uncle shrugged and after a moment, Joey reached out and grabbed the line from her. She didn't have to go far to find another reindeer. Twinkle, always curious, had come to see what was going on. Sparkle's sister quickly let her attach a second line and lead her over to Joey.

"All right. Now you see that wagon over there? We're going to hook them up so they can help us today. Just hold on to the lead there and come with me."

"Are you sure this is safe?" Rafe asked.

"Perfectly," she assured him. Joey's sullenness seemed to have disappeared and he looked entranced as he followed her through the gate, leading the sweet and docile Sparkle behind him.

He looked nervous but still absolutely thrilled at the responsibility. At the wagon, he held Sparkle's lead while she harnessed Twinkle and then he stepped away while she did the same for Sparkle.

Just as she was finishing, they were joined by Louisa and Barrett, wearing jeans and cowboys hats.

"Mom says we can help you on The Christmas

Ranch!" Louisa said breathlessly, as if she had run all the way down from the main house.

"Did you finish your chores?" Hope pressed.

"Yep. And I didn't have any homework and neither did Barrett."

"I finished my math worksheet in class," Barrett said proudly. "Now all I have to do is read for twenty minutes to Mom and we do that at bedtime, only sometimes she falls asleep before I'm done."

Her heart squeezed for her sister, who was running harder than Hope was, trying to keep the Star N going.

"Excellent job. Homework and chores first, then you can help me. That's the deal I made with your mom."

Louisa made the sort of disgruntled face only a nine-year-old girl could manage. "I know. She said. Only then it will be time for dinner and almost bedtime."

"I have a feeling you'll have plenty of chances to help before Christmas is over," Hope assured her.

Louisa gave Joey a friendly smile. "Hi. I'm Louisa Dustin and this is my little brother, Barrett."

Barrett eyed Joey up and down, taking particular interest in that world-class shiner. "Hey. I know you. You're a second grader, too, aren't you? You have Ms. Sheen, right? I'm in Mrs. Billings's class."

"Yeah," Joey mumbled. He looked uncomfortable around the other children, but she figured after a few minutes of Barrett's chatter, he would unwind.

"I had Ms. Sheen two years ago," Louisa said. "She's super nice."

Joey didn't look as if he particularly agreed and Hope had to wonder if teachers weren't quite as nice to troublemaking boys as they were to sweet, well-behaved girls.

Hope fought a sudden urge to straighten the boy's wool beanie and tighten his scarf. Something about this unhappy little boy made her want to hug him close and promise everything would be all right, even though she knew it likely wouldn't—not when his mother was heading for prison.

"So what's the plan here?" Rafe asked. "Do you want me to start on the repairs at the lodge?"

"Actually, I had another idea in mind, if you don't mind. These boxes are the lights that go on the Christmas village. I figured while the weather is somewhat nice, we can hang them all and then test the elves to make sure they work."

"Oh, yay! That's my very favorite part!" Barrett exclaimed.

Louisa suddenly looked sad. "We always helped our dad and Uncle Claude do it."

Hope gave her a quick, sympathetic hug. "I know, honey. I'm sorry."

Louisa let out a sigh but quickly turned her attention to other things, in the way of children. "Can I help lead the reindeer?"

"I was hoping you would, darling."

"Wouldn't it be easier to use a pickup truck?" Rafe asked.

She made a face. "Easier, yes. But this isn't about easy. It's tradition to have the reindeer help with this part."

He looked doubtful but followed along holding Joey's hand after Louisa ordered Twinkle and Sparkle to "Walk on" then led the reindeer pulling the dozen or so boxes of lights about three hundred yards to the area surrounded by a picket fence that contained eight small structures they lovingly called the Christmas village.

Uncle Claude had made each little cottage and the animatronic figures inside. It was one of her favorite parts of The Christmas Ranch—from several buildings containing little wooden elves who actually appeared to be hammering and sawing toys to one containing a family opening presents to Mrs. Claus's kitchen, where the animatronic Mrs. Claus perpetually removed cookies out of the oven for Santa.

The village even had a little church—steeple, nativity scene and all—as well as two little animatronic church mice who raced back and forth.

"Cute," Rafe said as he took in the scene.

"It *is* cute. It's adorable. Kids go crazy for the village, especially at night when all the scenes are turned on and the figures are moving around. It's Christmas magic at its very best."

She was almost daring him to disagree. Something told her Rafe hadn't had enough Christmas magic in his life.

To her delight, he only nodded. "I can imagine. Where do we start?"

"The lights are pretty self-explanatory. Uncle Claude and Travis were both great at organization, which makes it easy on us. Each building has a couple boxes of lights that go to it. They are all clearly marked and there should be a picture of the finished product in each so you know how to hang the lights. You and the boys take a couple of buildings and Louisa and I will take a couple. We should be able to finish in a few hours."

He looked doubtful at that estimate and she couldn't blame him. Every job she had started on The Christmas Ranch was taking longer than she expected, which didn't exactly bode well for the opening—but they had to start somewhere and the Ranch's beginnings seemed the perfect place.

Chapter 7

He could think of worse ways to spend a November afternoon.

The air was clean and pure, scented with pine and sage and something earthy that wasn't at all unpleasant. Raw mountains towered over the ranch on both sides—it was in a canyon, after all—yet even with their snowy crowns they seemed warm and comforting, rather than forbidding.

As the sun went down, the shadows lengthened, stretching out across the landscape in fanciful shapes. The temperature was chilly but not freezing. He heard the cry of a hawk soaring on the current and the distant whinny of a horse—or maybe it was a reindeer. What did he know? Did reindeer whinny? He had no idea.

He wasn't a country boy. Never had been. He grew up in the gritty streets of urban Los Angeles, with concrete and gangs and graffiti.

But there was a peace here he had found in very few other places.

Joey seemed to have picked up on it, too. He had lost his shyness somewhere during that walk out here with the reindeer and now he and Hope's nephew, Barrett, were chattering away like best friends.

He strung another line of lights around the window of the little village church while he listened to them talk about their favorite Star Wars character and how the Clone Wars cartoon series was better than the original series. He strongly disagreed but decided to keep out of the discussion for now.

After a moment, the conversation drifted to what they wanted for Christmas.

"I want a new snowboard," Barrett said. "After Christmas, we can ride the tow rope up the sledding hill anytime we want and snowboard down. It's so fun. You should come try it. If I get a new board, you can use my old one."

"I won't be here after Christmas," Joey said, with a dark look at Rafe, who pretended he wasn't paying attention. "We're moving to California right when Christmas vacation starts."

"California? Why would you want to go *there*?"

"Because he's going to get a job there or something, I guess. I don't know. It sucks."

Barrett digested this for a moment, then glanced at Rafe and said in what he probably thought was a low voice but which carried clearly in the cool air, "How come you live with your uncle? Where's your mom and dad?"

Joey frowned. "I don't know where my dad is. He's a *pendejo*."

Rafe winced and hoped Barrett didn't repeat the word to his aunt, who was sure to know it was a particularly nasty pejorative.

"I don't know what that word means," the other boy admitted.

"It means he's a dumbass," Joey said, which wasn't a much better word. Out of the corner of his gaze, Rafe saw his nephew give him a careful look to see if he was paying attention. When he continued to focus on hanging the lights, the boy continued, "He ran off when I was born."

"What about your mom?"

"She's in trouble and has to go away for a while, so I have to live with my uncle."

"That *does* suck," Barrett said. After a moment, he offered a confidence of his own. "My dad died this summer."

"Did he get shot?" Joey asked, which just about broke Rafe's heart that his nephew had any exposure to a world that would lead him to jump immediately to something so violent.

"No. He died in an accident. I miss him a lot. So now I just live with my mom, my aunt Celeste, my great-aunt Mary and now my aunt Hope, I guess, since she came back."

"All girls?"

Barrett nodded. "I know! I'm the only boy, except for Jack Frost. That's my dog."

"Dogs don't count."

"Jack does because he's super smart, the smartest dog in the whole wide world. He can commando crawl across the room and he can wash his face with his paws and he even kicks a soccer ball."

"No way!"

"Seriously. Maybe if you come back tomorrow, I can bring him and show you."

The two boys went on to discuss the brilliance of Jack Frost, who apparently wasn't even white, despite his name—go figure!—but was a very light-colored yellow lab. They were still at it, stopping only when he would ask them to hand him something up on the ladder.

He was almost finished when a new voice intruded into the nonstop conversation.

"How's it going, guys? It looks fantastic from here."

He looked down from his position on the ladder to find Hope standing just below him. The fading sun picked out the golden highlights in her hair and she looked as fresh and beautiful as the mountain landscape around them.

"We're good. Almost done with this one," he answered.

"That's good. I was thinking we should probably stop for the night. It's after six and it's going to be dark in a minute. If I don't get Louisa and Barrett back to the house before dinner, Faith will be after my head for keeping them out this late."

"I just want to finish this structure. I'm close."

She nodded and turned to Louisa. "Why don't you and Barrett take Sparkle and Twinkle back to the pen and unhitch them?"

"Really? Can I?"

"Sure. You've had plenty of experience. I know your dad let you take care of them all the time."

The girl beamed, thrilled at being given the responsibility.

"Can I help?" Joey asked.

"You'll have to ask your uncle that."

Joey gave him a pleading look out of big brown eyes, the same expression Rafe always had a tough time resisting. "Please, Uncle Rafe?"

He glanced at the reindeer with those big, scary-looking antlers.

"You're sure it's safe?" he asked Hope again.

"Very safe. They're as gentle as a lamb. More gentle, actually. I've known some pretty aggressive sheep in my day."

It was only a few hundred yards to the reindeer pen. From the ladder, he should be able to see them go the whole way.

"I guess it's okay, then."

"Can we ride on the wagon?" Barrett begged.

"Sure," Hope said, "as long as you sit still and don't move around to shift the weight."

Joey and her nephew climbed onto the back of the wagon and held on as Louisa took the lead line on Sparkle and ordered the reindeer to walk on.

His nephew was riding on a wagon pulled by reindeer, led by a girl only a few years older than he was. He supposed that wasn't too strange. In Afghanistan, he had seen girls not much older than Louisa who lived with their family goats by themselves in the mountains for weeks at a time.

"They're fine," she assured him. "Let's finish this so you can get out of here."

"Right."

He turned back to the last string of lights he had to hang and continued attaching them to the little light holders along the lines and angles of the building.

The whole time he worked, he was aware of her—the

pure blue of her eyes, her skin, dusted with pink from the cold, the soft curves as she reached over her head to hand him the end of the light string.

"That should do it for me," he said after a moment. In more ways than one.

"Good work. Should we plug them in so we can see how they look?"

"Sure."

She went inside the little structure at the entrance to the village, where she must have flipped a few switches. They had only finished about half of it but the cottages with lights indeed looked magical against the pearly twilight spreading across the landscape as the sun set.

"Ahhh. Beautiful," she exclaimed. "I never get tired of that."

"Truly lovely," he agreed, though he was looking at her and not the cottages.

She smiled at him. "I'm sorry you gave up your whole afternoon to help me but the truth is, I would have been sunk without you. Thank you."

"You're welcome. I can finish these up when I get here in the morning, after I take Joey to school. Now that I've sort of figured out what I'm doing, I should be able to get these lights hung in no time and start work on the repairs at the lodge by midmorning."

She smiled at him again, a bright, vibrant smile that made his heart pound as if he had just raced up to the top of those mountains up there and back.

"You are the best Christmas present ever, Rafe. Seriously."

He raised an eyebrow. "Am I?"

He didn't mean the words to sound like an innuendo but he was almost certain that sudden flush on her cheeks had nothing to do with the cool November air.

"You know what I mean."

He did. She was talking about his help around the ranch. He was taken by surprise by a sudden fierce longing that her words meant something completely different.

"I'm not sure I've ever been anyone's favorite Christmas gift before," he murmured.

She gave him a sidelong look. "Then it's about time, isn't it?"

As soon as she said the words, she quickly changed the subject. "Louisa is probably just about done taking care of the reindeer. I should head over to make sure she doesn't need help."

"What about the other lights? Where do you want them?"

She glanced at the few remaining boxes he and the boys had unloaded from the wagon that hadn't been hung yet. "Let's just store them in the front cottage so they'll be ready for tomorrow."

Between the two of them, it only took a moment for them to carry the boxes to the cottage and then Hope turned off the lights and they walked side by side back to the reindeer pen.

"Barrett said something about how fun it would be to have you home for Christmas, for once. You're apparently one of his favorite aunts."

She chuckled. "I hope I at least make the top three, since that's all he has, if we count Aunt Mary."

"Why haven't you been home for Christmas, since you obviously love it so much? What were you running from?"

It was a question he hadn't intended to ask and one that she obviously wasn't expecting. She stared at him, bristling a little. "Why would you automatically assume I was running from something? Maybe I was running *to* something. Or maybe I just like running."

"Is that it?"

"My sisters and I grew up traveling around the world. Our parents were medical missionaries. My dad was trained as a physician's assistant and my mom was a nurse and they opened medical clinics slash outreach centers all over the world. We never spent longer than six months anywhere. Liberia, El Salvador, Papua New Guinea, Cambodia. You name it, we probably lived there. Until I was thirteen, I probably spoke other languages more than I ever had the chance to speak English. I guess it was just natural for me to inherit the travel itch from them."

He didn't need to ask what had happened when she was thirteen. Again, he had the impression that now was the time to tell her he had participated in the rescue but he ignored it. He was enjoying this tentative friendship they were developing and the heady attraction simmering between them too much to ruin it yet.

"You're home now," he pointed out. "Does that mean you've scratched the itch sufficiently, then?"

She was quiet as they walked through the field, their boots crunching on dry growth. "I don't know. I'm supposed to start another teaching job after the new year but I'm beginning to think perhaps I need to stay here and help Faith and Celeste and Aunt Mary. Things are kind of a mess around here."

"Will you be able to stick around in one place?"

"That is an excellent question, sailor." She gazed

up at the mountains around them. "J.R.R. Tolkien said something about how not all who wander are lost. I agree with that. I also believe sometimes a person can be perfectly content wandering around for a long time and then...she's not. I think it was time for me to come home. Past time, probably."

"I hope it's everything you want."

She smiled at him and he had the thought that he could get used to this, too. Walking with a lovely woman across stubble fields as the sun dropped behind the mountains and the stars began to peep out. "Thanks. What about you? What are you going to do now that you've left the navy?"

He was much more comfortable *asking* the deep questions than answering them. "I don't know that either. We're sort of in the same boat. I've got a buddy in private security back in San Diego. He's offered me a job but I haven't decided yet. Who knows? I might want to try my hand at construction. I guess we're both at a crossroads with our lives, aren't we?"

She looked struck by that observation. "It's scary as hell, isn't it?"

He laughed gruffly. "Terrifying," he admitted. "At least you're not responsible for a troubled kid."

"There is that," she said with a smile.

He suddenly wanted rather desperately to stop right there in the field and kiss her senseless, even though they were just a few dozen yards from the reindeer pen where he knew the children waited. He was drawn to her in ways he didn't quite understand. His entire adult life, he had kept his relationships casual and uncomplicated. He had never been this fiercely, wildly attracted to a woman.

He couldn't be completely certain but he suspected she was feeling the heat spark and seethe between them, too. She blushed when he looked at her and he had caught her gaze more than once on his mouth, as if she were wondering what he tasted like.

He let out a breath. This was *not* the time to put that to the test, as tempted as he might be. And he was *very* tempted.

He was glad he resisted when Barrett and Joey hurried over to greet them just seconds later.

"*There* you are," Joey exclaimed. "What took you so long? Guess what, Uncle Rafe! I got to help take the harness off Sparkle and he's not scary at all. He licked my face and it tickled. I fed him a treat *and* I got to pet a dog named Tank and Barrett has his own horse named Stinky Pete and he said maybe I could ride him sometime and I'm going to borrow his old snowboard when it snows more and guess what? You don't even have to walk back up the hill 'cause you just hold on to a rope and it tows you back up and it's fun as can be. Can we come back when it snows more?"

Rafe struggled a moment to make the shift from sheer, raw lust to trying to make sense of a seven-year-old boy's rapid-fire chatter.

"Whoa. Slow down, kid."

"Can we come back tomorrow? Maybe I can ride Stinky Pete then."

"We're coming back tomorrow," he said.

"Yay!"

"But you have work to do, remember? You're paying back Ms. Nichols for breaking her window. We won't be here to play."

His face fell. "Oh, yeah."

"Tell you what," Hope said with a warm smile to Joey. "If you work really hard to help us tomorrow and Friday—and if you and your uncle aren't too busy on the weekend—you can come back and ride Stinky Pete then. Deal?"

"Yes. That would be great. Thanks. Thanks a lot!"

He blinked a little, taken by surprise at Joey's excitement. Who would have guessed that some reindeer and a floundering Christmas attraction would be the things to hit the right button with his nephew and help him feel a little joy again?

He never would have expected it but he wasn't about to look a gift horse—or reindeer—in the mouth.

Chapter 8

Hope had a million plates spinning and all she wanted to do was find a warm corner where she could curl up and take a nap.

She yawned for about the hundredth time and checked her watch. It was barely 9:00 a.m. and she had already been up for hours—with no naps on the horizon in the foreseeable future.

Mustering all her strength, she shoved the small posthole digger deeper into the hard ground, then set the stake in, tamped the dirt around it hard and moved on to the next spot. Three down, only about a thousand more to go.

Each walking path to the Christmas village, the sledding hill and the main house was usually bordered by waist-high strings of white lights, hung on stakes spaced at regular intervals—and each year, the stakes needed to be reset into the ground.

She drew in a breath and let it out in a huff of condensation then shoved down the post-hole digger, thinking how much easier this would have been on a warm day in September than now, when the ground was almost frozen.

"What are you doing and why don't you let me do it for you?"

She had been so focused on the job, she hadn't heard Rafe arrive. He stood beside her wearing a flannel work shirt over a dark green henley. Her knees suddenly felt wobbly but she told herself that was simply because she had only slept a few hours.

"Oh. Hi! Sorry. I didn't hear you come up."

"You looked a little busy."

She made a face. "It's a stupid job. I don't know why Uncle Claude or Travis didn't install these posts permanently so we wouldn't have to reposition them each year. I guess they wanted flexible walking paths in case they wanted to change things up, but it makes tons more work. I thought about skipping it this year but it really does help people know where to go and keeps the crowds contained a little."

"Give."

He was obviously a man used to giving orders. Must be a military thing. The woman-power part of her instinctively wanted to bristle at his highhandedness— but on the other hand, woman power was all well and good but not when it came with a side of stupid. She was tired, her shoulders were already aching after only three posts and he had all those lovely muscles to help with the job.

She handed over the post hole digger with alacrity. "You don't have to order me twice, sir."

He smiled at her pert tone. "Looks like you're spacing them about six feet apart."

"Yes, just so the light strings will drape nicely. It goes faster as a two-person job. If you dig, I'll set the posts."

"Sounds like a plan."

For the next several moments they worked in a companionable silence, settling into a comfortable rhythm. It was hard work but his help took a formidable task and made it much more manageable.

"Thanks for coming," she said. "I wasn't sure if you would really show up or not."

"I told you I would. Did you doubt I meant what I said?"

She had a feeling he was definitely a man of his word. "No. I just thought you might have come to your senses in the night and realized we were fighting a losing battle here." The list of things she needed to do kept growing larger by the minute and she was beginning to fear the disheartening reality, that her sisters were right and she could never whip The Christmas Ranch into shape in only a week and a day.

"I've been in my share of battles. If you want, I can give you all kinds of cheesy idioms about sticking to your guns and so forth."

"Please don't."

He chuckled. "Okay. But how about this one— sometimes you just have to buckle up, put your head down and plow through whatever comes until you get through?"

"I'll take that one," she said. Her sudden yawn on the tail end of the word came out of nowhere and took her completely by surprise. "Sorry."

"Rough night?" he asked, with a mix of amusement and concern in his expression.

"Too short, anyway."

She probably looked like death warmed over. She suddenly had a completely vain wish that she had bothered with a little concealer that morning for what she was sure were probably king-size circles under her eyes. Or any makeup whatsoever, for that matter.

"I can sleep in January, right? I need to strike while the iron's hot and all that. Is that a battle idiom?"

He shoved the post-hole digger into the next position, twisted it and with what seemed like hardly any exertion managed to do in about three seconds what had taken her a good five minutes. "I think that one falls more in the blacksmith category. Either way, that doesn't mean you should wear yourself to the bone over this place. How late were you working out here?"

"I didn't do anything else down here on the Ranch. I was up at the house. I'm working on a little side project."

"Because you obviously need a few more of those."

She made a face at his dry tone while she stuck the next stake in the ground in the hole he had dug. "This project is more for fun than anything else. My sister wrote this great story about Sparkle the reindeer and how he uses cleverness and a little magic to save Christmas at the North Pole. I decided to illustrate it and have some copies printed up to sell at the gift shop."

"Of course you did."

"I've got this friend who was in the Peace Corps with me. Now she and her partner own a printing company in the Seattle area and she's agreed to rush print a couple hundred of them for me. If I can get the illustrations to her special delivery by Saturday, there's a chance they'll be here next week but definitely the week after the opening."

"Like you didn't have enough to do?"

"I know. But the story is wonderful and I wanted to share it with the world. I think it will be a huge hit—and the illustrations I've come up with are actually really cute, if I do say so myself. Some of my best work. I've been working on it at every opportunity. I finished the cover last night. I've got a couple more pages to finish tonight before I send it off to Deb and Carlo in the morning."

"Another all-nighter, then?"

"I slept a few hours. Not enough, but a few. Anyway, it will be worth it. It's adorable. Wait until you see the book. The title is *Sparkle and the Magic Snowball.* Isn't that perfect?"

She pushed a strand of hair out of her eyes and smiled at him.

"Perfect," he agreed.

"I'll give Joey a copy before you leave, so he can remember his time working for the crazy Christmas lady."

He shook his head and headed for the next spot. "I don't think he'll need a picture book to remind him of his time here, but I'm sure he'll appreciate it. He couldn't talk about anything else last night at dinner. He can't wait for the chance to ride Stinky Pete."

"He seems like a great kid—now that he's sworn off throwing snowballs at cars and breaking windows, anyway. Barrett was bubbling over all night at dinner about his new friend. They really seemed to hit it off."

"It's good to see him making friends. The kid has had a tough road. My sister hasn't exactly been the most stable of mothers, moving him around the country from boyfriend to boyfriend, dead-end job to dead-end job."

She had a feeling he needed to talk to someone and she was more than willing to provide a listening ear, especially since she found everything about him fascinating.

"Is that what brought her to Pine Gulch? A man?"

He grunted and shoved the post-hole digger into the ground with more force than strictly necessary. "Yeah. A jackass by the name of Big Mike Lawrence. He runs a tavern in town. The Lone Wolf."

Her grimace was involuntary. The place always gave her the creeps. It was decent enough, the time or two she went there with friends during visits home, but she always had a weird feeling there. In comparison, The Bandito—Pine Gulch's dingy, preferred drinking establishment—seemed almost warm and inviting.

Rafe didn't miss her expression. "Yeah. That's the sense of the place I get, too. She met him through an online dating service and after only a few weeks of chatting, he talked her into quitting her waitress job in California and coming out here to work for him."

"I'm guessing it wasn't a wise decision."

"You could say that. He turned out to be selling illegal prescription drugs out of the back room and embroiled her in the whole thing—using and selling. Four months later, she was arrested after a DEA undercover investigation. She agreed to plead guilty in exchange for her testimony but she's still going to serve time. She should have walked away when she showed up in Pine Gulch and discovered her new romance wasn't all he pretended to be online."

He loved his sister. She could hear it weaving through the frustration. "Sounds like she got in over her head."

"I guess. He didn't pull her into the drug operation until she had been here a month, though I have a feeling he got her using right away. It wouldn't be the first time. By then, she claimed she used all her savings to get established here and didn't have anywhere else to go. I don't know why she didn't just call me. I would have helped her. I would have come in and busted any heads necessary and gotten her the hell out of here."

Hope didn't know his sister at all but from her short acquaintance with Rafe, she already knew he wasn't the kind of man a woman wanted to disappoint. His sister probably knew Rafe would come in swinging and might end up hurt.

"She called you to help with Joey, didn't she?"

"I guess."

They had reached the entrance to the Christmas village. He crossed the path to head back to the entrance and shoved the post-hole digger into the ground at the next spot with more force than absolutely necessary. She was grateful she had given him a physical task— or he had taken it over, anyway—to work off some of that frustration.

"What kills me most is that Cami knew better. *Knows* better. We lived it, you know? Our mom threw her life away on drugs and alcohol. When she wasn't stoned, she was sleeping off her last binge or out looking to score her next one. We were in and out of foster care or couch surfing with relatives through our whole childhood."

"Oh, Rafe. I'm so sorry." She thought of her own childhood. It might have been ramshackle and even dangerous in some people's eyes, but until her parents died, her family life had always been filled with laughter, with fun, with love. Her parents had always cared passionately about their family, their faith and the people they served.

She couldn't imagine what sort of uncertainty and pain he must have known, in contrast.

He looked embarrassed, as if he regretted saying anything. "I can't understand how Cami could live through what we did, knowing the toll it took on us firsthand, yet still be out there making some of the same mistakes."

She tried to picture him as a little boy Joey's age, trapped in dark circumstances beyond his control while he tried to be protective of his sister. Many young men would have taken the easier route, into that world of drugs and crime and despair. Instead, he had joined the navy and become someone good and honorable, a man who would give up his career to take care of his family.

"My dad used to tell us that everybody has demons," she said softly. "You can't judge a person by the path they've traveled, only the direction they're heading now."

"What would your dad say about the two of us, who don't quite know what direction we're heading right now?"

She smiled a little. Her father would have liked Rafe. She suddenly knew it without a doubt. "He probably would have said we'll figure things out in our own way, that perhaps we're only waiting to find the right door and that when we do, we'll know just which one we need to open."

She shrugged. "But then, some would say he should

have left a few doors closed in his life or picked a different one."

"Why would they say that?" His voice sounded interested but his gaze was focused on the post-hole digger.

She pictured her father the last time she saw him, quite obviously dead on that jungle path while soldiers shoved her and her sisters into the helicopter. Hope fell silent as she waged an internal debate about whether to tell him.

It wasn't as if she lived her entire life around the events of that Christmas day but they had certainly served as a pivotal moment of her life. It had shaped everything that came after, had really shaped the woman she had become, and she suddenly wanted him to know.

He had shared dark, difficult aspects of his life with her and she had a sudden, inexplicable need to do the same—though it was something she rarely discussed, even with close friends.

"When I was a girl, we lived in a remote area of Colombia for a few months while my parents opened a medical clinic there—until one day my family was kidnapped by leftist rebels, hoping to score a large ransom. The only problem was, my parents really weren't associated with any big umbrella organization. There was no one to pay the ransom. We were held for three weeks, until we were eventually rescued by the US military. My dad died during the rescue and my mom died two months later of a fast-moving cancer that could have been prevented if we had lived in a place with halfway decent medical care instead of out in the middle of nowhere without even a satellite phone to call for help."

He had paused digging to focus on her as she spoke and listened with an unreadable expression. Tension seemed to vibrate off him like the fragile wisps of condensation coming off the warmer dirt they overturned.

"I'm sorry, Hope. So sorry."

Her gaze flashed to his at the low, intense note in his voice. He was genuinely upset by what she said, she realized. Instantly, she regretted saying anything. She shouldn't have brought it up—she probably *wouldn't* have, if she hadn't been exhausted.

"No. I'm sorry. That sounded bitter, didn't it? I'm not bitter. My parents genuinely wanted to help people. My mother used to quote Mother Teresa all the time, that a life not lived for others is not a life. My parents lived their convictions, which is both rare and admirable in this world."

"That doesn't comfort a lost thirteen-year-old girl, does it?"

She narrowed her gaze. "How did you know I was thirteen?"

He turned back to his work and made another hole. "I don't know. I think the other day you mentioned coming here when you were that age. I guess I did the math."

"Well, you're right. I was thirteen. Fae was fifteen and CeCe was eleven. We were lucky. Relatively speaking, I guess. After our dad died and our mom was diagnosed and put on hospice, we came here to live with Mary and Claude."

Despite the difficulty of the memories, she still had to smile. "Let me tell you, that was some serious culture shock. We went from living all over the world and speaking a dozen languages and dialects to a cattle ranch in small-town Idaho."

"Did you have a tough time fitting in?"

She shrugged. "You can't grow up the way we did

without developing some chameleon-like tendencies. We did okay. Celeste and Faith thrived with a little more structure and permanence. I guess I was the odd one out, who wanted to see what was over the next mountain range."

"And what did you find?"

She told him a little about the places she had lived, about some of the amazingly courageous women she had met in Morocco and the earnest, hardworking people she had been privileged to know while in the Peace Corps in Thailand. Before she knew it, they had once more worked their way back to the main parking lot.

"Looks like that's it," Rafe said.

She looked around. "Wow. I was so busy talking your leg off, I didn't realize how close we were to the end."

"You sure you don't need me to dig another hole while I'm in the groove?"

"No. Which I'm sure is a relief to your poor arms. Thank you! I can't tell you how much time you saved. See what a few muscles can get you."

"I always figured they'd come in handy some day."

She smiled. Not only was she fiercely drawn to Rafe on a physical level but she was discovering she genuinely liked him. He was a good listener, he seemed to respect her opinion and he had rare flashes of wry humor that seemed to come out of nowhere.

"You are proving to be invaluable, sailor. Who would have guessed the day your nephew threw a snowball through my window would turn out to be such a lucky break for me?"

He gazed at her for a long moment and then cleared his throat. "Where does this go?"

"We store it in the equipment shed. I'll show you."

She led the way to the small shed and opened the door. The place was small, dim and smelled like motor oil. "We usually store it there by the snowblower."

He carried the post-hole digger in and set it in the corner. When he turned back around, she realized how very little room there was inside the shed. They stood only a few inches apart and she was suddenly fiercely aware of him, the strength of him and the overwhelming *maleness*. Instinctively, she took a step back and stumbled against a small workbench.

"Whoa." He reached out to catch her before she could fall and somehow in the process of trying to correct her balance, she ended up caught in his arms—whether by accident or design, she couldn't tell. Not that she was able to give it much rational thought when this was exactly where she wanted to be.

"Careful," he murmured, which seemed to be a particularly appropriate warning.

"Sorry. I'm sorry."

She gazed at him, trying not to think about how warm he was, how comforting that strong chest felt against her.

His hazel eyes glowed from a shaft of light glowing inside the dim storage shed from the open door. Like a jungle cat, she thought. Her blood began to pulse, thick and sweet, and her insides began to buzz with awareness, with hunger, with anticipation.

He didn't seem in any hurry to let her go. They stood inside the doorway of the storage shed wrapped together for several seconds—or maybe minutes or hours. She couldn't be sure. Finally his gaze dipped to her mouth and he murmured something she didn't quite catch—a curse or a prayer, she wasn't sure which—and then he pulled her closer and lowered his mouth to hers.

He tasted delicious and his mouth was warm and determined. She caught her breath. After the first burst of heady shock—wow, the man could *kiss*—her arms slipped around his neck and she gave herself up to the moment and threw her whole heart and soul into returning the kiss.

Chapter 9

Who knew the doorway to heaven could be found inside a dingy little storage shed behind the St. Nicholas Lodge?

The moment Hope returned his unwise kiss, heat and hunger crashed over like a thirty-foot swell. She was soft, curvy, warm—and tasted heady and sweet, like some sort of thick, forbidden cinnamon and almond pastry he wanted to gobble up in one bite.

On some deep level, he knew this was a mistake but he couldn't seem to help himself. As they had worked together the past hour, he had been desperately aware of her, the lithe curves and the sun-warmed skin and her sweet little mouth that hadn't stopped moving. She was lush and lovely and he was having a very hard time resisting her.

It didn't help that there had been something vaguely

sexual in pounding the post-hole digger into the ground time after time—the sweat, the rhythm, the physical exertion. He finally had to force himself to stop watching her bend over to place each stake into the ground.

Yeah, he had been without a woman for a long time if he could get worked up over digging a bunch of holes in half-frozen Idaho soil.

Was it any wonder he hadn't been able to help himself from taking advantage of the moment when she stumbled into his arms? What normal red-blooded— not to mention already half-aroused—male could possibly resist?

Only a kiss, he thought. Just enough to ease both his hunger and his curiosity. He might have been content with that—though probably not, he acknowledged— until she started kissing him back, sweet and sultry and eager.

All thought flew out of his head and he yanked her against him and just devoured her.

The kiss was hot, wild—his hands under her jacket, hers tangled in his hair. A flat surface. That was all he needed. The analytical part of his brain that helped him survive difficult missions was already scanning the storage shed for something that might work even while the rest of him was busy enjoying the kiss. A cot, a table, anything.

The work bench she had stumbled against might have to do, though its narrowness wouldn't be comfortable for either of them...

He was just about to lower her to it, comfort be damned, when a sudden cold gust of wind rattled the door of the shed. She shivered in his arms and he felt as if that wind had sucked the air right out of him.

What was he doing? This was crazy.

He stepped away, his breathing ragged. She still had her eyes closed, her face lifted to his, and it took every ounce of strength he had not to reach for her again.

She was a dangerous woman.

For several days—since he met her, really—he had been trying to convince himself of all the reasons he couldn't allow himself to give in to this attraction seething through him. One kiss and all that careful reasoning headed for the hills.

This wild, urgent need, the edgy hunger, was completely out of his experience. In truth, it scared the hell out of him. He liked being in control of every situation and right now he felt about as in control as a churning leaf caught in a whirlpool.

He drew in a deep breath and then another, fighting for calm. This was stupid. If she knew who he was, what he had done, she would be bashing him over the head with that post-hole digger instead of looking at him with those soft, dazed eyes that made him want to yank her against him and kiss her all over again.

For a long moment, the only sound in the shed was their ragged breathing and then she let out a surprised-sounding laugh.

"Well. You certainly know how to take the winter chill off the morning."

How did she do that? He had half expected her to yell at him for distracting her with a kiss. Instead, she laughed and tried to defuse the tension—making *him* want to laugh, too, even when his thoughts were in a tumult.

He decided to respond in the same casual vein. "Just

doing my humanitarian duty. I wouldn't want your lips to freeze off."

She smiled a little. "Thanks. I appreciate that. I'm pretty fond of my lips."

He was growing quite fond of them himself. "They are certainly memorable."

She laughed again, a soft bell of a sound that seemed to slip beneath his jacket and lodge somewhere in the vicinity of his heart.

"Um. Thanks, I guess."

"Right." He paused. "Despite how memorable I find them, I will do my best to forget. Kissing you was… inappropriate. I've been trying to talk myself out of doing it for days but apparently I don't have the iron-clad self-control I always thought I did—at least when it comes to you."

"You've really been trying to talk yourself out of kissing me for *days*?"

"Something like that." It seemed like eons—vast, endless eternities. He sighed. "I'm sorry."

"You have nothing to apologize about. We don't need to make a big deal about this, Rafe. You're a great-looking guy—all that sexy warrior mojo you've got going on—and I'm obviously attracted to you. But I'm not in the market for a casual relationship right now. Neither are you. We both have stuff going on. I get that. This was a mutual, uh, lip-warming. Now that we are sufficiently heated, we can get back to business. For me, that business is the thousand and sixteen things I have to do today, not fretting about a moment of craziness that isn't going to happen again."

He should be relieved that they were both on the same page. Instead, he wanted to toss the whole book in the air, push her farther into that little shed and kiss her until they created their own tropical microclimate.

He nodded, forcing down the urge. "Good. That's good. I guess I'll get going on some of the things I wrote down yesterday."

"You still want to help?"

"Of course. Why wouldn't I?"

"I… Great. Thank you. I need to take care of some things in the office. You can find me inside the lodge if you need me."

If he needed her. That was a laugh. He needed her like he needed water and air—but he was going to have to accept he couldn't have her. "Got it. I'll see you later."

She waved and hurried away, leaving him aching and aroused.

Hope hurried inside the St. Nicholas Lodge, pausing only when she was certain she was quite concealed from view.

Inside, she sagged against the wall, fighting the urge to bury her face in her hands.

What in the world just happened there?

That kiss.

She drew in a shuddering breath, grateful for the steady support from the wall. Her knees still felt shaky and she was afraid if she stepped away she would teeter. She tried to tell herself it was merely exhaustion from only catching a few hours of sleep but she knew it was a lie.

Oh, she was in big trouble here.

She pressed a finger to her lips—her apparently *memorable* lips—and closed her eyes, still tasting him there, like coffee and mint and all things delicious.

For several long moments there in the supply shed, she had forgotten everything she had to do. All she wanted to do was stay there. In the circle of his arms, she had been aware of a strange but powerful feeling of security, of safety, as if he would protect her from everything ugly and dark in the world.

Yeah. Big, big trouble.

It was only a kiss, she tried to remind herself. But why did she feel as if something monumental had just shifted in her world?

She could fall hard for a man like him. How could she resist the combination of quiet strength, inherent decency and raw gorgeousness?

As if she needed one more thing to worry about right now! She didn't have *time* for a broken heart, darn it.

For one crazy moment, she wanted to march out there and tell him that while she appreciated what he had done so far, she didn't need his help and he could now just go on his merry way finding some other *memorable* lips to warm, thanks very much.

He would know as well as she did that was a lie, that she was nothing short of desperate. If she wanted to open the day after Thanksgiving, she needed every bit of help she could eke out—even from a man she sensed might have the potential to leave her battered and broken.

She needed Rafe's help. Pure and simple. That had been reinforced to her quite emphatically that morning when his muscles and strength had turned a seemingly impossible job into a big checked-off item on her to-do list.

Where on earth would she find someone else on short notice to take care of everything that needed to be done—and how could she possibly find the time to start the search?

Rafe was here, he was more than capable and for reasons she didn't understand, he wanted to help her.

She would simply have to do her best to forget about that kiss—which just might be harder than the task she had set out for herself to bring Christmas to Cold Creek Canyon.

She wasn't sure how much longer she could keep going at this frenetic pace.

Tuesday night—five days after that stunning kiss, which, of course, she hadn't been able to forget whatsoever—Hope let herself into the darkened ranch house at ten minutes to midnight. Her family was probably sound asleep. Oh, how she envied them. She was so tired, her left eye had started to twitch hours ago, but she still had at least a few hours of work to do before she could give *both* eyes a rest.

For the umpteenth time, she wondered if she was crazy to have ever started this whole thing with The Christmas Ranch. The odds still seemed stacked sky-high against her. With each passing hour, she grew more and more certain she simply wouldn't have time to accomplish everything necessary to open to the public.

Maybe she would have been better off throwing all the time and energy she had expended the past week into the cattle side of the Star N. At least then she would feel like she was actually helping Faith and the rest of her family, not entangling them all in this ridiculous holiday attraction that would probably be a huge bust this year.

She had one more full day and evening to accomplish

everything on her list. The day after that was Thanksgiving and she had vowed she would take off at least part of the day to be with her family.

She wouldn't have even come close to being ready for the opening if not for Rafe Santiago.

He showed up as soon as Joey went to school and left only long enough to pick his nephew up and then the two of them would come back and help out until after dark. He was a relentlessly hard worker and didn't stop going from the moment he showed up until he left.

She had no idea how she would ever repay him.

Hope was painfully aware that since that kiss, both of them made a conscious effort to avoid being alone together. Awareness still seemed to shimmer between them, bright and dazzling, but he had been careful to focus on jobs on the other side of the Ranch from wherever she was working.

When they spoke, it was polite, even friendly, but they exchanged no more of those confidences they had shared that day while digging the holes for the pathway light stakes.

That hadn't stopped her from watching him when he wasn't looking and remembering those heated moments in his arms.

She pushed away thoughts of Rafe, which had the strangest way of sneaking into her mind when she could least afford the distraction. She still had a few hours of work to finish before she could sleep but she needed a little fuel to keep her engine going.

With any luck, Aunt Mary or her sisters—depending on who had cooked that night—might have left her a plate of whatever the family had for dinner.

After hanging her coat in the mudroom, she headed

for the kitchen and was shocked to find a light on and Celeste working at the table with art supplies spread out all around her—googly eyes, colorful feathers and construction paper.

"Wow. You're up late!"

Celeste shrugged. "I had a few things to prep for the Thanksgiving storytime I'm doing at the library tomorrow. We're making paper plate turkeys and I've learned the only way to keep things halfway sane is to throw all the kits together ahead of time."

"Those are darling. The kids are going to love them."

Hope knew Celeste adored her job as the children's librarian at the small city library in Pine Gulch and she was wonderful at it—dedicated and caring and passionate.

"Thanks," Celeste said, then gave her a somewhat sheepish look. "Okay, these handouts are only part of the reason I'm still up. I could have done this in my room, but I was waiting for you. I've been dying of curiosity."

"Oh?" For a crazy moment, she wondered if Celeste was going to ask about the big, gorgeous man who was working at The Christmas Ranch, but both of her sisters were so busy, she wasn't sure they were even aware of Rafe and all his efforts on her behalf.

"You got a FedEx delivery this evening. Two big boxes from Seaberry Publishing."

"What?" she exclaimed, her exhaustion instantly sluicing away. "They're here? Oh! That's fantastic news! The best!"

"What's here?"

"Our book! *Sparkle and the Magic Snowball*. My friend Deb was going to rush the print job but she warned me not to expect anything until next week at the earliest. I'm so happy the first shipment of books will be here for the opening!"

"You said you wanted to print up a few copies," Celeste exclaimed, looking suddenly nervous. "Exactly how many was a few?"

"Um. Five hundred." She winced, waiting for her sister's reaction.

"Five hundred!" As she might have expected, Celeste's jaw sagged and her eyes filled with horror. "What are we going to do with five hundred copies of a book no one wants? How much did that cost you out of pocket?"

More than she wanted to share with her sister. She had used a big chunk of her savings but fully expected to earn it back—when the books completely sold out— and enough to give her sister a nice royalty. "Don't worry about it. I got a good deal from Deb and Carlo."

"Five hundred copies!"

She reached for her sister's hands. "CeCe, it's a delightful story, full of heart and wisdom and beauty. The best sort of children's story. Deb absolutely adored it. She asked if she could print some extras to give as Christmas gifts to her daughter's friends and reduced our cost accordingly. I hope that's okay."

Celeste swallowed hard. Her eyes looked huge in suddenly pale features. "Oh, Hope. What have you done?"

"We talked about this, remember?"

"You said a few copies!"

"It's always cheaper per item if you print more quantity at the same time. That just makes good business sense."

"But what are you going to do with all those books?"

"We don't have to sell them all this year. We can keep them in the gift shop for years to come."

"If we even have The Christmas Ranch after this year!"

She wasn't going to think about that yet. Not tonight, when she finally had something wonderful to celebrate.

"You will love it, I swear. I can't wait to see the finished product. I can't believe you didn't already open the boxes!"

Celeste looked pale, her eyes huge in her narrow face. "They were addressed to you. I couldn't snoop through your personal mail."

Hope certainly would have snooped, but then she and Celeste were two completely different people. Her sister was sweet and gentle and kind and Hope was…not.

She squeezed Celeste's hands. "I'm so glad you stayed up until I came home. It's only right that we look at them for the first time together. The author and the illustrator. How cool is that?"

Celeste was all but wringing her hands as Hope lifted one of the boxes onto the table and grabbed some scissors out of the kitchen catch-all drawer to carefully split the packing tape.

She pulled the flaps back and her heart gave an excited little kick at the delicious new-book smell that escaped.

There it was, in bright, brilliant colors. She reached inside and pulled one out. Had she really drawn that darling, whimsical picture on the cover, of a reindeer with a wreath around his neck and his little bird friend Snowdrop perched in his antlers?

It seemed only right that she handed the first copy

over to Celeste, who took it with hands that trembled. "Oh. Oh, my," her sister breathed, gazing at the picture book as if it contained all the secrets to the universe.

Celeste ran a finger over the little reindeer and for the first time, Hope felt a qualm or two or ten, hoping she had done the right thing.

"It's such a charming story," she said softly. "I'm afraid my illustrations haven't quite done your words justice."

"No. No, they're perfect. You hit exactly the right note between sweet and warm, without being corny."

She flipped through the pages, stopping on one or two to look more closely. "This is crazy. These are fantastic, Hope! When could you possibly have had time to do this? You've only been here a little more than a week!"

"Oh, here and there. A lot of it was at night after everyone was in bed."

This was the reason she was so tired, because she had spent three nights straight without sleep, trying to get all the details right on the twenty illustrations.

"They're wonderful. I love Snowdrop. He's my favorite. Oh, and the way you've put that darling little holly wreath in all the pictures."

She flipped another page with a soft smile. "You're very good," she said. The note of surprise in her sister's voice probably wouldn't have bothered Hope so much if it didn't serve to emphasize the distance that had crept up between her and her sisters the past few years, mostly by her own doing.

"Tell me this," Celeste said. "Why are you off teaching English in far-away countries when you could be a professional illustrator?"

She harrumphed. "You don't need to exaggerate. I'm not *that* good."

"I know books, Hope—especially children's books. It's what I do. These illustrations are fantastic—whimsical and charming and full of wonder and heart. People are going to love it. How could they not?"

"I hope so. I have five hundred copies to sell." At least one of her harebrained ideas just might pan out, though it was too early to know until visitors to the gift shop were able to get their hands on the book. "You'll be receiving fifty percent of the profits, by the way."

Celeste shook her head. "Just put it back into the Ranch. Buy a few more strings of lights or something."

She hoped the book would result in far more sales than that but she didn't say anything now to her sister. It was hard enough for Celeste to know she had printed five hundred copies so she decided not to mention that Deb and Carlo were prepared to go back to press at any moment once they gauged the demand.

"We make a pretty good team, don't we?"

"I guess we do." Celeste smiled, looking soft and lovely. Her sister's beauty was the sort most people tended to overlook. She had always been quiet and perhaps a little introverted—more so after their parents died and the sisters moved here to Pine Gulch.

Perhaps having a published book would give Celeste a little more confidence in herself and all she had to offer the world.

"We should do another Sparkle story together," she said impulsively. "Not this year, of course—I won't have time before Christmas, but will you let me take a look at some of your stories after the holidays? Because of the time crunch this time, I couldn't really consult with you about the illustrations but I'd love more collaboration, if we do another one. I also want you to consider the possibility of creating a digital version to sell online, if we get enough interest with the print version."

Celeste blinked, looking stunned and a little overwhelmed. Hope took pity on her.

"Not tonight. We can talk about it another time, when we're both not so tired and you're not up to your eyeballs in turkeys."

Celeste nodded, her gaze still on the book in her hand.

"And speaking of story times," Hope went on, "you must take a few copies to the library for the children of Pine Gulch. Three or four, at least. And don't you think it would be perfect if Mrs. Claus—perhaps a professionally trained storytelling version of Mrs. Claus—could come and read *Sparkle and the Magic Snowball* to the children who visit The Christmas Ranch while the real Sparkle is there, too?"

Her sister pushed a strand of overlong hair from her face. "You don't give up, do you?"

"Not when it's about something and someone I care about so much. I would love you to do this. I know I can find someone else to be the official Christmas Ranch storyteller—even Aunt Mary—but no one would be as good at it as you, especially since you wrote the story yourself."

Celeste gazed down at the book in her hands then back at Hope. "I don't know. I'm not sure I can read my own writing aloud. It's such an intimate, personal thing."

"All the more reason you should be the one sharing it with the world. It's your choice. Just think about it.

I won't push you, other than to say that I don't think anybody else can really do the story justice, CeCe."

With a sigh, her sister folded her arms, tucking the book against her chest. "You're impossibly stubborn, just like Dad was. I suppose that's one of the reasons we all love you."

"If I weren't stubborn, I never would have taken on The Christmas Ranch. I would have let that Closed Indefinitely sign stay up, well, *indefinitely*, and would have spent the past week getting in everyone's way here at the house and fretting about my next job."

Instead of burning the candle at both ends *and* in the middle—not to mention nurturing a serious crush over a man she couldn't have, but she didn't mention that to Celeste.

After a long silence, Celeste spoke, her words hurried as if she had been thinking them for a while and only needed the chance to let them out.

"This is hard for me to admit, but…but I think what you're doing with the Ranch is a good thing. The *right* thing. For all of us."

"Oh. Oh, CeCe." Her throat suddenly felt tight and her eyes burned, though she told herself it was only the unexpected approval from her sister.

"The children have been happier these past few days, with something to keep them occupied. Even Faith has remarked on it, though she might not admit it out loud to you. Mary is happier too and even Faith seems to have more energy. We were all completely frozen in our grief over Travis. Maybe we just needed you to come shake things up. I'm glad you're here and I'm glad the Ranch is going to open after all."

"Does that mean you'll help out as Mrs. Claus?" she pressed.

Celeste rolled her eyes. "You don't give up, do you? I'll think about it. That's the best I can do right now. And now I really need to catch some sleep if I'm going to be able to cope with thirty preschoolers tomorrow."

"Good night. I'll be right behind you. I'm going to grab a bowl of cereal and read this beautiful story written by my brilliant baby sister one more time."

The brilliant baby sister in question only gave a rueful smile and, clutching the book, headed for her room, leaving Hope behind to wonder whether she was really doing the right thing for her family.

Chapter 10

The next afternoon, Hope made the finishing brush strokes on the project in front of her, then sat back on her heels to admire her work.

Beautiful. Exactly the look she wanted. She had found the big piece of scrap barnwood from an old demolished outbuilding behind a shed on the Star N and that weathered red was exactly the shade she wanted.

Okay, it hadn't been a top priority, but she didn't mind the extra time she had spent on it, especially with her sudden conviction that the sign would provide the perfect finishing touch.

Maybe CeCe was right. Maybe she should have tried to be an illustrator. She had always loved to draw and paint and had a fair talent at it. She had a degree in art history but had always thought she didn't have the chops to do it professionally.

The last few years while in Morocco, she had turned to photography, not only because the country was so very photogenic but because it seemed a far more portable medium—it was easier carrying a camera and lenses through a crowded, twisting medina than a huge canvas and box of paints.

Photography was definitely an art form but she did love the immediate, hands-on, almost *magical* connection between her brain, her eyes, a canvas and the brush in her hand.

She stood up, pressing a hand to the small of her back that ached from an hour crouched over the floor in the back storeroom of the St. Nicholas Lodge.

"What's all this?"

She turned at the voice and found Rafe had come in while she was patting herself on the back over her work. He looked gorgeous, dark and tough and ruggedly handsome in another of those heavy cotton work shirts over a soft henley, this one blue.

Her palms suddenly felt itchy and her insides trembled. "New sign for the reindeer enclosure," she managed.

"Home of the Original Sparkle," he read aloud.

She was particularly proud of the cute reindeer on the sign and the way the word *Sparkle* seemed to come alive.

"Remember I was telling you about the delightful story my sister wrote and the illustrations I was doing for it?"

"Right. The reason you haven't been getting any sleep since you came back to Pine Gulch," he said.

"Well, the books came last evening and they're absolutely wonderful, every bit as magical as I dreamed."

"Sparkle is one of the reindeer you had pull the wagon that day we put the lights on the Christmas village, right?"

"Yes. We all adore him. He's gentle and kind and definitely a favorite. I've got to show you something. You get to be the first one to see it."

Overflowing with excitement, she hurried over to her big tote bag in the corner. She reached inside and pulled out the little project she had made up after mailing off the finished pages of the book to Deb and Carlo in Seattle—a stuffed fabric reindeer based on her illustration, made out of sparkly fabric, complete with a ribbon and child-safe jingle bell around his neck.

"Ta da. It's Sparkle."

She thrust it at him. The toy looked a little girlish and silly in his big, rough hands as he turned it this way and that for a better look. "You did this?"

"I like to sew. All of us do. It's something our mother taught us."

"You sew, you paint, you teach English in undeveloped areas of the world. Is there anything you *don't* do?"

Besides protect her heart against big, gorgeous navy men? She was discovering she wasn't all that terrific at that particular skill.

"Don't you think the kids will love it?" she asked, ignoring his question.

He gave her a look filled with amusement and something else—something warm and bright and even more glittery than the little stuffed fabric creature he held in his hand. "They will adore it. I just have one question."

"What's that?"

"Do you ever stop moving?"

She shrugged, though she had been living in a state of perpetual exhaustion for days. "I'll stop after the opening Friday."

"No, you won't. You're going to work yourself into the ground until Christmas is over. You can't do everything you want to, Hope. If you don't pace yourself and figure out the definition of the word *enough* you're going to find yourself flat on your back in bed."

She would like to be flat on her back in bed—as long as he was there beside her, cuddled in front of a fire, with a nice cozy quilt wrapped around them and nothing else.

The impulse came out of nowhere, probably a product of her exhaustion. Suddenly she tingled *everywhere*. Stupid imagination.

"I know. I don't need a lecture from you, Dr. Santiago."

He made a face. "You need to listen to someone. You need to slow down, Hope. You're wearing yourself out. I'm…worried about you."

"Oh."

Warmth fluttered through her, sweet and seductive.

"You don't need to worry about me. I'll be fine. Great. Only two more days and then the Ranch will open and everything will be perfect."

"And you'll be in a hospital bed, suffering from exhaustion. What do you have to do this afternoon? Just give me your list and I'll do what I can to check things off while you go take a nap."

"I wish that were possible, but it's not. I have too much to do if I'm going to make this happen."

"Let me help you, Hope."

"You are helping me! You've been amazing, Rafe. Anything I need, you're there, from fixing the tow rope to building that little shelter where people wait in line for the sleigh rides to all the repairs you've done inside and out. I honestly don't know what I would have done without you. Are you sure you don't want to come work full-time for me on The Christmas Ranch?" she joked.

"Depends," he said, his voice husky. "What kind of benefits can you offer?"

All at once, she knew he wasn't talking about 401(k)s or long-term disability insurance. The air between them was suddenly charged, thick and heady, swirling with the currents of awareness they had both been ignoring all week.

Walk on, she told herself, just as if she were one of the reindeer pulling a sleigh. *You're hanging by a thread here anyway and don't need his kind of trouble.*

Apparently she wasn't very good at listening to her own better judgment. She took a step forward, unable to help herself.

"I'm sure I could come up with something…enticing."

His laugh sounded rough and a little strained. "I don't doubt that."

She wanted to kiss him again. All week, the memory had simmered beneath her skin. They had both worked so hard. Surely they deserved a little reward…

She stepped closer and he suddenly looked wary, as if he regretted ever starting this.

"Um, Hope."

She kept moving, until she was only a foot away from

him. "I've been telling myself all week that kissing you again wouldn't be a very good idea."

He cleared his throat. "Yeah. I get that."

"Right now, I don't care. I'm going to do it anyway. Is that a problem for you, sailor?"

He laughed again, his pupils a little dilated. "Ask me that again in a few minutes," he said, his voice a low rasp that shivered down her spine. He didn't wait for her to kiss him, but reached out and tugged her against him and lowered his mouth.

Oh. Wow.

Their kiss in the little storage shed had been raw and wild. This one was soft, sweet, tender—and completely devastating.

He explored her mouth with his, each corner, each hollow, licking and tasting and seducing with every passing second. She was fiercely grateful for his muscles and his strength. Without him holding her up, she would have collapsed right onto her cute little reindeer sign.

"You taste so good," he murmured. "I've dreamed about it every single night since that morning last week. I thought I imagined it but you're even more delicious than I remembered."

She didn't care about anything right now, not the Ranch, not the storybook, not her to-do list. All that mattered was this moment, this man and the amazing wonder of being in his arms again.

She wrapped her arms around him, savoring the heat and strength of him. A warm tenderness seemed to unfurl somewhere deep inside, something she had never known before that made her want to hold him close and take away all his worries. She didn't want it to ever end.

He slid his mouth away and began to trail kisses across her cheekbone to her throat and then worked his way back to her mouth.

Yeah. She would have no problem standing right here and doing this for the rest of the day. Or week. Or year.

"Oh."

The soft exclamation—and the realization that someone else was there—finally pierced the soft, delicious haze that seemed to have surrounded them. It took her a moment to collect her scattered thoughts enough to be able to ease her mouth away from his.

She turned and found Faith standing in the doorway, watching the two of them with her mouth open and an expression of raw shock on her features.

Rafe had suddenly gone still, like an alert, dangerous panther, she realized, though she wasn't quite sure why. Maybe the same reason why she suddenly felt mortified, though she was a grown woman who had every right to kiss an incredibly hot—and even more amazingly *sweet*—man if she wanted to. And she *so* wanted to.

"Faith. Um. Hi."

Her sister continued to stare at them, though her gaze was fixed on Rafe.

"Um, Faith, this is Rafael Santiago. The man I told you about, who has been helping me out with the Ranch."

"You never mentioned his name."

Why did that matter? Hope shrugged. "Didn't I? That's funny. I'm sure I must have."

"No. Believe me, I would have remembered."

After the sweet intensity of that kiss, Hope could barely focus on remembering to breathe, forget about trying to figure out why her sister was behaving so oddly—and Rafe, as well, for that matter. Why would he be watching Faith with that strange, alert expression?

She was suddenly reminded forcefully that he had just spent twenty years in the military, facing dangerous situations.

"What are you doing here?" Faith demanded, in a weird, almost hostile tone that was totally unlike her usually gentle sister.

"Faith," she exclaimed, mortified. "I would think that was fairly obvious." *And if you would please go away, we can do it some more.*

"Not *that*," Faith said. "I'm asking what *he* is doing here?"

"Helping out your sister," Rafe answered for himself.

"Why?"

"Because she needed it. And because I wanted to."

Faith stepped forward and Hope was surprised to see some of the color had leached away from her features.

"Why are you in Pine Gulch, of all places?" she pressed. "That seems an odd coincidence, don't you think?"

"That's exactly what it was, actually. Believe it or not." A muscle worked in his jaw as he turned to look at Hope with an expression she couldn't read, almost like an apology, though she had no idea what was happening here.

"It's also a long and complicated story."

"Is it?"

"My sister is in jail in Pine Gulch. I'm here caring for her son until after her sentencing."

"And you just happened to bump into Hope and offer to help her with The Christmas Ranch?" Faith asked, skepticism in her voice.

"That's about the size of it, yeah."

Okay, this was ridiculous. She knew her sister felt a great deal of responsibility for her and for Celeste but this was pushing things. She was thirty years old, for heaven's sake, and had spent most of her adult life not only living on her own but residing in a completely different country.

"Faith, cut it out. Why are you being like this? Rafe has been an amazing help to me. I never would have been ready for the opening Friday if not for him."

Her sister narrowed her gaze at Hope, looked at Rafe, then back at her with an intensity that suddenly made her uncomfortable. "You don't know who he is! You don't remember him at all, do you?"

Hope frowned. "Remember him? What are you talking about?"

"Special Warfare Operator Rafe Santiago. He was there, in Colombia. One of the navy SEALs who came to our rescue."

Her heart gave a hard, vicious kick at the words and for a moment, she could only stare. "That's ridiculous," she said, when she could find her voice again.

"It's not," Faith insisted. "I remember every single name, every man. I wrote them all down so I wouldn't forget afterward."

"You sent thank-you notes, care of our lieutenant," he said, his voice gruff.

Through her shock and disbelief, she saw Faith's too-pale skin suddenly turn blotchy and pink as she blushed. "It seemed the right thing to do."

She shifted back to Rafe, suddenly flashing back to that horrible Christmas day, to stunning hazel eyes in a tense, hard face.

She remembered gunfire and shouting in Spanish and the helicopter and then screaming and screaming for her father while a young soldier yanked her inside.

"That was…you?"

Rafe had grown even more still in that eerie way he had, that jungle cat, as if he were fusing himself into the background, merging his skin and his bones to his surroundings.

"Yes."

"You said you were in the navy. You never said you were a SEAL."

He said nothing. Where was the man who had kissed her so tenderly? Who had held her and whispered delicious words about her mouth and how she tasted?

This man seemed like a stranger—dark, dangerous, indestructible.

"You've known all this time and you never said a word about being there. We even *talked* about Colombia and you still didn't mention anything. Why?"

"It was…wrong not to say anything, especially when you brought it up. I should have. I'm sorry now that I didn't. I tried a few times but the moment never seemed quite right."

This was the reason he had helped her, she suddenly realized. Not because they were friends, not because he was coming to care about her as she was him. It was all tangled up in the past, in that pivotal moment that had altered the course of her life. The fear and the pain and the helplessness she couldn't outrun, no matter how far she traveled.

She stared at him, feeling as if everything had changed in a matter of moments, as if all the soft, hazy daydreams she was beginning to spin about him had just turned into the dark, ugly stuff of nightmares.

Chapter 11

Okay, he had seriously mucked this whole thing up.

Rafe did his best not to stagger beneath the combined weight of the glares delivered by the two Nichols sisters.

He thought he had been doing a good thing, helping the family out by making The Christmas Ranch ready for guests, but somehow he had made several serious errors in judgment.

He should have told her. In retrospect, he wasn't sure why the words had been so difficult. At first, he hadn't wanted to dredge up something he knew must be difficult for her or add another layer of stress when she was already dealing with so much.

Later, after he had come to know her better and—yes, he could admit it—to *care* about her, he had put off telling her because he had been trying to avoid this moment, the shock and betrayal in her eyes.

He supposed some part of him had also worried that when she found out he had been involved in her family's rescue, she would tell him to stop coming to The Christmas Ranch. That would have broken Joey's heart, since his nephew loved coming here every afternoon—and without his help, she never would have been able to whip the place into shape in time.

In the back of his mind, he had known she would find out eventually. It was as inevitable as deep snow in the mountains around here.

"You knew who I was from the beginning," she said with dawning realization. "That very first day, when Joey threw a snowball at my pickup truck."

"Not until you told me your name," he said. "After that, yes. I knew you and your sisters had come to Pine Gulch after everything went south in Colombia. Our lieutenant made a point of keeping track of your whereabouts and passed that intel along to those of us he knew were concerned about you all."

"You've probably been on hundreds of missions since Colombia," Faith said. "How could you possibly remember three girls you met seventeen years ago?"

"I remember everything about that day." He didn't tell them it was his first mission as a SEAL and his first actual combat experience and it would have been indelibly etched in his brain even if everything hadn't fallen apart as it had. "When Cami called me and told me she was in jail in a little town she was sure I'd never heard of called Pine Gulch, Idaho, I was stunned at the way fate could twist and turn like a python."

He should have told her, damn it. That very first day, he should have mentioned they shared a history. Each and every time the thought had come to him over the past week that *now* would be a good time, he should have acted instead of sitting on his ass and waiting for the perfect moment.

He might have told himself he was thinking about her feelings but the truth was, withholding the information hadn't been fair to her.

"Before that day with Joey and the window, I always intended to come out here and meet all three of you. In the back of my head, I guess I thought maybe I would check and see how you were, all these years later. I couldn't quite figure out how to just show up on your doorstep and say, 'Hey, surprise. Remember me?' I guess I just never expected to meet one of you on the other end of a broken car window."

The explanation didn't appear to ease any of the stormy emotions he could see building in Hope's expression. She faced him, all tangled blond curls and kiss-swollen lips and flushed cheeks.

"You've been working here a week and you didn't think it was important to bring it up once. You *kissed* me—multiple times, I might add—and you still never told me."

Faith cleared her throat. "I should, uh… I've got some things to do at the house."

Right. Just come on in and interrupt in the middle of an epic kiss, ruin everything, then leave again.

He knew the thought wasn't fair. He was the only one to blame in this whole mess.

"You don't have to leave," he and Hope both said at the same time.

"I think I do. I only stopped to see how things were

going down here and...to see if you need a hand with any last-minute things."

"Oh, Faith." Something he didn't understand passed between the sisters, something intense and emotional. Hope crossed to her sister and hugged the other woman, though he wasn't quite sure why.

"Thank you. I can't tell you how much that means."

Faith hugged her back for just a moment then extricated herself. "I'll come back after I, um, finish some things at the house."

She clearly wanted to escape. Rafe couldn't blame her. He wouldn't mind slipping away either. Before he could, Faith approached him and gave him a steady look. "Has Hope invited you and your—nephew, is it?— for Thanksgiving?"

The question took him unawares and he had to collect his thoughts for a moment before he could answer. "Yes," he admitted.

"I've invited them over a few times," Hope said, with dawning awareness. "He refused each and every time. Now I'm beginning to see why. You couldn't be sure Faith or Celeste wouldn't be as ditzy as I apparently am. You figured one of them would recognize you."

Yeah, that had been part of the reason for his continued refusal, but not the entirety. "I told you I didn't want to intrude on your family dinner."

"It's no intrusion," Faith assured him. "Come to dinner, if you don't already have plans. It's the least we can do to repay you—not only for what happened seventeen years ago but for all the help you've apparently given Hope these past few days."

She waved to both of them and hurried out of the lodge, leaving a heavy silence behind.

"Well," Hope finally said. "This is an unexpected turn of events."

He drew in a breath and faced her. Her usually bright, open expression had become hard, almost brittle, in the past few moments.

"Hope. I'm sorry. I should have told you."

"Why didn't you?"

"Stupid reasons," he admitted. "I see that now. I didn't want to upset you when you were already stressed and exhausted."

He exhaled. He might as well get this over with, tell her the rest of it while every ugly secret was bubbling up like an acidic mineral pool.

"At first, I didn't tell you because, well, I didn't know how to bring it up. Later, I suppose it was...self-protective, in a way."

"What are you talking about?"

"I made mistakes in that raid. Mistakes that have haunted me ever since. They're hard to admit, especially now that I've come to know you and better understand the cost of my mistakes. It was my first mission and I screwed it up. That's why I never forgot any of you, why I was interested in your well-being after the mission was over. That's also why I didn't want to tell you after we became...friends. I guess I didn't want you to hate me."

She stared at him, eyes huge in her delicate, lovely features. "What mistakes? How did you screw up?"

"We don't need to go into this now, do we?"

"What mistakes, Rafe?" she pressed, her tone relentless. He knew that stubbornness. The same grit had kept her on the go constantly the last week, until she was about to drop from little sleep. She wouldn't let up until he told her everything, each ugly misstep.

"We can at least sit down."

Not knowing quite what else to do, he gestured toward the chairs arranged around the huge Christmas tree she and the children had decorated a few evenings earlier, near one of the massive river-rock fireplaces.

He sat down next to her and fought the urge to reach for her hand. This was much harder than he expected. He had spent seventeen years as a freaking navy SEAL and had scuba dived, parachuted and prowled into all manner of hazardous situations. So why was his adrenaline pumping harder than he ever remembered?

"First of all, I guess I should tell you, this was my very first operation as a SEAL. I was a dumb twenty-one-year-old kid just weeks out of BUD/S. I spent my first few years in the navy stationed on an aircraft carrier and had never been in actual combat."

She was silent, watching him out of eyes that didn't seem to miss anything.

He swallowed. "It was supposed to be an easy extraction, just sneak in during the early morning hours when everyone was sleeping, separate you and your family from Juan Pablo and his crazy militants and take you all back to the helipad. But something went wrong."

"Yes. It did."

He closed his eyes, reliving the confusion of that night. "Your father was my responsibility but he wasn't being held where he was supposed to be, where our intel reported."

"They moved him to another hut a few days before Christmas to keep him separate from our mother and us, thinking he wouldn't try to escape without us and we couldn't escape without him."

"My partner and I finally found him. He was being

guarded by one small kid who looked like he was no more than thirteen or fourteen."

His sister's age, he remembered thinking. "I should have taken him out in his sleep but I...didn't."

He should have at least immobilized the kid and removed any threat with a sleeper hold, but the kid had already been sound asleep, snoring like an elephant and he and his partner had made the disastrous decision to leave him sleeping.

"We managed to get your father out of his restraints and the hut where they were holding him. But just as we were heading to the extraction site, something awoke his guard—the kid I didn't have the stones to take out in his sleep. He yelled and all hell broke loose as you all were loading up. I turned to fire but I was too slow."

"And?"

He swallowed. "If I had been a fraction of a second faster, your father might still be alive."

He waited for her to get angry or hurt or *something*. She only continued to stare at him out of those huge eyes.

"You said the mission haunted you for all these years," she finally said. "Is this the pack full of guilt you've been carrying?"

"Not all of it, but it makes up a few of the heaviest stones I've got back there."

"Well, you can set those down right here. What happened to my father wasn't your fault. He made his own choices, all along the way. He was the one who chose to drag his family to that particular area, despite all the warnings. My father was a great man whose heart was always in the right place but he was also an idealistic one. He believed in the inherent goodness of people and he refused to accept that some people and some situations couldn't be fixed by an outpouring of love or charity or generosity of spirit."

"My single moment of hesitation cost your father his life."

She shook her head. "You don't know that. A helicopter was landing outside Juan Pablo's camp. Do you really think that guard or Juan Pablo or anyone else would have slept through that? You risked your life for us. All of you did. That's the only part that matters to me about your actions of that day."

She genuinely meant it, he realized. He had expected tears and recriminations, anger, pain. Instead, she was offering *solace.*

What an amazing woman.

Her words seemed to seep into his heart, his conscience, like a balm, healing places he hadn't realized were damaged, and he didn't trust himself to speak for a long moment.

"I'm not angry with you about anything you did that day. I couldn't be."

Her voice abruptly hardened. "Don't think for a moment that lets you off the hook for keeping this from me since the day we met. You owed me the truth from the very first."

"I did," he said, his voice gruff. How could he tell her he hadn't wanted to risk damaging this fragile, tender friendship that was becoming so very important to him?

"I don't know if I can get over that, Rafe. It's going to take some time." She stood up. "That said, Faith is right. You and Joey should come to Thanksgiving dinner. You have no excuse to say no now. We eat about three. I'll tell Mary and Celeste to expect you."

She rose, gave him a long look, then hurried away from him into the office of the lodge and closed the door.

By the time she made it to the office, Hope was almost running, though she hoped Rafe couldn't see her from where he still sat by the fireplace.

With a pretend casualness she was far from feeling, she closed the door with great care so it didn't slam then sank down into Uncle Claude's big leather chair, desperately needing the comfort of the familiar.

She had barely had time to absorb the sweetness and aching tenderness of that kiss and *this*.

She didn't have time to even think straight right now. In forty-eight hours, The Christmas Ranch would be opening to the public and she still had a hundred last-minute details to attend to—not to mention more reindeer to sew, if she could find time.

She had promised herself she would take Thanksgiving afternoon off to be with her family, which left her tonight, a few hours in the morning and Friday throughout the day, before The Christmas Ranch had its traditional opening at dusk on the day after Thanksgiving.

Now she had this stunning revelation to contend with.

Rafe was there. He was a navy SEAL and had been involved in her family's rescue that fateful Christmas day seventeen years go.

Now she realized why he had seemed so familiar. She had blocked many things out about that day but now that she knew the truth, memories flooded back in a heavy deluge.

She couldn't have pinpointed any particular features

among any of the other SEAL team members who had rescued them except those eyes, so unexpectedly and strikingly hazel in his otherwise Latino features.

Now she could picture him as clearly as if she had a photograph of that day—young, tough, dangerous.

Why hadn't he told her?

She still didn't understand. She thought they had been able to push aside their obvious attraction for each other and had started to develop a friendship of sorts.

She had even begun to think maybe she was falling in love, for the first time in her life, even though she had known nothing would ever come of it.

How could it?

For one thing, he obviously didn't share those burgeoning feelings if he could continue perpetuating a lie by omission. More important, he was completely focused on his nephew right now, as he should be. In a few weeks' time, he would be moving back to San Diego to start a new life with Joey and she had all but decided she was going to stay here in Pine Gulch with her family.

For another, how could she ever trust him now?

She buried her face in her hands for only a moment, surrendering only briefly to the pain and frustration churning through her. She had worked so hard to move past that life-changing day, to tell herself she was stronger than what had happened to her. She wouldn't let the ideas of some misguided zealots control her life.

Now, when she had finally met a man she thought she could fall in love with, the events of that day reared back to consume everything good and wonderful in her world.

After a momentary pity party, she dropped her

hands, rubbed them briskly down her legs and stood up again. She didn't have time for this. The people of southern Idaho didn't care about her petty problems. They needed a little Christmas spirit and she was going to deliver it, damn it, no matter what the cost.

Chapter 12

They shouldn't have come.

Standing beside him on the front porch at the Star N Ranch house, Joey vibrated with excitement. It was like a force field of crackling energy around him.

"Can I ring the doorbell?" he asked.

"Sure. Go ahead."

The boy rang it, waited about two seconds, then rang it again. He was about to go back for a third time two seconds after that but Rafe held a hand out to block him.

"Whoa. That's good. Give somebody time to answer the door."

"I'm starving. I can't wait for turkey!"

Before Rafe could answer, the door opened and a vision appeared, silhouetted in the doorway. It was Hope, but as he'd never seen her before. She was wearing makeup for the first time he remembered and all that luscious hair had been curled. It fell past her shoulders in blond waves that made him want to trail his fingers through it.

She wore dressy slacks and a soft-looking sweater in rich blues and greens.

His mouth watered—and not because of the delicious aromas emanating from the warm doorway.

"You came," she said, her features politely distant. "I wasn't sure you would."

"You basically ordered me to," he answered.

She made a face before returning her features to that cool mask he couldn't read. Was she happy to see them? He didn't know. She seemed to have walled up some central part of herself since that earthshaking kiss the day before and the awkward way it had ended, with her sister's interruption.

"Hey, Joey." She beamed down at his nephew with a much more genuine smile that made his chest suddenly ache.

Yeah. They shouldn't have come.

"Hi, Hope. Uncle Rafe said we should bring you a hostess gift, so I made this." He thrust the handprint turkey he had made that morning.

"I love it! Thanks. That one is going on the fridge, for sure. Come in. You don't have to stand out in the cold."

They walked into the house. He had caught delicious smells while standing on the porch, but once inside, Rafe was just about bowled over with sensory overload from multiple delicious things cooking. Potatoes and turkey and stuffing and pie, all mixed together in one luscious package.

Through it all, he could still pick up Hope's scent,

though, that subtly exotic cinnamon and almond scent of her.

"Where's Barrett?" Joey asked as soon as he handed over his coat.

"He and his sister are down the hall with a few of the neighbor kids, engaged in a vicious Mario Kart competition in the den. I believe there's always room for one more. Third door on the right."

"Yay! Thanks!" He hurried away from them, leaving Rafe and Hope alone in the foyer.

"You brought goodies," she said, gesturing to the casserole dish he held.

"Er. Yeah. I believe we've already firmly established I'm not much of a cook but I've been known to make a pretty good guac from one of my grandmother's recipes. I brought chips, too."

"Wow. Thank you. Those will go fast. Everybody's in the kitchen. Come on back."

He followed her toward those delectable scents and found the open kitchen and family room more crowded than he expected. To his relief, he wasn't going to be the only male at the Star N family Thanksgiving. Two other men were in the room.

An older woman, plump and comfortable, looked him up and down from her spot at the long kitchen table where it looked as if she was snapping beans. "So this is your navy SEAL."

"He's not mine," Hope said, her voice tight. "But yes. This is Rafe Santiago. Rafe, this is my aunt Mary and these are a few of our neighbors, Chase Brannon—who has a ranch just up the road—and Justin and Ashley Hartford. Yeah. That Justin Hartford."

He stared for just a moment at the familiar face of the

man holding out his hand before he recovered enough to shake it. He didn't get starstruck, but every single one of Hartford's films was in his top ten list of favorite films. He knew the man had left Hollywood more than a decade earlier and disappeared from public view. Now he knew where he'd gone.

"And you know my sisters already."

He nodded warily at the sisters, not sure of what his reception would be now that everyone in the family knew he had been involved in that ill-fated rescue.

The youngest sister—the quiet one who wrote stories about reindeer and worked as a children's librarian, he remembered—rose from the table and approached him. To his great surprise, she reached up and kissed him on the cheek.

He was still reeling from that unexpected sweetness when she pounded him lightly on the chest. "You should have told us."

He squirmed. "Yeah. Hope has already given me the lecture."

"Told you what?" Ashley Hartford, blonde and pretty, asked him.

"It's a very long story." Faith stood at the stove stirring something he couldn't see from here while the big, burly rancher handed her ingredients. "Let's just say our family owes him a huge debt that all the Thanksgiving dinners in forever could never repay."

That was so far from the truth they weren't in the same time zone, but this didn't seem the time to argue about it.

"So what brings you to Pine Gulch?" Justin asked. "Are you visiting or are you new in town?"

"Another long story," he said, trying not to think how

weird it was to be making small talk with a man whose movies he had watched too many times to count. "Visiting, I guess you'd say. I'm only here until Christmas. I've got a...family situation in the area."

"Well, if you have to be stuck somewhere for a while, Pine Gulch isn't a bad spot," Hartford said with a smile.

"True enough," Rafe answered, surprised to realize he meant the words.

When he first came to town, he had felt a little claustrophobic with the mountains looming big in every direction, as if he didn't quite have enough room to breathe or a ready escape route in case of trouble, as ridiculous as that seemed. With each passing day, he was coming to appreciate the wild beauty of this corner of the country and the inherent kindness of the people.

Now that he was apparently becoming a more familiar face around town, neighbors had started to wave to him when he drove past, parents in the car pool lane at school stopped to chat and one of the checkers at the grocery store had even special ordered a certain kind of protein drink for him, after he couldn't find it the other day.

He would be sorry to leave—something he never would have expected three weeks earlier when he rolled into town.

"Can I do anything to help in here?" he asked.

Faith shook her head. She still hadn't smiled at him and he wondered if she would—not that he was narcissistic about it. The woman had just lost her husband. She had plenty of things on her plate that had nothing to do with his sudden reappearance in their lives.

"I think everything is just about ready," she said in

answer to him. "In fact, now that the gravy is done, I think it's safe to call in the kids."

The meal wasn't the awkward experience he might have expected. The food was delicious and beyond plentiful and the company quite convivial. All the children—Faith's and the Hartfords's—were included at the main table. Joey seemed to fit right in and he only had to remind him once, in a subtle, private way, not to talk with his mouth full.

The neighbors were obviously good friends—he got the impression Ashley Hartford was particularly close friends to Faith and Celeste and the big rancher Brannon seemed protective and solicitous of all the Nichols women.

Listening to the conversation, it was obvious Hope and her sisters loved each other and their aunt and all of them doted on Faith's children.

After dinner, everyone helped clean up, even the kids. He had some vague expectation that he and Joey would take off as soon as the dishes were done, as he planned to make a visit to Cami at the jail before visiting hours ended, but his nephew jumped right back into playing video games with the other children in the den and he didn't have the heart to drag him away yet.

The adults moved into the family room, where Chase Brannon had turned on a football game.

"Oh, look," Celeste exclaimed, gazing out the window. "It's starting to snow a little again."

"Keep your fingers crossed it stays that way," Hope said darkly. "The little part, I mean."

"Don't say that!" Justin said with a laugh. "After that dry autumn we had, we need all the precipitation we can find."

"You can have your precipitation, cowboy, as much as you want. The day *after* tomorrow," Hope said.

"A big storm on opening day is bad for business," Faith explained to Rafe, still without smiling at him. "A few inches, like we had overnight, is just perfect but people don't like to brave nasty weather just to watch some little twinkling lights come on."

"One year we had two feet of snow on Thanksgiving night," Mary said.

"Keep your fingers crossed we get a few picturesque inches and that's all," Hope said. "Which reminds me. I've got to run down to the barn."

"You promised you would take the afternoon off," Faith said.

"I know, but I left a mess down there. I was oiling and polishing the reindeer sleigh and checking all the bells and I'm afraid I let the time get away from me. I just need to put all the cleaning supplies away and hang all the harnesses back up. It will only take a minute."

"Can't it wait until tomorrow?" Celeste asked.

"It could, but I don't want to risk one of the barn cats knocking anything over and making a bigger mess. I'll be back in a minute."

She rose and though he knew it was likely a mistake, Rafe rose, as well. She hadn't given him more than that polite smile all afternoon and he wanted to get everything out in the open between them if possible. This might be his only chance to clear the air.

"Need a hand?" he asked.

"No. I'll be fine."

"Don't be silly," her aunt Mary said. "With two people, the job will take half as long. Plus, he can make sure you don't get distracted by a hundred other tasks you find to do once you walk out that door. I'll tell you one thing, missy, we're not waiting on you all night to break into those pies."

He could tell she still wanted to refuse his help and was clearly reluctant to have him come with her. The thought stung, though he knew he deserved it.

After an awkward moment, she shrugged. "Sure. I can always use help with the heavy lifting."

In the foyer, she handed him his coat and he helped her into hers and they walked out into the crisp November night. A light snow was falling and even though he judged it was only about four-thirty in the afternoon, the cloud cover made it seem later and darker.

"Thank you for a wonderful dinner," he said, as they headed down the path toward the St. Nicholas Lodge. "I'm not sure Joey has ever enjoyed himself so much."

"I didn't do much," she admitted, "but I'll be sure to pass along your thanks to Mary and Faith. You said Joey enjoyed himself. What about you?"

"Everyone was…more kind than I expected." Or deserved, he thought, but didn't add. He also didn't mention that by *everyone*, he meant present company excepted, since she wouldn't even look at him.

He didn't like the distance between them but didn't have the first idea how to bridge it. "What will you need my help with tomorrow?" he finally asked as they neared the reindeer barn. "Joey and I can be out first thing."

"I was going to talk to you about that, actually. I'm glad you brought it up."

"Oh?"

"Joey has worked so hard this week. Throw in the work you did that you won't let me pay you for and we are more than square for the broken window on my truck. I could have replaced it three or four times over for the in-kind work you have done."

This wasn't about the window and it hadn't been since almost the first day.

"I'm just saying, you've done more than enough. You can stop now. You don't have to come out tomorrow and Joey can consider his debt more than paid after all his hard work—not to mention yours."

"We'll be here tomorrow," he said firmly. "If you don't need me after that, okay, I can accept that. But do you really think I'm willing to put all this work into something and not stick around to see the payoff?"

She sighed. "Fine. Thank you. I do still have many things to do before dusk tomorrow and I'm sure we will encounter some crisis or other that will benefit from your carpentry or mechanical skills."

He didn't feel like he had much of either one but he had learned quickly while he had been helping out this week—everything from repairing the motor on a couple of the little animatronic scenes in the Christmas village to figuring out the electrical load capabilities of the wiring inside the lodge and how many strings of Christmas lights it could safely support.

As they neared the barn next to the reindeer enclosure, Hope lifted her face to the cold air, heedless of the snowflakes that landed on her cheeks and tangled in her eyelashes. His chest ached with some indefinable emotion as he watched her. Regret? Longing? He wasn't sure.

"This storm has me nervous," she finally said, taking the last few steps to the barn. "The weather forecasters are saying we're supposed to get several inches. It could be a disaster."

"Or it could put everybody into even more of a holiday mood. You never know."

She opened the door and flipped on a light switch. Most of the reindeer were outside, preferring the cold weather, he supposed, though they could come in and out of the barn through the open door on one side.

The place smelled of leather, oil and hay—a combination he found more appealing than he might have expected.

A small fancy red sleigh that looked like it could only hold two or three people was parked in one concrete stall.

"Wow. I haven't seen this before. That's impressive."

"It's been in the other barn closer to the house. We just brought it down this morning. Uncle Claude loved this. He babied it all year long. It's kind of silly to go to all this work to polish it up, since we only use it a few times during the season for special events."

"Why?"

"The reindeer aren't that crazy about being hitched up together so we don't do it very often—mostly for photo ops. We park it in front of the lodge some afternoons and hitch one or two of the reindeer to it. Kids love to have their picture taken in it since it looks like they're driving Santa's sleigh."

"I can see that."

They spent a few minutes picking up the cleaning supplies she had left out and storing them in a cabinet in what she called the tack room, then they hung up the leather harnesses adorned with bells that jangled as they hung them up.

"Thanks," she said. "See. I didn't need your help. What did that take? All of five minutes?"

He shrugged. "I would rather be here with you than inside talking to people I don't really know."

Even if everyone inside the house had been lifelong friends, he would still rather be out here with her in the quiet peace of this barn, while snow fluttered down outside and the sun began its slide behind the mountains.

"Are you going to the jail to see your sister today?"

So much for quiet peace. He sighed at the uncomfortable topic. "Yeah. I figured we would stop by after we leave here. The jail is open for special visiting hours on Thanksgiving. I promised her I would bring Joey, even though I don't think it's an environment he needs to spend much time in, you know?"

"I get that."

"This whole thing is such a mess. Frankly, I have no idea how Joey is coping."

"He seems to be doing okay. He's a hard worker and he's obviously a smart kid. He has been nothing but polite to me while he's been working around here for me. Once the two of you get back to San Diego and settle into a routine, he'll be fine. You'll both get through this."

He still wasn't convinced of that. The idea of returning to San Diego held much less appeal than it had a week ago, even though his buddy with the private security firm had called him twice this week, wondering if Rafe could start right after Christmas.

"Thanks. I appreciate the vote of confidence. Every day I feel like I'm discovering another part of raising a kid that hits me completely unprepared."

"You're doing fine, Rafe. Better than fine. Joey

seems happy and healthy. He's a very lucky boy to have you."

Her words seemed to seep into his heart and he wanted to keep them there. "Do you mind calling me about twenty times a day to remind me of that?" he joked. "That should just about be enough."

She smiled, the first genuine one she had given him all day. She looked so beautiful there in the rustic old barn, with her wild, pretty hair and the delicate touches of makeup. He felt a little tug in his chest, remembering that earthshaking kiss of the day before.

He knew he had no right to kiss her again but the emotions welling up in his chest basically made it impossible for him to do anything else.

The moment his lips touched hers, everything inside him seemed to sigh with joy. He didn't understand this emotional pull between them. It was unlike anything he had ever experienced, rich and fierce and *real*. Maybe it had something to do with the past they shared or maybe it was simply because of her, this amazing woman who had come to mean so much to him. He didn't know. He only knew that kissing her was the best kind of magic and he never wanted to give it up.

On some deep level, Hope knew she should push him away. How could he kiss her again, as if nothing had changed between them, when *everything* was different now?

This wasn't, she amended. The sweetness and peace she found in his arms was somehow the same, despite everything else between them. How could that be? She wasn't sure, she only knew she wanted to hold on to it as tightly as she could manage.

She had a wild wish that they could stay right here, sheltered together in this warm barn while the snow-flakes twirled outside and the wind began to moan a little in the rafters.

Oh, how she wished everything could be different between them, that they had met each other at a different time, a different place and without all the ghosts of the past haunting them.

"Hope," he murmured against her mouth. Just her name, and her heart seemed to tumble in her chest.

She was in love with him.

The realization washed over her with stunning clarity.

She loved Rafe Santiago. Rescuer, navy SEAL, reluctant guardian.

Oh. What was she going to do? Not open herself up for more emotional devastation, that was certain.

"Stop. Rafe. Stop. Please."

He groaned low in his throat and rested his forehead against hers.

This was heartbreak. It was a physical, tangible pain in her chest and she wanted to cry, much to her horror. The tears welled up in her throat, behind her eyes and she had to take a moment to force them all back before she could speak.

"What are we doing here?" she whispered.

He eased away. "If you don't know, then I obviously must be doing something wrong."

She made an impatient gesture. "Here. You and me."

He looked wary suddenly. "What do you mean?"

This was a mistake. She should be casual and light, pretend their kisses meant nothing to her. She didn't need to flay herself open to him.

She couldn't do that. This was too real, too important. She could feel her hands trembling and she folded them together "Every time you kiss me, you turn me inside out. You don't have any idea, do you?"

He stared at her, those beautiful hazel eyes wide in his dark features and a little wary. "I...do?"

She wanted to be angry with him for being so oblivious to his effect on her but she couldn't. How could she blame him, when she was the fool here?

"You probably also don't have the first clue that I could...easily develop feelings for you. I'm halfway there. I could fall hard for you, Rafe. I don't want that and you don't either, trust me. I need your help to make sure it doesn't happen."

It was only a little lie. She wasn't halfway anything, but he didn't need to know that part—especially when he didn't bother to conceal his shock. He swallowed hard, staring at her. "Hope—"

She gave a short laugh. "I know. It's a mess. Believe me, I don't *want* to care about you. This *thing*—this heat, this attraction, whatever you want to call it—is crazy and intense and completely the last thing I need right now. When you kiss me, I lose track of everything I want, everything I've worked for. All I want is to stay right here in your arms."

He cleared his throat. "Why is that a bad thing, again?"

She ground her teeth, fighting the urge to smack him. He didn't get it. He didn't see she was fighting to earn her family's respect. She owed them. She suddenly remembered another Mother Teresa quote her mother used to say—*Bring love into your own home, for this is where love must start.*

She hadn't done that. She had left her family behind while she went off trying to change the world in some misguided effort to do what little she could to carry on her parents' legacy.

Meanwhile, she hadn't been here for her family when they needed her after Travis died. This was her chance to make things right for them. By making The Christmas Ranch a success, she might be able to help save the Star N—but not while she continued to let him distract her, while she fell apart each time he kissed her.

"If I let you, Rafael Santiago, you will break my heart." She straightened and gave him the most steady look she could muster. "There's only one solution to that. I just won't let you."

"The last thing I want to do is break your heart."

"And the last thing I want to do is fall in love with you and then have to stand by with a broken heart while I watch you walk away."

"What if I don't? Walk away, I mean?"

Despite his careful tone and guarded expression, she felt a tiny flutter of joy, fragile and sweet—which she firmly squashed beneath her boot.

"You would. You have a life in San Diego and you need to return to it. I get that."

"I don't have to go back to California. You said it before. We're both at a crossroads."

"If you didn't—if you stayed—I would always wonder whether you are doing it for the same reason you volunteered to help at the Ranch in the first place. Because of some wrong-headed sense of guilt, to make amends for something you were never responsible for in the first place."

She knew she was being ruthless and even a little

cold, using the Colombia card to win her argument, but it was the only way she could protect herself—and she suddenly had the epiphany that she had been protecting herself for a very long time. Maybe even since that fateful Christmas day.

Her relationships were always casual, light, fun... and completely without depth and meaning. She had never had any problem leaving any of the men she dated behind when she went on to the next job, the next adventure.

With Rafe, everything was different. She knew that instinctively. Her heart would break time after time and she couldn't put herself through that.

"Please don't kiss me again. I won't beg but consider this the closest thing to it. If you can possibly feel you owe me anything because of what happened in Colombia, after everything you've done this past week to help around here, *this* is all I would ask. I would prefer if you didn't come around after tomorrow's opening. Will you do that for me?"

She folded her hands together, her nails digging into her palms. She hated asking him. Worse, she hated the hurt in his eyes as she basically told him she didn't want him there anymore. They had begun a friendship before he ever kissed her and she was basically throwing that away, as well.

What other choice did she have?

"I don't know what to say."

"Don't say anything. This is hard enough."

She headed for the door, knowing if she didn't leave now she wouldn't be able to find the strength. "I'm going to head over to the Ranch office in the lodge and finish a few things. Thanks for your help here and with…everything, but you should probably go get Joey from the house so you can visit your sister. I would imagine visiting hours at the jail are limited, aren't they?"

He gave her a long, measured look, his expression murky. She had a feeling he had plenty of things he wanted to say to her but she didn't give him a chance, only turned and walked out of the barn without looking back.

Chapter 13

"Where is everybody?"

Aunt Mary's question was bewildered and completely genuine but it still gouged under Hope's skin like uncoiling barbed wire.

She forced a smile for her aunt and leaned forward to hug her, setting off the little jingle bell on her ridiculous elf hat. "That's a pretty bad snowstorm out there. On a night like tonight, most people want to be home cuddled up by the fire watching *It's a Wonderful Life* or something. They don't want to tramp around in the snow and wind to look at a few lights."

Opening night at The Christmas Ranch usually was one of their biggest events. They offered free hot cocoa and cookies, a live band playing Christmas music and of course the big event itself, when they turned on all the lights in the vast display.

Instead of the two hundred people she had anticipated, she could only see a fraction of that, maybe thirty
or so, mostly close neighbors and friends who lived in
Cold Creek Canyon.

The Dalton brothers—Wade, Jake and Seth—were
there along with their wives. They all stood talking to
the Dalton matriarch and her second husband, who happened to be the mayor of Pine Gulch.

Caidy and Ben Caldwell and his children had come,
along with Caidy's brother Ridge Bowman and his wife,
Sarah, and daughter. The wealthy and powerful Carson McRaven and his wife, Jenna, who had provided
the refreshments for the evening, stood talking to the
Cavazos—Nate and Emery—as well as Faith's best
friend, Ashley Hartford, and her hottie former action
movie star husband, Justin, who had just been there for
Thanksgiving dinner.

Those who lived in Cold Creek Canyon were always
supportive of The Christmas Ranch, which meant the
world to Hope and her family.

It wasn't quite enough, though, she thought, looking at the sparse crowd. This was close to a disaster.

"Did you put an ad in the paper, honey?"

She put on a fake smile for her aunt. "Sure did. I
called them earlier in the week, but I was too late by
then to make the deadline for yesterday's edition. They
couldn't run anything until next week's issue since all
the Black Friday ads had already been scheduled. Our
ad will run in the Pine Gulch community paper as well
as the Idaho Falls, Rexburg and Jackson Hole papers
next week. A radio spot started yesterday on all the
area stations. And I put flyers up on all the community
boards I could find in the region."

She was quite certain it hadn't helped their attendance any that for weeks that blasted Closed Indefinitely sign had hung over the gate. She couldn't seem to get the message out—everybody in town still seemed to think they were taking the year off because of Travis's death.

Was she supposed to go door to door throughout town to let everybody know the Nichols family had changed its collective mind—well, okay, she had changed it for them—and the Ranch would now be open for business as usual?

This was no one's fault, she reminded herself. Not Aunt Mary's. Not Faith's or Celeste's. Not really hers either, since she had worked her tail off trying to get ready for tonight. None of them could control the weather or alter newspaper deadlines.

"Things will pick up," she assured her aunt, wishing she believed it herself. "Now, go mingle and have a good time. I'm going to grab another tray of appetizers."

She hurried to the little kitchen off the office and grabbed one of the beautifully prepared trays. At least they had good food. Jenna was an amazing cook, which was why her catering business was enormously successful.

She adjusted her stupid hat a little with one hand then headed back out.

"Can I give you a hand?"

Her heart skipped a little beat at the low voice and at the sight of Rafe, big and strong and gorgeous.

He and Joey had come out earlier in the day to do a few last-minute adjustments to the tow rope on the sledding hill but she had been busy in the office and hadn't spoken with him. Now, seeing him here dressed up in a button-down shirt and trousers, her breath caught and her knees felt ridiculously weak.

"I like your outfit."

Oh. Son of a *nutcracker*, to steal her favorite epithet from Buddy the Elf. He looked gorgeous and masculine…and she looked like Buddy's dorky little sister.

"I couldn't talk Faith or Celeste into wearing it so I guess I was stuck. Somebody had to."

Though why, she suddenly wasn't sure. No one was even there to see her dressed in the stupid elf costume. "This is a disaster. Only three dozen people—and they're all friends and neighbors."

He looked back through the doorway into the party. "Don't worry. Things will pick up. Word of mouth will spread. As soon as word gets out that you're open this year after all, the crowds will follow."

She didn't deserve his reassuring words, not after the things she had said to him the day before. She couldn't believe he'd even showed up tonight.

All the work the two of them had done ahead of time. For what? A handful of people? She thought of all the money she had poured into this, most of her savings, all the promises she had made to her sisters. This was supposed to be her chance to show them she could contribute to the family.

She gripped the tray harder, fighting the urge to sink down to the floor, appetizers and all, and cry.

"I wish I could believe that."

Rafe gave her a searching look and she knew he must see the emotions swimming in her expression. His hard, formidable features softened. "Yeah, maybe the turnout tonight isn't what you'd hoped, but give yourself a break. It's only the first night."

"I know. I just had such high hopes."

"You've done a good thing here, Hope. You've thrown your heart and your soul into this and people are inevitably going to respond to that. You've brought Christmas magic to Pine Gulch. Everyone needs a little of that right now."

"Even you?"

He looked out at the brightly lit lodge with its big Christmas tree, the blazing fires, the grand Santa throne where Mac Palmer presided in his glorious costume.

"*Especially* me," he said quietly. "I'm honored I had the chance to be part of it."

Her throat felt tight, achy, and she wanted nothing more in that moment than to fall into his arms. How could she possibly resist this man?

He gave her a sudden, unexpected grin that sent heat spiraling through her. "One thing, though. You might want to try to smile a little. Trust me, there's nothing more depressing than a grumpy elf."

She laughed, as he intended, even though her heart seemed to ache. Everything she said the day before had been completely ridiculous, she thought again. She wasn't in any danger of falling in love with him. How could she be, when she was already there?

"Point taken. I will put on my perkiest smile. Thanks for the reminder, sailor."

"Anytime."

Except he wasn't only a sailor. He was a navy SEAL—the toughest, most hardened of warriors—and he wouldn't be here in a few more weeks for pep talks or anything else.

The reminder was as coldly sobering as if someone had just shoved her into a snowbank.

Ignoring the ache in her chest, she pasted on a smile so big it made her cheeks hurt and headed around the crowd with her platter of cookies and hot cocoa.

By the time Monday morning rolled around, Hope was afraid her face had permanently frozen in that rictus of a fake smile.

She pulled the quilt up under her chin, gazing out the window at the pale morning. She could see daylight, which meant it had to be late—on these shortest days of the year, the sun didn't rise above the mountains until almost eight.

She had slept in, the first time in *weeks* she had done that. So why did she still feel achy and exhausted? Maybe because she hadn't dropped into bed until after two in the morning, up late sewing more little reindeer toys so they could at least have twenty or thirty on hand in the gift shop, just in case.

She flopped over onto her back and stared at the ceiling of the odd-angled bedroom that had been hers since she and her sisters came here, lost and afraid.

She was seriously tempted to punch her pillow, pull the covers over her head and go back to sleep for another three or four hours. Why shouldn't she? Why was she putting so much time and energy into what was turning into her most spectacular failure ever?

The crowds had picked up a little on Saturday as the winter storm slowed but on Sunday, attendance had been *way* down.

At this rate, they would barely break even for the season. All her good intentions about helping ease Faith's burden would remain only that. Pipe dreams. Pretty little ice sculptures that melted away into nothing.

She should have just let The Christmas Ranch stay closed and thrown her energy into the cattle side of the Star N operations. She wasn't sure what she could have done there but it would have been better than creating false expectations.

With a sigh, she sat up. As much as she might like to, she had too much to do to stay hidden away up here feeling sorry for herself.

She pushed away, swiveled to the edge of the bed and was just about to stand up when her cell phone rang from its spot charging on the bedside table.

She stared at it for a long moment, recognizing Rafe's number flashing across the screen

She couldn't escape the man. He was in her thoughts, her dreams, and now on her phone. She almost didn't answer it but finally picked it up, unplugged it from the charger and answered.

"Hello." She tried for a brisk, businesslike, *didn't I ask you to leave me alone?* sort of tone.

"Are you watching this?" he demanded, with more excitement in his voice than she had ever heard.

"Watching what?" she asked, not wanting to tell him she was still in bed and wasn't watching anything except a few cobwebs up in the corner.

"The television. Channel six. Are you close to one?"

"Yes." There was a small flatscreen atop the carved old-fashioned bureau, since Faith used this as a guest room when Hope wasn't there. She wasn't sure it worked since she hadn't had time to turn it on once since she had been back in Pine Gulch.

"*Hello, Nation.* Turn it on, right now!"

"Why?" she asked warily.

"Just trust me. Channel six," he said again. "They

were teasing a story right before the commercials I think you're going to want to see."

The floor was freezing against her bare feet as she padded to the television, the phone in the crook of her shoulder. "Not your usual sort of show, is it? Or maybe you like all that celebrity gossip."

"Joey wanted to watch a cartoon this morning before school. I flipped through the channels to find something and happened to catch a couple minutes of this one. It really doesn't matter why I was watching. Just turn it on. Hurry."

She flipped the television on and found the channel. They were just coming back from a commercial to a man and woman sitting together on a set decorated with poinsettias and a Christmas tree.

"Welcome back, Nation. I'm Paloma Rodriguez."

"And I'm Mitchell Sloan. We hope you're having a lovely Monday, wherever you are."

"So, Mitchell. You know my husband likes to ski, right?" Paloma said.

"From what you've said, he likes to ski and you like to sip hot toddies by the fireplace."

"Exactly. I'm not much of a skier. This year we decided to take the kids to Jackson Hole, Wyoming, for Thanksgiving. It's such a fun little town. We spent a week there and Kent and our older son had a wonderful time skiing. Meanwhile, toward the end of the week, the younger two were starting to drive me crazy—until I happened upon this wonderful little family attraction a short way from Jackson. It was called The Christmas Ranch and look at this."

The woman pulled out a darling little stuffed reindeer—*her* darling little stuffed reindeer!—and Hope shrieked.

"Ow," Rafe said in her ear and she realized she was still holding the phone.

"Sorry! Sorry! That's Sparkle! Are you seeing this?"

"I am."

The camera panned to some home video of two little children bundled up in snowsuits—sledding down the hill behind the Ranch, then cut to them gazing, awe-struck, at the reindeer, stars in their eyes.

"This place was so magical," Paloma Rodriguez said with definite gush in her voice. "It's truly wonderful, the most charming place I've seen in a long time. They have live reindeer for the children to pet and even their own little mascot."

She made the stuffed toy do a little dance. "This is Sparkle and he has his own story that is absolutely ador-able. Charming and sweet and heartwarming. Alicia and Julio begged me to read it to them at least a dozen times on the airplane ride home and I'm still not tired of it. It's that cute. *Sparkle and the Magic Snowball*. If you're in the area, you should visit. The Christmas Ranch, just outside Pine Gulch, Idaho. It's less than an hour from Jackson Hole and well worth the trip, for the cinnamon hot chocolate alone."

"Great travel tip, Paloma," her cohost said with a practiced smile. "Linda and I are heading to Jackson Hole between Christmas and New Year's. I'll definitely have to try some of that hot chocolate. And speaking of hot. I hear we have some spicy news on the celeb-rity romance front."

They started chatting about a picture that was appar-ently exploding all over the internet of a young starlet and her much older leading man in a heated off-screen embrace.

Hope paused the show and flopped back onto her bed.

"Oh. My. Word."

She was still holding the phone to her ear, she realized when she heard Rafe's low chuckle in her ear. It seemed only right that she share it with him since he had worked every bit as hard as she had this past week to get everything ready for the opening.

"That was amazing. You were just on national TV. Wow. I can say I knew you when."

"We were on TV!" she exclaimed. "*Sparkle* was on TV! This is amazing. I have to call Celeste! Do you know what this means?"

"I hope only good things," he answered.

Warmth trickled through her at the sincere happiness in his voice. He meant his words. He wanted only the best for her, from the very beginning.

How could she possibly go on without this man in her life?

She pushed away the dark thought, focusing instead on this incredible turn of events.

"I have to call the printer and order more books and make more toys and maybe hire more people."

"Take a minute to breathe first," he advised. "You should savor this. You worked hard and you deserve the success. Don't rush past it looking at the tasks ahead of you until you've embraced this moment."

"I've got to record this. How do I do that? I've got to figure out how to do that." She spent a minute trying to work the controls on the DVR and finally got it right just as the door to her bedroom was shoved open and Celeste burst in, eyes wild and her cheeks flushed.

"You need to see the news! We were just on *Hello, Nation*! The *national* news!"

"I know! Rafe called me and I caught it just in time. Did you hear what Paloma Rodriguez said? *Charming and sweet and heartwarming*. That's you she's talking about! Your story. Isn't it wonderful?"

She suddenly realized her sister didn't look convinced of that. She sank down onto the bed, the color beginning to leach out of her cheeks.

"I'm not ready for this!"

She laughed—until she realized Celeste was completely serious. Her sister looked terrified.

"Rafe, I have to go," she said into the phone.

"Okay."

"Thank you for calling. Just...thank you."

"Sure."

He ended the connection and her heart gave a little spasm, wondering when—or even *if*—she would have the chance to talk to him again.

She sat down beside her sister on the bed and gripped Celeste's icy fingers. "This is wonderful news, CeCe. Now everybody else will know how brilliant you are, too. You wrote a beautiful story and it's only right that it has an audience beyond our family, don't you think? What would Mom and Dad say about sharing our gifts, not hiding our light under a barrel? You have an amazing gift and it needs to be out there, glowing for all the world to see."

"That's easy for you to say. You've always been comfortable glowing in the world. To me, this is a terrifying thing."

"It's a wonderful thing," she corrected. "Think of how many people you can touch with your words. Mom and Dad would have been so proud of you, honey."

Celeste gave her a shaky smile, then her eyes filled with tears. "Until you came back, I was perfectly happy writing Sparkle stories for only Barrett and Louisa."

"See? I knew there was a reason I needed to come home."

A reason that had nothing to do with a certain gorgeous former navy SEAL, she reminded herself, and slid from the bed with one more hug for her sister.

"I guess I'd better get dressed. Ready or not, I have a feeling The Christmas Ranch is about to get much, much busier."

Chapter 14

"Are we almost there? I can't believe we're finally here. I finally get to sit on Santa's lap and tell him what I want for Christmas. Do you think I'm too late?"

Rafe glanced in the rearview mirror at Joey, who was just about bouncing out of his seat with excitement. He didn't begrudge the kid a little happiness, especially after the past rough three weeks. As sick as he had been, listless with fever, it was good to see him being excited about *anything*.

The week after Thanksgiving, Joey came down with what Rafe thought was just a virus but it had turned into a nasty bronchitis. Two visits to Dr. Jake Dalton's clinic and a round of antibiotics later, he had ended up missing seven days of school and had only returned for the previous week.

Now, the night before Christmas Eve, this was the

first chance they'd had to come to The Christmas Ranch.

Rafe didn't want to endure another few weeks like they'd just passed through. He had a whole new appreciation for the challenges parents faced on a regular basis. Nothing could break a parent's heart like a sick kid.

"The dude in red is pretty good at last-minute orders," he finally answered, "but I can't make any promises. Anyway, we wrote him a letter while you were sick, remember? I'm sure he got that, so you're probably golden."

He was pretty sure he had covered all the Christmas bases, at least from a gift standpoint. The kid's wish list had been short enough, actually, that Rafe had double-checked to make sure Joey had included everything he wanted.

His nephew only asked for a couple of LEGO sets—that Rafe had actually ordered online just after Thanksgiving when they were first mentioned—and a Marvel superhero backpack he had managed to pick up in Idaho Falls the week before, after Joey finally went back to school.

He had found a few other things on that shopping trip—probably too many, actually. He didn't have a good handle yet on appropriate Santa gift quantities. He had even managed to wrap everything over the weekend after Joey went to bed, though none of it would win any prizes in the gift-wrap department.

"I can't wait!" Joey said, then coughed a little with the lingering bronchial spasms he hadn't quite shaken. "What should we do first? The sledding hill or the sleigh rides?"

"Why don't we get the Santa thing out of the way,

since that's your first priority, and then you can decide
the rest?"

"That's a good idea. Look! There it is!"

Sure enough, the bright and welcoming lights of The
Christmas Ranch beat away the dark December gloom.
A light snow fell, adding an even more picturesque
quality to a scene that already looked warm and festive.
He drove beneath the sign he had tacked up for Hope
that first day he had come here and was aware of a little
bubble of nerves coursing through him.

He was looking forward to this, probably more than
he should, given the way things had ended with Hope.

Joey's sickness had been tough enough to cope with
this month. Throw in Cami's sentencing the day before
and he was definitely in need of a little holiday spirit.

He hadn't seen Hope in more than three weeks, since
the Ranch opened. True to his word, he had stayed away
as she had asked him. It was just about the hardest thing
he had ever done and he was honest enough to admit
that he might have caved and gone to see her anyway,
if not for Joey's illness.

How many times had he wanted to drive up here, just
to talk this out and tell her she was being crazy? He
had even turned up the canyon twice after Joey went
back to school the week before but had ended up driving past and turning around, feeling like a stupid kid
riding his bike past the house of his elementary school
crush in hopes of catching a glimpse of her.

He had to drive through the parking lot twice before
he found a parking space. The place was hopping, as he
had fully expected. That little bit on the national news
had spawned all kinds of other publicity. The weekly
newspaper in town had done a big spread on The Christ-

mas Ranch and on the runaway success of *Sparkle and The Magic Snowball*, which was racing up bestseller lists after she had digitized it and put it online as an ebook.

He had read every word of the article and had held the newspaper in front of him for far too long, gazing at the photograph of Hope. It was lovely and sweet, a picture in the snow and sunshine with Sparkle all decked out in his holiday jingle bell gear. Even so, he was aware the image had captured none of her vitality and spirit, the energy and enthusiasm and creativity that made her so amazing.

He parked the SUV and helped Joey out of the backseat. His nephew slipped his hand in Rafe's as they walked toward the lodge, which sent a little shaft of warmth settling in his chest.

The illness had at least served one good purpose—he and Joey finally seemed to have bonded over coughing fits and sniffles and nebulizer treatments. His nephew at last seemed to have accepted that Rafe wasn't going anywhere. The night before, he had even told Rafe he thought he was pretty cool. High praise, indeed, from a seven-year-old. It made him feel almost as good as surviving BUD/S.

When they walked inside, they were met with noise and laughter and a jazzy Christmas trio playing in the corner. The scent of pine and cinnamon filled the air.

They made their way through the crowd inside toward the ticket counter, though it wasn't easy. The place was packed as this was the last night the St. Nicholas Lodge was open—though he had read in that article he had all but memorized in the local newspaper that the Nichols family apparently kept the Christmas village open on Christmas Eve with free admission, their gift to the community.

The sleigh rides and sledding hill would continue to operate until after New Year's Eve.

He bought all-access tickets for him and Joey, which would allow them to enjoy all The Christmas Ranch activities. Just as he was hooking the green-and-red-striped wristband on his nephew, Barrett Dustin rushed up to them.

"You're here! Finally!"

"I told you I might be coming tonight," Joey said to the boy who had become his best friend.

"Have you seen Santa yet?"

"Not yet. We just got here."

"I've already sat on his lap like a hundred times but I'll stand in line with you again if you want. Tonight you get M&M's bags instead of just candy canes after you talk to him! I already had one but I want another one."

"Can I, Uncle Rafe?"

"Sure. Go ahead. I'll catch up."

The boys raced off, giggling together. Rafe was fastening his own wrist brace when he became aware of some subtle shift in the atmosphere in the room. Joey—who adored all things Star Wars and had made him watch far too many Clone Wars cartoon episodes while he was sick—would have called it a disturbance in the Force.

He shifted and there she was, just a few feet away from him, speaking with a couple he had met in Jake Dalton's waiting room. Cisco and Easton Del Norte, he remembered, along with their little girl who looked to be about five, chubby-cheeked and adorable, and a very cute toddler little boy.

She must have felt that disturbance in the Force, too—or maybe just the weight of his gaze. Her attention shifted from the couple and for just a split second when she first saw him, he saw a world of emotions in her beautiful blue eyes—shock, discomposure and a wild, unexpected joy.

She blinked away everything and said something to the couple then approached him a moment later. "Rafe. Hello."

He wanted to stand there staring at her all night, absorb every detail he had missed so much. These past three weeks, without her smile and her laughter and that sweet, lovely face, nothing had felt right.

"Hi."

After an awkward moment, she reached out and hugged him in the way of friends who haven't seen each other in too long. He closed his eyes for just a moment, soaking in the scent of her, cinnamon and almonds, and the *rightness* of having her in his arms, even for this quick, meaningless hug.

Too soon, she stepped away, her expression guarded.

"How have you been? How's Joey? I've been worried sick about him."

"He's doing better. Thanks. He's so relieved to finally have a chance to see Santa that I think he would have walked here if I hadn't finally agreed to bring him tonight."

He wanted to make perfectly clear that was the reason he was there, not because he couldn't go another hour without seeing her—though that was probably closer to the truth.

"Oh, and I need to give you a belated thank-you for

the care package you sent over with Faith and Barrett when they stopped by. It helped."

She had sent drawing paper and colored pencils as well as a copy of her and Celeste's book and one of her little handmade stuffed Sparkle toys, which he had been afraid his Transformers/Iron Man/Anakin Skywalker loving nephew might think too girlish. On the contrary, Joey had been delighted with it, especially because Hope had made it. His nephew had come a long way since calling her mean that day he broke her window.

She smiled softly. "You're welcome."

Before he could respond, a tired-looking woman holding hands with a child on either side of her jostled Hope, who stumbled and would have fallen if he hadn't reached out to catch her.

"Sorry. I'm sorry," the woman said, with a frazzled look. He wanted to tell her not to apologize. In fact, he would have paid her twenty bucks to do it over and over if it would give him the chance to hold Hope in his arms again.

She remained there for a fraction of a moment, gazing up at him with a startled look in her eyes before she swallowed and eased away again.

"Wow," he said. "This place is packed."

She smiled, looking heartbreakingly beautiful. "If I could ever meet Paloma Rodriguez in person, I would smooch her all over her face. Seriously. We've been hopping ever since she featured us on *Hello, Nation.* I've had to hire a dozen temporary workers to keep up with the crowds and I've got eight women in the local quilting guild sewing Sparkle toys for us—and we *still* can't keep up with the orders."

"That's terrific."

He was so happy for her success, mostly because he knew how important it was to her.

"What's going on with Cami?" she asked. "I've been wondering. Was she sentenced this week?"

He nodded grimly. "Yesterday. She got three to five, which was a little longer than her attorney expected, and she won't be eligible for parole for twenty-four months. She was transferred from the county jail to the state penitentiary right after her sentencing, though she got to see Joey for a few minutes before they took her."

"Oh, Rafe. I'm sorry."

He shrugged. "She made a long string of poor choices and they had consequences—one of which is, I guess, that I get to be a father figure for at least the next two years."

"Not a father *figure*. A father."

"Right."

The magnitude of the task somehow seemed less overwhelming than it had a month ago. He figured they would get through it as they had this month—one moment at a time.

"Looks like Joey and Barrett are almost to the front of the line," she said. "You'd better go if you want to get any pictures for his scrapbook."

"I don't expect I'll have time for much scrapbooking the next few years, but you're right. I should at least take a picture or two to capture the moment."

"Find me before you leave tonight," she said. "I have something for you. I was actually going to bring it over to your house tomorrow but if it's okay, I'll give it to you tonight instead."

That shocked him enough that he wasn't quick

enough to come up with a response before she slipped away through the crowd. He watched her for a moment, then turned to freeze Joey's moment with Santa for posterity.

It was too noisy inside the lodge for him to hear what the boy requested from Santa. As soon as his nephew hopped down, he asked him, just to make sure he wasn't missing a big-ticket item on the wish list.

Joey gave him a solemn look. "That's between me and Santa."

He suddenly had fears of the boy coming up with something entirely new, something Rafe wouldn't be able to deliver since he had no idea what it might be. The way he figured it, this was probably the last year the kid would believe in Santa. He was already beginning to express a few qualms about the physical logistics of one man making it all around the world in one night.

Rafe wanted to hold on to the magic as long as he could. He would hate to disappoint the kid in their first Christmas together, especially given all Joey had been through the past few months and the fact that it would be tough enough this first year without his mom.

"Want to give me a hint?" he asked, a little desperately, as they stood in line for the horse-drawn sleigh rides that made up the next thing on Joey's list.

He thought Joey wasn't going to answer him, but as they walked toward Sparkle and the others in their enclosure, he looked up at the sky, speckled with a few stars that peeked out from the clouds, then back at Rafe. "I asked if we could stay here," he finally said. "I like it in Idaho. I don't want to go to San Diego."

He didn't know what to say. "Why not? San Diego

is great. It has beautiful beaches and nice weather all year round and lots of fun things to do."

"But it doesn't snow there," Joey said. "I like snow. I like throwing snowballs, I like sledding, I like making snow angels and going on sleigh rides. All those things. I like snow and I like all my friends here. I don't want to leave Barrett or Sam or any of my other friends."

Rafe wanted to tell him he would make new friends, but he had a feeling the promise would sound hollow.

He didn't have a chance to continue the conversation until they were loaded onto the sleigh with several others and the driver started out on a well-worn trail through the snow.

"What did Santa say, when you asked him if you could stay here?"

"He said he couldn't make promises about where people live. It's up to their parents." Joey looked disgusted, his shoulder bumping Rafe's arm as the horses jostled them. "I told him I didn't live with my parents right now and he said it was up to whoever I lived with. He also said sometimes what you think you want is different from what you really need."

The words seemed to hit Rafe with the force of a rocket-propelled grenade.

Sometimes what you think you want is different from what you really need.

In his case, he knew what he wanted *and* what he needed—and they were exactly the same thing.

Hope.

He loved her. *That* was the edgy feeling that had been under his skin all this time.

He was in love with Hope Nichols, the scared thirteen-year-old girl he had helped rescue from a terrorist camp in Colombia, another lifetime ago.

This wasn't simply attraction or friendship or affection. He needed her in his life—and Joey did too, he suddenly realized.

He gazed up at the wintry night, at the dark silhouette of the mountains and the full moon that peeked just over the top of them. He loved this place, too, and didn't want to leave it.

Like Joey, he wanted to stay in Pine Gulch.

How could they make it work? He could help her run The Christmas Ranch but it was obviously a seasonal enterprise. What could he do the rest of the year?

He gazed at the mountains, thinking of a hundred possibilities. He was heading back to San Diego to work private security for his friend Jim. Why not see if Jim wanted to open a satellite operation here in Jackson Hole? He could definitely see a need, with all the wealthy visitors and celebrities who visited there.

If that didn't pan out, he could always start a construction company. The home-building industry in this part of the West was vibrant, spurred by all those celebrities and wealthy folks who wanted to build second homes.

He had no doubt he would come up with something. He had spent seventeen years as a navy SEAL, trained to find solutions to tough situations.

The main job ahead of him would be convincing Hope she needed him too.

Hope couldn't seem to shake her melancholy mood.

She told herself it was only because this was the last night the lodge would be open for the season. After the frenzy of the past month, it was only natural to focus a little on endings, on goodbyes.

Her melancholy certainly had nothing to do with a gorgeous hazel-eyed SEAL or his adorable nephew.

She would miss this, as crazy as things had been since Paloma Rodriguez had changed their world. When the season was over, she would suffer a little bit of a loss. Reviving The Christmas Ranch had given her purpose and meaning and she wasn't quite sure what would happen next.

Right now, she decided to focus on that and not the much larger heartache awaiting her in the form of that particular man she didn't want to think about.

"One of the elves told me you were the one in charge."

She turned at the statement and found a woman in her early thirties. She was quite pregnant but wore a fashionable maternity coat and a lovely knit scarf and matching hat. Behind her stood a handsome, well-dressed man holding a girl of about four while a boy around Barrett and Joey's age stood nearby.

"Yes. I'm Hope Nichols," she said warily, afraid the woman wanted to lodge some sort of complaint. "May I help you?"

The woman's serious features suddenly dissolved into a watery smile. "This is probably going to sound strange but…can I give you a hug?"

"I… Sure."

The woman offered her a quick embrace then stepped away, looking embarrassed. "You must think I'm crazy."

"Not at all," Hope assured her. "Is everything okay?"

At the woman's sudden sniffle, the man handed her a tissue and rubbed her shoulder in a warm, familiar, loving gesture that sent an ache lodging under Hope's breastbone.

She wanted that—the steady comfort of knowing she had someone to lean on when times were hard and someone to celebrate with when wonderful things happened.

"I just have to tell you how grateful I am to you and your family for giving us this treasure. I'm so happy you opened this year after all. It feels like a gift you gave just to me. I was devastated when I heard it was going to be closed early in the season. I... My name is Jane Ross. This is my husband Perry. We live in Pocatello and each year since I was a teenager, my family has come here during the holidays. It was the highlight of our Christmas season."

Hope smiled, heartened to hear what wasn't an unfamiliar tale. *This* was the reason she wanted to open the Ranch, because of families like this that found joy and togetherness here.

"This has been the hardest holiday season for me ever," the woman said softy. "My parents both died within the past year, my mother just a few months ago."

"Oh. I'm so very sorry."

"The holidays have been incredibly tough. I miss them so much and I didn't know how I could bear it. I haven't felt like having Christmas at all. It just seemed like too much work, you know? But I had to anyway." She gave a helpless shrug. "The children needed Christmas. I put the tree up and decorated the house, but I've only been going through the motions, just trying to make it through and crying just about every night because I missed my parents so much. Then I saw an article about you in the newspaper, about how you were going to close because of a recent family tragedy but had decided to stay open after all. I told Perry we had to come and I'm so very glad we did."

The woman squeezed her fingers. "Coming back here," she went on, "bringing my own children and continuing the tradition, I feel such a connection to my parents again. For the first time, I'm remembering the joy and magic and meaning of Christmas again. I can't express how much that means to me. Thank you so much for helping me find that again."

"You are so welcome." Hope embraced the woman again, sniffling a little along with her.

"We picked up one of your books and the Sparkle toy, as you can see."

She pointed to the little girl, who was hugging it tightly.

"You can be sure it's going to be enjoyed for many seasons to come. Merry Christmas and God bless you for what you've given us."

She waved them on, her heart overflowing—and her tears, too.

"That was lovely."

She whirled around and found Rafe standing nearby, looking big and warm and comforting.

"You heard?"

"Most of it. Does that sort of thing happen a lot?"

"Once in a while. That was…special."

She wanted to sink into his arms. It was an almost visceral need. How had she forgotten how happy her heart was when he was near?

"Where's Joey?" she asked, mostly to distract herself.

"Barrett took him up to the house so they could exchange Christmas presents."

"Ah." The crowd was starting to thin, she saw, but it was still packed inside the lodge. "Have you eaten? Aunt Mary brought down a bunch of goodies for all the workers, including a big batch of minestrone soup in the slow cooker. It's kind of our goodbye celebration at the lodge, even though we'll partially reopen up again the day after Christmas."

"I'm not really hungry," he said, a strangely solemn look on his handsome features.

She had missed him desperately. Seeing him again only made her realize just how much.

Her emotions, already raw from the interaction with Jane Ross, threatened to consume her.

She swallowed them down and forced a smile. "I told you I have something for you and Joey. It's back in the office."

He nodded and followed her as she led the way. Inside the office, he closed the door behind him, as if he didn't want to be disturbed, and her heart started to pound.

"I'm...glad you stopped by tonight," she said.

"Even though you asked me to stay away?"

She sighed. She ought to simply hand over the present, wish him Merry Christmas and safe travels back to San Diego and say goodbye.

She wasn't particularly good at doing what she ought to. Why break her record now?

"That was kind of a stupid thing for me to ask of you, wasn't it?"

"If by *stupid*, you mean insanely difficult, then yes."

Something about the intensity of his voice sent her resident troupe of butterflies pirouetting through her insides again.

"It didn't work very well anyway," she muttered and felt his attention sharpen on her.

"What didn't work?"

"Nothing. Never mind. Let me just grab your gift."

She hurried to the corner where she had left the large flat package. "Here you go."

"Thanks."

"Go ahead. Open it."

"Are you sure?"

She wanted to see his reaction. What was the fun in giving a gift if she couldn't see how it was received? He ripped the paper away and held out the large framed photograph.

"Wow. That's wonderful."

It was of Joey. The boy had his arm around Sparkle's neck and his smile was as big as the brilliant blue sky behind him.

"I shot it one day when you were helping out, before we opened. Isn't it great? I sent it away to be printed on canvas and then I had Mac Palmer, one of our Santas who does some woodworking, make a frame for it out of the extra barn wood we had around the Star N. I wanted both of you to have a keepsake from The Christmas Ranch so you can remember your time here."

He gazed down at the smiling boy and the sweet-faced reindeer, a soft light in his eyes. "It's lovely. Thank you."

"You're welcome."

He didn't return her smile. "One question, though. Do you really think I'm going to need a photograph to remember my time here?"

Her heart started to pound again. "Won't you?"

He set the photograph down on the desk and moved

closer to her, those stunning hazel eyes intense, determined. She thought of that nocturnal predator again and a nervous thrill shot through her.

"I could never forget you, Hope."

She swallowed, unable to look away. "Um, sure. We have a…history together."

"I wish we didn't," he said fervently. "I wish I had met you for the very first time that day Joey broke your window."

That would certainly have made their tangled relationship much easier but she couldn't agree. Their lives were inextricably entwined and had been for a long time.

She thought about fate—about how the past and the present could sometimes twist and curl together like ribbons on a Christmas tree.

He had been an integral part of her life since she was a girl—she just hadn't known it.

"Don't say that," she murmured. "Our lives are bound together because of the past."

He reached for her hand and she was stunned to feel his fingers tremble a little, her amazing, hard, tough navy SEAL. "I would rather our lives were bound together because of right now, this moment. Because of our feelings for each other."

She hitched in a breath and met his gaze. "Rafe—"

"I love you, Hope. I knew at Thanksgiving, I just didn't want to face it until you said you were afraid you were falling for me. These past weeks without you only showed me how very cold and empty my life is when you're not part of it. I need you. Your laughter, your energy, your amazing creativity. All of it. I love every part of you."

He gave her a lopsided half smile that completely shattered the last of her defenses. "That's why I wish we'd never met. So we could leave behind all the baggage—the mistakes, the regrets—and simply be two people finding each other at last, like some kind of Christmas miracle."

She couldn't seem to order the tangled chaos of her thoughts into anything resembling coherency. All she wanted to do was kiss him desperately.

At her continued silence, he gave her a long, steady look.

"I know what you said the last time we were together. Hell, I've gone over that conversation in my head so many times I've got every word memorized. Has anything changed? Is there any chance you might be able to accept the past for what it was and see me for who I am right now, today? A man so in love with you, he can't seem to think about anything else?"

She exhaled on a sob that was half laughter, half tears. "Rafe. Oh, Rafe."

She threw her arms around his neck and he groaned a little then kissed her with all the pent-up, aching need she had been pushing back throughout this endless December.

He kissed her for a long time while Christmas music played and the crowd buzzed behind the closed door. She never wanted it to end.

Eventually they came up for air, but she couldn't seem to get close enough to him. She rested her head on his chest—that broad, let-me-take-all-your-troubles chest—and had never felt so safe and warm and loved.

"This has been the craziest month," she murmured. "I can't even tell you. We have been so incredibly busy, every day I hardly had time to take a shower, but the Ranch has had its biggest year ever. Our profits are quadruple what they've ever been. We're going to have enough to more than cover our operating expenses and even to help offset the operating cost deficit on the Star N side of things, too."

"I knew you would do it. Didn't I tell you?"

She smiled, humbled and overwhelmed at his constant faith in her. "Here's the thing. I was so happy that all our hard work paid off and especially happy for CeCe as I watched people fall in love with her writing and want more. I should have been over the moon. But I missed you so much, I couldn't truly enjoy the success. A hundred times a day, I wanted to share some little triumph with you. To laugh with you or be frustrated or get some of that sometimes annoying but usually spot-on advice you always seem to have."

"I'm going to remember you said that."

His laughter was a low rumble against her cheek and she had no choice but to kiss him again.

"I love you, Rafe," she said, some time later. "I loved you and I missed you and Joey so much I could hardly breathe around the ache in my heart. I'm sorry I couldn't be there while he was sick."

"We got through it. Your care package helped. You can be there next time."

She felt a little thrill at the idea—not that Joey would ever get sick again, she didn't want that. But that Rafe wanted her in his life to help him through, if it were to happen again.

"I realized something while we were apart," she said softly. "Since I graduated from college, I have been traveling around the world in search of something I couldn't even name. Oh, I genuinely wanted to make a difference in the world and enjoyed experiencing other cultures, seeing new things, helping people as much as I could in my small way. But something was always missing."

She smiled at him, feeling as if she would burst from the joy that bubbled through her. "I finally know what it was."

"Oh? Let me guess. Cinnamon hot cocoa."

"Well, that and something else." She smiled tenderly and kissed his jaw. "I'm talking about you, Rafael Santiago. Isn't it funny that I could travel all over the world seeking something without knowing it and I only found it when I finally came back home?"

He pulled her close again and kissed her sweetly, gently, while outside she heard Christmas carols and the sound of children's laughter and the occasional hearty *Ho Ho Ho*. She had done this—brought joy to other people and a little holiday spirit. It had been hard, backbreaking, intense work but worth every moment.

In return, she had received the very best gift of all, the only one that really mattered.

Love.

* * * * *

Dear Reader,

Being a writer is a magical thing. What a marvelous opportunity—to be able to create people out of only my imagination. By the time I've finished a book, my characters always feel like real friends to me. They become people I care about, who inevitably have a lasting impact in my life. That's why it was such a delight to revisit the Dalton family in *A Cold Creek Holiday*. I've written other books set in Cold Creek and have had characters of previous books make guest appearances occasionally, but never to the extent of this story. So many of my previous characters played significant roles in the story of Emery Kendall and Nate Cavazos. In a way, seeing them all again was like a warm, crazy, fun family reunion. It definitely felt like coming home.

And isn't that what the holidays are all about? My very best to you and yours this holiday season.

RaeAnne

A COLD CREEK HOLIDAY

Chapter 1

Few things gave a woman a sense of her own vulnerability like driving on an unfamiliar mountain road in the dark through a snowstorm.

Her knuckles white on the wheel of the small SUV she had rented at the Jackson Hole Airport, Emery Kendall squinted through the blowing flakes the wipers tried to beat away, desperate for any sign she was even on the right road.

The GPS unit on the rental wasn't working—naturally—and the directions she had printed off the internet had already proved fallible twice.

She let out a breath. Stupid. This whole thing was a colossal mistake. What had seemed like such a logical plan in September, even a welcome excuse to escape the weight of her pain and grief and memories during the holidays, had lost a great deal of its allure the first

time her tires slipped in the two or three inches of unplowed snow and the vehicle slid toward the ominous
stretch of river ribboning beside the canyon road.

She had every reason to hate driving in the snow. It
brought back too much pain, too many memories, and
she couldn't help asking herself what on earth she was
doing here. She should be safe at home in Virginia, snug
in her townhouse with a fire crackling in the grate and
a mug of hot cocoa at her elbow while she tried to wrap
her recalcitrant head around her latest project.

Alone.

She clicked the wipers up to a faster rhythm as she
approached a slight break in the dark silhouette of trees
lining either side of the road.

A log arch over the side road was barely visible in her
headlights, but she saw enough to make out the words
burned into the wood.

Hope Springs Guest Ranch. Finally.

The owners really ought to think about a few well-
placed landscaping lights so weary travelers knew they
were in the right place.

Not that it was any of her business how they ran their
guest ranch. Right now the only thing she cared about
was reaching her rented cabin, hauling her things inside
and collapsing on the bed for the next two or three days.

She turned into the driveway, which was unplowed
with no tracks indicating anyone else had driven this
way recently, at least not since the snow started to fall.

As the tires of the four-wheel-drive whirred through
the virgin powder, that sense of vulnerability and unease returned, not so much from the weather now as
the sobering realization that she was heading alone to a
strange place—and, she had to admit, from the knowl-

edge that the Cold Creek Land & Cattle Company was only a mile or so up the road.

The Daltons. Three men, brothers. Wade, Jake and Seth.

A tangle of conflicting emotions tumbled through her, but she quickly pushed them all away, as she had been doing since the September night when her mother's dying confession had rocked the entire foundation of her world.

Not now. All that could wait. At the moment, the more pressing need was to get out of this snow before she became hopelessly stranded and ended up freezing to death in a snow bank on the side of some obscure mountain road.

No Christmas lights illuminated the night, which she found odd for a guest ranch. Even a little string of white lights along the fenceline would have provided a much more cheery welcome than the unrelenting darkness.

Just when she was wondering if she had imagined that sign out front, she reached a cluster of buildings. A white-painted barn and a two-story log home dominated the scene and she was relieved to see the house ablaze with light.

The woman she had spoken with when she made the reservation months ago told her to check in at the main house. She had confirmed her reservation a few weeks ago and received the same instructions, though this time from a rather flighty sounding girl who had been somewhat vague, even as she assured Emery everything was in order for her arrival.

A cold wind dug under her jacket as she walked up the steps to the wide front porch, and she was grateful for her wool scarf and hat.

She rang the bell beside a carved wooden door and a few seconds later she heard from inside the thud of running feet and a decidedly young female voice. "Doorbell! Somebody's here! I'll get it, Uncle Nate."

Three heartbeats later, the door swung open and a dark-eyed girl of perhaps seven or eight peered out.

She didn't say anything, didn't even smile, just simply gazed out in her blue thermal pajamas, as if finding a bedraggled traveler on their doorstep in the middle of a stormy December night was a daily occurrence.

She supposed it likely was. They did run a guest ranch, after all.

Despite the girl's impassive expression, Emery forced a smile. "Hi. I'm Emery Kendall. I think I'm expected. I'm sorry I'm so late."

"It's okay. We're not in bed yet. Just a minute." She shifted her head and called over her shoulder. "Uncle Nate. It's a lady in a really pretty hat."

Emery touched her cloche, one of her own creations.

The girl held the door wide-open, but Emery didn't feel quite right about walking inside, invited only by an eight-year-old. Conversely, she also didn't feel right about standing in the open doorway, allowing all the delicious warmth from inside to wash past her and dissipate in the storm.

Before she could make up her mind, a man in a dark green wool henley, flannel shirt and Levi's walked into the entry.

He exuded danger, from his hard eyes to his unsmiling mouth to the solid, unyielding set to his jaw.

She had that unsettling cognizance of her own vulnerability again. Who knew she was coming to Idaho?

Only Lulu, the manager of her store, and Freddie, her best friend.

Solitary Traveler Shows Up at Dark Mountain Lodge in a Storm, Never to Be Heard from Again. She could just see the headline now.

Or maybe she had spent too many sleepless nights in the past two years watching old Alfred Hitchcock movies on the classic film channel.

Just because the man *looked* dangerous didn't mean he necessarily was. How many serial killers sent little girls who called them Uncle Nate to greet their victims?

"Yes?" he asked, in a decidedly unwelcoming tone.

"I'm Emery Kendall."

He met her gaze with raised eyebrows and a blank look. "Sorry, is that supposed to mean something to me?"

If not for that sign out front, she would have worried she had the wrong place. Now she just wondered what wires had been crossed about her arrival date.

Either that, or this was the most inhospitable guest lodge it had ever been her misfortune to find.

"I have a reservation to stay in one of your cabins until the twenty-seventh of December," she said, fighting down that unease again. "I made the initial reservation several months ago and confirmed it only a few weeks ago with a woman named Joanie something or other. I have the paperwork if you'd like to confirm it."

"Joanie ran off." The pajama-clad girl had followed the man back into the room and she spoke in a matter-of-fact tone. "Uncle Nate is really mad."

"Uncle Nate" did indeed look upset. His mouth tightened even more and his eyes darkened to a hard black. She felt an unexpected pang of sympathy for the unknown woman. She wouldn't like to have all that leashed frustration aimed in *her* direction.

"Damn fool woman," he muttered.

For one crazy moment, she thought he meant her, then realized he must be referring to the absent Joanie.

"Is there a problem?" She couldn't help stating the obvious.

"You might say that." He raked a hand through short dark hair. "We run a pretty low-key operation here, Ms. Kendall. This isn't your average five-star hotel. We've only got a few guest cabins that are mostly empty in the winter."

"I understood that completely when I made the reservation. I saw the Web site and reviews and talked at length about the amenities with the woman who initially took my reservation. I'm perfectly fine with the arrangements."

She didn't add that they were ideal for her purposes, to be left alone for the holidays, away from the gaiety and the frenzy and the memories.

Not to mention the proximity of Hope Springs Guest Ranch to the Cold Creek ranch.

"Yeah, well, we've got one employee who usually handles everything from reservations to making the beds. Joanie Reynolds."

"And?"

"And three days ago, she ran off with a cowboy she met at the Million Dollar Bar and I haven't seen her since. You want the truth, we're in a hell of a mess."

He didn't look apologetic in the slightest, only frustrated, as if the whole mess were *Emery's* fault.

She was exhausted suddenly from the long day of traveling, from flight delays and long security lines and two hours of driving on unfamiliar roads. All she wanted was to sink into a bed somewhere and sleep until she could think straight once more.

"What do you suggest I do, then? I had a reservation. I made a deposit and everything. And I've been traveling for eight hours."

She heard the slightly forlorn note in her voice and wanted to wince. Nate Whoever-He-Was must have heard it, too. A trace of regret flickered in the depths of those dangerous dark eyes.

He sighed heavily. "Come in out of the cold. We'll figure something out."

She hesitated for just a moment, that serial-killer scenario flitting through her head again, but she pushed it away. Little girl, remember?

Inside the house, she was immediately struck by the vague sense of neglect. The furnishings were warm and comfortable, an appealing mix of antique, reproduction and folk art pieces. Through the doorway, she glimpsed a great room with soaring vaulted ceilings. A lovely old schoolhouse quilt had prominence against the wall and she fought the urge to whip out her sketchbook and pencils to get those particular umber and moss tones down on paper.

But she also didn't miss the cobwebs in the corner of the space and a messy pile of mail and unread newspapers scattered across the top of the console table in the entryway where she stood.

Nor did she miss the wide, muscled shoulders of the man, or the way they tapered to slim hips.

"Is there anywhere else close by I could stay?" she asked, more than a little aghast at her inconvenient and unexpected reaction to him.

He turned with a frown and she sincerely hoped he couldn't see that little niggle of attraction.

"Not really, I'm sorry to say," he answered. "There are a couple other guest ranches in the area, but everybody else closes down for the winter. There's a motel in town, but I couldn't recommend it."

"Why do you stay open when everybody else shuts down?"

He made a face as if the very question had occurred to him more than once. "We have some hardcore snowmobilers who've been staying since the ranch opened to guests five years ago. Their bookings are being honored, though we haven't taken new ones since...well, probably since you made your reservations."

A muscle flexed in his jaw. "Look, do you mind waiting here while I check the computer?"

"I have a copy of my reservation in the rental. I can get it for you."

"I believe you. I just want to figure out what Joanie has done. For all I know, we're hosting a damn convention she forgot to mention to me before she ran off. Just give me five minutes."

He walked away, leaving her standing in the entryway with the little girl—who was suddenly joined by another girl who looked perhaps a few years older. Her hair wasn't quite as long and her features were thinner. But just like her sister—they looked so much alike, they could be nothing else—she said nothing, just regarded Emery with solemn, dark eyes.

Something strange was going on at the Hope Springs Ranch. She couldn't help noticing a large artificial Christmas tree in the great room, but it was bare of lights or ornaments, and as far as she could tell, that was the only concession to the holidays within her view.

"I really like your hat," the younger girl who had answered the door finally said to break the silence.

She smiled at her, despite her exhaustion. "Thank you. I made it."

"You made it?" The older girl's eyes widened. "Like you sewed it and stuff?"

"Yes. And I designed the material."

The girl frowned, clearly skeptical. "Nobody designs material. You just buy it at the sewing store. That's what our mom used to do anyway."

"Before she died," the younger one added.

"Be quiet, Tallie," her sister snapped. "She doesn't need to know *everything*."

Emery wanted to tell them she might not know everything, but she did know about losing a mother. Her own had only been gone a few months. But she supposed the experience of a twenty-seven-year-old woman losing her mother was quite different than that of two young girls.

"You do pick out material in a fabric store," she answered. "But someone has to design the material in the first place and decide what color dyes and what sort of fibers to use. That's what I do."

She didn't add that her fledgling textile line had recently been called "innovative, exciting and warmly elegant" by the leading trade magazine.

"Can you show me how to make a hat like that?"

"Me, too!" The younger girl exclaimed. "If Claire gets to make one, I want to. I can give it to my friend Frances for Christmas."

"Ooh, maybe I could make two," her sister said. "One

for Natalie and one for Morgan. They're my very best friends."

"Can I make a pink one?" Tallie asked. "I *love* pink, and so does Frances."

"Ooh, I would like purple," her sister said. "Or maybe red."

Emery shifted, wondering where in Hades their uncle had disappeared to and how the situation had suddenly spiraled out of her control. It must be the fatigue—or perhaps her complete lack of experience with young girls.

"I don't even know if I'm staying here yet. Your uncle and I are still working out the details."

The expression on both faces shifted from excitement to resignation in a blink and she wondered what in their young lives had contributed to their cynicism.

She hated sounding like such a grump, especially toward two girls who had lost their mother. "If I'm staying, we can see," she amended.

That was apparently enough for them. For the next few moments the girls talked about colors and patterns until their uncle returned to the room.

"Your reservation wasn't on the main calendar in the office, but I found it on a deleted copy of her files from the hard drive backup. I don't know what happened. Everything is in such a mess."

"Is the cabin I reserved available, then?"

He sighed. "Nobody else is staying there, so I suppose you could say it's available. But Joanie basically ran the lodging side of things and I haven't had time to replace her yet. I'm going to have to scramble just to find maid service. It might take me a few days, so you might want to reconsider and find a place in Jackson Hole. We'll of course fully refund your deposit."

"I don't need maid service. I can take care of myself. I just need a quiet place where I can get some work done."

He studied her for a long moment then finally shrugged. "I think you're crazy, but what do I know? If you want to stay, I suppose it wouldn't be fair of me to turn you away since you've had a reservation for several months. Let me grab my coat and I'll take you down and open the cabin."

"Yay! You're staying." Tallie beamed at her as Nate reached into a closet in the hallway and emerged with fleece-lined ranch coat. "Now you can show us how to make a hat."

"She only said we could see," the older girl warned her sister. "That usually means no."

"Ms. Kendall is our guest," their uncle said with what she was beginning to consider his characteristic frown. "You girls are not to pester her. You know the rules."

Though Emery had been seeking a tactful way to discourage them, she had a sudden obstinate urge to do exactly the opposite.

"Give me a day or two to settle in. I brought my sewing machine and some fabric samples we could probably use."

"Who packs a sewing machine for a holiday visit to the mountains?"

She forced a smile. "I'm not here to ski, Mr...."

"Sorry. Cavazos. Nate Cavazos."

"Mr. Cavazos. This is a working vacation for me. I just need peace and quiet to finish several projects awaiting my attention. The setting doesn't really matter."

That was an outright lie, but she decided it was none of Nate Cavavos's business exactly why she had come to Cold Creek.

Damn tourists.

Nate grabbed the key to the biggest and best of the four small cabins his sister and her husband had built along Cold Creek.

If he had his way, he would send Miss Fancy Kendall back to Jackson Hole, just be blunt and tell her in no uncertain terms that there was no room at the inn.

What the hell did he know about running a guest ranch? He was a highly trained military specialist with a background in explosives. He knew about blowing things up and planning clandestine operations. Organized chaos was his specialty, not fluffing pillows and fetching tea for sleek city women who drove Lexus SUVs and looked as if they just stepped out of some après skiwear catalog.

Damn the woman and damn Joanie Reynolds for running off and leaving such a mess behind.

"If you'll follow me, you can park your vehicle next to the cabin. I'll unlock it for you and make sure the heat's working, then help you with your bags."

"That's not necessary, really. Both of us don't need to go out into the storm. I can take the key and let myself in if you'll just point me in the right direction."

He ignored her and opened the door. "Claire, keep an eye on Tallie for me, okay? I'll be back in a minute. I've got my cell with me if you need me."

"Okay."

She was too agreeable, his oldest niece. He hadn't seen her a great deal in her eleven years, just the occasional visit between deployments, but he remembered her as always being eager to please. In the three months since her parents died, she had become even more so, though she still tried to boss her younger sister around as if she were trying desperately to control that one little corner of a chaotic universe.

"When can we make the hats?" Tallie asked.

"What hats?"

Emery Kendall pointed to hers. "They were admiring my cloche. I told them I could perhaps help them sew one of their own."

He didn't know what the hell a cloche was. It sounded French and vaguely sexy, especially to a man who hadn't been with a woman since before his last tour of duty.

"Girls, you're not to bother our guests. You know that."

"They weren't bothering me," she protested. "I told them we could see in a few days, once I settle in."

His mouth tightened. That was the *last* thing he needed, for his grieving, emotionally hungry nieces to suddenly decide to latch onto this stranger who was only going to be here for a week or so.

They missed their mother and father terribly. The hell of it was, he had come to the conclusion he was far worse at parenting than he was at running a guest ranch.

"You don't have entertain Tallie and Claire," he said, his voice gruff. "Especially when you've got work of your own to do."

She looked as if she wanted to argue, but he wasn't at all in the mood to tangle with her anymore tonight. He wanted to get the blasted woman settled in to her cabin and come back to the house so he could figure out where the hell his life had gone so disastrously off-track in a few short months.

"You girls go on up to bed," he said. Though it was an order, he tried not to phrase it as such. He had learned the first few weeks after Suzi and John died that eight- and eleven-year-old girls didn't respond like trained commandos to terse commands. "I'll check on you when I come back inside."

Without waiting for their answer—or to see if Ms. Kendall followed him—he turned up his collar, pulled down his Stetson and headed out into the lightly blowing snow.

He was halfway down the driveway he hadn't had time to plow yet and trudging toward the cabins a few hundred yards away from the house before he heard her vehicle start up behind him.

He had to admit, his sister and her husband had picked a good spot for guest cabins. When he was a kid, this part of the struggling ranch had held rusting old farm equipment and a ramshackle shed or two. But Suzi and John had cleared all that out and built four comfortable log cabins out of old salvaged timbers and white chinking so they looked as if they had been there forever.

In the daylight, the place had a nice view of the west slope of the Tetons and of Cold Creek Canyon. And Suzi had made the inside of each cabin warm and welcoming.

He didn't know much about this sort of thing. As long as he had a sleeping bag and a tight-weave tent to keep out the worst of the bugs and the sandstorms, he was fine. But he imagined the guests of the ranch Suzi had renamed Hope Springs probably appreciated the handmade curtains and the lodgepole pine furnishings.

He unlocked the first cabin and immediately switched on the electric fireplace in the main room and the smaller fireplace in the bedroom. Between the two of them, they did a surprisingly effective job of keeping the place toasty in only a matter of minutes.

He walked back out onto the porch and found the blasted woman trying to wrestle a huge suitcase out of the cargo space of the SUV.

"I said I'd help you with your bags," he muttered.

Despite the dim light from the porch and the swirl of snow, he didn't miss the cool look she sent him out of lovely blue eyes he didn't want to notice.

"I appreciate your...courtesy."

He didn't miss the slight, subtle pause before she said the last word. Though he wanted to bark and growl and tell her where to shove that delicate hint of sarcasm, he forced a tight smile.

"Here at Hope Springs, we're nothing if not courteous," he said in a benign sort of voice that matched her own.

He reached down and pulled the suitcase away from her then lifted another one out. The back was chock-full with five suitcases and several bags of groceries. At least Joanie must have had the foresight despite her typical ditziness to encourage their guest to shop for food before she arrived. He was grateful for that, at least. The ranch didn't provide any meals and the nearest restaurant was six miles down the canyon in Pine Gulch, but the cabin was outfitted with a full kitchen.

Between the two of them, it only took a few trips to

empty out the back of her vehicle and set everything inside the now-toasty cabin.

When he returned inside with the last load, he found her in the kitchen, putting away food from the grocery bags.

She had taken off her coat and beneath it she wore a pale blue turtleneck that showed just how nicely curved she was in all the right places.

He didn't want to notice. "The kitchen should have everything you need in the way of pots and pans and that sort of thing. If you're missing anything you need, you can call up to the main house."

"I'm sure I'll be fine."

"The reservation said you're staying until the twenty-seventh. Is anyone else joining you?"

He wondered if he imagined the way she tilted her chin in a rather defiant sort of way. "No."

She was staying here by herself through Christmas? He wasn't big on celebrating the holidays himself, but he had to wonder what would make a soft, pretty woman like Emery Kendall leave everything familiar and hide out in the Idaho wilderness alone during Christmas.

None of his business, he reminded himself. He had enough on his plate without spending a minute wondering why she wanted to hole up here by herself.

"If you need anything, the number to the main house is the top button programmed on the phone," he said.

"I'm sure I'll be fine. Thank you for your help." She paused. "Actually, there is one thing. When I made the initial reservation, I was told I was welcome to use any of the Hope Springs horses during my stay."

"That's generally the policy. If you need help saddling a horse, you can usually find me or Bill Higgins, the hired man, somewhere around the place."

"I shouldn't need help. I've been around horses most of my life. But thank you."

A woman who sewed fancy hats, wore her clothes with the kind of flair that belonged in a fashion magazine, drove a rented Lexus SUV and apparently had plenty of experience with horses. He gave a mental head shake as he said good-night and walked back into the December night.

He wasn't sure what to think of her. Nothing, he reminded himself. He didn't need to spend one more minute than necessary thinking about the woman. She was a guest at the ranch, that was all. One he would be thrilled to send on her way at the earliest possible opportunity.

Chapter 2

She slept better than she had in months.

It was an unexpected boon. She had never been able to sleep well in a strange bed. Coupled with the insomnia that had troubled her since before her mother died, Emery had anticipated a rough night.

Perhaps she had only been exhausted from the long day of travel and the complications of her arrival. Whatever the reason for her deep sleep, she awoke invigorated, her mind racing with ideas for the boutique hotel redesign she was working on for one of her favorite clients, Spencer Hotels.

This is exactly what she hoped might happen, that escaping from her routine in Warrenton might help her recapture some of the joy she had always found when a new project started to click in her head.

What she had taken to be a blizzard the night before

left only about three or four inches of new snow on the ground. She opened the rather ordinary beige tab curtains to the alpine scene outside her windows and spent the morning with her sketchbook.

The hotel Eben Spencer had recently purchased was in Livingston, Montana, gateway to the north entrance of Yellowstone. He wanted mountain chic with an edge, and custom everything—window coverings, upholstery, bed linens.

By early afternoon, she had filled her sketchbook with several possibilities she thought would work for the property. After a quick bowl of canned tomato soup and half a sandwich, the lure of the brilliant blue sky—the pure clarity of it against the dark green pine topped with snow—was too powerful for her to resist.

She bundled into silk long johns and her warmest outdoor gear and decided to check out the ranch's equine offerings.

As she walked past red-painted outbuildings toward the large horse barn and corrals she had spied the night before on her way in, she saw no sign of her reluctant host. Her only companion was a magpie who squawked at her from atop the split-rail fence then hopped away in a flash of iridescent wings.

At the horse barn, a half dozen horses munched alfalfa that had recently been spread for them in the snow-covered pasture and it appeared as if that many again preferred the warmth of the barn.

She stood at the railing, admiring the quarter horses. She could see a couple mares were ready to foal and all of them looked well-fed and content.

After a few moments, a strong-boned dappled gray

gelding wandered over to her spot and dipped his head for a little love.

"You are a pretty boy, aren't you," she murmured and he whinnied and tossed his head as if in complete agreement.

"That one was our mom's horse."

She whirled around and found the girls from the night before watching her from the corner of the pasture. Claire and Tallie, she remembered.

They wore jeans and parkas and mismatched gloves and Tallie's hair was slipping out of her braid. Had her sister fixed it or had Nate? The idea of that dangerous-looking man trying to wrangle his niece's hair tugged at her emotions.

"Hi," she greeted the girls.

"That was our mom's favorite horse," Claire repeated.

"He's beautiful," Emery answered.

"His name is Cielo. It means *cloud* in Spanish," the younger girl said. "You can ride him if you want."

"Oh, I don't…"

Tallie didn't wait for her to answer. "Annabelle was our mom's other favorite horse, but she's having a baby after Christmas so you can't ride her."

"Which one is Annabelle?"

"The black with the white stockings," Claire said, gesturing to a lovely mare currently drinking from the water trough.

"So do you want to ride Cielo?"

She did, suddenly, but she was wary about riding a horse that had been a favorite of their deceased mother.

"If you're sure it's okay."

"Sure," Tallie answered, then her gamine features

lit up. "Hey, she could come with us! Then we could go now."

"Where are you going?" Emery asked warily.

"Just a friend's house," Claire said.

"By yourselves?"

The girls exchanged glances. "We're allowed to ride as long as we have someone with us," Claire finally answered, an explanation Emery didn't completely buy.

"What were you planning to do before you ran into me here?"

"Wait." Tallie heaved a put-upon sigh. "We've been waiting all morning, and Uncle Nate is *still* busy with the man who came from Idaho Fall."

"The lawyer," Claire said. "He's talking about our mom and dad's state."

It took Emery a moment to deduce their uncle and the attorney must be discussing their parents' estate. Poor little things, to lose both their mother and their father.

Let that be a lesson to her. Just when she was tempted to wallow in self-pity at the strange journey her life had taken over the past few years, she was completely gobsmacked by someone whose path was even tougher.

"I'm sure they'll be finished soon."

"But we have an important mission," Tallie declared. "We can't wait much longer. We really can't."

Emery couldn't help her smile. Had she been so dramatic at eight? "What could possibly be so urgent?"

"Our friend Tanner has been home sick from school for three whole days."

Again, Emery had to swallow a smile at the gravity in the girl's voice. "Oh my goodness. I hope it's nothing serious."

"He had the flu and was throwing up and everything.

He said it was really gross. But his stepmom said he's feeling tons better."

"That's a relief." Emery was surprised to find herself enjoying her interaction with these cute girls.

"Yeah, only I brought home all his homework papers yesterday and I just *have* to get them to his house so he has time to finish them before school on Monday or he'll be in big trouble."

"I can see why you're in such a hurry, then."

"So will you come with us?" Claire asked. "We can help you saddle Cielo."

She looked at the powerful horse and then back at the girls. She had been considering a ride. And by the looks of him, riding Cielo would indeed be like riding a cloud. What would be the harm in going along with the girls and saving Nate Cavazos a little work?

"We'd better make sure it's all right with your uncle."

"I'm sure he won't mind," Claire said. "This way he doesn't have to find the time to take us."

"Why don't you ask him anyway? I would feel better if he gave his okay. Tallie and I will saddle the horses and meet you at the house in a few minutes, all right?"

Claire gave a reluctant sigh, but nodded. "Tallie, you get Junebug for me. And don't cinch her too tight."

"I know. I've only done it a million times."

Claire returned to the barn a few moments later, just as they were saddling Tallie's small paint pony, a pretty little mare she called Estrella.

"Did he say it was okay?"

"Yep," Claire said, her attention turned to her own horse.

"Good," Emery answered, surprised at how much

she was anticipating a good, hard ride. "Does it take long to reach Tanner's house?"

"It's not far. Maybe a mile," Tallie answered. Before Emery could ask if she needed a hand into the saddle, the girl clambered up like a little monkey and settled easily on the horse's back.

Both girls looked completely at home in the saddle and Emery, who had been riding since she was younger than either of them, though with an English saddle, felt like a veritable greenhorn in comparison.

"Come on. Let's go," Tallie insisted, nudging the heels of her boots into the horse's side.

The younger girl led the way down the snowy driveway and both of the other horses followed Estrella with alacrity, tack jingling softly and their gaits smart, as if they were thrilled to be out in the cold, invigorating air.

The mountains loomed over them, raw and jagged, their peaks a dramatic contrast of snow and pine.

At the end of the long, curving drive, they followed the canyon road along the creek for perhaps a half mile. In that time, they encountered no vehicles.

"Are we getting closer to Tanner's house?" Emery asked after a few more moments.

"Not very far. Look, there's the sign for it."

She followed the direction of the girl's outstretched hand and her heart clutched in her chest.

A huge log arch spanned the driveway, much bigger than the sign for the Hope Springs Guest Ranch had been. This one declared Cold Creek Land & Cattle Company in black iron letters.

Oh, dear heavens.

She wasn't ready. She still hadn't decided if she

would *ever* be ready. She needed more time to figure out if she wanted to face any of the Daltons yet.

She wanted to whirl Cielo around and ride as fast and as hard as she could back to the relative safety of Hope Springs.

"What's the matter, Ms. Kendall?" Tallie's mouth puckered into a concerned frown. "You look funny."

She didn't feel funny. Far from it. She felt panicked and vaguely nauseous, the canned tomato soup suddenly turning to greasy sludge in her stomach.

She drew in a breath. She could do this. The Daltons knew nothing about the revelations that had completely rocked her world four months ago. As far as they knew, she was only a guest staying at a neighboring ranch.

"Nothing." She forced a smile and eased her hands on the reins. "Nothing at all."

Her heart pounded as they rode under the arch and headed up a long driveway that wound around a stand of lodgepole pine and bare-branched aspens.

The house was a grand, imposing log structure with a long front porch and several gables, surrounded by several outbuildings. Some distance from it, she could see a large, sprawling metal-framed building. She guessed that was the Cold Creek equine training facility she had read about on the internet.

Her heart felt as if it would pound right out of her chest and she couldn't seem to catch her breath in the cold air. She hadn't had a panic attack since she graduated from college, not even during the worst of her pain and loss during the past two years, and she really didn't want to start again.

Breathe, she ordered herself.

When they neared the house, the girls jumped down from their horses and Emery knew she couldn't go inside.

"I'll just wait for you out here with the horses," she told them. "You go give your friend his homework."

The implications of the connection began to sink through. Tanner must be one of the Dalton children. Wade's, probably, since as far as she could determine, he was the only brother with grade-school-age kids, although Seth had older stepchildren. That made Tallie's friend Tanner her...

She jerked her mind away. "Go ahead. I'll be fine."

"Okay, but we might be a few minutes. You might get cold. I told Tanner I would explain our math assignment to him and I don't know how long it will take."

Before she could come up with an answer, a tall, dark-haired man with a definite air of authority walked out of a nearby barn. He stopped short when he spied them, then his handsome features lit up.

"Well, hello there, Miss Tallie and Miss Claire," he called as he approached them. "What brings you all the way up to the Cold Creek on such a wintry day?"

Emery drew in a calming breath and then another one. He looked just like the picture she had of his father. Which brother was it? Her guess was Wade. He ran the family's cattle operations, from what she could determine, while the youngest brother, Seth, was in charge of the horse training facility. A third brother, Jake, was a family physician in Pine Gulch.

She could have hired a private investigator to find all this information, but she hadn't needed to go that far. A few clicks on the computer and she had found all she needed to know and then some.

"I've got Tanner's homework, Mr. Dalton."

"That is sure nice of you girls to ride over for that. It will give him something to do besides snipe at his brother and sister. He'll be real glad to see a little company. And who's your friend?"

"Her name is Ms. Kendall and she's from Virginia," Claire answered.

Emery didn't feel she had any choice but to dismount. She prayed her shaking legs would hold her up.

"I'm Emery Kendall. I'm staying at Hope Springs through the holidays."

He wore a battered leather work glove, but he removed it and reached out his hand. She shook it then quickly dropped her fingers.

"Nice to meet you, Miz Kendall. You picked a beautiful time of year for a visit. This area of eastern Idaho is pretty year round, but there's something special about the place during the holidays, as long as you can stand the cold."

She had only seen the one picture, but she knew his father shared that same smile, that same thick, wavy, dark hair.

"Let's tie your horses so you can come in out of the cold for a minute and I'll let Tanner know you all are here," he said. "And don't worry, he's not contagious anymore. Just grumpy as can be."

The girls giggled at that and followed him back up the porch steps and into the house.

The house was huge and warm and welcoming. Here were the Christmas decorations the girls' home lacked. A massive Christmas tree decorated with plaid ribbons and hundreds of ornaments brushed the top of the soaring vaulted ceiling and pine garlands with matching ribbons draped the river-rock fireplace and hung from the log staircase.

Whoever decorated the place had used a pleasing mix of color and texture to create a sense of brightness and warmth.

She was studying a particularly lovely embroidered sampler on the wall when a woman with blond hair and fine-boned features entered the room.

"Tallie and Claire Palmer. Two of my favorite people!"

"We brought Tanner's homework assignment. Mrs. Peterson said he can turn it in when he goes back to class."

"He'll be so excited to see you," the woman said with a warm smile. "Come on back to the kitchen. I just took a tray of cookies out of the oven. You'd better come grab one before the hungry little mouths around here gobble them all up."

"And the hungry big mouths."

The man owning the hungry big mouth in question swooped the woman into his arms and planted it on hers and kissed her soundly, apparently unembarrassed by the presence of a stranger.

"You'll have to fight Cody for them, I'm afraid," she answered after he released her. "He's already snitched three off the cookie sheet before I could even transfer them to the cooling rack. I'm sure he had to have burned his tongue, but he'll never admit it."

Wade Dalton chuckled, then apparently remembered his manners. "Sorry. Carrie, this is Emery Kendall. She's staying at Hope Springs and was nice enough to ride with the girls over here to bring Tanner's homework. Emery, this is my wife, Caroline. If you'll excuse me, I'm going to go fight off my kids for the cookies. It was nice to meet you."

"Thank you," she murmured. Only after he left the room did her heart rate seem to settle down.

"Tanner and Nat are in the family room playing video games," Caroline said to the girls. "I'm sure Tanner would love some company besides family for a few minutes if you've got time to visit."

The girls looked to Emery as if for permission and she wasn't quite sure how to respond. Right now she didn't feel in charge of anything, not even her own breathing. "A few moments, I suppose. Then we'd better ride back before your uncle begins to worry."

"I told Tanner I would explain the math assignment," Tallie said. "We're subtracting fractions and stuff and it's really hard."

"That is so kind of you to help him," Caroline said with a warm smile. "I don't know what we would have done without you."

Though it was only a first impression and she could be way off-base, for all she knew, Emery thought the other woman seemed completely sincere in her gratitude, the sort of person who could lift even the most defeated spirit just with her smile.

She would have been very much inclined to like her, even if she hadn't already read and admired Caroline Montgomery Dalton's self-help books on finding your life's direction before she knew of the connection to the Daltons of Cold Creek Canyon.

"Emery, where did you say you were from?" Caroline asked when the girls hurried from the room.

"Virginia. Warrenton, an hour outside Washington, D.C."

"Lovely country there. Are you in Pine Gulch visiting family?" Caroline asked.

Under the circumstances, Emery didn't quite know how to respond to that particular question.

"I guess you could say I needed a change this Christmas. It's been a…difficult year. My mother died of cancer in September."

"Oh, I'm so sorry for your loss. I can only imagine how hard the holidays must be for you."

Though she didn't physically touch her, the concern in her voice was somehow just as comforting as an embrace.

"The grief is still very painful, especially as she was my…only family. I wasn't quite ready to face the parties and celebrations of the holidays and was looking for a change this year. I read about Hope Springs Guest Ranch online and it seemed just the place to spend the holidays."

"It's a very peaceful spot," Caroline said softly. "I've always thought it had healing energy. I know Suzi, the girls' mother, felt the same."

She didn't expect to find healing. She only wanted to figure out how everything she thought she had known about herself could turn out to be a lie.

"I'm surprised Nate is taking new guests. I was under the impression he's working toward closing the place, which is really a shame after all the work and heart and soul Suzi and John put into it."

"I made my reservation back in September. There was some mix-up with it, but Mr. Cavazos agreed to honor it."

"He has his hands full, that man."

Before Emery could answer, a timer dinged from somewhere in the house. Caroline glanced behind her.

"My cookies are just coming out. Listen, do you mind coming back to the kitchen with me? I don't want to leave you out here by yourself, but if I don't take them out, they'll burn. Of course, they'll still get inhaled around here, no matter how crispy they are."

"I don't mind," she answered. She followed Caroline down a hallway toward the origin of the delicious smells of almond and butter and sugar. The hallway was lined with photographs, old black-and-whites, framed snapshots and some that looked like professionally taken portraits. Emery's head swiveled as she took in the barrage of images and she had to stop so she could absorb them all.

"This is…your family?"

"Yes." She noticed the direction of Emery's gaze, a candid shot of three men in Western-cut suits standing at what looked like a wedding. They were laughing and lighthearted, each of them extraordinarily handsome. "Those are my husband's brothers, Jake and Seth. That was taken at Seth's wedding. They both live nearby, which is wonderful for all of them. We're very close with them and their wives."

She couldn't stand here gaping at someone else's family, not without making Caroline Montgomery Dalton think she was crazy, so she followed her down the hallway into the kitchen, doing her best not to cast longing looks over her shoulder.

In the kitchen, she found Wade Dalton sitting at a long, scarred pine table with a blonde toddler in pink overalls on his lap and a little boy of about five or six chattering a mile a minute at his side.

"I got to help make the holes for the jam, Dad. Only even though they're called thumbprint cookies, Mom wouldn't let me use my thumbs to make the dents. I had to use the lid of a marker. Don't you think that's weird?"

"Extremely," he answered with a grin toward Emery and Caroline. "But probably a little more sanitary."

"There's a method to my madness," Caroline said. "That way the jam doesn't ooze out the sides as easily. It's all in how much pressure you apply when you make the hole, isn't it, bud?"

The boy nodded emphatically. "And I'm just right, aren't I?"

"You're perfect."

Emery stood aside, observing their interaction while Caroline pulled the cookies from the oven in one smooth motion and replaced that tray with another filled with dough cutouts.

When she had set them on a cooling rack, she turned back to Emery. "So what do you do in Virginia, Emery?"

"I design textiles. I've got a shop outside D.C. that sells custom fabrics for interior designers, furniture makers, that sort of thing. We're moving into the retail market in the fall with a new midrange consumer line."

"How interesting," Caroline exclaimed. "I wish I could sew, but I'm afraid it's not one of my skills. How did you get started in that particular business? It seems rather obscure."

Emery knew from her research that Caroline Montgomery Dalton was a life coach who probably excelled at convincing people to talk about their hopes and dreams, but she was still flattered by the woman's interested expression. "I waffled between graphic arts and interior design in college, but realized my real love was creating at the sewing machine. After I interned with one of the bigger textile design firms, I decided to branch out in my own direction."

"I'd love to see some of your fabrics while you're here. Did you bring any swatches?"

She laughed. "Only about four boxes' worth. This is sort of a working vacation for me. I'm working on a design project for a hotel in Montana that wants custom fabrics from the ground up."

"I just had a great idea." Caroline said suddenly. "You should come to the party we're having next week."

Emery blinked, astounded that the woman would invite a perfect stranger who was only in the area temporarily to socialize with them. "What kind of party?"

"A friend and I are throwing sort of a celebration for the neighbors in Cold Creek Canyon. Everyone in the canyon is invited. Even though you're only here temporarily, that means you."

"You and a friend are throwing it," Wade said, a little dimple teasing at his cheek. "Except it's at Jenna's house and she's doing all the cooking."

"I'm helping!" Caroline protested. "I sent out all the invitations and I'm making cookies to take. Anyway, we capitalize on our strengths, right? Can I help it if she has a huge house with an indoor swimming pool and just happens to be a gourmet cook?"

Wade grinned and picked up one of the warm cookies. His mouth widened in appreciation as he bit into the soft treat. "You can take her down, honey. At least when it comes to your thumbprints."

"I'll make sure to tell her you said so, especially

when you're going to town on those magic bars she makes that you love so much."

She turned back to Emery. "Seriously, it's going to be a blast. All the neighbors from Cold Creek Canyon are invited. We would love to have you. I hate the idea of anyone spending the holidays alone."

Oh, sign her up to go to a party where the only reason she had been invited was because everyone felt sorry for her. That was a big part of the reason she had opted to leave Virginia this year, so her friends wouldn't feel obligated to invite her to their own holiday gatherings out of pity.

On the other hand, Caroline was offering her the perfect opportunity to spend a little time with the Daltons in a social situation. She hadn't specifically said Wade's brothers were attending, but Emery knew from her research that they both lived in the canyon, Seth in his own home here at the ranch and Jake a bit closer to town. Besides that, Caroline said the brothers were close so she would guess they would all attend the party.

"I'll think about it," she finally said.

"Wonderful. Nate and the girls are invited, of course, but I haven't heard from him. Maybe you could work on persuading him."

As if she could convince the man of anything. In the few moments she had spent with him the night before, he hadn't made it a secret that he wasn't exactly thrilled to have her staying at the ranch in the first place. She had a feeling he wouldn't respond favorably if she tried to manage his social life while she was there.

She was spared from having to come up with a polite answer by the arrival of Tallie and Claire, in company with a blond boy in sweats and a Utah Jazz sweatshirt—and with a definite gleam of mischief in his eyes.

"Get the homework situation straightened out?" Wade asked them.

"I guess," the boy muttered, his expression disgruntled. "I still say it's not fair I have to do homework when I'm sick."

"If you feel well enough to play video games, you can do homework," Caroline said, her voice firm even as she held out a cookie for the boy.

The girls chatted for a few more moments with Caroline and Wade and it was obvious to Emery that they were no strangers to the kitchen. She let them visit for a while she tried not to steal surreptitious glances at Wade. Finally, though, she was afraid her not-so-subtle interest would become too obvious. She glanced at her watch, then interjected into a break in the conversation.

"We'd better start heading back."

"Do we have to?" Tallie moaned.

"Your uncle will be looking for us," she answered, though in truth, she was just as reluctant to leave. She wanted to sit here awhile longer enjoying the warmth of this family and the tensile connection to old secrets.

Tallie gave a few more put-upon sighs, but Claire only looked disappointed for a moment, then she rose. "Come on, Tal. Let's go."

"Thanks again for bringing the homework," Wade said to the girls, then turned to Emery. "It was nice to meet you."

Somehow she managed to smile back over the renewed pounding of her heart. Would he say that if he knew the truth? She had to wonder. As she ushered the girls toward the door, Caroline and Tanner followed them. On the porch, she held out two lunch bags Emery hadn't even noticed she had been carrying.

"What's this?" Emery asked.

"Cookies, a bag for you and one for Nate and the girls. And just in case I didn't mention it, they're made with jam from our own raspberry canes in the garden. I don't have very many specialties so I'm pretty proud of this one."

Caroline hugged both Tallie and Claire goodbye, sympathy in her eyes for the two little girls. To her surprise, she hugged Emery, too.

"It was great to meet you. I really would love to see some of your fabrics."

She didn't know what to do with all this warmth, especially when some insane part of her wanted to sit right down on the porch and tell Caroline Dalton everything.

"I'll see what I can do," she answered, then she and the girls headed off the porch, mounted their horses and took off down the driveway toward Hope Springs.

Chapter 3

They were all mostly silent on the way home. Emery was lost in thought, wondering if this whole trip had been crazy. What place could she ever have in the Daltons' lives? As much as she had instinctively liked both Wade and Caroline Dalton and despite the ties they didn't even know about, she was a stranger to them. What right did she have to burst into their lives, dredging up the past?

She was so wrapped up in her thoughts, she didn't pay much attention to anything until they turned onto the Hope Springs access road. As Cielo moved alongside Claire's horse, she had the first clear view of the girl in several moments and she was stunned to see silent tears trickling down cheeks reddened by the cold.

The sight jerked her from her own self-absorption and she nudged the horse closer so she could reach out to touch the girl's shoulder. "Oh, honey, what is it?"

"Nothing," Claire sniffled.

"It's the cookies Tanner's mom made," Tallie said. She looked close to tears, as well, though she seemed to be holding them back.

"What's wrong with the cookies?"

"Nothing," Claire said. "It's just...we haven't made any this year. Not real ones, anyway."

"Our mom always made Christmas cookies with us. Every year. It was so fun," Tallie said sadly.

"We made sugar cookies and wedding balls and almond ones dipped in chocolate," Claire said, her voice breaking on the words. "I miss them so much."

She let out a sob and Emery stopped her horse and pulled the girl into as much of a hug as she could manage when they were both on horseback.

"We made cookies with Uncle Nate," Tallie reminded her sister. "They were okay."

"They were from store-bought dough. That's all Uncle Nate said he could make. And we still burned them."

Emery did her best to ignore the fluttering in her stomach at the image of the tough, virile man who could lift her heavy suitcase without a blink standing in the kitchen in an apron making cookies with his nieces.

"I'm so sorry, honey," she murmured. She wasn't the only one missing her mother or the life she used to have this Christmas, though what these two little girls were suffering seemed so much harder.

"Listen, I'm not the greatest baker, but I do have a few good cookie recipes. Maybe we could find a day before Christmas and the three of us could whip something up."

Tallie, on her sister's other side, looked ecstatic at the offer. "Really? You mean that?"

"As long as your uncle doesn't mind."

"He won't mind," Claire assured her as she wiped at her eyes. "He loves cookies. He just doesn't know how to make them."

"Can we still make a hat like yours if we're making cookies?" Tallie asked.

"I'm sure we can figure out a way to do both," she answered, and was greeted with delighted smiles.

So much for her claim that she wanted to avoid Christmas this year, she thought as they spurred their horses toward the house. Now she was committed to helping the girls make cookies and sew a few presents. The biggest surprise of all was that she actually looked forward to it.

Claire's tears dried by the time they reached the barn. As they dismounted and began removing the saddles from the horses, she and Tallie chattered about Christmas and the things they had asked for that year. Emery was carrying the saddle to the tackroom when she heard the outside door open.

"Where have you two been?"

She frowned at the anger in Nate's voice and quickly set the saddle on its form and returned to the stalls.

"We went for a ride," Claire answered.

"You went to the Daltons, didn't you?"

"I had to give Tanner his homework," Tallie said. "I told you."

"And I said we would drive over as soon as I finished with the attorney. You know the new rules. You know you're not supposed to take the horses on your own, no matter what your parents might have allowed. I have to know where you are."

"We weren't on our own," Tallie protested. "You said we couldn't go unless we were with an adult. We had Ms. Kendall with us."

He turned on her, his features thunderous.

"You had no right to just ride off with them. Do you have any idea how worried I've been? I was just about ready to start a search party."

"I left you a note," Claire said. "You were busy with the man and I didn't want to bother you."

"I didn't see any note."

"I put it on the hall table. That's where we always put stuff for Mom and Dad to see."

He raked a hand through his hair, his features still taut and angry, though Emery saw the echo of worry in his eyes. "I must have missed it."

"We gave all the homework to Tanner and now you don't even have to take us, since you don't like going to the Cold Creek," Tallie said, her voice cheerful.

"Tanner's stepmom was making cookies," Claire added, holding out the bag to him. "She sent a bunch for us."

"Did she?"

"Yep," Tallie said. "And then Claire was sad about the cookies since we didn't make the ones we usually do and Emery said she'll help us make Christmas cookies this year. Wasn't that nice?"

Nate shifted his dark-eyed gaze in her direction and he didn't look at all pleased by what she thought had been a rather kind offer.

"I'm sure it was." He put enough doubt in his voice

that it sounded as if he believed exactly the opposite. "Listen, why don't you girls head up to the house where you can get warm and set the table for dinner? I'll finish up with your horses and be up in a minute."

They agreed readily enough and a moment later, she was alone with him in the barn.

"I'm sorry if I overstepped," Emery said. "It won't happen again."

"I shouldn't have gone off on you like that. I was just worried. A storm's coming and I was afraid they would be caught up in it." He paused, giving her a careful look. "They told you they could go, didn't they?"

She remembered Claire's claims that she had told her uncle they were going. "I might have been given that impression," she admitted slowly. "But I should have made sure."

He led Cielo into a stall and began brushing the horse with practiced motions that told her even if he hadn't lived here in some time, he was no stranger to horses or ranching.

"Their parents gave them a little more freedom to come and go as they please. They're used to riding all over the ranch and even to the neighboring ranches, something I'm not completely comfortable with. It's been one of many small adjustments over the past few months."

"How long have their parents been gone?"

"Since September."

She wanted to ask him what had happened to them, but he spoke before she could come up with a tactful way to broach the subject.

"Look, you're only here for a few days." His words

were clipped, abrupt. "I would appreciate it if you would stay away from the girls."

She stared, the words of sympathy she had been gathering crumbling to ash in her mouth. "Excuse me?"

He shrugged. "Nothing personal. I'm sure you're a nice lady and all. But Tallie and Claire have suffered enough loss the past few months. We're all struggling to find our way here together. It's hard enough for them to have strangers coming and going in their lives. That's one reason I'm thinking about scaling down the guest ranch part of the operation here. I'm doing my best to keep them separate from the few guests we still have. Going for horseback rides with you, making cookies, sewing hats. It's all too much. They're going to think they have some kind of relationship with you. When you head back east to your life, the girls are going to feel abandoned by one more person in their lives."

"A rancher and an armchair psychiatrist. An interesting combination." She tried and failed to keep the bite from her voice.

She was beyond annoyed, suddenly. Had she ever asked for the girls' company? No. Her whole intent in coming to Hope Springs had been to spend the holidays alone, not to suddenly find herself responsible for the emotional well-being of two orphaned little girls. She was only trying to be kind to them, not trying to insinuate herself into their lives.

"I'm no psychiatrist, armchair or otherwise," he answered. "Or a rancher, for that matter. I'm only an army Ranger who's far more at home with my M4 carbine in my hands than a curry comb these days. I don't know a damn thing about raising two little girls. I'm going completely on instinct here—that's all I can do, really—and my gut is telling me it's not good for them to become too close to you."

Emery fought the urge to pick up the hayfork leaning against the stable wall and bash him over the head with it. Of course, if he was a highly trained soldier, he would probably have it out of her hands before she could even think about using it.

He was the girls' guardian, she reminded herself. It was his right—and obligation—to act in whatever way he thought was in their best interest.

"I will certainly do my best to stay out of their way," she finally answered. "But I refuse to be cold or rude to them when our paths cross, just to pander to your paranoia. It's not in my nature."

"I can see that. I wouldn't want you to be rude," he answered and she could almost see his tongue dip into his cheek at the words.

She scowled. "The girls asked *me* to go riding and to help them sew hats for their friends. I did offer to help them make cookies, but only because Claire was distraught over missing that particular holiday tradition, not because I was trying to worm my way into their lives. I have work enough of my own to do. I thought I was coming to Idaho for seclusion and peace, not to entertain two lost, lonely little girls. Maybe before you start warning your guests to stay away from Claire and Tallie, you ought to ask yourself what they're missing from *you* that prompts them to latch onto the first kind stranger who comes along."

He drew in a breath, but she didn't give him an opportunity to respond to her counterattack; she just turned on her heels, thrust open the barn door and marched out into the fading December afternoon.

He deserved that, he supposed.

Nate watched his guest flounce out of the barn and winced as he remembered his accusatory tone. He had certainly botched yet another of his interactions with her. What was it about the woman that brought out the worst in him? He considered himself a pretty decent guy, for the most part. He usually tried to treat women with respect and appreciation. But without even trying, Emery Kendall seemed to hit all his hot buttons. She was sleek and cultured and sophisticated.

In comparison to all that blond perfection, he felt stupid and rough-edged. Just the poor dumb Mexican kid of the town whore.

He checked the horses one last time then left the barn. He really sucked at this whole hospitality thing. He wanted to shut the gates of Hope Springs and keep everybody out, guests and interfering neighbors alike.

He supposed that made him sound like some kind of hermit. He wasn't. He liked people, for the most part, and considered the others in his unit a genuine brotherhood.

But coming home to Pine Gulch seemed to bring out the worst in him. All the childhood pain and shame and confusion, those demons he had worked so hard to exorcise after he left came bubbling back up from somewhere deep inside, like one of those sulfur hot pots not far away in Yellowstone, oozing and ugly and acrid.

He looked over at Emery's cabin, where the lights glowed merrily against the gathering twilight.

She was only looking for a quiet place to spend the

holidays, she had said. She was paying for a quiet escape. Whether he wanted to be running a guest ranch or not, he had opened the gates and allowed her in, so he was stuck—at least until he figured out what to do with Hope Springs and with the girls who had been left in his care.

Whatever she might be running from, whatever the cause of those secrets he could see in the deep blue of her eyes, he owed it to her not to let the hot mess of his life, both past and present, spill over and burn her.

Emery woke up to pitch darkness, bitter cold and the vicious howling of wind beneath the eaves.

For a moment, she couldn't remember where she was, but as her eyes adjusted to the darkness, she registered the thick weight of the down comforter, the sturdy hollows and curves of the log ceiling above her, the flannel sheets that were worlds different from the 600-thread-count Egyptian cotton she used at home, but somehow comforting nonetheless.

Idaho. She was staying at a cabin in Cold Creek Canyon, just a short distance from the Daltons.

That deduction left her with two further mysteries for her sleep-numbed mind to work through. Why was she so blasted cold? And what had awakened her from fragmented dreams of her empty arms and her empty heart?

A loud banging rang out through the cabin from the other room, far too sharp and urgent to be something random from the wind she could hear howling under the eaves.

She really didn't want to leave the protection of the blankets in order to check it out. If she was this cold with the covers tucked to her chin, how much worse would it be when she pushed them away?

"Ms. Kendall? Emery?" a man's low voice pushed through the howling wind and the stubborn cobwebs of sleep. Nate Cavazos, she realized.

"Coming," she called out, trying to gather her scrambled thoughts together. She reached for the bedside lamp, still not completely familiar with the cabin's layout to make her way in pitch darkness.

The light didn't switch on and she frowned. *That* must be why it was so dark and so cold in here. That storm howling out there must have cut the power, which meant the electric fireplace wasn't working, either.

Though everything inside her protested the invasion of even more cold, she managed to push away the covers and scramble in the blackness for the slippers she had left by the side of the bed. She might have to climb out of what little warmth she had left, but she wasn't about to touch her bare feet to the icy wood floor.

"Ms. Kendall?" Nate called again, raising his voice louder to be heard over the roar of the wind.

"I'm coming. Just a moment."

Groping her way in the dark, she made her way through the doorway of the bedroom then cursed when she cracked her knee on the mission rocking chair her outstretched hands must have missed.

She finally found the door, more by instinct than sight, and fumbled with the locks. She yanked it open then caught her breath as wind and snow swept inside in a mad icy rush.

Through the swirling snow, she could barely see Nate in the glow of the small lantern he held. He looked big and dark and dangerous. She remembered their tense discussion earlier in the barn and every instinct cried out for her to shove the door against him.

She ignored them all and opened the door farther. "It must be brutal out there. Come inside out of the wind." Her voice still sounded raspy and she tried to clear the sleep out of it as he pushed past her into the small cabin.

She was instantly aware of the heat emanating from him despite his snow-covered winter coat.

"Power's out. Guess you figured that out by now. I tried to start the generator for you behind the cabin, but the damn thing's being stubborn."

Ah. No wonder she was quickly turning to a solid block of ice.

"Does this happen often?" she asked, grateful she could see enough from his lantern light to grab the nubby throw off the back of the couch and wrap it around her.

He shrugged. "Sometimes. When I was a kid, I remember the power would go out just about every time we had a bad snowstorm. I think it's a combination of the wind and the heavy snowfall dragging down the power lines that run up the canyon. I don't expect it will be out for long. Maybe a few hours. Meantime, I'm afraid you'll have to come up to the house while we wait for the power crews to fix it."

She wrapped the throw more tightly around her. "Why? Don't you think I should be warm enough if I huddle under the blankets and put my coat on?"

"You have no idea how the windchill can work its way even through the best chinking in these log structures. I don't feel right about leaving you down here in the cold. We've got another generator at the house, plus a couple of wood fireplaces that can keep things plenty toasty. The girls are already camped out in the great room with their sleeping bags. We can find space for one more."

Near the girls he had warned her in no uncertain terms to stay away from? She might have a difficult time doing that when they were sharing the warmth of a fireplace. "Aren't you afraid I'll suck them further into my dastardly plan to break their little hearts when I leave Pine Gulch?"

He frowned and she felt bad for her sarcasm when she saw his mouth tighten with discomfort.

"This is an emergency and can't be helped," he answered. "These walls don't have much insulation. I can't leave you down here with no heat source. Even an hour in this cold could be deadly."

The gravity in his voice disconcerted her. She swallowed. As much as she wanted to lash back after his blistering words this afternoon, perhaps this wasn't the time. He *had* come down in the howling storm to make sure she was warm and safe. She ought to be grateful he didn't let her freeze to death.

"Can you give me a moment to change my clothes and put a coat on?"

"As long as it's only a moment. I don't like leaving the girls alone up at the house in this kind of weather. Here. Use the lantern. I've got a flashlight."

She nodded and reached outside the throw to take it from him. As she did, something hot flashed in his dark eyes for just an instant then was gone, and she realized that while her silk long underwear wasn't what anyone could call sexy, it still clung to every curve.

Her heart pounded at what she considered completely unreasonable speed. She snatched the lantern from him and hurried to the bedroom, closing the door firmly behind her. Inside, she quickly slipped a soft mint-green velour workout suit over her long underwear, then ran a brush through her sleep-tangled hair and pulled it back into a ponytail.

If she had any sense, she would pack up her rented SUV right this moment, head back to the airport and catch the first flight back to Virginia.

Whatever happened to her peaceful escape? She never expected Mother Nature to thrust her into this awkward situation, forced to spend even more time with a man who obviously wanted her out of his life.

Her sigh puffed out a little breath of condensation. She could handle this. With luck it would only be for an hour or two, then the power would be back on and she could hole up back here at the cabin until she finished the Spencer Hotels project, not venturing out until the holidays were over.

When she returned to the living room, she found Nate waiting for her just inside the door. Unfortunately, her boots were on the mat right beside where he was standing and there was no room around the furniture in the small space for her to grab them without being practically on top of him, an image she absolutely did *not* need racing through her head right now.

"I, um, need my boots," she said, gesturing to them.

"Oh. Right." He moved as far as he could in the other direction, but she still barely had space to squeeze past the table and grab them.

She was aware of the heat emanating from him. If there were more light in the small space, she wouldn't be surprised to see steam puffing off his coat. Was he always this warm or was it only the contrast between his body heat and the icy air inside her cabin?

She pushed away the question as completely irrelevant and focused on shoving her feet into her boots and throwing on her coat.

"Ready?" he asked, barely veiled impatience in his voice.

"As I'll ever be," she muttered.

He opened the door and the breath was snatched from her lungs by the cold and stinging snow.

"I'll take point on the way back to the house," he said, and she remembered him referring to himself as an army Ranger. She could easily see him parachuting out of an airplane over hostile territory or leading a team into a hostage situation somewhere.

"Just hold on to my coat and follow my tracks in the snow and you should be okay," he growled over the wind.

She might have thought the warning was overdramatic, maybe even intended to scare her, but the moment they stepped off the porch, the wind and snow raged even harder. She could see nothing but black with frenzied swirls of snow beyond the pale light from the lantern and the more focused beam of his flashlight.

As they began their painstaking trudge through the snow, she almost laughed when she remembered how she had thought the snow the night before was a blizzard. Compared to this, that was just a mild flurry. She could barely make out any kind of landmark in the darkness without any ambient glow from a porch light or a vapor light, and what she could see was buried in snow.

She remembered reading in school once about how early pioneers were sometimes forced to run a rope between their house and barn during blizzards so they could hang on to it to safely while they made their way back and forth to take care of their livestock. Without that anchor, they could become hopelessly lost in moments and freeze to death before they found their way back home, not ever knowing they might be a few feet from their door.

She clutched the hem of Nate Cavazos's coat like it was her only lifeline, the only safe thing she had to hold on to in this surreal landscape.

At last, when her lungs were heaving from the cold and from the rapid pace the man set for them through knee-high snow, they reached the porch. He gripped her elbow to help her up the steps that hadn't yet seen a shovel and then he opened the door to the main ranch house.

Though she could still see the condensation of her breath here, blessed warmth from the fire crackling in the great room eased its steady way through the house and into her aching muscles.

Compared to the fury that lurked outside the door, it felt like the tropics in here.

She set the lantern down on the console in the hall and shook snow off her coat and took off her hat, this time a wool creation her assistant at the store knitted out of one of their custom yarns.

"Go ahead and hang your coat on one of the hooks," he said. She shrugged out of her coat and complied, aware as she did that he wasn't removing his own. Was he really going back out into that storm? she wondered. Before she could ask, though, two little dark heads peeked around the doorway.

"You're back!" Tallie exclaimed. She came into the

entry with a brightly striped afghan wrapped around her shoulders. Beneath it, Emery saw she wore blue footie pajamas. Claire followed close behind with a matching afghan around her shoulders, but a plaid flannel nightgown several inches too short and fuzzy pink slippers peeking out below.

Tallie hugged her uncle, despite the clumps of snow clinging to his coat. "We thought maybe you were lost in the storm, Uncle Nate. You were gone *forever*."

The girl sniffled and Emery heard the deep fear in her voice. Her heart ached for this child who would probably never stop worrying she would lose someone else she loved.

For a moment, the man looked a little panicky at her tears, but after an awkward moment, he pulled her into a hug and kissed the top of her glossy hair.

"Nope. I'm right here. I just had some trouble with the generator at the cabin so I had to bring Ms. Kendall back with me before she turned into a Popsicle. It sure is blowing out there. If not for the snow and the cold, it would be a good night for flying kites."

Both girls giggled, as Emery realized he had intended. Though she wasn't inclined to like him very much right now she had to approve. His teasing hit just the right note with his two frightened nieces.

"I'm so glad you're safe," Tallie said. "And you, too, Ms. Kendall."

To her shock, the girl left her uncle's side and slid her arms around Emery's waist. She smelled of shampoo and laundry detergent with an undertone of smoke from the fireplace and Emery felt a curious tug at her heart.

"Come in by the fireplace. It's *freezing* out here," Claire ordered.

She followed her into the great room and wanted to just stand and bask in the heat from the fire blazing merrily in the river-rock hearth.

She was struck again by how bare the room was, with that empty Christmas tree and that massive rock mantel that cried out for some sort of natural garland of pine boughs.

The room was large, with two different furniture settings, two large sofas and an easy chair that made a U shape around the fireplace and a separate sitting arrangement in one corner near the Christmas tree. Both sofas were covered in blankets that had probably been dragged from other rooms in the house.

It was a comfortable room that could be genuinely lovely with a few little touches. But that was none of her business, she thought.

"I need to go back out and check on the livestock and bring in some more logs," Nate said. "Will you all be okay in here?"

"Do you have to?" Tallie asked, a plaintive, worried note in her voice.

"Sorry, bug, but I do."

"Be careful," Claire said in the bossy tone Emery was beginning to realize was second-nature to the girl.

"I shouldn't be long," he said. "There should be plenty of wood to keep the fire going. Stay warm in here."

Though the girls looked worried after he left, they quickly shifted their attention to Emery.

"You can sleep on one of the couches," Claire said in a managing sort of voice that reinforced Emery's earlier impression that the girl was used to doing all she could to keep order in her world.

Still chilled from trekking through the snow, she sat as close as she could to the fire and wrapped a soft wool blanket around her shoulders. Tallie immediately sat beside her, only a few inches away, though the couch was broad and longer than normal.

"Will the horses be okay?" Tallie asked.

"I'm sure they'll all be fine. Horses are smart creatures and they'll head for any available shelter during the storm. Don't worry."

A particularly intense gust of wind rattled the huge picture window suddenly and the younger girl gasped and moved even closer.

"I really don't like the wind," she muttered.

"Don't be such a baby," Claire made a show of rolling her eyes, but Emery was quite certain she saw apprehension in the other girl, as well, as she sat on her other side.

"I don't like the wind, either," Emery admitted.

"But you're a grown-up."

"Sometimes grown-ups are afraid of things too," she answered calmly. Heaven knows, she could bore them senseless with all the things that kept her up at night. "Shall I tell you a story my mother used to tell me when I was a little girl?"

"Please," Tallie begged, snuggling closer.

She settled deeper into the sofa. "The north wind and the sun one day had an argument about who was the stronger and could more easily remove a traveler's coat…"

She dragged the story out as long as she could, embellishing with several details that had never been in the original story. Then she added another and another and by the time her voice trailed off, both girls were half-asleep. Tallie stirred a little as Emery stopped speaking, but then eased back down again.

Emery closed her eyes as the fire crackled and hummed, its warmth both a physical and a mental comfort. This wasn't at all a bad way to spend a snowy night, she thought, just before she drifted off.

Chapter 4

When Nate returned to the house an hour later, exhausted and chilled to the marrow of his bones by the intense storm, he found the power still out, the fire burned down to embers and Emery and both girls sleeping on one couch.

He added another log to the fire and watched to make sure the embers would ignite it, then turned back to the sleeping females.

Emery dozed on one end, her cheek on the armrest, and both girls were cuddled together like puppies at the other.

The familiar, heavy weight of duty pressed down on his shoulders as he looked at his nieces. He loved them and had from the moment each was born, though he hadn't had much more than a distant, avuncular interest in them over the years.

That love had certainly grown in the past four months, but he had also discovered that instant fatherhood was far more terrifying than any challenge he had ever faced. Even being trapped in an Afghanistan mountain pass by a Taliban ambush and having to wait thirty-six hours for their exit transport had been easier than finding himself responsible for the emotional and physical well-being of Tallie and Claire.

It was enough to make even the most hardened of soldiers long to just pack up his gear and go AWOL.

He wouldn't. He owed his sister far too much for that, but sometimes he wondered how the hell he could survive the task ahead of him. Just thinking about them turning into teenagers and all that would come with that was enough to turn his hair gray.

Day by day, he reminded himself. That was the only way the three of them could make it through. One feeble, awkward step at a time. He just hoped to hell it would get easier.

He shifted his gaze to the other end of the couch toward his unwilling houseguest. In sleep, she was remarkably lovely, with those elegant debutante high cheekbones and that silky tangle of hair in a loose ponytail over her shoulder. His hands itched to pull it free, to bury his fingers in all that softness…

He had been far too long without a woman.

He sighed. That part of his life was in an indefinite holding pattern, much to his regret. How could he even think about women, about easing those particular appetites, when he had all these other damn plates spinning? The girls, the ranch, working out the details of Suzi and John's estate?

If ever there was a woman who might make him

change his mind about that, it was Emery Kendall, with that luscious mane of hair and her long, sleek legs and blue eyes that reminded him of a mountain lake on a clear, pure July afternoon.

As he watched, her long lashes fluttered and then opened. Disoriented confusion flickered in her gaze for an instant, followed quickly by alarm. He frowned. Why the hell would she be afraid of him, especially after he had risked frostbite to get her up here to the ranch house in safety?

He was only slightly appeased when she made an effort to steady her nerves. She sat up and wiped at her eyes.

"Sorry I woke you," he murmured. "I was just adding another log to the fire."

"No power yet, I guess," she whispered.

"Not yet. If lines are out around the valley, it might take the power company until morning to get out this way."

She nodded and extricated herself from the girls, who didn't even stir as Emery slid from the blankets, rearranged them and stood silhouetted by the fire's glow.

His unruly body stirred. She definitely had curves in all the right places, something he *didn't* want to notice right now. He also didn't want to see how pretty and warm and slightly mussed she looked just waking up.

To his dismay, she walked nearer, probably so they could talk without disturbing the girls. Unfortunately, her proximity only intensified his awareness of the quiet intimacy here in the darkened house and the seductive scent of her, of vanilla and cinnamon and luscious, sleepy woman.

"How are the horses?" she whispered.

It took all his control not to step away from temptation. "Okay, as far as I can tell. Annabelle, one of our foaling mares, seemed a little restless but I'm sure she was just edgy about the storm. I'm afraid we're going to lose the roof on one of the hay sheds. It's metal and some of the sheets don't seem as secure as I'd like, but it's not safe in the dark and the wind for me to climb up and check."

"I should say not!" she exclaimed, slightly louder than a whisper. Claire stirred a little, but then seemed to settle back down.

He eased away from the fireplace toward the other end of the great room where they could speak slightly above a whisper. The fire's warmth reached here, though she still picked up a blanket and wrapped it around herself before she joined him.

"Were the girls all right?" he asked.

"Tallie doesn't like the wind. She was a little nervous at first, but Claire and I managed to settle her down. We told some stories and then they both fell asleep."

"I guess it was good you were here so I didn't have to leave them alone longer than necessary."

"They were worried about you."

"Yeah. They're both a little paranoid something's going to happen to me."

She was silent for a long moment and he braced himself, sensing the direction of her thoughts even before she spoke.

"What happened to their parents?" she finally asked.

He sighed, hit again by the grief for the sister he had loved. "Plane crash. John was a pilot with a share in a little Cessna in Idaho Falls. They left the girls with friends—the Daltons, actually—for a weekend so they could fly up to Glacier National Park for their anniversary. They had engine trouble on the way back and the plane lost altitude. John tried to make an emergency landing in a rainstorm, but he didn't have a clear spot and they ended up crashing into the mountains up near Helena."

He hated thinking of his sister's last moments, the terror she must have experienced as the plane went down. He was quite certain her last thoughts would have centered on what would happen to her girls. He only hoped she had somehow known he would step up, no matter how hard it might turn out to be.

He was also fully aware of the irony. He had been the special forces soldier, performing dangerous mission after dangerous mission, but it had been soft, homebody Suzi who had died so tragically and unexpectedly.

"Oh, those poor girls," Emery murmured. "No wonder Tallie is so nervous about bad weather. Where were you when it happened?"

"My third tour in the war against terror. Afghanistan, this time."

"So you came home?"

He hadn't seen any other choice. The girls had no one else. He could have sent them into foster care, but that would be a miserable way to repay the sister who had sacrificed so much to take care of him.

"I was close to the end of my commitment so I was able to work it out with the army to take the rest of the leave coming to me and get out early."

He hadn't wanted to. He had expected to make the army his career as long as they would still have him. But sometimes life threw a curveball and you either had to hit back or get cold-cocked in the face.

"May I ask you a question?" she asked after a moment.

"Shoot."

"I know it's presumptuous of me and you don't have to answer if you don't want to. It's really none of my business. But why isn't the Christmas tree decorated? Christmas is only a week away."

He glanced at the bare tree as guilt pinched him. Here was yet another way he had failed the girls. The three of them had brought the artificial tree down from the attic the week before and put it together, fully intending to decorate the blasted thing, but that was as far as they'd gotten.

Every day he told himself he would put the lights on it, but something always came up. A problem with one of the horses, a meeting at school, this blasted endless wrangling with the attorneys executing John and Suzi's estate.

Here was just another way he was failing the girls, though they hadn't once pushed him to finish decorating the tree all week. On some level, he suspected they were struggling just as he was to find a little holiday spirit somewhere.

"It's on the list. None of us has been much in the mood for Christmas," he admitted now to Emery.

"I hear you there," she murmured.

He wondered again at her history, why she was choosing to spend the holidays hiding away here at Hope Springs. He didn't need to know, he reminded himself. She was a guest, nothing more, and he would do well to keep that in the front of his head.

"We'll get to it, though," he said. "I was thinking maybe tomorrow or Sunday."

"Good. That's very good. They're children. I'm sure

I don't need to tell you, but they need a Christmas tree. Stockings. Christmas cookies. All of it."

He had tried to make cookies, but the whole thing had ended in a disaster. Just like nearly everything else he tried.

"I have no idea how to throw Christmas for a couple of girls."

He hadn't meant to confess that and he was vaguely horrified that the words slipped out.

She gazed at him for a long moment and in the flickering light from the fire, her features looked fragile and as lovely as a painting.

"I could help you. At least with the decorating part."

He stared at her, stunned into speechlessness at the offer.

When his silence dragged on, she looked away and he saw annoyed frustration in her eyes. "Oh, right. I'm sorry, I forgot for a moment that you want me to stay away from the girls. I guess it slipped my mind while they were sleeping on the couch with me after you left them in my care."

His mouth tightened at her dry tone. Okay, he had been guilty of a bit of a double standard, grateful for her presence here with the girls during the storm when it was convenient for him, just hours after he told her he didn't want her spending more time with them.

He wanted to instinctively protest that he didn't want or need anyone's help, but that would have been a bald-faced lie. The second part, anyway. He might not want it, but he couldn't deny that he needed it, even to himself.

"What did you have in mind?" he asked warily.

"I could easily help the girls decorate the tree and

put a little Christmas spirit into the house, at least," she said. "It's…sort of my specialty."

"Decorating Christmas trees?"

"Decorating in general. I'm a textile designer. Curtains, pillows, furniture upholstery, that sort of thing."

He blinked at that. Here was yet another example of just how far apart his world was from Ms. Emery Kendall's. The closest he came to designer textiles was buying a bed-in-a-bag set at the Wal-Mart near the base between deployments.

He could just imagine her reaction to the mess the ranch was in right now. Joanie had been doing basic housekeeping for him here between her minimal guest ranch duties, but since she left, he knew he had let plenty of things slide around the house.

"We're pretty simple and straightforward around here. We just need a Christmas tree decorated, not some fancy froufrou interior design," he said slowly.

She smiled a little and he immediately wished she hadn't. She looked far too warm and approachable when she smiled and he needed to remember all those differences between them. "I can do simple. Trust me, Nate."

He wanted to. The impulse to trust her, to lean on someone else for something, just for a little while, shocked the hell out of him. What was the big deal? She was offering to help put up some Christmas ornaments, not move in and start redecorating the whole place.

He worried the girls would latch onto her and be hurt when she left. But he supposed if he talked to them and made sure they understood that her presence in their lives was temporary, they could make it through.

"Fine. Whatever. Even if they haven't been in a hurry

to put it up, Tallie and Claire will probably enjoy having a tree."

"You won't?"

He shrugged. "I don't do Christmas. Not really. It's been a long time since it meant something more than maybe a little extra chow in the mess hall to me."

"Do you miss it?" she asked quietly after a long moment. "The army, I mean."

He thought of the heat and the sand, the exhaustion and the constant, alert tension. He didn't think somebody who spent their time designing curtains would understand how he could miss it every single moment of every single day.

"This is my life now. The girls and the ranch."

She tilted her head to look at him and for a long moment, their gazes held. Something simmered between them, something bright, intense. Flames licked at the log in the fire, then consumed it in a shower of sparks.

He was powerfully drawn to her. If he moved just so, he could find out if that lush mouth was as sweet and delicious as it looked…

He leaned forward just a few inches, but the instant he realized what he was doing, he jerked back, furious at himself.

"You should sleep while you can."

Her blue eyes had darkened, he thought, until they were nearly the color of the Idaho midnight sky, but then she blinked and they seemed to go back to normal. "What about you?" she asked.

"I will. Eventually. I'd better go bring some more wood up to the house, just to be safe. If the power comes back on, I'll wake you so you can go back to your own cabin."

And out of my life, where you belong.

He didn't say the words, of course, though he wanted to. Still, he thought he saw something deep and bruised flare in her eyes as if she understood everything he had left unspoken.

"Good night, then."

She wrapped the quilt tighter around her shoulders and returned to the sofa by the fireplace.

He stood for a long moment in the doorway, watching her settle back in to sleep and fighting the impulse to go after her and apologize.

He finally slammed his hat onto his head and headed back into the storm. He had nothing to apologize for but his thoughts. He couldn't help it if he *did* think it would be better for all of them if she returned to her East Coast life and left him to deal with his two grieving nieces as he saw fit.

Still, she had been nice enough to offer her help with decorating the house. He couldn't turn her down, especially since he knew the girls would probably enjoy helping her.

He fought his way through the blowing snow to the woodpile and loaded his arms with as much as he could carry then trudged back to the house. He could come up with no genuine reason to refuse her help, unfortunately. But that didn't mean he had to pretend to be happy about it.

Emery awoke to the smell of coffee and burnt toast and the sound of giggling girls and machinery rumbling somewhere outside.

She blinked a few times, struggling to find her bearings. The soaring log walls came into focus and the gray stones of the fireplace and then she spied two little dark-haired girls peeking around the doorway at her.

Ah. Right. She was at the main ranch house because a storm had wreaked havoc through Cold Creek Canyon.

Through her sleep-numbed brain, she managed to put together a few salient points. The power must have come back on, unless Nate had the small appliances in the kitchen wired to the generator he had mentioned the night before. Or, she supposed, unless he had made his toast and coffee over an open flame.

That growl of machinery must be Nate digging them out with the tractor she had seen him using to plow the snow the day after she'd arrived.

She sat up and scrubbed her hands over her face as relief soaked through her that she wouldn't have to face him yet this morning. She had stayed awake far too long, reliving that moment when heat and hunger had flared in his eyes, when she had been quite certain he wanted to kiss her.

Sometime later, she had heard him come in. When he had walked into the room to check on the girls, she had fiercely feigned sleep, forcing her breathing to be slow and even, despite the pulse pounding loudly in her ears.

She drew in a breath now, remembering those long, drawn-out moments he had stood in the doorway before he turned and left the room. Either he had decided to stay up all night or he had found somewhere else moderately warm to sleep. He certainly hadn't used the other sofa. She would have known, since her own sleep had been light, unsettled.

"Oh, good! You're finally awake," Claire exclaimed now, hurrying into the room.

"What time is it?" Emery asked in a voice that only croaked a little.

"Almost seven," Tallie reported. "We've been up for *hours*."

"Hours? Wow. I guess I must have been tired."

"Uncle Nate said we should let you sleep so we were trying to be super quiet. But we made toast. Do you want some?"

Few things smelled as sharply awful as burnt toast, but she smiled anyway. "Toast sounds great. I guess the storm stopped."

Tallie nodded. "It snowed a *lot*. Uncle Nate said he could barely open the back door for the drifts."

She could imagine. From her vantage point, all she could see out the wide-pitched windows was a world of white.

"It's a good thing we rode over to Cold Creek yesterday to take Tanner's homework," Claire said solemnly. "Uncle Nate says the horses could never make it today. He said we'll probably have to stay inside most of the day and with all the snow, it's going to be ice-cold out there."

"I don't like to be inside," Tallie complained. "It's so boring."

Without their parents, she imagined the house must seem to echo with silence. Poor little things.

She stood up and reached behind to readjust her ponytail, which she could only guess looked pretty bedraggled right about now. "Well, I can promise, you won't be bored today. You'll only *wish* you could find a quiet moment. Girls, we've got work to do."

They gave her matching looks of suspicion out of

charmingly similar features. "What kind of work?" Claire asked.

Emery smiled at them both, marveling that the prospect of doing the very thing she had tried to avoid this year—wallowing in a little Christmas spirit—should lift her mood so effectively.

For a fleeting moment, she thought of her mother and how she had so enjoyed Christmas. Their house in Warrenton had always exploded with lights and ornaments and holiday cheer. She wouldn't have wanted Emery to firmly close the door on the holidays this year out of her grief and sorrow. Her mother would have been the first one to help these lonely little girls.

"You'll see," Emery said. "I think you're going to need a little more than toast for breakfast. What do you say to pancakes?"

"I say de-lish," Tallie said with that adorable grin of hers.

"Yum," Claire said. "I've been thinking I should learn how to make pancakes. Uncle Nate tries, but his are all squishy and gross."

She smiled. "Give me a few minutes to freshen up a bit and then we'll eat. And then, my dears, we go to work."

Chapter 5

Thirty minutes later, she was frying a package of lean bacon she'd found in the refrigerator and overseeing Claire at the griddle while Tallie colored at the kitchen island.

"Now see, when the batter starts to bubble on the top, that's when you know they're ready to be turned."

"That must be where Uncle Nate goes wrong," Claire said, her brow furrowed. "I wonder if he knows the batter is supposed to bubble."

"I'll be sure to mention it to him if I get the chance," Emery said, unable to completely hide her smile.

"Here he comes," Tallie proclaimed. "You can tell him now."

Sure enough, a moment later, she heard boots thudding on the back steps and a moment later, the mudroom door off the kitchen opened.

Her stupid, reckless heart caught in her chest as she remembered those intense few moments the night before, the flare of heat in his dark eyes when she had been quite certain he wanted to kiss her.

"Hey, Uncle Nate!" Tallie called. "Emery knows why your pancakes never taste very good."

She flushed as he walked into the kitchen, stomping snow off his boots.

"Does she?" he asked slowly.

"She says the pancakes have to bubble first before you flip them. I think these are just about ready," Claire said, then she tucked her bottom lip between her teeth and shoved the spatula under one of the pancakes with all the solemn intensity of someone trying to extract explosives from a landmine.

"Remember, flipping is all in the wrist," Emery said.

Claire nodded and turned the entire batch just right, except for one that landed half on another.

"I messed up," she said with a disappointed frown.

"Just one," Emery said with a warm smile. "That's no big deal. Nobody can turn every pancake perfectly. You did great. They're going to taste delicious."

"Did you see that, Uncle Nate?" Claire exclaimed.

"I sure did." He hung his coat on the hook by the door. "I hope you've got a couple to spare for me. Running that tractor works up a real appetite."

"You can have as many as you want," Claire promised him. A moment later, she flipped a tall stack onto a plate for him and handed it over to her uncle.

"Wow. Delicious. I only came in to fill up my coffee, but this all just smells as good as it looks."

"Would you like some bacon?" Emery asked. His dark gaze slid to hers and suddenly all the heat that had seethed between them in the quiet stillness of the night burned through her once more.

"Bacon would be good, if you've got some to spare."

Doing her best to ignore her ridiculous reaction to him, she put several strips on a plate for him and set it at his elbow as he pulled up a chair beside Tallie at the table.

For the next few moments, she listened to their interaction. He complimented Claire on the pancakes so effusively that the girl had a warm, rosy glow of pride. Between mouthfuls of pancakes and bacon, he also admired Tallie's drawings, making a special point of telling her specifics he liked about her picture, like the way the pine branches of the Christmas tree she drew looked all feathery and real.

He loved them. It was obvious in every word he said to them. How difficult this all must be for him. She had heard that note of longing in his voice when she asked him the night before if he missed the life he had given up for them.

Though they would probably always grieve for their parents, the girls were extraordinarily fortunate that Nate would give up his career, his life, to return to Pine Gulch and raise them.

She didn't want to feel this softening toward him, this flutter of tender feelings, so she forced her voice to be brisk. "How much snow did the storm leave?" she asked.

He cast a quick glance at her then turned his attention back to his plate. "Hard to say, exactly, because of the wind. I'm guessing maybe eighteen inches, but we've got drifts four feet high in places. It's going to take most of the day to clear them out. Hope you weren't in a hurry to head down the canyon. I doubt the county will be getting to Cold Creek Canyon Road until tonight at the earliest."

She was trapped here with them. Or at least at the ranch. Since the power was back on, she could return to her cabin and spend the day in isolation, trying to finish her sketches for the Spencer Hotels project.

"We're not going anywhere anyway," she answered. "Not for a while, at least. The girls and I have plans."

"Except you haven't told us what they are yet," Tallie complained.

"I'm sure you'll find out soon enough," Nate said with a sidelong smile to Emery that made her ridiculous heart kick up a notch.

"I hope it's something fun," Tallie said, trying to wheedle a little more information out of them.

"As soon as you're finished eating, why don't you to go change out of your pajamas into some clothes you can work in," Emery suggested.

"I'm done," Tallie jumped up and headed for the door.

"Me, too." Her sister quickly joined her and Emery could hear them racing each other up the stairway.

Too late, she realized her suggestion for them to change would leave her alone with Nate.

After a few more moments of eating in an uncomfortable silence, he pushed his plate away, finished off his coffee, then rose.

"I don't know how long I'll be out there. After I get us cleared out, I've got to see what I can do about fixing the hay shed. The wind took out a big section of the roof."

"Can you repair it by yourself?"

"I'll have to figure something out until I can get somebody out here to do the job right." He cleared his throat. "I hope it's okay if I leave the girls with you. I usually don't like to be gone from the house too long, but I don't have much choice. It's too cold for them out there."

"We've got plenty to keep us busy," she assured him. "Don't worry. We'll be fine."

He met her gaze again and she could swear she felt her heart knock against the walls of her chest. Ridiculous. She really had to reel in this insane reaction to him.

"Thanks. For breakfast and for...everything."

"You're welcome." She forced a smile, hoping it looked more genuine than it felt.

He studied her for a moment then slid away from the chair, reaching for his cowboy hat just as the girls hurried back.

"That was the quickest change on record," he said with a mock look of astonishment. "You two are like a couple of firefighters heading out on a call."

Claire rolled her eyes at him, but Tallie giggled.

"Are you going back in the cold?" the younger girl asked.

"Yeah. I've still got a lot of digging ahead of me. You girls do what Ms. Kendall says, okay?"

They gave him hugs as he bundled up.

"Be careful on the tractor," Tallie told him, her voice solemn. "Drew Wheeler's dad died in a tractor wreck."

"I'll be careful, I promise." He kissed her nose, wrapped his scarf around his neck and headed out into the cold again.

The kitchen was curiously empty without his presence. Both girls looked a little forlorn, but Emery summoned another smile.

"Let's clean up these dishes, then get to work."

"Your pancake recipe is very good," Claire said, her voice solemn. "Thank you for showing me how to make them. From now on, I won't forget about the air bubbles."

This serious child needed to laugh a little more often, Emery thought. The truly tragic thing was, she saw entirely too much of herself in Claire, a child so eager to please the remaining grown-ups in her life that she became an adult far too early.

Emery made a vow that she would do her best to see the girl enjoyed herself while they decorated the Christmas tree.

"Now will you tell us what we're going to do?" Tallie begged.

She hugged the girl's shoulders. "Get ready. The three of us are going to make some magic."

The storm kept Nate away from the ranch house most of the day.

After all the ranch access routes were plowed out and he had spent a couple hours doing a credible, if somewhat makeshift, job covering the exposed hay until the weather wasn't so cold and he could repair the roof properly, he headed down the canyon with the tractor to see if any of their neighbors needed digging out.

On the way, he passed Seth Dalton out on a tractor, as well, working on the driveway of Guillermo and Viviana Cruz, the Daltons' nearest neighbors. He lifted a hand in greeting to the man before he continued on his way.

He really wanted to despise all the Dalton boys, on principle if nothing else. He had certainly hated their father. Half of Pine Gulch did, though few of them had as personal a reason as Nate.

As far as Nate was concerned, Hank Dalton had been a genuine son of a bitch. He had lied and stolen and basically manipulated his way into owning half of Cold Creek Canyon. He had respected no boundaries.

Nate's hands tightened on the tractor controls. He hated Hank Dalton, even two decades after his death, but he couldn't quite bring himself to feed that hate by turning it against the man's sons.

They were difficult men to dislike.

Wade Dalton, who had taken over running the ranch after his father's death, seemed a fair man in his few dealings with him. Nate had seen him around town with his wife and a passel of children and it was obvious he doted on his family.

Jake, the middle brother, was the family physician in town. Nate had taken both girls to him in a panic a few months back when they'd both caught some bug and run fevers of a hundred and one. Doc Dalton had been patient and calm with the girls and had even taken time to allay Nate's brand-new-parent phobias about germs.

Seth, the youngest, had been Nate's own age and while they hadn't exactly been friends, they hadn't been enemies, either. Seth had seemed most like his father, at least where women were concerned. He used to run through them like irrigation water through a sprinkler pipe, even in high school.

Nate had been shocked to come back to Pine Gulch and find Seth married to, of all people, the very respectable elementary school principal, a woman he liked and admired. By all appearances and the rumors he'd heard, theirs was an extraordinarily happy marriage and Seth's wild reputation seemed firmly in the past.

He supposed he and the Daltons could never be best friends. The vein of bitterness against their father ran too deep inside him for that and he couldn't seem to get past it. But they were neighbors for the time being, until he figured out whether he was going to sell the ranch, so he did his best to be polite.

He frowned as he reached the next ranchette down from Rancho de la Luna as another little detail on his to-do list nipped at him. The girls were begging him to take them to a neighborhood party Caroline and Wade Dalton were throwing along with Carson and Jenna McRaven.

He had been putting them off and hadn't let the McRavens or the Daltons know whether he was going to show up. He was going to have to make a decision on that. But not right now, he thought as he lowered the snowplow. The party wasn't until Wednesday. That gave him three more days to make up his mind.

By late afternoon, he was cold and hungry and knew he had taken extreme advantage of Emery Kendall's presence at home with the girls. He had to get back and figure out what to fix them for supper, his least favorite part of instant parenthood.

He drove back to the ranch, hurried through the afternoon chores, then headed up to the house, bracing himself to face her wrath.

He entered by the front door, since it was closer to the barn, and walked into a winter freaking wonderland.

He stared around the house, delicious scents eddying

around him. Onions and garlic and tomatoes, along with the underlying sweetness of something tasty baking.

Garlands of pine boughs and red and gold ribbons draped the log staircase and just about every doorway in sight. A vast collection of wood-carved Santas he vaguely remembered from one of the few visits he made back to the ranch during the holidays took up an entire corner display cupboard and a trio of thin evergreens stood in what had been an empty corner, draped in twinkling white lights and more of those red and gold ribbons.

He walked into the great room. This morning the tree had stood barren and forlorn in the window, but now it was ablaze with lights and ornaments and more of those red and gold ribbons. It was topped by a huge gleaming tinsel star, one of the few Christmas traditions he remembered from his own childhood. What should have looked tawdry and outdated amid all the other decorations somehow looked wondrous and bright in the gathering dusk.

Had Suzi really tucked away all these ornaments somewhere or had Emery and the girls made some of them this afternoon?

He looked around, marveling at the difference a few little touches could make. This morning when he left to plow the snow, he thought it had been a nice, comfortable house. A little cluttered and dusty, maybe, since Joanie took off, but not a bad place. Certainly nicer than it had been when they were kids, for all the work Suzi and John had poured into it.

In the space of a few short hours, apparently Emery Kendall had gone to town and turned something average into something extraordinary.

She and the girls must have scoured every inch of the house and the attic to find all the decorations. A couple of quilts in Christmas colors had been hung on the walls alongside the one that traditionally hung there. The mantel was covered in a wild cluster of red, gold and white candles in a variety of thicknesses and heights.

The place looked warm and inviting. Happy, even.

He should have done this for them. This was a connection to their past and he couldn't let them lose it.

He drew in a breath, took one last look around at the wonder Emery and the girls had created, then turned to follow the delectable scents to the kitchen. They didn't hear him come in, probably because Christmas carols were blaring from the small under-cabinet stereo in the kitchen and Emery and the girls were all singing along.

The kitchen was a mess. Flour covered the surface of the island and at least three or four dozen sugar cookies cooled on racks on every inch of the countertops.

"Oh, look, here's a shape we haven't used yet," Emery said as she sorted through one of the bottom drawers he wondered if he had ever even looked inside. "It's a really cute angel. Look at those darling wings."

"Ooh, I want to cut out that one," Claire exclaimed, looking more animated than Nate had seen her since he came back.

"I'm going to put yellow wings on it and maybe a halo," Claire added.

"I don't want to use that one," Tallie said with that stubborn look she sometimes wore.

"Why not?" Emery asked, surprise in her eyes at Tallie's tone.

"Because it's fake. There are no such thing as angels."

The cynicism, so unusual in the typically bright and open Tallie shocked him. Nate frowned, lurking there on the other side of the door, just out of view.

"Why do you say that?" Emery sounded as surprised as he felt.

"My mom used to tell me we all had a guardian angel to watch over us," Tallie answered. "But I don't think that can be true at all. If it was, why didn't Mommy and Daddy's guardian angels hold up their airplane so they wouldn't crash?"

He drew in a sharp breath, quite certain Emery must be able to hear the sound of his heart shattering into pieces. Every once in a while, the girls' raw grief reached out and socked him in the gut. He wished with everything inside him that he could ease this pain for them, make their world right again.

Maybe if he was a better substitute parent to them, they wouldn't have to stay up late at night thinking about these sorts of things, like guardian angels who had apparently fallen down on the job.

"Oh, honey." Emery's voice was soft and sad. "Sometimes even the very best of guardian angels can't stop bad things from happening. That doesn't mean you don't have angels watching out for you. The other night when I was driving here in a storm, I was sure my mom was with me making sure I made it here safely."

"Maybe she wanted you to get here so you could help us put up the Christmas tree," Claire said.

Emery laughed, though Nate was quite sure it sounded a little trembly. "You're probably exactly right."

"So why didn't the angels help my mom and dad?"

Tallie asked plaintively. "Didn't they know me and Claire needed them?"

"I don't know the answer to that, sweetheart," Emery said after a long pause. "There are a lot of things I wish I knew the answer to. I can only tell you that I'm positive your parents would have wanted to stay with you more than anything. But I bet they're so happy you have an uncle who loves you deeply."

He must have moved or made some kind of sound, because Emery's head whipped around and their gazes met. So much for stealth, he thought as she gave him a charged look. He could tell she was wondering how much of the conversation he had overheard.

More than he wanted to, he thought, wishing again that he could make everything okay for the girls.

"Hi, Uncle Nate!" Apparently the moment of cynicism and disbelief had passed as Tallie greeted him with one of those rapid-fire mood shifts that always disconcerted him and left him wondering if it was more a function of her age or her sex, as chauvinistic as he knew that made him.

"Hi." He returned her hug, still somewhat stiff and awkward at these spontaneous displays of affection, though he wanted to think he was improving. "So where are you hiding all the elves?"

"What elves?" Tallie asked.

"The ones who have been going crazy decorating the tree and hanging garlands everywhere and even making cookies."

Tallie giggled and even bossy, serious Claire broke a grin.

"No elves, Uncle Nate," Tallie assured him. "It was

only us. Ms. Kendall and Claire and me. We did all the work. Every bit of it."

"Wow. I couldn't believe it when I walked in. I was sure I had come to the wrong place and walked into that Christmas store in Jackson Hole by mistake."

"You can have a cookie," Claire told him in that managing tone of hers that sometimes bugged the heck out of him, but just now seemed sweetly concerned for his well-being.

"Thanks. Don't mind if I do. Which one should I try?"

"A snowman," Tallie said. "I decorated that one with the red hat, see?"

He took a bite of the sugar cookie. It was soft and chewy and perfect. "Wow, that tastes terrific."

"I mixed the dough my very self," Tallie announced, looking pleased. "Claire only helped a little."

Her sister snorted. "Only because I was busy helping Miss Kendall make the rolls!"

Almost effortlessly, Emery stepped in to avert one of their potential bickerfests that could turn fierce in an instant. "I don't know what I would have done without help from each of you today. They knew where all the decorations were stored and helped me scour through every box."

"You all did a great job. The house looks…perfect."

Emery smiled at him and for an instant, the kitchen seemed to fade away and they were once more in the hush of the darkened house, talking quietly in the night while the girls slept. Just as the evening before, he wanted to kiss her with a ferocity that astonished him.

What the hell was the matter with him? She wasn't at all his type, he reminded himself. Beyond that, she was a guest at the ranch and beyond *that,* they were standing in a flour-covered kitchen with his two nieces looking on, for crying out loud.

"Would you like some soup?" Emery asked. "It's beef barley. I hope you don't mind, I helped myself to the ingredients in the pantry and found plenty of packaged meat in the deep freeze. I thought you might like something warm when you came in from outside."

"That would be great. It's been a long day."

"I'll get it for you, Uncle Nate," Claire said. He thought about telling her he was perfectly capable of dishing his own bowl of soup and she didn't have to wait on him, but she looked so eager to please he didn't have the heart.

"I'll get you one of the rolls," Tallie said. "They're really good, too. I had three of them."

"Thanks. I'll start with two."

For the next few moments, the girls fussed over him, pouring him water, fetching utensils, grabbing a napkin, while Emery looked on with amusement.

He had to admit, it was kind of nice, though not a particular pleasure he was very accustomed to. It had been a long time since he'd been mothered. Longer still since it had been his own mother filling the role.

Emery had done all this, given the girls something to focus on besides their loneliness. He was grateful for her, but that didn't help the nagging worry.

They already were crazy about her. He could tell by the way Claire sought her opinion about decorating a cookie and how Tallie looked to her for approval as she rolled out more of the dough.

Hell, he could be halfway there himself if he spent any more time sharing quiet confidences in the dark.

He would just have to make sure that didn't happen, he told himself. And though the soup tasted delicious, he had a tough time eating more than a few spoonfuls past the sudden apprehension tightening his throat.

Chapter 6

Her soup must be truly terrible, if a man who had been working out on the ranch all day in the cold could barely stomach it.

Maybe she needed to double-check the seasonings. A bit too much pepper, perhaps? She couldn't quite believe that, especially since she had tried it earlier with the girls. They had eaten every bite and she had found it delicious, savory and rich and warming.

Nate, though, was glowering at it like it was flavored with alum and vinegar.

She had spent all day trying to make the ranch house more comfortable for him and for the girls. A little thanks might be nice, instead of this scowling, surly stranger who would barely look at her.

Maybe it wasn't the house or the soup he didn't like. More likely, it was her. He had made that plain enough the past few days, though she had hoped things might be different between them after the night before.

She wouldn't allow herself to be hurt. He *was* a stranger, one whose opinion shouldn't matter to her.

With a forced smile to the girls, she reached to untie the holiday-themed apron she had borrowed from the hook inside the pantry, the one Tallie had softly told her had been Suzi Palmer's favorite.

"That's the last batch of cookies. I think you can decorate the rest of them on your own, girls. I really need to head back to my cabin."

"No!" Tallie exclaimed. "You don't have to go yet."

"You should sleep here again," Claire said, worry clouding her eyes. "What if the power goes out again?"

Emery smiled, even as her heart clutched that this girl felt she had to shoulder responsibility for everyone in her world.

"No worries," she answered, hugging Claire's thin shoulders. "If the power goes out, I'm quite sure your uncle won't mind at all if I come back to the house, will you?"

Something flared in his eyes at the challenging note to her voice, but he didn't rise to the taunt. "Of course not," he said, his voice cool. "The storm has passed and has headed across Wyoming by now, but you can stay here tonight if you're worried."

She shook her head. "I'll be fine. I will take a little soup home with me if you don't mind, to warm up in the microwave for lunch tomorrow."

It took a few more moments than she would have liked to dish some of the soup into a container she had spied earlier in the cupboard, when she had been looking for measuring cups for the cookie dough.

While she thrust her feet into her boots and put on her coat and scarf, Tallie and Claire continued to plead with her to stay one more night—and she continued to gently insist she needed to return.

Finally, Nate set the spoon back in the half-eaten soup bowl and scraped his chair back. "Girls, that's enough. Emery is staying at the ranch as our guest, not as your new favorite plaything. I'll walk you back," he said to her.

She gave him her best snotty debutante look, the one she and her girlfriends had perfected at their private girls' school for moments just like this, when they were faced with a stubborn, interfering male.

"That's completely unnecessary. I believe I know the way by now. Go ahead and finish your soup."

Nate didn't seem swayed by either the look or by her cool tone as he put his still-damp coat back on. "I need to make sure the power's working at the cabin anyway before I feel right about you staying there for the night. You girls finish up the cookies, then when I come back you can give me the grand tour of everything you did today, okay?"

"I'll keep an eye on things," Claire said, sounding about thirty years old instead of only eleven.

"Thanks," he answered, then thrust open the door for Emery. "You ready?"

Not wanting to argue with him in front of the girls, she only nodded stiffly and followed him outside.

She hadn't been outside since the middle of the night, that arduous trip through the blowing snow to the house. The wind had stopped, she was relieved to discover, but the cold still snatched away her breath. After only a few breaths, she was quite sure her lungs would freeze into icicles.

She was grateful to reach the cabin, even if it did look dark and cheerless compared to the festive ranch house they had left behind. He opened the door for her, flipped on the light inside, then, to her dismay, he followed her into the cabin.

"I'll just check the heat," he said.

"I can think I can flip the switch to turn it on all by myself. I'm not one of the girls. I've been taking care of myself for a long time."

He tilted his head as he studied her while the fan on the electric fireplace whirred to life, pouring blessedly warm air into the room.

"Why is that?"

"What?" she asked, confused.

"Why have you been taking care of yourself for so long? I'm sure this sounds chauvinistic, but I'm just wondering why there's no man in your life."

"How do you know there's not?" she snapped, not quite sure why she was so angry, but grimly aware she was more furious than she'd been in a long time.

He shrugged. "I might just be a dumb soldier from Idaho, but I can put a few minor details together and get the big picture. What kind of man lets his woman come out to the middle of nowhere to spend Christmas by herself? That tells me you've probably had a bad breakup in the not-so-distant past."

"You're not as smart as you think you are, Mr. Cavazos."

"I don't think I'm smart at all," he muttered. She thought she heard him add something else under his breath like "at least I haven't been since you showed up", but she didn't hear the words clearly and she wasn't about to ask him to repeat them.

"You're wrong about a recent bad breakup. My divorce was final eighteen months ago and the marriage was over six months before that. And there's been no one else."

She thought of that terrible Christmas two years earlier, when her perfect little world—everything rosy and bright she thought she had attained—came crashing down at her feet with only a few words and a careless moment behind the wheel.

Nate leaned his hip against the edge of the table, crossed his arms across his chest and studied her carefully with a baffled look in his eyes.

"What kind of damn fool walks away from a woman as beautiful as you, who can make beef barley soup that tastes like heaven?"

She stared at him, heat soaking through her at his words. She didn't want to think about the first part so she focused on the second. "I thought you hated the soup. You barely tasted it."

He raised an eyebrow. "Are you kidding? I wanted to stick my face in the bowl and just inhale the whole thing, but I figured that would probably be bad manners in front of the girls. After they're in bed, though, I might just have to dish up another bowl."

Nate Cavazos was a complicated man, she decided. Not as easily pegged as Jason or any of the other men she had known.

"That's beside the point. The question is, why the divorce?"

None of your damn business, she wanted to say. It was nothing less than the truth and was exactly what she should have said and what she intended to say when she opened her mouth. But somehow completely different words came out.

"Turns out, if a man cheats on you when you're college sweethearts, he's probably not going to change after you're married."

It had only been that one time, Jason had claimed. He had been drinking, she had been a sorority girl who came onto him. That had been the only time she had *known* about in college. She had stupidly taken him at his word when he said it was a one-time fling and meant nothing. If she had listened to her gut, she could have avoided so much pain later.

"He *must* be an idiot, then," Nate said now. "But at least you didn't have to drag any children through the mess of a divorce."

Her throat closed and she fought the instinct to cover her abdomen. Nate didn't need to know *everything.*

"Lucky, wasn't it?" she said, then cleared her throat, hoping he didn't hear the slightly ragged note in her voice. "Anyway, that's all in the past. I've *completely* moved on. Jason had nothing to do with my decision to come to Hope Springs for the holidays."

"Then why are you here?"

None of your damn business, she almost said again, but refrained. "Work. My mother died in September. She was…the only family I had left and I didn't want to face the holidays without her in the midst of all my friends and familiar surroundings. I needed a change."

"I guess you found that. Idaho blizzards are certainly out of the norm."

"True enough. I didn't expect quite the adventure I've discovered so far, but it hasn't been all bad."

"Well, thanks again for everything you did today. I should have decorated the tree weeks ago, not left it this late."

"The girls and I enjoyed ourselves."

"I could tell. A little too much, maybe." He made a rueful face. "I'm going to be taking down decorations until Valentine's Day."

"Take everything down now, if you hate it so much," she retorted sharply.

He looked baffled by her sudden attack, as well he should be, she thought. It had been unprovoked and unnecessary. *Just say good-night and push him out the door,* she thought.

"Did I say I hated any of it?"

"Not in so many words, maybe. But it's obvious you're not happy with how the girls and I spent our day."

He looked at her as if she were crazy. She *felt* a little crazy, and tired and out of sorts. She should have just kept her big mouth shut.

"Why do you think I don't like the decorations? I said thank-you, didn't I? I'm pretty sure I did."

Just go, she thought. "You did. I'm sorry. I'm just tired and cranky. It's been a long day following an... unsettled night."

There it was. The reason she was upset. She hadn't slept much, too stirred up by that moment when he had nearly kissed her—when she had desperately wanted him to, something she hadn't admitted until right this moment.

Suddenly the tension in the cabin ratcheted up a notch and when she finally looked up, she was afraid he could read her thoughts. He was staring at her mouth, his eyes intense, half-closed in a sexy sort of way.

"Well, good night," she finally said, about five blasted minutes too late, but even to her own ears, her voice sounded thready, smoky, even, and an instant later—before she could even think to take a breath— he stepped forward in one smooth, determined motion and captured her mouth.

She froze in shock. He smelled of the cold, like pine trees drooping with snow, but the heat of his mouth on hers made an arousing contrast. He tasted of coffee and her soup and the sweet aftertaste of the girls' sugar cookies.

And something else, something male and sexy and indefinably Nate.

She didn't intend to kiss him back. She slid her hands to his chest, fully intending to push him away. Instead, she suddenly found her fingers curled into the soft weave of his shirt beneath his unzipped coat. She could feel the enticing heat of him and she wanted to sink into it, into him.

With a soft little sound, she opened her mouth to his, all the curiosity and disappointment of the night before forgotten in a moment as that heat curled through her and wrapped around them both.

She didn't know how long they stood inside her cabin, their mouths tangled and the world outside her door forgotten. She only knew it had been entirely too long since she had felt this clutch of desire, this churn of her blood, the heat and wonder from a kiss that completely stole her breath and her reason in one fell swoop.

He was the one to break the connection. One moment

he was there, hard and muscled and male, then next he was taking a step away from her and cold rushed in to take the place of all that heat.

They gazed at each other for a long moment, the only sound in the cabin their ragged breathing and the whir of the electric fireplace.

Finally he shook his head just a little, as if he couldn't quite believe what had just happened.

"Don't say anything," she said, her voice low as her cheeks flamed with embarrassment and lingering desire. She had never responded to a man with such instantaneous heat. "That should never have happened."

"No?"

"No! We're… You don't even like me."

"I wouldn't say that, exactly," he drawled.

What *would* he say, exactly? She didn't want to know, she told herself. "It was a mistake. We're both tired and the day has been…eventful. Let's both just pretend it didn't happen and move on."

"Right." His tone was skeptical, but he reached for the doorknob.

Emery thought of her mother, always scrupulously polite and well-mannered, the perfect hostess and law firm partner's wife. She tried to adopt the tone Catherine had perfected. "Thank you for walking me back. Good night."

He still looked somewhat dazed and she was almost certain his gaze dipped to her mouth again, but he only turned the knob.

"You can pretend all you want, I suppose," he finally said. "Good luck with that. But I have to tell you, I'm a pretty basic kind of guy. I'm afraid my powers of imagination won't stretch quite that far. I don't think I'll be forgetting it anytime soon."

He left before she could offer any sort of reply to that and she closed the door after him, wondering how one man could be so full of complications.

She pressed two trembling fingers to her mouth, to the heat and taste of him that still lingered there.

Good heavens, the man could kiss. For a brash, abrupt soldier, he had seduced her lips with consummate skill.

She hadn't been this attracted to a man in…well, ever. Yes, it had been a while since she had been involved with a man. She hadn't dated since her divorce, too busy first grieving the loss of the cloud castles she had created for her life and then coping with her mother's cancer diagnosis and her fight against the disease that eventually claimed her.

Perhaps that was the reason she wanted to melt in Nate Cavazos's arms like an ice cube tossed onto a sizzling hot engine.

She let out a breath. She wanted to believe her past two years of abstinence were responsible for her reaction to him, but she couldn't quite make herself buy that explanation.

Nate was the most powerfully physical man she had ever known. Men in her world wore designer suits and comfortably talked about the difference between twill and chambray.

Nate was all soldier, rough and dangerous and irresistible.

Some instinctively feminine part of her responded to all that energy, all that heat, and she just wanted to soak it all in. She sighed. It didn't matter the explanation for the unwilling attraction. She simply had to ignore it. In a week, she would be back in her real life and this would all be just a memory.

Mistake or not, she knew their kiss would linger in her mind for a long, long time.

Chapter 7

He couldn't stop thinking about Emery Kendall and that kiss that had curled his toes.

Twenty-four hours later, Nate stood by the Christmas tree she had decorated in front of the big window, looking at the lights of her little cabin twinkle in the darkness.

Every once in a while, a shape moved past the curtain and he caught his breath, feeling like some kind of a damned voyeur.

That kiss. It had haunted his dreams through the cold night and then seemed to follow him around all day as he had hurried the girls off to school, spent the day at chores and doing a proper job on the hay shed roof, and then hurried into town after school for the parent-teacher conferences he would have blown off if not for a fortuitous call from the school secretary.

He couldn't forget the taste of Emery's mouth, lush and inviting and far more sensually responsive than he might have expected from her.

His insides still clutched with hunger when he remembered that moment when she had curled her hands into his shirt and pulled him closer.

He shook his head at his own ridiculous reaction. He was in serious danger of making a fool out of himself over her. Polished society-type women didn't have the time of day for rough soldiers with the sand of the Middle East still stuck under their fingernails and an entire footlocker overflowing with problems and responsibilities.

He gazed at the reflection of the Christmas tree she had decorated flickering in the window.

He wasn't sure how she had done it, but in a few hours the day before, she had changed the whole mood of the house, brightened it somehow.

She hadn't made any huge changes. No long-forgotten antiques had been dragged out of the attics or anything. But a few little touches lent a warmth and homeyness to the place and seemed to push back the darkness a little.

He hoped the girls sensed it. He wanted to think they had been a little happier, especially Claire. Maybe it was the impending holiday or thinking about Christmas vacation that started in a few days, but he thought she had lost some of that pinched, uptight look around her mouth. After school when he was meeting with her teacher, she had smiled a little more than he was used to and had even laughed a few times on the drive home.

That laugh had stuck in his memory, mostly because

he personally hadn't found much of anything amusing after his conversation with Jenny Dalton, the principal of the elementary school and Seth Dalton's wife.

There was another woman who apparently thought he was doing a lousy job taking care of the girls. Oh, she had been kind enough when she gently asked if he needed any help Christmas shopping for the girls.

What, did she think he was going to leave their stockings empty, for crying out loud?

And then she had just as gently asked him if he would mind if she and her daughter Morgan, one of Claire's friends, took her shopping for new clothes during the Christmas vacation.

He looked out at the ranch, his face burning all over again. Apparently, Claire had hit a growth spurt and he had been too busy trying to survive all the changes in his world that he hadn't even noticed. Her parka was a couple inches too short at the wrists and the jeans she told him she and her mother had bought only that summer for back-to-school now looked like floods on her.

While he wasn't paying attention, she was growing tall and slender, just like Suzi had been.

He should have noticed. Instead, someone else had been forced to point out the obvious. A Dalton, no less, even if Jenny was only a Dalton by marriage.

For one dicey moment, he had wanted to tell her to go to hell. But as he watched his oldest niece talking with Morgan and with Tallie, he had been forced to admit she was right. Claire looked like a raggedy urchin and Tallie wasn't much better.

He could afford entirely new wardrobes. Money wasn't the issue, since he had saved virtually all his combat pay the past dozen years and had built a healthy nest egg.

But what he knew about girls' clothing could just about fit inside that dust speck on the inside of the glass.

Under the best of circumstances, shopping wasn't his favorite activity. He had done most of the girls' Christmas shopping online and had found other gifts their parents had left them hidden in the back of the master bedroom closet.

Just the idea of an hour or two at the mall made him break out in a cold sweat.

He didn't miss the irony. He had spent more than a dozen years parachuting into hot spots around the world, packing around seventy pounds of gear as he faced down enemy combatants, constantly aware that he was only a mistake away from going home in a body bag.

But the idea of browsing the shelves of a department store for girly stuff made his palms itch and the hair on the back of his neck prickle.

He needed help. That was the hard, nasty truth, and was most of the reason he stood here gazing out at Emery's cabin and trying to gather his nerves.

Some things a man just wasn't qualified to handle on his own. If Joanie hadn't taken off, he would have dragged her into this. And if Jenny Dalton wasn't married to Seth, he probably would have taken her up on her offer.

But Joanie wasn't here and Jenny wasn't a viable option. He knew what he had to do. His gaze flicked again to the light coming from the window of the cabin, casting its tiny, warm glow against the December night.

He just needed to suck it up, he supposed, and get to it.

Emery Kendall was the most put-together woman he had ever met. From her tasteful earrings to her endless scarves to the tailored cut of her shirts, it was obvious she knew clothes and accessories. Even after she had spent the other night sleeping on his couch and then had chased two girls around the house decorating and making cookies and soup and otherwise spreading holiday cheer, she had looked composed and beautiful.

She would know just the things Claire needed, and Tallie, as well.

If he could think of anyone else to ask for help, he would do it, rather than have to face Emery again after that stunning kiss.

But he was drawing a complete blank here and didn't know what the hell else to do. Since the only other option was to wing it on his own and spend a day making a complete disaster of things in the girls section of Nordstrom's, he supposed swallowing his pride was a small price to pay.

With a strange mix of resignation and dread, he checked on Tallie and Claire to make sure they were soundly sleeping then shrugged into his coat and headed out into the night.

How was it possible for one woman to create such chaos in only a few hours?

Emery looked around the cabin and frowned at the mess. Scraps of fabric covered every surface, she had knocked over a box of ribbon spools and had been too busy to pick them up again, crumpled sketchbook pages had been discarded everywhere and the various shears she was forever losing peeked out from the oddest places.

When her creative muse was upon her, she completely lost track of time and space. She always intended to be so methodical, so careful. But then her mind would race with ideas and before she knew it, her workroom ended up in this complete shambles.

The process of decorating the ranch house with Tallie and Claire the day before seemed to have turned on the spigot of her creative juices. Now she couldn't manage to shut them off.

First thing that morning, as soon as she heard the squeal of brakes on the school bus and realized the canyon had been plowed, she had driven into Idaho Falls. The fabric store options were rather limited there, but between what she found and what she had already brought along of her own designs, she had made huge strides in her plans for the Spencer Hotels project.

She had more than enough for her meeting after Christmas with Eben Spencer and the designer working on his Montana property.

Once she was on a roll, she couldn't seem to stop. She had sewn up a dozen charming ornaments for the rather scraggly little tree she had purchased in town. She had made two tree skirts, one for her little tree and a much larger one for the ranch house, then she had stitched several stockings and now she was throwing together a couple of cloches for the girls.

And she had another idea, one she would have to talk to Nate about. If he agreed, she could give the girls something truly memorable for Christmas. It would take hours of work, just about every available moment she had between now and Christmas, but she was almost positive she could pull it off in the few remaining days.

If he agreed, anyway.

She shouldn't get involved any more than she already was. She knew it perfectly well, but somehow the girls had wormed their way into her heart and she couldn't help wanting to do whatever she could to ease their pain, even just a little.

Ideas and patterns danced across her mind as she went through the comforting, mechanical motions of working the sewing machine, something that had brought her peace since the first little Singer she'd begged for when she was Tallie's age, sewing her own Barbie clothes.

Finally, the ideas were flying at her so quickly she had to move away from the sewing machine and pick up her sketchbook. She had just begun to make a few rough lines on the paper when the doorbell suddenly rang.

Drat. And double drat.

She thought about ignoring it, about returning to this idea that suddenly seemed so ripe with possibilities. But that wasn't really an option, she supposed. Who else would be stopping at her cabin door but Nate or one of the girls? Since Tallie and Claire ought to be in bed this late on a school night, she could only guess it was Nate.

Her breathing seemed to quicken and she couldn't stop thinking about the taste of him and the hard strength of his arms around her, that kiss that had haunted her memory for the past twenty-four hours.

All the more reason not to open the door.

But he knew she was in here. Her rental vehicle was out front and all the lights were blazing. Somehow she knew the blasted man would only continue ringing the bell until she answered, so it was absurdly self-indulgent to leave him standing out there all night.

But, oh, she was tempted.

Sure enough, the doorbell rang again. She sighed and set her sketchbook facedown and covered it with a fabric swatch for good measure, then she drew in a breath and reached for the doorknob.

He blinked a little when she pulled open the door. She must look a sight, she suddenly realized, with her hair pulled up out of her way in a haphazard knot and the reading glasses she wore for close sewing work on a chain around her neck.

"I'm interrupting."

Yes. "No," she lied. "Come in."

Despite all the clamoring of her instincts, she held the door open for him. He walked inside and his eyes widened further.

"Wow. Looks like a dress shop imploded inside here."

She shrugged. "Something like that. Every once in a while I find my groove and I can't seem to stop."

"I saw your lights on late last night."

The idea of him looking out from the ranch house to her cabin gave her an odd, jittery feeling inside. Had he been thinking about their kiss, too?

I'm a pretty basic kind of guy. I'm afraid my powers of imagination won't stretch quite that far. I don't think I'll be forgetting it anytime soon.

"Ideas started coming after…after yesterday with the girls." *After you kissed me senseless,* she thought, but of course didn't say.

He raised a skeptical eyebrow at the fabric samples spread out everywhere. "Is that a good thing?"

Despite the nerves jumping through her like little frogs on a summer night, she managed to smile. "In this case, it was a very good thing. I have a big presentation right after the holidays for a hotel I'm helping decorate. My idea well has been a little dry lately so I was relieved to make some progress. And then when I was happy with the designs I came up with for that project, the ideas still kept coming."

She moved aside a swatch of folded chintz until she found what she was looking for. "That reminds me. These are for you and the girls."

She held out the three stockings she had made for them, but he didn't reach for them, only stood staring at her. "You made Christmas stockings for us? Why?"

Emery shrugged, feeling foolish. "Impulse. I thought maybe the girls might like new ones for a new start."

He took them, his features still astonished. Though she had chosen a bold green-and-gold striped damask for them, they still looked ridiculously delicate and frilly in his dark, masculine hands. She had embroidered their names on the top cuff in a straightforward serif font.

"You really made these? For us?"

As if she knew any other Tallulahs, Claires or Nates. She flushed and began picking up and carefully folding some of the swatches, simply to have something to occupy her hands. "If you don't like them or if the girls don't, you don't have to keep them."

"I'm stunned. I don't know what to say."

She snapped out a length of jacquard in her own design. "Don't say anything. It's a gift for the girls."

She paused, her hands smoothing the texture of the weave. "You might have noticed we didn't have any stockings hanging yesterday while we were putting up the Christmas decorations."

"I did. I just figured you hadn't found them in the boxes."

"We did, almost right away. But Claire became upset when she saw them—four matching stockings with their names and their parents' names on them. It seemed painful to her to hang those empty stockings, or worse, to just put up their two and leave the other two in the box, so I thought a completely new start might be good for them. But I promise, you won't hurt my feelings if you think they would rather use their old stockings for tradition's sake."

A muscle flexed in his jaw and he cleared his throat. "No. These are great. Really nice. How did you do the names?"

"I have an embroidery stitch on my machine. It's not that hard."

"Well, thank you. Really. Thanks."

"You're welcome. Here, let me put them in a bag for you in case it's still flurrying. You probably don't want them to get wet." She forced her voice to be brisk as she took the stockings from him again and dug through another pile of material until she found a plastic sack from the fabric store.

He lapsed into silence and all those tangled knots in her stomach returned. She held the bag out to him.

"Here you go," she said.

He reached for the bag and as their hands touched, a spark jumped from his fingers to hers. His dark gaze flashed to hers and those knots pulled tighter at the flare of hunger she saw in his eyes.

"Was there something you needed?" she asked, then was mortified at the throaty note in her voice, especially when she was almost certain his gaze shifted to her mouth for just a heartbeat before he jerked it back to meet hers and veiled his expression.

"Actually, yes," he finally said and she didn't miss the slight shadow of hesitation in his voice. "I came to ask a favor, but it seems presumptuous now, after you've gone to all this work already for the girls."

"That was really nothing. It only took me an hour, I promise, and I enjoyed it. Go ahead and ask your favor."

He sighed. "I wouldn't drag you into this if I had another choice. Let me just throw that out there up front."

"Okay," she said slowly, not sure whether to be offended or relieved.

"I had a talk with the principal of the elementary school today."

She waited, but he didn't seem inclined to add more. "Is one of the girls having trouble in school?" she guessed.

"Academically, no. They're both doing okay in that area. Better than I ever did, that's for sure. But the principal seems to agree with you that I'm neglecting them."

She glared at him. "When did I ever say you were neglecting them?"

"Not in so many words, maybe."

"Not in *any* words. Why would I say it when I certainly don't believe it? And neither should this principal! What is he talking about?"

"He's a she. And in this case, Jenny's right. Claire is desperately in need of some new school clothes. Everything she has is worn-out or too small. Tallie's wardrobe isn't much better, but she at least has her sister's hand-me-downs to fall back on."

"What did she suggest?"

"She offered to take Claire shopping, but I didn't feel right about it. I'm their guardian so it's my responsibility." He looked about as thrilled by this particular responsibility as an ant faced with moving a dump truck full of seed pods.

"I noticed a few nice shops in Idaho Falls when I was buying fabric this morning," she said, trying to put as much encouragement in her words as she could muster.

"So you'll do it?" he said quickly.

She blinked. "Do what? You want me to shop for the girls?"

"It would help me more than I can ever repay."

"You're their guardian," she pointed out. "You just said it's your responsibility. What's the difference between the principal taking Claire shopping and me doing it?"

He frowned. "Okay. None. But training bras and that sort of thing are a little outside my area of expertise. I thought maybe you could just pick up some things and I could give them to the girls for Christmas."

That would be the easy way out for all of them. Given the tension between them and the kiss she couldn't forget, she was no more eager to spend an afternoon in his company than he was to scour the stores for the girls.

"You're going to have to figure it out sometime."

He sighed. "I know. Just like I've had to figure out how to put hair in braids and make more than just ramen noodle soup for dinner and spray the monsters under Tallie's bed with Suzi's patented anti-monster spray. I just thought in a few years the girls will want to do their own shopping anyway, won't they?"

"What's the saying about taking a man fishing versus teaching him to fish? Unless you're planning to get married in the next month or two, someone's not always going to be around to bait the shopping hook for you, Nate."

He looked disgruntled. "You won't help me unless I endure the torture right alongside you, will you?"

She shook her head. "Sorry."

His eyes narrowed and she might have thought he was annoyed if not for that spark she could see there. She was absurdly conscious again of her loose updo and the glasses she had at least pulled off so they hung around her neck on their chain as if she were some sort of flustered librarian.

"Since you're not giving me a choice, I suppose we might as well get this over with. Are you free tomorrow while the girls are in school? They've only got two school days left before Christmas vacation."

She tried to picture a day spent with Nate Cavazos doing something so domestic as shopping for clothes and those knots inside her became a hopeless tangle.

"I'm sure I can drag myself away from my fabric for a few hours."

"Thanks, Em. About nine-thirty work for you?"

She was so flustered at his shortened use of her name that it took her a moment to reply. "Yes. Nine-thirty should be fine."

"Thanks. I'm saying that entirely too often to you lately, aren't I?"

Since it was a rhetorical question that didn't require an answer, she only smiled and opened the door for him.

After he left with the bag of stockings, the cabin seemed quiet and a little forlorn.

That was only the mess, she told herself as she bustled around trying to making a little order out of the chaos. It certainly had nothing to do with a dark-eyed soldier or the memory of his mouth devouring hers.

Chapter 8

He would rather be standing in the middle of a damn Al-Asra sandstorm than the girls' clothing aisle at Dillard's.

The woman was insane. Why the hell would two young girls need all this stuff? So far she had him carrying three shopping bags crammed to overflowing with sweaters, shirts, slacks, shoes, skirts, underwear and those dreaded training bras.

"How are they both on pajamas?" she asked.

"No idea," he was forced to admit.

"Why don't we start with three pairs each, on the assumption they've got some at home they can still wear?"

"Sounds fine." He had never been a pajama wearer, but had started since he had come back to Pine Gulch. While it had been fine to sleep in skivvies in the army, it didn't feel quite right with two young girls in the house.

"And if you don't mind a suggestion, my…parents always gave me a new nightgown on Christmas Eve so I had something new when my grandparents descended on Christmas morning."

He had heard that hesitation before when she spoke of her parents and he wondered about it. Had they left behind some kind of bitterness?

Maybe they had more in common than he thought, if that were the case. Heaven knows, he had enough bitterness toward his mother to fill a C-130.

She held up two nightgowns that looked basically the same to him except one was plain red and the other plaid. "Which one?" she asked.

As if he gave a…

"You pick," he tried for diplomacy. "You're better at this than I am."

"You're going to have to shop for them eventually, you know. I'm not going to be here next time they need pajamas."

The thought of life at the ranch after she left gave him a funny, hollow feeling in his gut he decided he was probably wiser not to examine too closely.

"Why don't you get one of each? The plain one in Claire's size and the plaid for Tallie?"

"Good choice," she answered with a smile. "I think that should just about do it, unless you can think of anything else for Christmas you need to buy while we're in town? Stocking stuffers? Christmas dinner?"

"I haven't given that much thought," he admitted.

It *would* be a relief to wrap up the whole shebang today and be done. Except for putting together any items that might need assembling. And wrapping. And shoving all this stuff under the tree on Christmas Eve. And fumbling through Christmas dinner.

"It's harder than I ever dreamed, taking care of all the details," he confessed.

Her eyes softened at what he was suddenly afraid sounded like desperation in his voice. She rested a hand on his forearm and squeezed gently and he was intensely aware of her. "You'll figure things out, Nate. Right now everything seems new and overwhelming, I would guess. Once you get into a routine, it will probably all seem easier."

He wanted to bask in that concern in her eyes, the warmth of her skin that penetrated even through his jacket and shirt.

Too quickly, she removed her hand and he wondered why her cheeks looked a little more pink than usual.

He thought of all her hard work on those stockings and realized he needed something good to fill them. "I haven't given stocking stuffers much thought."

"Hmm." She pursed her lips. "What about a nice journal or some jewelry, since they both have pierced ears?"

"That sounds good."

"Or some things for their rooms, maybe."

"Again, I'll defer to your wisdom."

They walked to the jewelry counter and she helped him select a couple earring assortments for each of them, as well as some delicate necklaces with angels on them. Emery was so excited when she saw them and he couldn't help remembering the conversation he had overheard while they were making cookies, and Tallie's cynicism.

They spent another half hour looking for smaller

items until she finally declared herself satisfied with their choices.

The checkout line was already long with similarly overburdened shoppers, but Emery didn't seem to mind.

"I had an idea, actually, for a gift I would like to make for the girls," she said as they took their place behind a woman carrying only two bags instead of the three he held. "I meant to talk to you about it last night when you stopped by, but I didn't have a chance."

"You don't have to make them anything. I think you've done enough already."

"I know I don't *have* to." She smiled again and he thought how bright and lovely she became when she smiled, not at all like the stiff, elegantly detached creature he had thought her when she first arrived at the ranch. "It's a nervy suggestion and you might not like it, but it's something I'd really like to do."

"I'm all ears now," he said drily.

"The other day when I was helping the girls decorate the little trees in each of their bedrooms, I couldn't help noticing their comforters were nice, but they were starting to wear out. Not much, just a little. Textiles are my business so of course that's the first thing I see."

"It's about the last thing I pay attention to," he confessed. "I'm afraid I haven't noticed anything wrong with their comforters."

"I was thinking I would like to make a couple of quilts for their beds. I sketched out the patterns for them and everything…and then I thought, wouldn't it be wonderful if I pieced them using familiar clothing of their parents? A favorite dress of their mother's, maybe some ties or T-shirts of their father's. You haven't thrown away all of Suzi's and John's clothing, have you?"

He shook his head. "I had Joanie box it all up, but everything is still in the master bedroom. I keep thinking I need to take it all to Goodwill. Maybe after the holidays."

"Would you mind if I looked through the boxes and took some of the things to cut up for them?"

"It's three days before Christmas. How could you possibly finish a project like this by then?"

"I wouldn't have time to hand stitch them," she acknowledged. "But I'm a fast machine quilter. I know I can do it."

That she would even suggest such a project astonished him. The woman barely knew the girls, but she wanted to spend endless frenzied hours on a gift he knew both Tallie and Claire would find beyond price.

"You're supposed to be on vacation!"

"Working vacation, remember?" She smiled. "Anyway, this is what I love to do, Nate. Since I accomplished so much yesterday on my most pressing project, I've got plenty of time. I want to do this, if you'll let me. Please?"

He studied her, the sincerity and the hope in her eyes. She made him want to borrow a little of that hope himself and believe for a little while that everything would be okay.

"How can I say no, especially when the clothes would only go to a secondhand store somewhere? I know the girls would treasure such a gift, if you're sure this is something you really want to do."

"Positive." She smiled radiantly, brighter than the sun reflecting off the brilliant snow outside, but then it was their turn at the checkout counter so she dropped the subject.

By the time they paid for their purchases and left the mall, his feet ached in his boots as if he had marched twenty kilometers across the desert, his bank account had seen a substantial dent and he was ravenous.

"I owe you at least lunch for all this," he said after they had loaded the packages into the cargo space of his SUV.

"To tell you the truth, I'm so excited to get started on the quilts, I can hardly wait to go back to the ranch. But I suppose we have to eat."

"How do you feel about Mexican?"

"Love it!" she said, and he wondered again what put that color in her cheeks.

He took her to one of his favorite authentic Mexican restaurants in town, still around from his high school days. Over hot, salty chips and fresh-made salsa heavy on the cilantro, they talked about mostly inconsequential things—the ranch and her shop in Virginia and her plans for the Montana project. After their server brought their food and set it down with the warning that the plates were hot, as if they couldn't figure that out from the nuclear-reactor-type hand mitts she used, he finally asked the question that had been burning through him for days.

"Why are you here, Em?"

Surprise flickered in her gaze and something else, something almost furtive. "I'm having what looks like a really great chicken quesadilla."

"You know I don't mean here at Lupe's. I mean here in Idaho. Who comes to the middle of nowhere to be alone for the holidays? I know there's more of a story here. You told me you were divorced, but what about family? Aunts, uncles, cousins? Why would you choose to be alone?"

She took a sip of her raspberry lemonade, avoiding his gaze. "I...don't really have any family. My parents were both only children. My mother died in September after being diagnosed with non-Hodgkins lymphoma two days before Christmas last year. My...father died a few years before that."

She was evading the question and he still wondered why. "No significant other in the picture?"

"I haven't really dated anyone since the divorce. My mother's cancer diagnosis a year ago sort of took center stage in my life."

Maybe that was the reason she wanted to be alone. Maybe she still hadn't gotten over her cheating ex. He didn't like to think about her marriage. And because it bugged him, he decided to probe further. Sort of like the time he'd been hit by a sniper in Kirkuk during an engagement and for weeks after had hung that dented Kevlar above his bunk so he could look at it every night before he crashed.

"Even if you wanted the divorce, I imagine it's still tough to close the book on a marriage you probably thought would last forever."

She gazed at him, shock widening the blue of her eyes, then released a soft sigh. "Yes. It has been difficult. But not for the reasons you might think. It wasn't the divorce itself so much as...everything else."

She was quiet for a long moment, then she let out a breath, fidgeting with her napkin.

"I told you my husband cheated," she spoke in a rush. "I didn't tell you he had his little affair with a coworker while I was pregnant with our first child."

What kind of bastard would even consider looking at another woman while his own extraordinarily lovely wife grew big with his child? Nate uttered a couple of pungent military words out of pure disgust at the man.

Her short laugh sounded surprised, but not offended, much to his relief since he hadn't realized he'd cursed aloud.

"Excellent analysis, considering you've never met him," she said.

"What can I say? I'm a keen judge of character."

She smiled in return, but it quickly faded. "I was not quite six months pregnant when Jason told me he was leaving me for her on Christmas Eve two years ago, on the way home from dinner with my mother," she said after a long moment. She spoke the words dispassionately, but he sensed far more emotion stored behind her words than she allowed to seep through.

"Merry Christmas."

"Right. We were on a snowy road and I was driving. In my shock and confusion and, well, fury, I guess, I became distracted and I wasn't paying proper attention to the road. We slid on a patch of ice and hit a tree."

He swore again, more gently this time, somehow sensing what came next.

"I broke my arm and a few ribs, that was all. Nothing really serious. Jason only had a concussion, I'm sorry to say."

He would have smiled at that, if not for the anguish in her eyes. "But…the airbag deployed and I went into premature labor. My daughter only survived a few hours and died just before midnight Christmas Eve. She was three and a half months early and just too fragile to survive such a trauma."

He stared at her, stunned at the sorrow she had endured. How could he have thought her cold when she first arrived at the ranch? It was all a smokescreen, just the fancy veneer she wrapped around all this pain.

A lump rose in his throat and he wanted to pull her into his arms and hold on tight. Since this didn't seem quite the place for that, amid the bustle of waiters and the cooks in the open kitchen talking loudly to each other in Spanish, he settled for picking up her hand and lifting it to his mouth.

It was an uncharacteristic gesture for him, but it somehow seemed just right. "I am truly sorry, Em."

She looked flustered, but didn't pull her hand away. "I guess you can see why Christmas isn't my favorite holiday. The past few haven't been the greatest. Three years ago, my...father died just a week before Christmas, my mother was diagnosed with cancer last year just a few days before Christmas. And between those particular events, I spent the Christmas two years ago in a medicated haze amid the ruins of my life."

She finally withdrew her hand and folded it with the other one in front of her. "This year I just wanted to escape it all. The memories and the heartache and the craziness."

"And then I put you in a position where you couldn't avoid it. First by decorating the house then Christmas shopping with me today." He remembered their conversation earlier and suddenly frowned. "And the quilts. The last thing you need to be doing is taking on such a huge Christmas project like making quilts for Tallie and Claire. It's a great idea, but maybe I can find someone in town to do it after the holidays."

"Not on your life!" she exclaimed. "I want to do this for them, Nate."

"Are you sure?"

"Positive. Working at my sewing machine is cathartic for me, I promise."

He was about to argue when he suddenly heard someone calling their names.

"Nate Cavazos! And Emery! Hello."

He turned and found Wade and Caroline Dalton approaching their table with bright smiles, carrying a couple of doggie bags. They must have been seated in the other dining room of the restaurant or he would have seen them when Nate and Emery came in.

He couldn't quite figure out their warmth toward him. He'd done nothing to encourage it, but since he'd been back in Pine Gulch, they had never treated him with anything but open friendliness.

He ought to be able to see beyond the surface resemblance, but every time he saw Wade Dalton, he saw Hank, big and handsome and commanding.

Caroline Dalton reached her hands out to squeeze Emery's. "How are you? It's so lovely to see you again!"

"Emery was kind enough to help me finish some last-minute shopping for the girls," he said. He wasn't sure he liked the speculative gleam in her eyes.

Wade gave him a commiserating sort of look. "Shopping, huh? Misery loves company, I guess. I was dragged along today, too, mostly to be the sherpa, I think. Though I can't imagine someone climbing Mt. Everest needed to carry more stuff than this."

Caroline rolled her eyes. "We have four children, Wade, and multiple nieces and nephews. The packages tend to pile up." She turned back to Nate. "I'm sure you're finding that, aren't you, even though you've only got two?"

"Right," Nate replied.

Emery said nothing and he suddenly realized with consternation that in the past few moments, all the bright animation on her features had drained away and her mouth was drawn into a tight line.

Why? He thought of her intention to retreat from the craziness of the holidays. Maybe she didn't like Caroline Dalton's reference to their close-knit family and the craziness of it, since she had none of that.

"Are you both coming?"

He jerked his attention back to the conversation. "Coming?"

"To the party tomorrow night at the McRavens."

Oh, right. The party he was supposed to RSVP to, the one he'd completely forgotten.

"I know the children are so excited about it. The girls love swimming at the McRavens. You'll be there, right? And Emery, you, too."

"I don't…"

"You might as well say yes," Wade said with a broad smile to Emery that somehow only seemed to deepen those shadows in her blue eyes. "She's just going to keep badgering you until you agree."

"I am not," Caroline protested. "I asked nicely. Of course, I'm not taking no for an answer. Tomorrow night, seven o'clock. We'll see you both there, and the girls, as well."

With one last bright smile and wave, Caroline towed her husband toward the door, leaving an awkward silence in their wake.

"Why don't you like the Daltons?" Nate finally asked when the silence had drawn on for several beats too long.

Her gaze flashed to his and he saw a furtive flicker there for just a moment before she became serene and composed once more. "Why would you think I don't like them?"

"I don't know. Just a vibe. You don't seem any more thrilled at the party invitation than I am. Am I wrong?"

She pursed her lips. "I like them well enough," she said slowly. "We've only met once and Caroline was nothing but kind to me."

"But you still don't want to go."

Again that mysterious *something* glimmered in the depths of lovely blue eyes that reminded him of someone.

Tell me, he wanted to say. He almost thought she was going to. She opened her mouth and drew in a little breath then closed it again.

"I wasn't expecting to socialize when I came to Pine Gulch," she answered, twirling her fork through the food she had barely touched. "I'm not part of your community. Why on earth would they even want me at their neighborhood Christmas party when I'm definitely not part of the neighborhood, especially when I'm only here until the end of the week?"

He knew damn well he shouldn't have this little clutch in his gut at the thought of her leaving, at how empty he knew Hope Springs would feel when she was gone. Before he could come up with an answer, she turned the tables back on him.

"What about you? What's your objection to the Daltons as neighbors?"

He didn't want to bring up the whole sordid past,

but he couldn't completely lie to her, either. Not when she had shared such painful pieces of her life with him.

"Our families have a somewhat...tangled history."

"Oh?" She set down her fork and gave him an oddly intent look.

"Long story," he answered. One he wasn't about to delve into right now with her. As far as he was concerned, it was all in the bitter past and he hated remembering it.

He glanced at his watch in a lame attempt to change the subject. "Do you want a box for that? You haven't eaten much, but we should probably wrap this up if we want to make it back to the ranch in time to hide the goods before the girls' bus shows up."

"I don't need a box. It was delicious, but I'm finished."

So much for their pleasant lunch, he thought as he helped her into her coat. Secrets and grief and the Daltons all in one convenient package.

It was enough to sour him on Lupe's for a long time.

Chapter 9

This had all been a terrible mistake.

Not just the day spent with Nate, though she had a sinking feeling she would have an even more difficult time extricating herself from his and the girls' world after today.

But coming to Idaho in the first place had been a foolish, rather pathetic attempt to forge a connection that didn't exist.

Coming here, meeting the Daltons, had seemed like such a good idea back in Virginia, wrapped in the familiar safety of home and still reeling from grief and shock after her mother's death. She had no one else, and this fragile connection had seemed the only thing she had to hang on to.

Mostly she had been curious about them. What kind of men were the Dalton brothers? Were they happy? Healthy? Did they treat their families kindly?

She never expected everything to become so tangled.

The truth was, just as she had told Nate, she was an outsider here and nothing would change that. And hadn't she spent enough time feeling like an outsider, even in her own family?

Her mother and father loved her. She had never doubted that. But they preferred to show that love from a distance, in between Junior League meetings and rounds of golf and social engagements.

Coming here changed nothing, except maybe to re-inforce how alone she was.

"Don't worry."

She blinked at Nate across the width of his SUV. "Sorry?"

"That frown of concentration. You look like you're scared to death I'm going to spin out and drive into a ditch. Relax. We're okay. The roads aren't slick. Besides, I've been driving in snow since I was fourteen."

"Except the years when you were driving in sand."

He smiled. "True enough."

She looked out the window and now that she wasn't lost in thought, she realized snow whirled around the vehicle and a few inches had piled onto the road while they had been shopping and having lunch.

"I'm not worried," she said, forcing a smile.

"Lie."

Not about the snow. "I'm sorry. I didn't realize you have a built-in polygraph unit in here."

"Don't need one. I can tell these things."

As she couldn't tell him the real reason for her frown, that she was regretting ever stepping foot in Pine Gulch, she decided to let him believe what he wanted. "All right. Distract me from the snow. Tell me what it was like to grow up in Idaho and why you're not thrilled to be back."

That last had been a shot in the dark, but the sudden tightness around his mouth confirmed her hunch.

He shrugged. "I couldn't wait to leave. I enlisted in the army the moment I was old enough for them to take me and I haven't looked back."

"Why?"

"Lots of reasons," he said, then added somewhat reluctantly, "most of them ugly."

She said nothing, waiting for him to tell her if he wanted. If he didn't, she respected his privacy enough not to pry. Heaven knows, she had enough secrets of her own.

For a long moment, the only sound in the vehicle was the swish of the wipers beating back the flakes and the tires whirring on the road.

Finally he sighed. "My dad died when I was ten. He had an aneurysm and drove his pickup off a steep embankment."

He said the words without emotion, but she heard the quiet sorrow behind them anyway and her heart squeezed. "Oh, Nate. I'm sorry."

He shot her a quick glance, but quickly turned his attention back to the road in order to slow down as they approached the turn into Cold Creek Canyon.

"Ten is a tough age for a kid to lose his dad, especially when, well, my mother wasn't exactly stable."

Again, she remained silent, allowing him to decide how much he would tell her.

"My mother didn't do well on her own."

"Some women don't."

"Right. She was definitely one of those women.

She...had her first affair about two months after my dad died. With a married man. A neighbor. I'm sure he offered her sympathy and a willing ear. Maybe advice around the ranch. Whatever. But because she was romantically involved with him, the bastard was able to cheat her out of some valuable pasture land along the river and a healthy portion of my dad's estate before he dumped her. I'm sure he would have taken the whole thing if he could have figured out a way."

"What did your mother do?"

His laugh was short and humorless. "She didn't take their break up well. That's an understatement. She was already depressed and I think she had been teetering on the brink of instability even before my father died. But when that bastard Da... When he dumped her, it sort of threw her over the edge. She started drinking heavily, sleeping with half the men in town. And not discreetly, either."

"Oh, Nate."

"I didn't mind so much for me, but it was tough on my sister to watch. The more my mother would drink, the more she slept around and the more she hated herself. The more she hated herself, the more she drank and slept around. It was an endless cycle."

"What happened to her?" she asked, though she was suddenly loath to hear the answer.

"When I was fourteen, she ran off with a trucker who came through town. Suzi was twenty-one. My sister dropped out of college in Pocatello and came back to run the ranch and get me through high school. Linda died a few years later. She was shot in a convenience store hold-up in Texas, which might seem like one of those genuinely unfair tragedies, except it was her current twenty-three-year-old boyfriend holding up the store."

She couldn't imagine how difficult that all must have been for him, a young man trapped in his mother's downward spiral, forced to watch her throw away her life with promiscuity and alcohol abuse.

"I guess you see why I feel so obligated to the girls," Nate went on as he drove under the Hope Springs arch. "My sister gave up her whole life to come back to Pine Gulch and raise me, rather than let me go into foster care. Suzi wanted to be a teacher, but she left school short only a couple semesters."

"I'm sure she had a good life here even without her degree. She and her husband were building something beautiful at Hope Springs. The guest ranch, the girls. Everything. I didn't know her, but I can only believe she was happy with her life by the love and care she poured into the house and her daughters."

A muscle worked in his jaw. "Well, even though I might hate Pine Gulch and want nothing more than to be back with my platoon, I feel like I have no choice but to do the same for Suzi's daughters that she did for me."

She thought of the men she knew back in Virginia, career-oriented, focused, driven. How many of them would be willing to give up what they loved most and enter a completely foreign situation in order to pay a debt of honor?

Few, if any. She was quite certain of it.

"They're blessed to have you," she murmured.

He shifted in the seat. "Don't know about that. But right now, none of us has much of a choice."

They drove in silence the remaining few moments

until they reached the ranch house and sprawl of outbuildings.

She was in grave danger, she thought as he pulled up
to her guest cabin. Her emotions were in turmoil. If she
wasn't careful, she just might go careening headlong
into love with this hard, dangerous, complicated man.

And wouldn't that just be a mess? She didn't need
more emotional torment in her world right now and
falling for Nate Cavazos would only result in heartache for her.

"Where are you going to put everything to hide it
from the girls?"

He shrugged. "They're sneaky and they know every
inch of the house. I wouldn't be surprised if they've already searched every closet and cubby."

"Where have you hidden everything else?"

"Under the bed in the cabin farthest from the house.
It's the one we rent out least often and nobody goes
there."

"Very sneaky."

Despite the tension still evident in his tight shoulders
after their discussion of his childhood, he managed a
lopsided smile.

"I'm an army Ranger. We're good at sneaky."

She returned his smile, even as she felt that precari-
ous shift and slide of her heart.

"I'll help you hide everything," she said. "You don't
have much time before the bus arrives, do you?"

He glanced at his watch. "I should be safe for a half
hour or so. But really, you've done more than enough."

"Listen, I didn't spend three hours at the mall for you
to mix everything up and forget who gets what. This
shouldn't take very long. I'll sort things into separate

piles. That way when you're ready to wrap, you won't have such a hard time figuring things out."

He didn't argue, only shrugged and climbed out of the SUV to unlock the cabin closest to the river.

She carried as many bags as she could inside and found this cabin very similar to hers. Hers was a little bigger, but they had the same layout, with one main living area and a separate bedroom and bathroom.

The main difference was in the color and tone of the decor. Her cabin was decorated in mountain chic, with deep reds and blues, while this had a slightly more feminine feeling, with tans and sage and a few lavender accents thrown in.

His sister had a natural flair for decorating, she thought. Both places were warm and restful. She thought again what a shame it would be if Nate decided to close the guest ranch after his sister and her husband had worked so lovingly to create these cozy havens for their guests.

He turned on the electric fireplace and by her second trip inside with more bags, the cabin had warmed considerably.

"I think that's everything," she said when he started to head out to the vehicle again.

He nodded and closed the door to keep out the icy air.

Even though they had just driven thirty miles together in the relatively small space of his SUV, somehow being alone together in the cabin had a different sort of intimacy. She pushed away that insistent awareness. Yes, he was dark and gorgeous and masculine. But he was also off-limits, she reminded herself.

Emery swallowed hard as she carried the last bags

into the small bedroom and began sorting their purchases into two piles.

He joined her and the room seemed to shrink until the only things she could focus on were Nate and the big queen bed with the antique brass bedstead.

"When do you intend to wrap everything?" she asked, hoping he didn't notice the way her fingers trembled a little as she sorted.

"I want to get everything out of the way. I was thinking maybe tonight after the girls are asleep."

"Do you need help?"

The moment the words were out, she wanted to drag them back, especially when he raised an eyebrow in surprise.

"An unusual offer for someone trying to avoid Christmas this year."

She couldn't rescind the offer now, as much as she might want to. "I just don't want you to make a mess of all my hard work picking the perfect gifts by shoving them into any old bag. Presentation is half of what makes a good gift."

He snorted. "Maybe for your country-club set. But the girls are eleven and eight. Hate to break it to you, but they're going to rip off whatever wrapping paper you put around them in about two-point-six seconds."

She laughed ruefully. "Well, for those two-point-six seconds, presentation is important."

He was silent for a long moment. When she looked up from the sweaters she was sorting, she found him studying her with an odd, intent look in his eyes. "You really need to do that more often, Em."

"Do what?"

"Laugh. It makes you breathtaking."

Before she could catch a single thought through her shock at his words, he brushed his thumb at the corner of her still-uplifted mouth. Her smile slid away and she froze at his touch and the glittery shower of sparks cascading through her.

Her gaze held with his for a long moment and she saw something dark and sultry kindle in his eyes. He leaned forward slightly, his lids half-lowered, but he didn't move those final few inches to press his mouth to hers.

He was leaving the decision to her, she thought, and somehow the discovery made it that much easier to arch across that small space between them and slide into his kiss.

The room was chilly, but his mouth was warm, focused. She wrapped her arms around his neck, vaguely aware she was still holding one of the little angel necklaces she had picked out for the girls.

Their kiss a few nights earlier had been raw and intense, shocking mostly because it had been so unexpected. But they had been building toward this one all day as they had shopped and walked and talked, sharing a meal and confidences and their private pain. It seemed inevitable, somehow, this coming together, like the first fledgling crocuses poking through the snow after a long, hard winter.

Everywhere she touched was solid, hard muscle and she wanted to sink into him.

"You taste like raspberry lemonade," he murmured against her mouth. "Sweet and tart and delicious."

His low words rasped across her skin and she decided she would drink no other beverage for the rest of her life. He deepened the kiss and she tightened her arms around his neck, lost in the wild torrent of sensation.

As they kissed and tasted for long, drugging moments, somehow they shrugged out of their coats, though she had no real awareness of it. A moment later, she could feel his hand at her waist and then the sizzling warmth of his fingers on her bare skin under her sweater.

She wanted him more than she had ever wanted anything in her life, this man with the bedroom eyes and the hard strength.

Their purchases covered just about every inch of the bed, but she didn't care. She wanted to sweep all her carefully sorted piles onto the floor and drag him down. But just as she started to reach behind her with some vague intent of making space for them, the sudden whine of airbrakes in the distance cut through the cold afternoon air.

At the sound, he dragged his mouth away and stared at her, his pupils expanded so that his entire irises looked black and dangerous.

Reality crashed down, harsh and unforgiving. She had completely lost control. Another few moments and she would have lost every ounce of good sense.

What on earth was she thinking? This wasn't her. She didn't have torrid affairs with men she had barely met and would probably never see again a week from now.

She drew in a sharp breath and eased away from him, fumbling to straighten her clothes that had become so disordered in their embrace.

"That must be the school bus." Her voice sounded thready and aroused and she quickly cleared her throat.

"I can finish up here and hide everything back under the bed. You had better go meet the girls or they'll be suspicious."

He raked a hand through his hair, looking just as stunned and disoriented as she felt. "Emery…"

"Go. They'll be looking for you."

After a long moment, he picked his coat off the floor and yanked it on, shoved on his Stetson she must have tipped off somehow, then walked out into the cold, leaving a yawning sort of silence behind him.

With mechanical movements, not daring to take a moment to even think about what had nearly happened between them, Emery quickly finished sorting the gifts and shoved them all under the bed with the others, then turned off the heat and closed the door behind her, making sure it locked securely.

When she finally reached her own cabin, she shut the door and sagged on to the sofa as everything inside her still seemed to tremble and sigh. She could still taste him, still feel that leashed strength under her fingertips.

This heat between them was crazy. Incendiary and fierce and completely out of control. She wasn't used to losing control like that. She liked things to be tidy, orderly. Or at least she always thought she did.

She thought of the chaos of her workspace when she was in the middle of a project. That was the only area of her life where she allowed disarray, since she had learned along the way that she did her most creative work when she just let herself be free and unencumbered by the expectations she always felt pressing down on her.

Maybe that was part of Nate's appeal. He didn't seem to expect her to be perfect.

She pressed a trembling hand to her chest, where her heart still raced. She had to put a stop to this. If she didn't, she was suddenly afraid she would end up leaving Pine Gulch more messed up than when she had arrived.

The girls tag-teamed him about the neighborhood party the minute they bounded up the driveway from the bus stop.

Tallie hit him up first. "Uncle Nate, have you decided if we're going to the party at the McRavens'? It's tomorrow! We have to decide, 'cause we're supposed to MVP or something."

"RSVP," Claire corrected with a "you big dork" tone to her voice. "It's when you tell someone whether you're going to their party so they know if they have enough food for everyone and nobody goes hungry. So are we going?"

"Can we, Uncle Nate? Can we? Huh?" Tallie dropped her backpack in the foyer and threw her arms around him for emphasis. "It will be super fun. Tanner says they're having Christmas carols and games and Santa Claus might even come. We *have* to go. Please say yes."

"We don't *have* to go," he muttered.

"But we *want* to. We really, really want to!" Claire exclaimed, with far more enthusiasm than she usually showed toward anything.

He gave an inward groan, not at all in the mood to tangle with them over this, especially after he was still reeling from the sheer stunning impact of Emery's kiss.

"I still haven't decided," he said firmly. "We can talk about it again after dinner. Meantime, why don't you show me what homework you brought home, then we can all get on to our chores."

Something about his firm tone must have gotten through to them. Or to Claire, anyway. When Tallie would have continued nagging and fretting at him like a puppy working a treat out of a rubber chew toy, Claire elbowed her in the ribs and muttered something in her ear he couldn't hear. Tallie gave a long-suffering sigh, but to his vast relief, she let the discussion drop—for a while, anyway.

She quickly picked it up again after they all came in from finishing their chores in the barn—and after he had made a quick, clandestine stop at Emery's cabin while the girls were busy to drop off the clothing she had asked for.

While he was warming up dinner, one of the pre-pared freezer meals he purchased from a company in Idaho Falls, Tallie started in.

"We should really let the McRavens know if we're coming to the party," she tried again from the kitchen table where she was supposed to be working on her homework. "Otherwise they might be mad."

"I'm sure they won't be mad."

"But what if they run out of food? Drew says Mrs. McRaven is the best cook. I don't want to miss the food."

"She is a great cook." Claire set aside her history worksheet. "Everybody always buys her cookies and cupcakes first when we have bake sales at school."

"And we can take our swimming suits and every-thing," Tallie reminded him for about the hundredth time. "On the bus this morning, Kip said they have a brand-new slide that curls around and goes into the deep end. It's gonna be so *awesome*. Don't you think we should call and tell them if we're coming?"

After about fifteen minutes of their pestering, Nate ground his back teeth, suddenly sick of anything to do with the word *party*.

What the hell had happened to his life? Five months ago he had been leading patrols, taking on bad guys, serving his country. Now he spent his days worrying whether the girls were drinking enough milk, whether they finished their math homework, if he had remembered to add the damn fabric softener to the load of whites in the washing machine.

Kissing his guests until he couldn't think straight.

"Look, I said I would think about it," he snapped in a harsh tone he didn't think he'd ever used with them before. "Let it go, both of you, or I'll say no just to shut you both up. Why do you have to hound me and hound me about everything?"

Tallie blinked in surprise and a little bit of fear, he was chagrined to see. She set down her fork beside her half-eaten casserole.

Her chin wobbled a little, but she didn't cry, which made him feel even worse. "I'm not hungry anymore," she said after five more minutes of tense silence.

"Me, neither," Claire looked down at the tablecloth and not anywhere close to his direction. "May we be excused?"

"Yeah," he said shortly. It was their night to wash dishes, but he decided not to push the matter, even though every child behavior specialist would probably tell him he should do exactly that. He'd already been told by Principal Dalton and others that he should do what he could to keep a regular, consistent schedule so the girls could begin to restore a little order and stability in their world.

They scraped their chairs away and he felt about three inches tall when they hurried from the kitchen without another word.

He sat there alone and doggedly finished his casserole even though he wasn't at all hungry, either, then stood and scraped their dishes, wishing Emery were there to talk him through this. She would know how to smooth this over, what he could say to make things right again.

The fact that he found himself wanting to turn to her made him nervous all over again about the impact she was having in their lives.

He sighed as he loaded the last dish in the dishwasher, added detergent and closed the door.

He really needed a housekeeper. With Joanie gone, the house was falling apart and he just didn't have the time to take care of everything and run the ranch, as well. That was right at the top of his list after the holidays.

But first he was going to have to go to the damn party, to smile and make conversation and basically put on a huge show that he was happy to be there.

It was just a party. He wasn't facing interrogation by an enemy combatant. He could be polite for a few hours. Other neighbors would be there besides the Daltons so he wouldn't have to sit and socialize with just them. For that matter, he could probably avoid the lot of them for most of the night.

Through the doorway, he caught sight of the Christmas tree Emery and the girls had decorated. None of them had turned on the lights at dusk so he hurried in and flipped the switch. After a moment of watching the colors reflected in the glass, he felt a little better. He remembered that happiness he had seen in Emery's eyes earlier when she had been talking about making the quilts. This was the season of joy, of hope, and he was acting like the world's biggest Scrooge.

He sighed and headed up the stairs, wondering if the crow he had to eat would taste any better than the casserole he had forced himself to swallow.

He found both girls on Claire's bed listening to her CD player with a headphone splitter.

They both gave him disgruntled looks when he opened the door and guilt poked at him. He sat on the edge of the bed, wondering if this would ever feel more natural.

"Look, guys, I warned you I would be lousy at the whole parenting thing. I don't know what the he—heck I'm doing. I've been straight with you about that. But that's no excuse for me to be mean. I'm sorry about earlier. I don't really want to go to the neighborhood party and I've been trying to come up with some excuse not to go."

They both opened their mouths and he could see arguments brewing in their eyes, but he shook his head to cut them off. "But since this is something you both want to do and since we're a family now and need to work together and compromise when we have to, I'll play nice and somehow make it through."

They both squealed and Tallie threw herself into his arms. "Thank you, thank you, thank you. It's gonna be so fun. You'll see."

Right. He couldn't wait. But at least the girls were talking to him again, so he supposed he could survive.

"Okay, a few more minutes and then it's time for bed. I might not have figured much out about being a parent, but I do know you both need sleep on a school night."

They groaned, but didn't argue with him, much to his relief, since he had an entire cabin full of Christmas presents to wrap.

Chapter 10

A smart woman ought to be wise enough to stay away from things she knew perfectly well weren't good for her. Things like strawberry cheesecake brownies and sappy movies when she was in a sentimental mood and half-off sales at her favorite designer shoe store.

And gorgeous army Rangers with big, dark eyes and wide shoulders and those impossibly long eyelashes.

Emery sighed, her gaze fixed on the glow coming from the windows of the last cabin in the row. The light had been on for the past half hour and she had stood here that entire time, gazing out the window and trying not to picture the scene.

He had to be wrapping presents for his nieces, ungainly thumbs and all. The idea of him sitting inside there surrounded by ribbons and tape and girly stuff gave her a funny little ache in her chest.

For the past eighteen hundred seconds, she had been debating the wisdom of walking the distance between them. Yes, she had offered to help him. But then he had kissed her instead of answering.

Didn't that rather negate her offer?

Spending time with Nate in a small, enclosed space would be about as smart as walking barefoot across the thin, crackly ice of Cold Creek, especially after the heat they had shared in that very same cabin just a few hours before.

But she *had* offered. And he *did* need help. She still firmly believed that all those lovely things they bought for the girls would lose some of their magic without proper wrapping and Nate himself had admitted he tended to be all thumbs.

Who was she kidding? Emery released a heavy sigh. He was right, the girls would rip the wrappings off in two seconds. The real truth was, she couldn't seem to stay away from him. Despite all her well-reasoned arguments all afternoon and evening to herself against putting herself in closer proximity to him, she wanted urgently to walk through the snow to that cabin to spend just a few more moments in his company.

All the more reason she should stay exactly where she was. She didn't come to Pine Gulch with any intention of finding herself entangled with anyone here. Not Nate or the girls, or even the Daltons.

Yet here she was, entangled whether she wanted to be or not.

She already cared for Claire and Tallie and she was wildly attracted to Nate.

What was the big deal if she was attracted to him? He obviously wasn't any more eager than she was to explore this heat between them. He had barely even looked at her a few hours earlier when he dropped off three boxes of clothing he had smuggled out of the house while the girls were busy with chores.

He had been taciturn to the point of rudeness when he told her she shouldn't feel obligated to follow through on her suggestion about the quilts, that he was only dropping off the clothing because she had asked for it. If she didn't want to go to all that trouble, she didn't have to, he assured her.

She had assured him right back that she still wanted to, but he barely even waited around long enough for her response, only said he had to go before the girls spotted him there and became too curious about the boxes.

Emery shifted her gaze from the window to the quilt pieces scattered around every corner of the room.

Heaven knows, she had plenty to do. Even though she had already sketched out both quilts and had started cutting out the pieces, she would be sewing day and night to finish two full-size quilts in three days.

But she could spare a few moments to help him.

She reached for her jacket. She was strong enough to handle any attraction between them. And if *she* wasn't, he would be.

She would just have to trust him. And if a girl couldn't trust an army Ranger who had just spent the day torturing himself by Christmas shopping for his two orphaned nieces, really, who could she trust?

He was making this much harder than it had to be.

Nate looked up from his position at the dining table through the doorway into the bedroom at the massive load of gifts still piled on the bed and the much smaller pile of wrapped presents next to him. The contrast between the two and the reality of how much work he still had to do made him want to bang his head against the chinked wall.

He had switched the little stereo in the cabin to a station playing Christmas carols in the hopes that it might help him get more in the mood for the task.

It wasn't working. He just wanted to bag the whole thing and toss the gifts under the tree as-is on Christmas morning.

Neither of the girls believed in Santa Claus anyway. They had told him so quite solemnly at Thanksgiving when they were watching the Macy's parade on TV instead of the football games he would have preferred.

He didn't need to go to all this fuss and bother. What would be the big deal if he just gave them unwrapped gifts in their stockings?

They would still be getting just as much stuff, after all. And it would sure be easier if he didn't have to try to figure out the proper way to wrap a stupid little tube of lip gloss, for hell's sake.

He picked up a little scrap of discarded silvery paper and rolled it around the tube of candy-flavored lipgloss then ripped a piece of tape off the dispenser and plastered down both ends.

It looked like crap, just like the rest of the presents he had wrapped. But the girls had very few bright spots in their lives right now and Christmas was going to suck enough for them. Maybe the extra time they had to spend unwrapping gifts would help distract them from the gaping void where their parents should be.

He hated thinking about Christmas Eve and Christmas morning, and dreaded how tough it was probably going to be on the girls not to have Suzi and John there watching them open their presents for the first time in their lives.

The first Christmas without their parents needed to be as close to perfect as he could manage. He only regretted that it had taken him until three days before Christmas to figure that out.

He picked up the next gift, a pair of furry pink boots Emery assured him Tallie would love. He was cutting paper to fit the box and listening to a really strange a cappella rendition of "The Little Drummer Boy" when somebody knocked on the door.

For just a moment, panic spurted through him. Had the girls woken up, seen the lights on down here and come to investigate? He was rather frantically looking around for a blanket he could toss over the jumble of presents when he heard a female voice that was definitely neither of the girls.

"Nate? It's me, Emery."

He probably should be relieved the girls hadn't found him, but he was depressed at the realization that his instant of panic didn't ease in the slightest.

"Yeah. Just a minute," he called, sliding his chair away from the table and hurrying to the door.

He opened it for her and told himself that the little leap in his chest at the sight of her, all rosy-cheeked and delectable, was only a little leftover indigestion from the tense dinner with the girls.

"I saw the light. Need a hand?"

He pulled the door open farther so she could enter the cabin. "I wish I could say no. But the truth is, I could use a million hands. Or at least two that know what they're doing here. I really stink at wrapping presents."

She held up her hands. "This is a little-known secret about me, but I majored in advanced ribbon-curling in college."

He laughed, entirely too drawn to this rare teasing side of her. She hadn't worn a coat for the short walk over, only a sweater and a red-patterned scarf wrapped in some complicated way that managed to look elegantly put-together.

He had turned on the electric fireplace when he came down to the cabin, but somehow the room still seemed considerably warmer when she walked inside and began to untwist her scarf.

He could smell her, that alluring scent of cinnamon and vanilla, and he remembered all-too-vividly the taste and heat of her a few hours earlier in this very place. Her curves pressed against him, the sexy little sounds she made when he nuzzled the slender column of her neck, the delectable softness of the skin just above her waist...

"Where would you like me to start?"

He blinked back to the present to find Emery had draped the scarf on the hook by the door and her attention was fixed on the presents piled everywhere.

He scratched the back of his neck, wrenching his mind from that blasted kiss. "I seem to have more trouble with the small stuff. Socks, earrings. Lip gloss. That sort of thing. If you don't mind taking anything smaller than a loaf of bread, I can handle the bigger gifts."

She smiled and he was struck all over again by how lovely she was and how that smile seemed to fill the entire cabin with warmth.

"A very wise and appropriate division of labor."

She gathered up a handful of smaller gifts and one

of the rolls of wrapping paper he had been fortunate enough to find in Suzi's stash of holiday stuff, and found a spot on the sofa where she could use the wide coffee table to spread out wrapping paper.

"Do you worry the girls might wake up?" she asked after she was situated and had started wrapping some socks.

"I thought when you knocked at the door I was busted for sure," he admitted.

"Lucky for you it wasn't the girls."

Funny, he didn't feel very lucky when it was all he could do to keep his hands off her. "They both have my cell phone memorized. I also left one of the two-way ranch radios as a backup." He pointed to the matching radio on the kitchen counter.

"You're prepared. Must be your military training."

He gave a rough laugh. "A dozen years in the army wasn't much preparation, I'm afraid, for a night spent wrapping mostly pink girly-girl presents."

"You're doing fine." She smiled.

"I haven't had much practice at this wrapping thing," he admitted. "I usually had the store gift wrap presents for my dad and Suz and my...mom."

She flashed a quick look of sympathy in his direction and he regretted telling her about his childhood. It wasn't a part of his life he liked to broadcast around and he didn't want her looking at him with pity in her eyes.

He would much rather see softness and warmth and...

He jerked his attention from all the things he knew he shouldn't want. He quickly changed the subject. "What about you? You haven't told me much about your family."

She was quiet for several moments while a jazzy piano version of "My Favorite Things" played softly through the cabin. When she spoke, her tone was casual, but somehow he sensed a great importance behind her words.

"My...father was a corporate attorney and my mother was in public relations. They married after dating in graduate school and I was born not long after."

"And you were an only child, right?"

Again she paused, far longer than the rather benign question warranted. Finally, he looked up from wrapping the pink boots for Claire to find her gazing into the small flames of the electric fireplace.

"Shortly before she died, my mother told me the man I thought all my life was my father really wasn't."

He stared, not knowing what to say. She didn't give him a chance to respond before she continued.

"Apparently, she had a relationship with a married man and I was the result," she went on. "In her family's rather blue-blood social circle at that time, illegitimate children still weren't quite acceptable, no matter what the rest of the world might be doing. So when she discovered she was pregnant, her college boyfriend agreed to marry her and raise me as his own. They never said a word in all those years until my mother's deathbed."

Her hands trembled slightly on the wrapping paper and her shoulders were tight and set.

"Whoa," he finally said. "That must have been a shocker."

She gave a ragged-sounding laugh. "You could say that. Apparently, I also have several half-siblings. That's why I didn't quite know how to answer your question. They have no idea about me, at least as far as I know.

I'm still trying to figure out if I want to work toward a relationship with them."

He whistled, long and low. "You do play your cards close to your vest, don't you?"

"It's not exactly a story I feel like telling to any stranger passing by. Or to my close friends, for that matter. Actually, you're the only other person who knows I'm not really one of the Kendalls of Kendall Park, daughter of Stephen and Julia Baird Kendall."

He shouldn't feel so flattered that she would confide this part of her life to him. He also shouldn't have the overwhelming urge when he heard that slightly forlorn note in her voice to drop the wrapping paper and tape, fold her into his arms and whisper that everything would be all right.

"You haven't met them?"

She shook her head. "I can't quite figure out how to just show up on someone's doorstep and say, Surprise! I'm your twenty-seven-year-old baby sister."

"That's a tough one."

"The truth is, I'm not sure I'm ready to suddenly parachute into the middle of an instant family."

He couldn't help a little smile at her vivid imagery. "You're right to be cautious. Trust me, that's solid advice coming from someone with experience, literally, at both parachuting and instant families. You don't want to jump into either unless you're a hundred percent sure about the way the wind is blowing, about whether you've got the stomach to make the jump, and about whether you're prepared for what you're going to find on the ground."

"I don't know any of that yet," she admitted as she coiled a ribbon in some elaborate way and adhered it to the package she was wrapping. "I guess that's what scares me most. What am I supposed to do now? I feel like everything I thought I knew about myself has been turned upside down."

"You'll figure it out."

"I hope so." Her voice was small and rather forlorn and his hands tightened on the wrapping paper. He wanted to pull her into his arms, to hold her tight and make all her worries and fears disappear. He wanted to kiss her until that lost look in her eyes began to fade, replaced by the desire he had seen there that afternoon.

He was suddenly afraid this wasn't only about physical attraction. If that was it, why would his insides be jumping around like a grasshopper on a hot July sidewalk?

No, this was more. He genuinely liked this woman. Something about her big blue eyes and her hesitant smile and that indefinable air of loneliness surrounding her reached right in and tugged at his heart.

He was very much afraid these fragile feelings could develop all too easily into something more.

This was tender and gentle and intimate. He wanted to tuck her against him and protect her from anybody else who might want to hurt her.

He didn't *want* this. God knows, he didn't need one more person to worry about. He couldn't handle the life *he* had parachuted into. The last thing he needed was to find himself wrapped up like one of these presents in someone else's troubles.

He ought to just shove her out the door into the cold night and assure her that while he appreciated her help, he could handle wrapping the remaining few gifts on his own.

All of his instincts were crying out for him to do just that, but he forced himself to ignore them.

Still, he sliced through the wrapping paper almost savagely. Damn her for blowing into his world at the most inconvenient time, when he could least afford the distraction and when he found himself in a lousy tactical position to protect himself.

What on earth had she done wrong?

Emery combed through their conversation of the past ten minutes and could think of nothing she might have said or done to turn his features dark and forbidding, to make that muscle in his jaw clench so tightly.

Was he disgusted that she was the result of an illicit affair? Or did he just not want to be dragged into her problems? In a few moments, he had shifted from offering her advice about parachuting to glowering at the girls' Christmas presents as if he wanted to toss the lot of them out into the snow-covered cattle pens.

They worked in a tense silence, those Christmas carols playing softly between them. Finally, when her pile had considerably dwindled and she only had a few items left to wrap, she decided she'd had enough.

She had spent her entire childhood trying to be perfect, studying hard for the best grades, applying to the right colleges, wearing just the right accessories.

Since her mother died, she had spent some serious time rehashing her life, examining the fierce perfectionism that had carried from childhood into her adult years. Now she could see it for what it was: a rather pathetic effort to gain the approval of a man who had been distant and reserved all her life.

She understood everything so much more clearly

now. Stephen Kendall had known she wasn't his biological child all along. Her mother had been clear about that. She could only imagine what he must have seen when he looked at her, another man's child. How could he be expected to give her that love and attention she had craved so desperately?

She had even married the son of one of his law partners to please him. Oh, she might have convinced herself she loved Jason when they started dating in college, but in reality she had been so happy to finally have Stephen Kendall's approval that she could have talked herself into anything.

Somehow she had transferred those efforts to please her father into making herself into the perfect wife, never complaining at Jason's late nights or his unexplained absences. He was working hard at the law firm he'd been folded into after he passed the bar, trying to establish himself so they could continue having their European vacations and their late-model cars and their big brick house in an exclusive neighborhood.

In the midst of all that perfection and despite his past history in college, she had stupidly never once suspected that Jason Markeson would turn out to be a cheating son of a bitch.

She was suddenly tired of it. Hadn't she vowed not to be so passive anymore, to reach out and seize what life had to offer?

"I suppose I have two choices," she finally said and her abrupt statement earned her a rather wary look from Nate.

"About what?"

"I can sit here stewing about what I might have said

or done to annoy you. Or I can stop wondering and just outright ask you."

He set aside a large package with a lopsided ribbon. "I'm annoyed?"

"You tell me. If you're not angry, what am I missing? Maybe the glower is just some army commando way of expressing undying gratitude for my help."

"I'm not angry," he said, then added almost under his breath, "Not with you, anyway."

She frowned, a little disconcerted. How narcissistic, she suddenly realized, that she would automatically assume she was the cause of his dark mood. He had stressors she couldn't even imagine, trying to run the ranch and raise his nieces and leave behind the military career he enjoyed.

"Who, then? The girls?"

He let out a long, heavy sigh. "Myself, mostly."

"Why?"

He didn't answer at first and when she met his gaze, she found him watching her with that half-closed look again, something in his dark eyes that sizzled through her insides.

"I don't know what to do about this."

"About…what?"

He sighed. "No matter how many times I tell myself I shouldn't want you, that I don't have time for this, that you're far too proper and polished for a guy like me, I can't seem to help myself."

She stared as that sizzle turned into a full-fledged burn. "Nate…"

"I know. It's crazy, isn't it?"

Her mouth was desert-dry suddenly and she had to force herself to take a deep enough breath to ease the sudden ache in her lungs. "Crazy. Right. Just what I was thinking."

He slid his chair back and the sound startled her into a little jump.

"I can't stop thinking about tasting you, putting my hands on you. All afternoon and evening, I've been wondering what might have happened if we hadn't heard the bus out front earlier."

She swallowed again, her insides hot and restless. "We both know what would have happened," she murmured. "We probably would have ended up on that bed over there."

"Which would have been a mistake for both of us."

"Huge mistake," she agreed.

"Enormous. Colossal."

Even as he said the words, he moved inexorably closer to her and her heartbeat accelerated. Without even being fully conscious of it, she rose.

"But just for the record," she said, her voice low, "I can't stop thinking about you...doing those things, either. I thought you should know."

Her last word was swallowed by his groan and then his mouth was on hers and all the heat from earlier roared back over them as if it had just been lurking between them on a low, steady simmer, ready to flare again.

Right. This felt right. All the reasons and arguments didn't matter when she was here with him, in his arms. She didn't need to be perfect with Nate. He didn't expect that from her and she somehow had a feeling he wouldn't be as attracted to her if he didn't see her for what she was, calluses and scars and all.

He lowered her to the sofa, his body all hard muscle

over hers, and she savored the strength of him above her. "I can't get the taste of you out of my head," he murmured, his body stretched along hers. "You're there all the time, no matter what I'm doing."

"I'm sorry."

He laughed roughly. "I'm only sorry the memory of it doesn't do justice to the real thing." He kissed her, his mouth fierce, almost possessive, and she clutched at his back, wondering just how she had come to care so much for this man in such a short time.

She could feel his arousal against her and she arched against him, seeking more. She wanted him, wanted this. The hunger was like a steady wind inside her, sweeping away all her uncertainties.

They kissed and tasted and explored while the soft carols played in the background and she wanted to remember every moment of this forever. He helped her out of her sweater, leaving only the white cotton blouse underneath. When his hands moved to the buttons of her shirt, she reached to help him. With each button that slipped through its opening, he pressed a kiss to the skin exposed.

And then, just as he reached for the last one, when her nerves had reached a fever pitch of anticipation for his touch, the sudden jangle of a cell phone rang through the small cabin.

Chapter 11

Both of them froze, their breath ragged. When the phone rang again he swore, low and vicious, wishing he could pound his head against the coffee table a couple dozen times.

"I can't ignore it," he said, fighting a groan. "I want to, more than I want to take my next breath, but I can't."

"I know."

She scrambled up, working the buttons on her shirt with fingers that trembled.

"It's got to be the girls. Claire knows to call me if she can't find me in the house. I always leave the phone by the side of her bed."

"Answer it."

With another quick, muffled curse, he reached for the phone. "What's wrong?"

"Uncle Nate, where are you?" Claire's plaintive cry

tore at his conscience. "Tallie had a nightmare again. A really bad one. She won't stop crying and I don't know what to do."

Walking barefoot out into the snow wouldn't have cooled the intense heat between them any faster. Though it was just about the toughest thing he'd ever had to do, he moved farther away from Emery and reached for his coat.

"I'm outside," he answered, which wasn't technically a lie since he was outside the ranch house.

"Well, can you come back in soon?" she begged. "She's really upset and she just wants Mom and Dad."

"Yeah. Yeah. Of course. I'll be there in a minute."

"Hurry, okay?"

"Hang on, honey. I'm on my way."

She hung up after his assurance that he would be there in a moment. Claire sounded far more composed than he felt. Sometimes he forgot she wasn't twelve yet, that she was still very much a child.

"Don't worry about anything," Emery said as he tucked his shirt back in. "I'll finish up out here and hide the gifts in the bedroom again."

He didn't know what to say that wouldn't make him feel like even more of a heel. "I'm sorry. More sorry than you'll ever know."

Her laugh sounded a little rough, strained. "The girls have excellent timing. First the school bus and now this. It's probably better this way. Neither one of us is in a good place for…anything."

"Em…"

She shook her head. "Go. The girls need you."

He gave her one more regretful look then hurried out into the cold December night.

* * *

An hour later, Nate stood in the darkened great room beside the Christmas tree, watching soft, puffy flakes of snow drift down. Tallie and Claire were finally settled again after a cup of instant hot cocoa and a half dozen stories.

For a good twenty minutes after he rushed to the house, Tallie had sobbed in his arms, distraught from her nightmare. He hadn't done much of anything except hold her and murmur soft little nothing words and promise her repeatedly that he wasn't going anywhere and neither was Claire.

Finally she had drifted back to sleep in his arms and at Claire's suggestion, he had put her in her sister's room in case she woke again.

Was there ever a moment in a parent's life that wasn't touched by guilt? He never should have left the house, even if Claire could reach him quickly on the cell. It wasn't fair that she had to deal with her sister alone in those first few tense moments after Tallie awoke.

Nate sipped at his own lousy powdery mug of hot cocoa then set it on the corner of the mantel. He was exhausted, emotionally and physically, and wanted nothing more than to unburden himself to a willing ear. The lights of Emery's cabin were on and her own little Christmas tree glimmered merrily in the window, but he knew he couldn't leave the house again tonight.

Even if he didn't have to consider the girls, it wouldn't be a good idea to seek her out again.

Too much was at stake. Not just his own increasingly powerful feelings for her, but more important, the girls. Tallie's nightmare was a stark reminder of the psychological trauma his nieces had suffered and how very far they had to go toward healing. Tallie was terrified that everyone she loved would leave her as her parents had done. The grief counselors he'd taken them to said only time and routine would provide the stability she needed.

He knew Emery's place in their world was fleeting. She would be returning to Virginia in a few days and all his instincts urged him to keep her at a distance, for the girls' sake.

But what about *his* sake? He craved her company like a canteen full of pure spring water after a long recon mission in the dessert. She was soft and sweet and when he was with her, he could forget about his worries and the uncertainty of the future and everything he had given up to do what was right for his nieces.

With Emery, he wasn't an ex-Ranger or a greenhorn parent or an out-of-his-league rancher. He was only a man wrapped around a beautiful woman who touched something deep inside him.

He sighed. Probably best that they'd been interrupted before things spiraled out of control, for everybody's sake. Somehow knowing that perfectly well still didn't seem to ease the yearning ache in his gut.

So much for those damn best intentions.

Nate gazed across at the passenger seat of his SUV where Emery sat with her hands folded and her mouth compressed into a thin line.

She looked even more lovely and sophisticated than normal, with her hair swept back into a shiny twist and her makeup so expertly applied, he could hardly tell she was wearing any.

"Why didn't you bring your swimsuit?" Tallie asked

her. "You won't even get cold because the pool's inside the McRavens' house!"

"I believe I've heard that," Emery said drily.

"You should go swimming with us, then!"

"I'll be too busy eating all the good food to go swimming," she said with a smile for the girls that seemed to reach right out and tug at his insides.

He really *had* intended to keep his distance. But he never counted on the girls finding Emery after school at the horse corrals on their daily visits to check on Annabelle, and inviting their guest to ride with them to the party.

A little warning might have been nice. Instead, a few minutes before they were heading out the door, Claire had casually mentioned they needed to pick up Emery because she and Tallie had offered her a ride.

"She said no at first, but we told her it wasn't good for the planet to take two cars," Tallie had confided.

"She couldn't say no after that. I hope it's okay," Claire had said.

It wasn't okay. Bad enough he had to go to the damn party in the first place. Tougher still, he now had to work to keep his hands off Emery, who looked sleekly delicious in a shiny white shirt, black slacks and another of her scarves, this one in jeweled holiday tones.

The woman was slowly shoving him straight over the edge.

They drove across the bridge that spanned the creek on the way to Raven's Nest, Carson McRaven's sprawling lodge. McRaven was a newcomer to Cold Creek Canyon and had purchased the ranch Nate had always known as the Wagon Wheel after the previous owner died in a ranch accident. Last summer, he had ended up marrying the widow who had sold him the land.

Nate had known Jenna Wheeler McRaven in high school. She had saved his bacon right after Suzi and John died by filling the freezer at the house with container after container of delicious food for them to eat in those first raw, terrible early days.

The McRavens' house was lit up, with a Christmas tree that had to be twice the size of the Hope Springs one blazing in the front window and lights framing just about every window.

He blinked a little at this exuberance. The few times Nate had met him, Carson McRaven didn't seem the sort to dive into the whole holiday spirit thing. But he supposed a man with four stepchildren probably had to make a few concessions.

The moment he parked the SUV and turned the vehicle ignition off, the girls climbed out and raced for the front door, leaving him to walk the short distance to the house alone with Emery.

He was intensely aware of her, her scent of cinnamon and vanilla and the roses the cold air put into her high cheekbones.

"How's Tallie today?" she asked just before they reached the steps into the house. "Did it take long for her to fall asleep again after the nightmare last night?"

He jerked his mind away from how badly he wanted to drag her against one of those porch supports and kiss her until they were both mindless.

"Okay," he answered. "A little quieter than normal, maybe. I really thought she was done with the nightmares. Right after the accident, she would wake up every night crying, but it's been several weeks since the last one."

"Poor thing. It makes your heart just break, doesn't it?"

"We all usually have a tough time going back to sleep afterward, but this one wasn't too bad. For the girls, anyway. I noticed your light was still on late."

She flashed him a quick look then turned her attention back to the step. "I was working on the quilts."

He had nearly forgotten them amid all that heated embrace and then all his angst over Tallie's nightmare. And, he was rather abashed to admit, over this stupid party he didn't want to attend.

"How are they coming?"

"Good," she answered, losing a little of the tension he'd noticed from the moment she slid into the SUV at the house. "I can't believe how fast they're coming together. Tallie's is nearly done and I should finish Claire's in plenty of time for you to put them under your tree tomorrow night."

Christmas Eve, he realized with a little spurt of shock. How could it possibly be here so soon?

Before he could answer, the door swung open and their host and hostess greeted them with friendly smiles.

"Nate!" Jenna wrapped him in a hug and kissed his cheek, reminding him anew why she had always been one of his favorite people at Pine Gulch High. "The girls rushed in a few moments ago so I figured you wouldn't be far behind. I'm so happy you made it."

He pulled away and introduced Emery, who was still hovering near the door. "Jenna, this is Emery Kendall. She's visiting the ranch from Virginia. Em, this is Jenna McRaven and her husband, Carson."

"Welcome!" Jenna exclaimed with another of her exuberant hugs while Carson shook Nate's hand.

"We're pretty casual tonight," Carson said. "The food is all set up buffet style in the dining room and most of the children are already in the pool. We've got adults stationed there to keep watch, don't worry."

"Thank you for inviting me," Emery said with a polite smile. "It's lovely to be included, even though I'm only visiting the area."

"We're happy to have you," Carson replied with a sincerity Nate hoped Emery didn't miss.

Before she could answer, though, Wade Dalton approached and held out his hand to Nate. Jenna, the proper hostess, began introducing Emery to him but Wade shook his head.

"We've met," Wade said with a smile. "Glad you decided to come after all."

Nate frowned. He'd always been struck by the resemblance between Wade and his father, but when he poured on the charm, the man was a dead ringer for Hank. He had a sudden insane urge to wrap his arm around Emery's shoulders and claim her as his for all the world to see.

Ridiculous. She wasn't his and she never would be.

That didn't stop him from having to swallow a growl when Wade gave her a broad smile.

"Carrie's going to be thrilled you're here. She's in the kitchen. I'll go let her know you and Nate are here."

She didn't answer, only nodded. But to Nate's shock, she didn't take her gaze off him as he walked away, following his progress away from them with a strange, intent expression.

Nate's stomach suddenly felt slick, greasy. He didn't

want to see her sudden fascination with Wade Dalton. He wanted to pretend he had been completely mistaken about it.

Like father, like son, apparently.

Old Hank Dalton had never let a silly thing like his wedding ring interfere with his love life.

"Can I get you a drink?" Carson asked.

He shook his head, but Emery asked in a rather strangled voice for some ginger ale.

"Coming right up," he said, and headed for a table laden with drinks, just as Maggie Dalton walked past them with a tray of little shrimp skewers wrapped in bacon.

Though they looked delicious and he hadn't eaten any dinner, he didn't think he could choke down even one. He had completely lost his appetite.

"Hey, Sergeant," Maggie said with a smile. He gave her a smart salute, as he always did when he saw her, more out of respect than obligation since they were both retired, indoors and out of uniform.

If she hadn't left the military a few years earlier, Maggie would have outranked him, since she had been an army nurse lieutenant stationed in Afghanistan who had been badly injured when her clinic had been fire-bombed by terrorists. He had been in country at the time and had managed to visit her for a few moments before she had been shipped out to Germany for better medical care.

Given the extent of her injuries, he had been pretty sure she wouldn't make it, but Maggie was a fighter. Though she had lost her leg below the knee in the attack, she didn't let her injury stop her. Besides raising two toddlers, she worked as a nurse practitioner in her husband's medical clinic and volunteered in many community activities.

"How are things with the girls?" she asked him.

"Fine. We're managing."

She shook her head with a rueful laugh. "You Rangers are always so verbose."

Despite his distraction, he managed to smile. "It's all part of our charm."

Before she could answer, her husband, Jake, walked into the room carrying one of their children, a little dark-haired boy with huge eyes and a wide, toothless smile.

"Hey, darlin'. Where's the diaper bag? This one stinks."

"Oh, I left it in the first bedroom off the kitchen when I changed Sofia. There's a changing table in there. Want me to take care of it?"

"No. I've got it," Jake said. "You can take the next one."

He kissed his wife on the cheek then turned to them. "Cavazos. Good to see you." He smiled at Emery. "Hi. I'm Jake Dalton. I don't think we've met."

Emery cleared her throat, a slightly dazed look in her eyes as she looked at the other man. "I'm Emery Kendall. I'm…staying at Hope Springs."

"Welcome to Pine Gulch. I'm sorry to run, but trust me, you don't want me hanging around with Mr. Stinkmeister here."

When he walked away, Maggie turned to Emery. "You're the fabric designer from Virginia Caroline was talking about! I'm sorry I didn't make the connection. She was hoping you would come. Nate, I'm stealing your guest so she can come back to the kitchen and dish with us girls."

Before he could protest, Maggie slipped an arm through Emery's and tugged her away, leaving him temporarily on his own.

Since he didn't feel like standing around making more small talk, he headed toward the vast three-story atrium that housed the pool, as he suddenly realized he should have done the moment they arrived to make sure the girls were well-supervised.

The noise level was considerably larger in the pool atrium, with screams and shouts of glee amplified by the echoing space.

He found a few adults in the pool and several more standing in groups, talking while they kept watch over the fifteen or so energetic kids splashing around in the pool. Seth Dalton was one of them. Though he was fully dressed and stood on the side of the pool, he was tossing a wet beach ball back and forth to several of the kids. He didn't seem to mind being splashed every time the ball came his way.

Nate supposed he should be grateful Emery wasn't around to fall for the youngest Dalton brother, too, since he was the one with the reputation of a heartbreaker, before he'd settled down and married the elementary school principal, anyway.

"Uncle Nate! Uncle Nate!" Tallie's yell from the diving board added to the din in the room. "Watch me. I'm gonna jump."

"Okay. I'm watching," he called back and had to smile as she did a perfect cannonball into the water before resurfacing and paddling to the side.

"Did you see me?" she called out when she reached the side.

"I did. You were awesome."

"I'm gonna do it again. Keep watching."

He smiled again. "You got it, kid."

He watched her jump two more times before she grew bored and started tossing the beach ball with the other kids.

"This has to be a big adjustment for you."

He looked away from the pool to find Seth had joined him. Though he wasn't very inclined to think favorably of any of the Daltons right now, he knew his jealousy was unjustified and unfair. The man was trying to make conversation and wasn't that the whole point of a gathering like this?

"It's not exactly where I expected to find myself, four months ago," he admitted. "But we're settling in."

"I can't say I know what you're going through. It must be tough to step in after all the pain those girls have been through. But I do know a little about suddenly becoming part of a ready-made family."

Jenny Boyer Dalton had two children from a previous marriage, Nate remembered. "How long did it take before you stopped feeling like you were completely out of your depth?"

"I'm waiting for that feeling to hit me any day now." Seth grinned. "But then, it's only been three years. I take comfort from Wade, who's been a father since Natalie was born eleven years ago. He has four kids now and still doesn't know what he's doing."

"That's why I was smart enough to marry a woman who's brilliant at the whole thing," another voice interjected and Nate looked over to find Wade had joined them.

Some covert ops specialist he was. He hadn't heard the man's approach over the noise from the pool. For one wild second, he wanted to shove the bastard into the water, but he knew that was unfair. Probably.

"We're comparing notes on being thrown into the deep end when it comes to kids," Seth said.

"My only advice is, just try to keep your head above water and paddle like hell. Not much else you can do," Wade said.

Despite his—okay, he could admit it—jealousy, Nate had to smile. "My arms are just about ready to fall off," he admitted.

"You've got it tough because you're on your own," Seth said. "Wade did that for a few years after his first wife died."

"It wasn't easy on anybody," Wade agreed. "At least I had my mom to help out. I don't know what we would have done without her."

His voice trailed off and he looked embarrassed for a moment, as if he'd suddenly remembered what had happened between Nate's mother and Hank Dalton and why Linda Cavazos wasn't in the picture.

"Caroline tells me you're thinking about closing the guest ranch," he said after an awkward moment.

"Thinking about it. I haven't made a decision yet, but as I've been going over the ranch accounts and familiarizing myself with the books, I'm figuring out it's a small part of our revenue base, but ends up taking a disproportionate expenditure of energy and resources. Besides that, I'm not sure I'm cut out for the hospitality industry."

"You planning to expand the ranching side of things, then?"

Why is it any of your damn business? he wanted to

ask, but he wouldn't be outright rude. "I haven't decided anything yet."

"I'm asking because I might have a lead on some summer grazing allotments that are coming up for bid, if you're interested."

He blinked, stunned by the offer. Grazing allotments from the federal government that allowed ranchers to move their cattle onto forest service land for the summer were highly coveted, more valuable around here than gold. "Why don't you want them?"

Wade shrugged. "We've used the same allotments for thirty years and they meet our current needs just fine." He paused. "I will add, though, that if you think you might end up selling Hope Springs altogether, I'd like first crack at it."

He stared at the other man as all his old feelings of resentment and suspicion welled up in his chest.

"I'm still weighing my options," he said firmly, when what he wanted to say was that he would sell the ranch to the Daltons the minute palm trees started growing at Hope Springs in January.

"Fair enough," Wade said. He didn't seem at all offended. "I just wanted you to know."

After Christmas he was going to have to make a decision. He couldn't continue waffling. Either he had to give a hundred percent to the ranch or he ought to sell it and take the girls somewhere else. Maybe not sell it to the Daltons, but to someone.

He didn't know what he would do besides being a soldier or a rancher, but he could figure something out.

If he didn't keep paddling, the only other option was to sink like a stone, and he wasn't ready to do that yet.

* * *

She didn't belong here.

The food was delicious, the conversation interesting, the company warm and friendly toward her. As she sat in the kitchen surrounded by women talking about their children and the holidays and memories they shared, Emery couldn't escape the inevitable conclusion that she was once more on the outside looking in.

She took a small bite of a cranberry tart. On some subconscious level she registered it was delicious, with just the perfect combination of sweetness and edge. But she was barely aware of what she ate.

Part of her longed, quite fiercely, to be part of their close-knit group. She wanted to be teased by Seth Dalton, to have the right to shower gifts on her nieces and nephews, to have these women as her friends and sisters.

This craving for a big, noisy, crazy family was as fierce as it was unexpected. Maybe it was because her mother had been her last remaining relative and her death left Emery unutterably alone. Or maybe that longing had always lurked somewhere inside her, buried deep by the reality of being an only child of only children.

Or not.

She swallowed the last morsel of the tart. For all she knew, maybe Hank Dalton had a dozen brothers, and she had a fleet of cousins she knew nothing about.

How would the Dalton brothers and their families react if they knew the outsider from Virginia shared half their DNA?

One brief sentence. That's all it would take. She

could tell Caroline or Jenny Dalton right now and the word would spread in a moment.

What would they think if they knew she was Hank Dalton's daughter with a tourist who had indulged in a brief affair twenty-seven years ago?

She sighed. The idea of spilling the news to them all seemed selfish and desperate suddenly. How could it be anything else? She was the one with everything to gain by sharing the information. She would have an instant extended family. Noisy children and darling chubby babies and three instant sisters-in-law to love.

What would they all have to gain? Only her. A boring textile designer who had spent her entire life trying—and failing—to be perfect.

She was quite certain telling the Daltons about her blood link to them would have unexpected ripples of consequence, like the ripples from a rock thrown into a pond.

"Emery, do you mind taking that plate of spinach pinwheels out to the great room?" Jenna McRaven asked. Her hostess was warm and friendly and, true to the girls' assurances, cooked like a dream.

"Oh, and don't let my husband near them or no one else will get any," Jenna said with a grin. "You can tell Carson if he puts up any kind of a fuss that I'm saving a private stash for him for later."

Emery managed to return her smile then walked into the great room where most of the guests had gathered. Several new people had arrived while she was in the kitchen. As she was setting the spinach rolls on the overflowing buffet table, an older woman in a glittery silver lamé blouse snatched one up.

"I love these things," she said with an expression of glee. "I was hoping Jenna would make them."

"They are good," Emery said politely.

"I don't think I know you," the woman said, squinting at her. "Are you a friend of the McRavens?"

"I'm actually a guest at Hope Springs until the end of the week. I'm here with Nate Cavazos."

The older woman's features lit up into a particularly lovely smile. "You must be the woman from Virginia. Caroline and Wade told me you might be coming. I'm Marjorie Montgomery. Used to be Dalton. Wade's mother."

If she hadn't already set the platter of food down, Emery was certain she would have dumped the whole thing all over Marjorie Dalton Montgomery's feet in her shock.

This was the wife Hank Dalton had neglected to mention to Emery's mother while he was busy seducing the starry-eyed girl fascinated by the romance of the West. The little she had eaten all night seemed to churn greasily in her stomach. Hank Dalton's wife. How foolish of her not to have even a moment of consideration for the woman in all this.

"How are you enjoying your stay?" Marjorie asked.

"It's been lovely," she managed to say through her suddenly dry mouth. "Everyone has been more than kind."

"Folks around here take care of each other, whether you've lived here all your life or just dropped in for a visit," she said with a warm smile. "Why, take my second husband. Four years ago, he moved here without knowing a soul but me. And Caroline, of course. She's his daughter. Which makes her my stepdaughter and my daughter-in-law both. Anyway, four years later, now Quinn has his own real estate office and he's on the Pine Gulch town council. Everybody warmed to him real quick."

"I've found everyone around here very friendly," Emery said.

"Carrie tells me you're a textile designer."

"That's right. I design fabric, mostly for the home. Pillows, curtains, that sort of thing."

"Fabric stores are my favorite places to shop!" Marjorie exclaimed. "I belong to a quilting group in town. It's one of my passions. We get together every other Thursday and do about eight or nine quilts a year, then we auction them off for charity every year."

"I'm making a couple of quilts right now, actually," Emery said. "I could have used your help today when I was piecing them."

They talked a few more moments about quilts, until a petite Hispanic woman who reminded Emery of Maggie Dalton approached them. After a few moments, their conversation shifted to a recent library board meeting.

As she listened to their conversation with half an ear about people she didn't know and future events she wouldn't be part of, the grim truth settled over her, dank and overpowering.

She couldn't tell the Daltons her identity. Not when doing so would force ugly secrets up like sludge from the ground. If she shared with them the story her mother had told her, she would have to tell Marjorie Dalton Montgomery that her husband had cheated on her when she had three young boys, the youngest probably only in kindergarten.

As much as she would love a ready-made family,

the chance to have a genuine place among them, how could she justify the hurt she would likely cause along the way?

Her chest ached at what she would be giving up, but she knew it was the right decision.

She should never have come to Pine Gulch. Better never to have met the Daltons and find them people she was almost certain she could like and admire than to have to carry that knowledge with her when she left.

But if she had never come here, she wouldn't have met Nate and the girls.

As if her thoughts had summoned him, she heard Nate's deep voice and then Tallie's higher-pitched one. She turned to find them in a corner of the room. His niece must have decided she was tired of swimming. She had dressed again and Nate was busy toweling off her dark hair with a beach towel decorated with The Little Mermaid.

Something fluttered through her chest as she watched the tough, dangerous soldier take care of the little girl.

Leaving them would be extraordinarily difficult. All three of them—Nate, Tallie and Claire—had somehow sneaked into her heart when she wasn't looking.

She would have to, though. And she would survive. She had endured the loss of her child and her marriage and her parents. She could endure few more losses.

At least she hoped so.

Chapter 12

Christmas Eve was her least favorite day of the year.

After the alarm on her cell phone buzzed her awake just before sunrise, Emery lay in bed and gazed at the log beams of her rented cabin, wishing she had more of a stomach for drinking so she could spend the day in an alcohol-induced stupor.

Her arms never felt as empty as they did on this day, little Gracie's birthday and date of her death.

If her world hadn't changed so painfully and abruptly two years ago today, her baby girl would have been toddling around their house in Hampton, pulling ornaments off the tree, gabbing away little nonsense words.

She would have been a good mother. Her experience the past few days with the girls verified that for her. She would have adored showing Gracie the magic and wonder of life in general and Christmas in particular.

She sat up and used the corner of the flannel sheet to dab at her eyes. She had far too much work to do to indulge in sitting here feeling sorry for herself, swallowed by her grief, and she was suddenly enormously grateful for that.

Though she had worked late in the night after the party at the McRavens' to finish Claire's quilt, she still needed to bind it and then finish machine-quilting Tallie's. She was going to have to sew her fingers to the bone in order to get them both done in time.

The reminder energized her, renewed her, and she slid from the bed. The best cure for self-pity and sadness was to pour all those negative energies into doing something positive for someone else.

Sewing those quilts for the girls was better for her psyche than months of therapy.

Several hours later, she sewed the last seam on the binding of Claire's quilt, then eased her chair away from the sewing machine, suddenly conscious that every muscle in her body ached, from her tense shoulders to her dry eyelids to the arch of her foot from pressing the sewing machine pedal.

She needed a long soak in a hot tub.

Or at least a nap.

She glanced at her watch and was stunned to see it was after four. She had been sewing virtually nonstop for ten hours. No wonder she felt as if she'd been trampled in a cattle stampede.

She picked up the quilt and carried it into her bedroom, where she had spread Tallie's quilt earlier in order to admire the finished product.

Though she had used the same mix of fabrics pieced from their parents' clothing in both of them, she had opted for different designs to show their individual personalities. Tallie's was whimsical and cute, a trail of colorful butterflies dancing across the pale pink background, offset by the brown edge. Claire's was a little more grown-up, a traditional Lone Star pattern with a large six-pointed star in the center, radiating color out to the edge.

She had used a mix of materials snipped from Suzi's and John's clothing in complementary colors and she had chosen brown backing for Tallie's and pink for Claire's. Considering the short time she had to work on them, she was amazed at how they'd turned out. She only hoped the girls would like them.

Her stomach grumbled and she frowned when she realized she hadn't eaten since the quick egg-white omelet she'd made for protein that morning.

She was standing at the refrigerator poring over her limited options for Christmas Eve dinner and had just about settled on a grilled cheese sandwich when she suddenly heard what sounded like muffled crying, followed quickly by a knock on her front door.

The girls!

"Coming. Just a moment," she called out, then rushed to the bedroom where the quilts were still spread and yanked closed the door, grateful she had already gathered all the scraps from the clothing she had cut up and tucked them carefully away in the boxes Nate had left on her doorstep.

Her tight shoulder muscles yelped in protest when she reached to open the door, but she forgot all about her aches and her worry that they would discover the quilts prematurely when she saw the two distressed little faces on the other side.

"What is it? Are you hurt? Is it your uncle?"

"Everything's ruined!" The cry was all the more distressing coming from Claire. Solid, dependable, serious Claire.

"What's ruined, honey? Come inside out of the cold and tell me what's wrong."

Both girls hurried into the room in tears, though at first glance it appeared to Emery that Tallie was crying more in sympathy with her sister than out of any real upset.

"We messed up everything," Tallie sniffled.

"I tried so hard," Claire said. "We wanted everything to be perfect for Uncle Nate but the *masa* is lumpy and gross and won't spread on the cornhusks and I burned my finger on the chili peppers and now the stupid tamales won't roll right."

She blinked, more than a little lost. "You're making tamales?"

Claire nodded. "We always have tamales on Christmas Eve. Our mama used to tell us *she* always had tamales on Christmas Eve so we thought Uncle Nate would like them. Joanie helped us buy the stuff before she ran off and I've been hiding it so Uncle Nate wouldn't know. Only I can't make them right and now everything is *ruined*."

Her tears seemed disproportionate to the current crisis and Emery pulled her close, her heart aching as she realized Claire's distress likely had more to do with missing her mother than out of any tamale-induced trauma.

"We thought maybe you could help us," Tallie said. "You can fix everything."

"Me?" She hoped her gulp wasn't audible to the girls. "I'm afraid I don't know anything about tamales."

"We have Mama's recipe book," Claire said. "I know what we're supposed to do, I just can't seem to do it."

She was exhausted, her muscles tight and achy, and cooking wasn't her area of expertise in the first place. But how could she simply ignore their suffering?

"Where's your uncle?"

"Doing chores," Claire answered. "He was supposed to be back already, but he called and said he had a problem with one of the horses and he'd be up as soon as he could. Dinner's never going to be done because tamales have to cook *forever* and we only rolled four of them."

"Will you help us?" Tallie begged.

"Oh, please." Claire added her voice. "Christmas Eve will be completely ruined if you don't."

They sounded so dramatic that she would have smiled if they hadn't both been perfectly in earnest.

This wasn't about tamales, she thought again. This was about two grieving little girls trying to hang on to traditions that had been lost with their parents. She didn't have the heart to refuse, even though she didn't think she would be any more proficient at the task than they seemed to be.

"Of course I'll help you." She ignored the twinge in her muscles when she reached for her coat and scarf. After she had put them on, she reached a hand out to each girl.

"Let's go. Christmas Eve tamales coming right up."

The girls were going to skin him.

He was late and they were going to be starving by the time he managed to heat up the lasagna from the freezer he had planned for dinner. He should have called again and had Claire put it in, but he'd gotten distracted in the barn and it had completely slipped his mind.

So dinner would be late. No big deal, he assured himself. Maybe if the girls stayed up later, they might have an easier time getting to sleep on Christmas Eve. Of course, they probably wouldn't be happy about having to wait for their dinner, but he hoped he could make it up to them when he explained the reason for the delay.

He pushed open the door. "Hey, girls," he called, "I have a surprise for you."

And then the scents washed over him, wave after wave, and he froze.

Suddenly he was a kid again, spending Christmas Eve surrounded by the delectable scents of corn flour and peppers and pork roast, in an endless agony of anticipation as he waited for their traditional tamales to steam.

What in the hell?

He followed his nose to the kitchen and had his second shock in as many minutes when he found Emery Kendall working at the kitchen island, wearing a splattered apron and looking decidedly bedraggled, her sleek blond hair falling out of its knot.

"Whoa. What's going on in here?"

"Tamales!" Tallie exclaimed, her little features flush with excitement. "We're making tamales, Uncle Nate. Can you smell them?"

"We always had tamales on Christmas Eve," Claire added, a little defiantly. "Mama said *she* always had them when you were kids and you did, too."

"We messed them up the first time and we were *so* upset," Tallie confided. "We thought Christmas was ruined for *sure* and then I said maybe Emery could help us fix them and Claire said that was a good idea and so we went and asked her and she said okay and this batch is just perfect."

"I wouldn't say perfect," Emery muttered. "But I hope they're edible."

He met her gaze and she looked frazzled and slightly helpless and completely beautiful, with her cheeks pink from the steam coming from the stove.

"Wow. I haven't had real homemade tamales in years."

He had a sudden vivid memory of this very kitchen, when he was probably a few years younger than Tallie, during the time he still considered the good years before his father died.

His mother would spend several days before Christmas making tamales from the recipe she learned from his *abuela*. They would have a big party with relatives and friends from all over southern Idaho. Cousins, uncles, aunts. It had been crazy and noisy and wonderful.

He tended to dwell on all the ugliness that came after with his mother and forget there had been plenty of good times along the way, before everything went wrong.

"They smell *delicioso*."

The girls both giggled and he smiled at them. His gaze shifted again to Emery's and something sparked between them, something sweet and bright.

"You are a woman of many talents," he murmured. "How does a blue blood Virginia textile designer know how to make tamales?"

She made a face. "I don't, as I'm sure you'll figure out when they're finally done. I followed your sister's recipe as best I could and then ended up making a frantic call to my friend Freddie—short for Frederica—and she walked me through it."

He peered into the steamer at two dozen pale rolled cornhusks and his stomach rumbled. "They look perfect. I just might have to eat them all."

"No!" Tallie exclaimed. "We get some, too. We're the ones who made them!"

"We'll have to see who's the quickest." He winked at her and found Emery gazing at him with an expression in her blue eyes he couldn't identify.

He wanted to bask in it suddenly, to burn this memory into his mind along with all those years of Christmas parties.

"How soon before they'll be done?"

"We actually had enough for two batches so you'll have some to freeze later. We're ready to put the second batch in now and the first batch will be done in about a half hour."

"Perfect. That will give me time to clean the barn off me." The words suddenly reminded him of the past two hours' effort. "Oh! I nearly forgot. I came in to tell you I've got a Christmas Eve surprise for you."

"What is it?" Tallie exclaimed. "Is it a present? Can we open it?"

"I guess you could say it's a present that's already been opened. Actually, it's not my surprise at all. It's Annabelle's. She had her foal three weeks early. That's what took me so long."

Why did girls always have to use that high-pitched squeal when they were excited? No "yeah, dudes" or fist-pounding around here. They just pierced his eardrums with their glee then hugged each other and danced around the kitchen.

"We have to go see it! Right now!" Claire exclaimed.

"After dinner, okay?" he said. "Otherwise the tamales will steam too long and they'll be ruined. You've put so much work into them, I want to do dinner justice."

They didn't look thrilled at the delay, but they didn't argue. "Uncle Nate, Emery can stay and have dinner with us tonight, can't she?" Tallie asked.

He shot a look at Emery at the stove just in time to see her mouth open a little in surprise at the backhanded invitation. Her surprise quickly shifted to discomfort.

"It's Christmas Eve, honey," she answered. "It's a time for families and I'm not really part of your family."

"But if you hadn't helped us with the tamales, we would have starved!"

She smiled a little at this dramatic wail, but he thought he saw sadness in her eyes. He wondered at it for a moment then suddenly remembered. This was Christmas Eve, the two-year anniversary of her baby's death. His chest felt tight, achy.

"I'm sure your uncle wouldn't have let you starve. He would have found something for you to eat."

"I had a lasagna in the freezer just waiting to be warmed up. But traditional tamales will be much, much better." He paused, wishing he could take her hand in front of the girls. "We'd love to have you join us. Will you stay?"

He waited for her answer, startled by how very much he wanted her to say yes.

"I'm starving," she admitted. "I didn't have lunch. And since the tamales won't be done for some time, I'd love to walk back to the cabin for a moment to clean up."

He wanted to tell her she looked beautiful, that see-

ing her with all her perfection a little bit messed up only
seemed to add to her appeal. Instead, he only smiled.

"Meet you back here in half an hour, then."

Dinner was an unqualified success.

The tamales were fantastic, rich and spicy and very
much like the recipe he remembered from his childhood.

Afterward, they laughed and joked while they
cleaned up together and then bundled up to walk down
to the barn to see Annabelle's yuletide present, all spin-
dly legs and big eyes and baffled expression.

"Oh! He's beautiful!" Tallie exclaimed while Claire
folded her hands together and tucked them against her
heart.

"He's a she," Nate said, completely enjoying their delight. "I figured you two could pick out a name for her."

"What about Holly?" Claire asked.

"Or Chrissy?" Tallie said. "For Christmas."

"What about Noël?" Emery joined into their name
game.

"Noël! I *love* it!" Claire said.

"Me, too," her sister declared.

"Noël it is, then. That work okay for you, Annabelle?"

The mare blew her lips out in a raspberry that
sounded very much like agreement and all of them
laughed.

The girls continued to be entranced with the foal,
but after a moment he saw Emery ease slightly away
from them to lean against the railing of the opposite
stall. Even though he knew in his gut the smartest

move would be to keep as much distance as possible, he couldn't seem to resist joining her.

"I finished the quilts this afternoon," she said in an undertone so the girls couldn't hear. "Actually, I had just sewn the last stitch about ten minutes before the girls rushed down to the cabin in the midst of the great tamale catastrophe."

"You did?"

"Yes. And even though this probably sounds terribly vain, I have to admit, they turned out beautifully. I think they'll love them."

"I'm sure they will."

"When I went back to the cabin to change before dinner, I wrapped them both up for you. If you want, you can pick them up when you transfer all the presents from the other cabin."

Oh, right. He still had to drag everything up to the house and put it under the tree later. In light of the fact that she had just spent two days sewing quilts for the girls, he had little to complain about, even if the prospect of filling stockings and making everything just right did feel a little overwhelming right about now.

"I have a better idea," he said suddenly. "We talked about giving them the nightgowns tonight, but let's give them the quilts instead. Then they can sleep wrapped in them and maybe it will feel a little like their parents are with them on Christmas Eve."

Her smile was soft and radiant, like sunshine creeping over the mountaintops on a frigid January day, and he wanted to stay here in this cold barn and bask in it.

"What a wonderful idea!"

No. He didn't want to bask in her smile. He wanted to capture it with his own mouth and absorb it inside him. Somehow that made it all worse.

"Let's do it now. We can pick them up at your cabin and then go back to the house for the girls to open them."

"I don't need to be there with you," she protested. "It's a family time."

He stopped her argument by taking her hands in his and squeezing her fingers, even though he knew touching her probably wasn't the greatest idea. "You absolutely *do* need to be there. I know you must have worked incredibly hard to finish them on such short notice. I want you there when the girls see them."

She shot a quick look at Tallie and Claire, still busy laughing at the foal's ungainly steps. "Are you sure? I don't want to overstep."

"You deserve to be there for the big unveiling." He paused, compelled to be truthful. "And without you, I'm afraid none of us would be having much of a Christmas. You made it all happen, Em. From the Christmas tree to the tamales. It was all you."

In the dim light inside the barn, he could see color rise on her high cheekbones.

"I'd love to be there when they open the quilts," she murmured. "If you're sure I'm not intruding."

He should say yes. He should tell her she had been intruding into his mind since the moment she showed up at the ranch with her deep blue eyes and her rented SUV full of suitcases.

But he only shook his head. "It's going to be great. Let's do it."

* * *

"Please tell us!" Claire begged for the twentieth time as they left Emery's cabin and headed back to the main house a short time later. "What's in the boxes?"

"You'll find out soon enough," Nate said with a grin. "You can open them after you change into your pajamas."

"But I can't wait that long," Tallie exclaimed. "I know I can't. The suspense is *killing* me," she added.

"I hope not," her uncle answered. "Because then the surprise Emery has for you will just have to go to some other eight-year-old with brown pigtails."

"Stop teasing me, Uncle Nate. You don't know any other eight-year-olds with brown pigtails."

"I'll just have to find one," he said pitilessly when they reached the door.

She glared at him, though she looked more excited than upset. "You will not. But okay. I'll go change into my pajamas. Do we have to take showers?"

"It wouldn't hurt," Emery said before Nate could answer. "We all got a little messy while we were making tamales and who knows what you might have picked up in the horse barn? But I bet you two can take the fastest showers on record."

"Me first!" Tallie exclaimed and she headed up the stairs. Claire rolled her eyes at her sister. She followed at a more sedate pace, but after three steps, she started taking them two at a time.

Too late, Emery realized the girls' defection left her alone with Nate, something she really hadn't been since that heated embrace on the sofa of the other guest cabin. "I'll just set this under the tree," she said after an awkward pause.

He followed her into the great room and she was painfully aware of him. They both set the large boxes next to the Christmas tree, then to her secret relief, Nate moved to the fireplace to stir the coals and add another log.

While he was distracted, Emery enjoyed the holiday scene, from the Christmas tree to the new stockings she had made for Nate and the girls, which now hung proudly from the mantel.

It was a wonderful room, with its soaring vaulted ceilings, log walls and the unpretentious decor. This was exactly the mood she wanted to capture in the textiles for the Spencer Hotels property in Livingston, this completely natural sense of the American West. Warm, homey, completely right, here amid the beauty of their surroundings.

Nerves fluttered through her like sparks shooting up the chimney when Nate finished at the fireplace and joined her on the sofa. She was again aware of him, the spicy, masculine scent that clung to his skin, the tiny hint of an evening shadow.

"I'm more excited than they are for them to open the presents," he confessed, "and I haven't even seen the quilts."

She smiled, doing her best to ignore her reaction to him. "Well, I've seen more than enough of them and I'm still over the moon. I just hope they like them."

"They'll love them. It's a wonderful thing you've done."

His dark eyes lit up with warmth and something else and she couldn't seem to look away.

"Emery—" he began, but whatever he intended to say was lost when they heard footsteps rocketing down the stairs. Those girls instinctively knew when to make an entrance, she thought wryly.

"I win! I win!" Tallie exclaimed and she raced into the room in a navy blue plaid nightgown.

"Not by much," Claire retorted as she skidded to a stop beside her sister. She wore waffle-weave long john pajamas with Tweety Bird on the front.

"Is it time?" Tallie asked. "Can we open them now?"

Nate slanted a look to Emery that she couldn't quite read, then he looked back at his nieces and cleared his throat. "In a minute. Sit down first."

The girls sat on the opposite sofa, though Tallie looked poised to start bouncing off the walls any moment now.

"I owe you girls an apology."

"Why?" Claire asked.

"Well, I should have asked you before about the Christmas Eve traditions you used to do with your mom and dad. I should have known about the tamales. Is there anything else we haven't done today that you used to do with your mom and dad?"

The girls looked puzzled for a moment, their brows furrowed, and then Claire spoke quietly. "Well, every year Dad used to read us the Christmas story before we went to bed. Not the ''Twas The Night Before Christmas' one. The one in the Bible."

Nate looked a little taken aback as if he hadn't quite been expecting that answer, but he quickly recovered. "Sure. We can do that, if you know where I can find a Bible."

"I know," Tallie said. She moved to the bookshelf in the corner and after a moment of searching through the spines, she pulled down a white leather book with gilt edges.

"It was our mama's," Claire said, her voice low.

Emotions swelled in Emery's throat as Tallie clutched the book to her chest for a moment then finally handed it over to Nate, who had moved to the plump easy chair.

Nate held it for a long moment, his thumb tracing his sister's gold embossed name on the front. He made no move to open it.

"Luke, Chapter 2," she said, trying to be helpful.

His looked up, his mouth quirked into a half smile. "I might not be a particularly religious man, but I do know that much. Thanks, though."

He opened the Bible, leafed through the pages and finally found the right book and chapter. Much to her surprise, as soon as he started to read, both girls joined her on the larger sofa, Tallie snuggling against Emery's shoulder until she put her arm around her and pulled the girl close.

Oh, she was going to have a terrible time leaving this place. The lump in her throat expanded. She felt enfolded in the warm, accepting love of these girls and knew it would break her heart into a million tiny, jagged shards to leave them. Next Christmas and every other Christmas would be painful and empty when she compared them to this one that she had started out dreading so much.

She wouldn't think about that now. Why waste this perfect moment by borrowing tomorrow's pain?

Nate finished reading, his voice solemn as he read the last words. When he closed the book, they sat in silence for a long moment and then he looked up.

He seemed surprised to find them all snuggled together and his eyes glittered with a sudden intensity.

"That was nice," Tallie said solemnly. "It gives me a really happy feeling inside."

"Me, too," Emery said in perfect accord.

"I think this is the perfect moment to open your presents," he said, his voice barely above a whisper in keeping with the hushed reverence in the house.

The girls brightened with excitement, but they didn't rip into the presents in a mad rush, as Emery might have expected. Instead, they knelt carefully on the rug by the tree and began to gently peel away the wrapping paper.

Tallie finished first and Emery held her breath as the girl folded over the flaps on the cardboard box. She reached inside and pulled out the quilt, her pixie features twisted with confusion.

"It's a blanket."

"It's a quilt," Emery explained.

She unfolded it, her eyes wide. "It's pretty," she said, then looked at her sister. "You got one, too!"

Claire pulled hers out, her hands gentle, almost reverent, as she spread it across the rug.

"I love the star!"

"Mine has butterflies," Tallie said. "Can you see them, Uncle Nate?"

"I see them. Does any of the fabric look familiar?" Nate prompted.

Claire picked it up and traced the most prominent fabric of the star pattern, lavender with tiny, pale pink flowers. "Mama used to have a skirt like this." She gasped. "And this one looks like Dad's favorite pajama bottoms."

"Emery used material from the boxes of your mom's and dad's clothing to make the quilt."

The girls looked stunned. "You did?" Claire gasped.

"I thought maybe when you had your quilts wrapped around you, it might feel a little bit like you were getting big hugs from your mom and dad."

Claire's eyes softened and she immediately wrapped her quilt around her shoulders. "You're right. That's just what it feels like," she whispered, looking thrilled.

Tallie did the same, but suddenly her eyes filled with tears and she let out a ragged little whimper that turned into another and another until she was sobbing.

Nate went to her and pulled her onto his lap, quilt and all. "You don't have to use it if it's going to make you upset," he said, sounding somewhat panicked by her tears. "I'll put it away. Maybe in a few years you'll want it."

"Oh, sweetheart, I'm so sorry," Emery added, feeling wretched. "I thought it would make you happy."

"No!" Tallie burst out when Nate reached to take the quilt from her. She held on to it tightly, even as her shoulders trembled. "I didn't mean to cry," she wailed. "I'm sorry. But please don't take it. These are sad tears *and* happy tears. I really want to put it on my bed. If I sleep with it, I know I won't have any more nightmares."

"Oh, sweetheart." Nate held her close, his chin resting on her glossy dark hair.

Her heartbreaking sobs subsided after a moment and she wiped her eyes on Nate's shirt, but he didn't seem to mind.

"Can you read us something else, Uncle Nate?" Tallie asked.

"Like what?"

"Mom's favorite Christmas story was *The Polar Express*," Claire said. "Maybe that one."

Nate seemed relieved to have something concrete to do besides holding a distressed little girl. "All right. One more story and then bed, okay?"

The girls agreed. This time, both of them sat snuggled in their quilts beside him, leaving Emery alone. That was as it should be, she thought. They were creating their own traditions, making their own version of family.

"All right," he said when he finished the last page. "Now time for bed. Santa can't show up until you're both asleep."

Since the girls had been emphatic more than once to her that they knew the whole Santa story, Emery was surprised at their ready compliance. She supposed there was something about Christmas Eve that allowed even doubters to put aside their skepticism for one night and believe in a little magic.

"I'm super sleepy," Tallie claimed.

"Me, too," Claire said, stifling a yawn that certainly looked genuine.

"Up you go," Nate said. "I'll come tuck you in."

"Can Emery come, too?"

He sent a swift look in her direction and she saw uncertainty flash there. She was about to let him off the hook by telling the girls she needed to sleep and should be heading back to her cabin, but Nate surprised her by nodding.

"Sure," he said. "If she doesn't mind."

"I don't mind," she said.

She helped Claire gather her quilt and carry the trailing ends up the stairs while Nate did the same for Tallie.

A few moments later, both girls were settled in their beds, their comforters replaced by the brand-new quilts that seemed somehow to fit perfectly in their bedrooms, as if they had always been there.

Emery kissed Tallie's cheek, touched to see the girl's fingers tracing the different textured fabric of the butterflies dancing across the quilt. Ridged corduroy from a pair of her father's slacks, denim from a work shirt, a deep purple satin poly blend from one of Suzi's blouses.

All the hours of work and the aching muscles were a distant memory, lost in the joy of seeing both girls find comfort in her creations.

"Sleep well, sweetheart," Emery said.

"Merry Christmas, Emery." She was quiet for a moment, then smiled sleepily. "It's a night for angels, isn't it?"

Tears burned behind her eyes, but Emery smiled. "I think so, sweetheart. Sweet dreams."

Part of her had that same wild wish that she had never come to Hope Springs, never had the chance to fall in love with these grieving girls. But she couldn't regret it when they had taught her so many lessons.

When she and Nate returned downstairs, he seemed a little distant and distracted. Probably wishing she would just go home and leave him alone, she thought. She opened her mouth to tell him she needed to do just that but he surprised her once more.

"I have no right to ask you any more favors since you've already done so much," he began.

"But?"

He sighed. "But I could use help with one more thing, if I haven't presumed entirely too much."

"How can I help?"

"I've never done the whole Christmas Eve thing. Putting out the stockings and the presents under the tree and everything. I'm pretty sure I'll screw it up on my own and leave everything a big jumbled mess."

She found his request almost unbearably sweet. "Of course. Although since I...don't have children, I'm not the world's biggest expert in that particular arena, either."

"But you know what looks good. You did such a great job decorating the house and then wrapping everything so nicely, I hate to just throw all the gifts under the tree. The only problem is, we're going to have to wait a few moments until they're asleep."

"Why don't I stay here with the girls while they fall asleep and you can go down to the cabin for the gifts? By the time you bring them all back, the girls should be asleep."

"Brilliant idea." He smiled a little. "See how much I needed your help?"

He tossed another log on the fire while Emery sank onto the sofa gratefully as her stiff muscles reminded her of the day's exertions.

When she heard him leave a moment later, she leaned back against the sofa cushion, watching the Christmas tree lights twinkle against the dark window and sorting through the emotions of the evening.

She had been dreading Christmas so much this year, the first holiday without her mother, the anniversary of Gracie's death.

How could she ever have guessed this would turn out to be the most perfect ever? From sewing the quilts to making cookies with the girls to decorating the house. She had loved all of it.

She closed her eyes, but the lights still seemed to glisten behind her eyelids. She would only rest for a moment, she told herself as exhaustion crept over her.

Just until he returned...

Chapter 13

Nate carefully loaded the last box of gifts into the cargo space of the SUV, closed the hatch, then paused for a moment to gaze up at the night. This Christmas Eve was a cold one, with no cloud cover to hold in any warmth. The night was clear and beautiful, with a vast glitter of stars overhead.

He couldn't help thinking about his past few Christmas Eves in the desert. Two years ago his team had been in southern Iraq and last year he'd been in the frigid mountains of Afghanistan.

This one was much better than any in recent memory, he was forced to admit. Between the tamales and the miracle of the tiny foal and that very tender moment when the girls opened their quilts, he felt more connected to life and the future than he had in a long, long time.

For the first time since he came back to Idaho, he was feeling good about what might come next. A year from now, he would be much more prepared for the holidays and everything the girls might expect from them.

The only problem was, this year was going to be a hard act to follow, especially without Emery.

The thought of her leaving seemed to take a lot of luster from the stars overhead. He pushed it away, just as he used to make himself ignore the frustrations and fears of the battlefield so he could focus on what needed to be done.

There would be time to miss Emery later. Right now, he needed to take care of business, which meant hauling the girls' Christmas booty up to the house.

When he drove back to the house, he let himself in the front door quietly, with a careful look up the stairs to make sure the girls weren't peeking down from the landing.

"So do you think the coast is clear yet?" Nate whispered as he entered the great room.

When no one answered, he was grimly aware of a sharp clutch of panic. But reason intruded. She couldn't have left already, not when he had asked for her help. That wasn't in her nature. His gaze swept the room and he exhaled with relief when he saw her stretched out on the same sofa she had slept on the night of the storm. She lay on her side, her blond hair drifting over her shoulders and her folded hands tucked under her cheek like a child's.

She was serenely lovely in sleep, her darker lashes fanning her cheekbones and those classical features relaxed. He wanted to push away a strand of hair from her cheek, but decided not to wake her.

How late into the night had she worked to finish the quilts for the girls? When he thought of her hunched over a sewing machine, pouring such care and compassion into the work for two girls she barely knew, he could hardly breathe around the ache in his chest.

Something soft and tender swelled inside him as he watched her sleep and for one crazy moment, he wanted to jerk her off the couch and send her away.

That panic returned a thousandfold, especially when he realized he would rather take on a hundred enemy fighters on his own from a vulnerable position in a box canyon than have to face these fragile, terrifying emotions that shimmered through him.

She gave a tiny little sigh and snuggled deeper into the cushions. Though he was wary about even coming closer to her, he lifted one of the knit throws from the other sofa and spread it over her, tucking in the sides to keep out the draft.

In her sleep, the corners of her mouth tilted up slightly, but she didn't open her eyes.

He couldn't stand here all night, watching her sleep. Beyond the vaguely creepy, covert surveillance factor, it was Christmas Eve and he still had parental responsibilities.

He forced himself to move away from her and with all the stealth in his commando bag of tricks, he carefully climbed the stairs, avoiding any creaky steps. What would the other members of his team think if they knew he was using all his mad Ranger skills to check on a couple of girls who should be sleeping?

Did he care? Not really. The realization took him by surprise and he paused outside Tallie's room to let it soak in.

This might not be how he anticipated his life turning out. Fate could sometimes be a heartless bitch. Suzi and John certainly never expected to die in a plane crash before their youngest kid was even double digits. Emery never expected to lose her baby on Christmas Eve at the same time her bastard of a husband dumped all over her.

Life happened. Coming home to Idaho and becoming an instant father figure to two girls who needed him might not have been in the plan, but it wasn't bad, either. He needed to man up and stop acting like some kind of martyr who had sacrificed everything he wanted to take care of his sister's kids.

He was getting plenty back from the deal. He had the ranch and the girls and neighbors who cared about them, whether he wanted them to or not.

Not a bad trade at all.

And Emery. Where did she fit in?

He pushed that puzzle aside again while he checked Claire first and then Tallie. Unless they were putting on award-winning performances, both girls appeared sound asleep. He even called their names softly, but neither of them so much as stirred.

Satisfied they were genuinely asleep, he returned downstairs for the work ahead to find that Emery hadn't moved on the couch, either.

Apparently he was on his own for the whole Santa Claus thing.

Though he tried to be as quiet as possible, something must have awakened her. When he returned with the last armload of gifts from the SUV, he found her sitting up on the sofa, doing the finger-swipe thing over her eyes.

"Hey," she said, her voice low and rough from sleep. "Sorry. I didn't mean to conk out on you."

"No problem. If you're too tired for more holiday fun, don't worry about it. I can give you a lift back to your cabin and wrap things up here on my own."

"I'm fine." She yawned as she stood up. "Really, I'm fine. A little nap was all I needed and now I've got my second wind."

He wasn't convinced, but she proved her words by setting to work immediately.

She took the girls' stockings down from the mantel and filled them first and then began arranging the gifts under the tree.

Finally, she stepped back with a satisfied sigh. "It's perfect. Don't you think?"

"Absolutely," he answered, wondering if she sensed he was looking only at her, not at the room.

"The girls are going to have a wonderful Christmas morning. I only wish I could see their faces."

"Why can't you?"

Surprise and then discomfort flitted across her features. "I'm sorry. That wasn't a hint. I don't belong there, Nate. You've been kind enough to include me in some of your holiday celebrations, mostly because the girls insisted, but Christmas morning should be just for you and the girls. This is your chance to start some new traditions of your own with them."

He wanted to argue, but some part of him knew she was right. She would be gone in a few days, as difficult as that was for him to face. He and Tallie and Claire had to make their own way.

"Thank you, though, for letting me have a small part in your holiday," she said, her voice subdued. "If you want the truth, I've been dreading Christmas. Especially tonight. Christmas Eve, the anniversary of...

the accident. This morning I was thinking I just wanted to sleep the day away and wake up about noon tomorrow. But I'm so glad I didn't. Tonight with the girls and with…with you has been wonderful. I'll never forget it."

He gazed at her in the multicolored light from the Christmas tree. Her sweep of blond hair reflected sparkles of red and gold and purple. All those tender emotions he had fought so hard against before returned stronger than ever and he couldn't help himself. He stepped forward and lowered his mouth to hers.

She sighed his name as he kissed her and her arms slid around his neck.

Now. *Now* the night felt perfect. Their kiss was slow and easy, like sinking into a soft bed at the end of a hard day.

Her mouth made him crazy. He thought he could spend forever just exploring every inch of those lips. He pulled her closer while the fire hummed and sparked behind them.

He wanted Emery Kendall more than any Christmas present he had ever wanted in his life put together. More than the official NFL leather football he'd begged and begged for when he was nine, more than the Element Fiberlight skateboard with the Independent trucks and the Bones wheels, more than the three-hundred-dollar twenty-year-old junker pickup truck he had bought himself for Christmas when he was seventeen.

He only wanted Emery.

But like the Ford Mustang he had *really* wanted that long-ago Christmas instead of a beat-up pickup truck, he suddenly realized he couldn't have this, couldn't have her.

What did he have to offer a woman like Emery Kendall except a faltering ranch and a couple of troubled, grieving little girls?

She was an elegant, sophisticated, country-club type with her own design company, while he had barely graduated high school and just walked away from the only profession he had ever been good at.

Oh, she was attracted to him. A man could sense when a woman shivered at his touch, when she leaned into his kiss for more.

He could probably seduce her right here, right now—or better yet, take her up to his bedroom to spend Christmas Eve in her arms.

But in the morning, he didn't doubt they would both regret it. She was leaving in a few days, returning to her life in Virginia, and he couldn't afford to let this crazy tenderness inside him lead him to do or say something stupid that he couldn't take back.

He eased away from her, though it was just about the toughest thing he had ever had to do, and forced himself to rise from the sofa.

"You need some sleep. It's late and you have to be exhausted."

She blinked, her eyes a little dazed. "Not really."

He was fiercely tempted to take up the soft invitation in her eyes, but he couldn't do that to either of them.

"You will be if you don't get some sleep. Come on. I'll walk you back to your cabin."

For a moment, she looked as disoriented as if he had just hauled her over his shoulder, packed her outside and tossed her off the porch into the snow. But after a moment she nodded slowly, her expression veiled. "You're right. It's been a big day."

She said nothing more while she pulled her coat and scarf out of the closet and slipped them on.

"I can drive you if you're too cold to walk."

After a swift look, she focused again on knotting her scarf. "I'm fine walking. You don't need to come with me."

In answer, he only put on his coat and held the door open for her. The temperature had dropped a few more degrees in the short time since he had brought the presents into the house, but he barely felt the cold. He was aroused and frustrated and wondering if he had just made one of the biggest mistakes of his life.

They walked the short distance to her cabin, their boots crunching in the snow and their breath clouding out ahead of them.

"Thank you again for all your help," he said when they reached her cabin door.

She smiled, but it didn't quite reach her eyes. "You're welcome. I hope you and the girls have a wonderful day tomorrow."

"Today, you mean. It's past midnight. Merry Christmas."

She smiled a little, her gloved hands gripping the doorknob. "Same to you."

He wanted to kiss her again. To press her back against that door and then to push them both through it and shut out the world and all the differences between them. Instead, he forced himself to smile as if his heart wasn't dented and sore.

"Good night," he said, then turned and headed back through the snow toward the house.

She had to leave. After a sleepless night, Emery came to the bleak conclusion that staying at Hope Springs was only postponing her inevitable pain.

She rolled onto her back, gazing up at the now-familiar log beams overhead. That stunning, tender kiss the night before had only reinforced what she had begun to suspect days ago.

She was in love with Nate.

This wasn't merely infatuation or sexual attraction, though there was plenty of that zinging between them.

This was the real thing.

She was in love with Nate Cavazos, army Ranger, reluctant rancher, brand-new parent. She loved his strength and his awkward gentleness with his nieces and the deep core of honor and integrity that brought him back to his hometown to repay his debt to his sister by raising her children.

She was crazy about the man.

How could she have been so very foolish? Nate wasn't interested in a relationship. If he were, he wouldn't have pushed her away last night when it had to have been obvious to him how very much she wanted to stay.

He had been pushing her away since she arrived. She could see that now. If he'd had his way, he would have barred the proverbial gate to her the very first night she showed up in the storm.

Maybe it would have been better all the way around if she had just turned around that night and headed for Jackson, as he had tried to convince her to do. At least then she could have spared herself the pain she knew waited for her back in her real life.

No. She couldn't regret it. Even though she feared her heart might never recover from this week in eastern Idaho, that part of it would always remain here, she couldn't be sorry. The time with Tallie and Claire had been priceless and she had to hope that her efforts might have helped ease their grief in some small way.

She sat up, looking out the window at the brilliant sunshine glistening off the snow. She needed to go now. Why postpone the inevitable? Every moment she spent here would make her leaving all that much more difficult. She didn't have a flight for two more days, but she would change her plans and find an earlier one.

Christmas Day itself was one of the slowest air travel days of the year. She remembered reading that somewhere.

As she slid from the bed, grabbed her toiletries and headed for the shower, she had to wonder just how far she would have to go next year to outrun the memories of her holiday here at Hope Springs.

Antarctica, maybe?

Or perhaps somewhere warm, like sub-Saharan Africa.

No matter where she fled, she had a feeling she was doomed for next year and each December 25 afterward to compare every Christmas to this one.

"Come on, Uncle Nate! The French toast is going to be cold by the time we get there."

Nate raised an eyebrow at Claire's bossy tone, but decided not to get on her case about it. The girl ought to think about a career as a drill sergeant. His own grizzled hardcase of a sergeant at basic training hadn't ridden him half as hard.

"I'm coming. Hold your horses." He paused and managed a smile. "Oh, yeah. I'm the one with the horses."

Both girls giggled at his lame joke, which he had to admit was one of the best things about being their guardian. They laughed even when he was being silly or stupid.

"I hope Emery likes it," Tallie said, gnawing her lip as she looked at the flat package he carried, covered in rather juvenile wrapping paper with grinning snowmen and penguins on it.

"I'm sure she will," he said.

The girls seemed to have had a good Christmas. Though they had all experienced moments of poignancy, even melancholy, about celebrating the holiday without John and Suzi, they had been excited about their gifts. Even now, they each wore one of the new sweaters Emery had picked out for them.

But from the moment they unwrapped the last present, their dark heads had been close together as they cooked up some scheme while he put together breakfast. They finally revealed to him as they ate their French toast that they had a present for Emery and could they take it to her, along with some breakfast?

He hadn't been able to come up with a good reason to refuse, so here they were. He carried the gift—a watercolor of the ranch, complete with horses in the foreground and the jagged mountains in the back.

They had given one very similar to him, along with a sweater they said Joanie had helped them pick out before she left and a box of his favorite kind of cherry chocolates.

Emery would probably love the picture, but he wasn't at all sure he wanted to be here. He didn't need a repeat appearance of all those terrifying emotions churning through his gut. After their awkward parting the night before, he imagined Emery wouldn't exactly be thrilled to see him, either.

"I'm going to knock," Tallie declared, racing ahead of them to scamper up the porch steps.

She answered the door a moment later and the slightly tousled woman who had awakened on his great room sofa last night was nowhere in evidence this morning. Now she looked sleek and elegant in gray wool slacks and a red sweater with her hair pulled back in that complicated twist thing and perfectly coordinating jewelry.

She looked as if she were preparing for a luncheon at some fancy club. Who dressed up like that just to spend Christmas Day alone?

Her gaze found him and something intense and unreadable flashed in her blue eyes for just a moment before she turned to the girls with a bright smile.

"Good morning! Merry Christmas to both of you. I was hoping I would see you today. How was your Christmas?"

"Cool," Tallie exclaimed. "We got a *ton* of clothes and earrings and a bunch of books. And I got a new bike with eighteen speeds since my old one is a little kid's bike."

"I got an iPod," Claire said. "Want to see?"

"Of course. Come in."

"We brought you breakfast," Claire announced. "It's French toast. We helped Uncle Nate make it from our mom's recipe and it's pretty good."

"I had four pieces," Tallie confided.

"Is that right?" Emery smiled faintly.

Claire held out the parcel in her arms. "We brought you a present."

Astonishment flickered in those eyes and then a soft

delight that somehow made all those crazy feelings start zinging around inside him again.

"You did?"

Tallie nodded. "We started it even before you gave us the quilts. But then we really wanted to give you something."

"How wonderful!"

Nate held it out for her and after an awkward pause, she reached for it. Their fingers brushed as she took the gift and it was all he could do not to yank her against him. Instead, he leaned a hip against the kitchen table as he watched her take the gift and begin to carefully unwrap it.

When she had pushed the last bit of paper aside, she turned it over and gazed for a long moment at the painting without saying anything.

Her reaction was everything the girls might have wished. Her eyes filled with tears and she gave a shaky-looking smile. "Oh, it's beautiful. Absolutely wonderful."

"We painted it together," Tallie said proudly. "Claire did the horses and the house and I did the mountains. I'm really good at mountains. And this morning after we had breakfast, Uncle Nate found a frame for us in the attic and helped us put it in it."

"This is the perfect gift for me to remember my time here when I go home. Thank you so much."

There was a strange note of finality in her voice and he wondered if either of the girls noticed. They didn't look very thrilled at the reminder that Emery's visit was temporary, but they didn't say anything, especially after she reached out and pulled them both into a hug.

"The picture will be priceless to me because you made it."

"There's a surprise in it," Tallie announced in a voice that, for her, sounded almost shy. "Can you see it?"

Emery studied the painting, her head tilted to the side as if she were standing in some fancy froufrou art gallery. She studied it for a long moment and then to Nate's surprise, her eyes filled up with tears.

"Oh, sweetheart," she murmured and pulled Tallie into a big hug.

Nate frowned. He hadn't seen anything unusual when he'd helped the girls frame it and now he craned his neck to see what all the fuss was about, to no avail.

"What is it?"

Emery pointed to a vee in Tallie's mountain peaks and he finally saw it, a small figure camouflaged by a couple of dark green pine trees. He looked closer and realized the figure had wings and a little gold-crayon halo.

Tallie, Little Ms. Doubter who wouldn't even make an angel sugar cookie out of her defiance and anger, had drawn a tiny guardian angel looking over the ranch.

A lump swelled in his throat and he cleared it a couple of times before he spoke. Even then, his voice sounded a little on the ragged side. "Nice," he said.

Emery might not have wings or a halo, but she had been an angel to them, he realized. She had helped them through what could have been a very emotionally charged time, had given them all faith that things would get better.

He owed her more than he could ever repay.

"I have the perfect place in my townhouse to put it, right above my desk. That way I can look at it every day and remember our wonderful Christmas together," she said.

He hated thinking about her leaving. About how empty the ranch would feel without her.

"We're going to go see Noël," Claire said. "Would you like to come with us?"

Emery was clearly not dressed for traipsing through the barn, but she nodded. "I'd love it. Let me grab my coat."

She moved to the hanger by the door and suddenly Nate had a clear view through her bedroom door...to the suitcase open on the bed and the case holding her sewing machine that sat beside it.

She was leaving. Not in a few days, but now, today. He suddenly realized what had seemed off to him in her cabin. All the personal little touches she had brought to her living space these past few days were nowhere in evidence, all packed away for her return to Virginia.

Panic clawed at him, raw and intense, and for a long moment, he couldn't think what to do, what to say.

He could say nothing in front of the girls, so he blurted out the first thing that came to his head.

"You girls go on ahead," Nate said. "We'll be along in a minute, okay? I need to talk to Emery."

Tallie and Claire exchanged curious glances, but shrugged. "Okay," Claire said. "Can we give Annabelle some sugar?"

"Sure thing," he said. "But not too much."

They left in a clatter of pink boots and Nate closed the door behind them, then turned to face Emery, who was watching him with a hint of apprehension on her features.

"You're leaving."

The blunt words hung in the air between them, harsh and unadorned.

"Yes." She lifted her chin.

"I thought you weren't flying out for a few more days."

"I decided to see if I can catch an earlier flight."

Which was stronger? he wondered. The hurt or the regret or that panic that still squawked through him like static on a badly tuned radio?

"Why? What's the big rush?"

She didn't meet his gaze as she busied herself tying her scarf, something she did when she needed to keep her hands busy, he realized. "I have work waiting for me back in Warrenton. I finished several projects while I was here, but everything is piling up."

Bull, he wanted to say. *You're running away.*

But why shouldn't she? He had given her no indication she should stay.

"Is that the only reason you're taking off?"

She flashed him a quick look, then reached to pick up a pile of magazines from the coffee table.

"What other reason would I have?"

He said nothing, consumed by the grim knowledge that everything would be colorless and bleak when she left.

"Don't…" *Go* he almost said, but the words tangled in his throat.

"Don't what?" she asked, an arrested look in her eyes.

He couldn't beg her to stay, even as the words tangled together in his throat. All those differences still remained between them, a deep, wide chasm he didn't have the first idea how to cross.

"Don't forget these things."

He picked up a stack of books from the end table and handed them out to her, then froze, his attention arrested by the top item. It wasn't a book, he saw now. It was a photograph in a dated wood frame. He pulled the picture off the stack and held it up so he could examine it more closely.

"What the hell is this?"

"Nothing. Just an old photograph." She reached for it, but he held it just out of her reach.

The French toast he'd eaten for Christmas breakfast with the girls seemed to have suddenly congealed into a hard, greasy knot in his gut. "Why do you have a picture of Hank Dalton? And who's the woman?"

He looked closer at the picture and he knew. Suddenly he knew. She looked very much like Emery, with the same high cheekbones and classical features, though her clothes and hairstyle were several decades out of date, and the stunning truth slammed into him like a runaway bull.

"This woman is your mother, isn't she?"

She nodded shortly, looking vaguely sick herself.

"Hank Dalton is your father. The married man you were talking about."

Chapter 14

He couldn't take it in. The woman he had come to... His mind shied away from the word he wanted to use and replaced it in his head. The woman he had come to *care about* shared blood with the man he despised.

"Apparently." Though her features looked distressed, she spoke calmly. "I don't have any real proof, but that's what my mother said and she would have no reason to lie. She was in Jackson Hole on a tour with some girl-friends and met him at a bar. He swept her off her feet. Wined and dined her for a week, never mentioning his wife or his three sons who lived just on the other side of the mountains."

Three sons. Wade, Jake and Seth Dalton were her half brothers.

Suddenly everything made a twisted kind of sense. Her tension every time Wade Dalton came around, her strange reaction to Wade *and* Jake at the McRavens' party.

She'd come here to meet them. That was the reason she had picked Hope Springs to spend Christmas, because of its proximity to the Cold Creek Land & Cattle Company.

An accident of geography. Not fate, not destiny. He was an idiot not to have figured it all out.

"Why didn't you tell me?" His voice sounded harsh, strangled.

Tiny lines furrowed between her eyebrows. "I did. The other night I told you I only recently found out my mother was pregnant with me several months before she married Stephen Kendall."

"You didn't tell me you were a damn Dalton."

She swayed a little and her features looked pale suddenly above the bright red of her scarf. "I would appreciate it if you would keep this information to yourself," she said after a moment. "I've decided nothing will be gained by disrupting the lives of the Daltons. They don't need to know their father was unfaithful to their mother."

He gave a harsh laugh at that, then couldn't contain another and another. He sounded like a damn hyena, but he couldn't seem to stop. The whole town knew Hank Dalton was a lying, cheating son of a bitch. His sons had to know that better than anyone.

"I don't think it's going to come as much of a shock to anybody," he finally said. "You remember me telling you about the neighboring rancher my mother had an affair with? The man who ruined her life and cheated her out of land and money?"

She stared at him and her blue eyes—Dalton eyes, he realized now—looked huge in her pale features.

"Yep. Dear old dad. Your mother wasn't the first or the last and neither was mine."

She looked stricken, suddenly, and he didn't miss the way her hands trembled as she reached to take the photograph he finally handed out to her.

He was sorry suddenly that he had been so harsh. It wasn't her fault her father was Hank Dalton, the man he hated above all others.

"I guess it's a good thing I'm leaving today, then," she murmured.

"Yeah."

"Will you… Can you tell the girls I changed my mind about seeing Noël? Tell them I wasn't feeling good or something. It's not really a lie."

"You're not going to tell them goodbye yourself before you leave?"

She looked as if she would rather just slip away, but she finally nodded. "I'll find you all before I go."

He nodded and opened the door, wondering when he had ever felt so completely wrecked.

"Where's Emery?" Tallie immediately asked when he reached the barn a few moments later without her.

He offered the half-truth she had given him. "She wasn't feeling well. But I'm sure you'll see her later."

They both look disappointed and he screwed his eyes shut. They were going to be devastated when she left. Their whole Christmas would be ruined.

This was exactly what he had feared, the very reason he had wanted to keep her from them. Now they were going to have to suffer one more loss in their lives, a woman they had both come to love.

A woman they had *all* come to love.

He gazed at the tiny foal in the hay nuzzling up to

her mother, their little Christmas miracle. The scene blurred in front of him and he blinked hard as the truth washed over him like a sandstorm.

He was in love with Emery.

Hopelessly, fiercely, irrevocably.

He drew in a ragged breath as all those well-reasoned arguments he'd been full of the night before crowded through his head. She was smart and sophisticated and beautiful. Nothing had changed. He still had nothing to offer her but a struggling ranch and a couple of orphaned girls who loved her.

So she was Hank Dalton's daughter. He couldn't blame her for her parentage anymore than he had any right to place the blame for their father's actions on the man's sons. Lord knows, his own mother wouldn't have exactly taken any prizes in the parenting department.

Tallie slipped a hand through his and he looked down to find her watching him with concern in her dark eyes.

"Are you okay, Uncle Nate?"

Far from it. He wanted to cry, for the first time since he was ten years old at his father's funeral.

"Yeah," he said, his voice gruff.

"I always get a little sad on Christmas day," Tallie confided in him.

"Why's that?"

"Because it's all almost over and we have to get back to real life. But don't worry, we can have an even better Christmas next year. We'll make tamales again and decorate the Christmas tree and maybe we'll even have two foals then."

He gazed at the motes of dust floating in a sunbeam like gold flakes from a glittery garland, a lump in his throat. Tallie was wrong. Next year wouldn't be better.

Without Emery, nothing would be. The thought of life on the ranch without her smiles and her gentleness and her kisses stretched out ahead of him, long and empty and miserable.

He straightened from the pen railing, his pulse pounding and determination uncoiling in his gut.

He couldn't let her go. At least not without trying to convince her to stay.

She refused to cry.

Though the emotions swelled up inside her in a hot, angry rush, Emery choked them all back, focusing only on gathering up the last of her belongings and stuffing them into the suitcase. She didn't care that she was wrinkling everything as she wadded and shoved and crammed.

She had to get out of here. Everywhere she looked were memories. Waking up the night of the blizzard to find Nate at her door. The tree where she and the girls had snipped evergreen boughs to decorate the house. The other cabin she could see through the window, where she had shared secrets and wrapped presents and kissed him until she couldn't hold two thoughts together.

And the girls. How was she ever going to get through saying goodbye to the girls? Just the thought of it had her fighting down a sob. She could hold it together for a few more moments, she told herself. She would be warm and casual with them and promise she would e-mail them after she returned to Warrenton.

Already her arms felt achy and empty, but she managed to hold on to her emotions as she began loading up the rented SUV. She left the food she'd purchased and the boxes of their parents' clothing she hadn't used in the quilts, but took everything else that belonged to her.

Finally the only thing she had left to load into the SUV was her largest suitcase. After one final sweep of the cabin, she rolled it out to the porch then bumped it down the steps. At the SUV, she reached to lift it with both hands, but it seemed as heavy as her heart. She wrestled it for a moment, pouring every ounce of her remaining strength into getting it off the snow-packed ground.

"Let me get that for you."

She froze at Nate's voice and prayed that the tears burning behind her eyes would just hang on for a few more moments.

"I've got it," she said stiffly.

"Do you?"

In that moment as he stood watching her trying to lift the heavy suitcase with that blasted unreadable expression, she hated him more than she had ever hated anyone or anything.

She hated him almost as much as she loved him.

"Go away, Nate. I can handle this."

He ignored her and reached for the suitcase with one hand. But instead of placing it in the cargo area of the SUV, he lifted it back up the steps and set it on the porch.

"Hey! What are you doing? I need that!" she exclaimed, following after him.

"I'll load it in a minute."

He made no move to explain himself, only stood on the porch looking down at her.

"Where are the girls?" she asked. Better that she could get this all out of the way now instead of having to drag out the goodbyes.

"They're still busy with Noël."

She was beginning to squirm under the intensity of that look, especially when he didn't say anything else. Could he see the desolation ripping through her when she thought about driving under the Hope Springs arch and leaving this place forever?

"If you will load up my suitcase," she finally said, hating that he was forcing her to ask, "I'll be on my way, out of your hair. You won't have to tolerate one of the terrible Daltons on your ranch another moment."

"Em."

She had been doing her best to avoid his gaze, but at the single word, she couldn't help it. She looked up and caught her breath at the expression in his eyes, dark and almost tortured.

"Don't," he murmured. Just that, nothing else.

Her heart gave one hard thump, then another and another. "Don't what?"

"Don't go. The girls want you to stay for Christmas dinner. I already put a ham in."

She curled her gloved hands into fists, furious suddenly that he was putting her through this. She couldn't keep up with him. One moment he looked at her with disgust, the next with that heat in his eyes she was helpless to resist.

"This is hard enough. Can't you see that? Please just give me my suitcase so I can go." She hated the small, distressed note in her voice, but couldn't seem to clear it away.

"Is that what you want?"

"You hate me because my father was Hank Dalton. I can understand that."

He shook his head. "I don't hate you. How could I?"

Finally, after far too much effort trying to contain them, one of the tears slipped through her defenses. In horror, she felt it slide down the side of her nose and she wiped at it with a violent gesture.

She heard Nate give a muffled groan and then an instant later, before she could even take a breath, he crossed the space between them and wrenched her into his arms.

"I don't hate you, Em," he repeated with stunning ferocity. "Far, far from it."

While she was still reeling from that, he kissed her with a softness and a sweetness that belied the intensity of his words and she didn't know what to do, what to say. She could only hold tight to his sweater with all her strength, afraid her knees would give out if she dared let go.

"Don't leave, Em. Stay, please. I'm sorry about earlier. About the way I acted. I was surprised, that's all. Will you stay? The girls would love it if you'd stay for Christmas."

A fledgling hope began to unfurl its tiny wings inside her, but she was afraid to give it room to soar yet. She could feel Nate's heartbeat under her fingertips and as she met his gaze again, she caught her breath at the emotions there.

"Wh-what about you?"

He was silent for a long moment, and then he smiled, something he did entirely too rarely. "I would love it if you'd stay much, much longer."

A wary sort of joy burst through her, but she was afraid to believe, after the misery of the past night and then this morning, and despite her best efforts to contain them, she could feel another tear slip through.

At the sight of it, Nate lifted his thumb and wiped it away and then he cupped her face in both hands.

"This is harder for me than anything I ever had to do in the army, and I've had to do some pretty tough things. But I'm going to come right out and say it. I'm in love with you, Em."

She stared, certain she must not have heard him right. "You're...what?"

"I think I fell hard for you the moment you walked in from the storm with your perky little hats and your complicated scarves and all the secrets in those Dalton eyes."

He kissed her again, his mouth warm in the cold Christmas air, and finally, finally, she let that hope begin to spread its wings.

"I know things are a mess here," he said. "But they're getting better, Em. I promise. I'm learning my way and figuring it all out. I don't have much to offer you, except a couple of girls who adore you and need you and a man who's crazy in love with you."

He paused, his gaze locked on hers. "The one thing I know for sure is that everything seems easier—better—when you're here, and it will kill me if you walk away. Please don't go."

In all her life, no one had ever said anything like that to her, had made her feel so very much wanted and needed. *This* was what she had been looking for when she came to Pine Gulch, she realized. Not her birth father's family. But this place.

This man.

This was good. It was right. It was every Christmas joy she had ever dreamed about magnified a million times.

She drew in a shuddering breath and then another one and then she flung her arms tightly around his neck and kissed him, laughing and crying at the same time, pouring everything she never thought she would have the chance to say into the embrace.

He made a rough, jubilant sort of sound and returned the kiss. When he pulled away several moments later, his eyes were dazed.

"I love you. Oh, Nate. I've been so miserable. It was devastating me to leave. I kept thinking this is the only place in my entire life that I've ever truly felt I belonged."

With that sexy groaning sound, he kissed her again, pushing her back into the cabin where it was a little warmer. And soon she was *much* warmer as he pulled her against his hard strength and deepened the kiss, his mouth hot and hungry on hers.

"Ewww."

Those girls and their impeccable timing again. Nate whispered an oath at the sound of Tallie's disgusted exclamation, but Emery only laughed against his mouth. She turned to find both girls standing in the doorway. Tallie's nose wrinkled at their embrace, but Claire's attention was fixed on the suitcase, her expression dark and troubled.

"You're leaving," she said in a betrayed sort of tone.

Emery opened her mouth to answer, but Nate beat her to it.

"She was going to. But I talked her out of it," he assured her niece. She looked as if she didn't believe him for a moment, then she tilted her head, taking in their embrace with first surprise and then a cautious hope.

"Is that true?" she demanded of Emery. "Are you staying?"

"I thought I would stick around for a while. Do you mind very much?"

Tallie squealed her approval and rushed to wrap her arms around both of them, but Claire still held back.

"How long is a while?" she asked.

Emery met Nate's gaze and smiled then turned back to his oldest niece. "I don't know. If it's okay with you all, I was thinking maybe forever."

Claire let out a small relieved laugh then joined them all in the embrace, and this time, as she was wrapped in the arms of their love, Emery didn't bother to hold back her tears.

Later that night when the girls were finally in bed after an exhausting day of board games, horseback rides and happiness, Nate sat on the couch in the great room with the Christmas tree lights sparkling and a fire in the grate and the woman he loved in his arms.

All day, he hadn't been able to stop touching her, to make sure she was real and that she was really his. Now, finally, she was in his arms and he felt truly at peace for the first time since he was ten years old.

"You're going to have to tell them, you know. Your brothers."

She lifted her head from his chest to stare at him and he wanted to smack his head with his open palm for bringing up the damn Daltons, when what he really wanted to do was continue making out on the couch.

"What about Marjorie?" she asked. "I don't want to hurt her."

He gave a rueful laugh. "I think that woman is long

past being hurt by anything Hank Dalton might have done twenty-seven years ago. She's a tough old bird. If you want my opinion, I think she'll be thrilled to find you and so will her boys. They're going to welcome you into their family quicker than a cricket in the chicken yard."

He thought of it, having the Daltons for brothers-in-law. Not that he was jumping his horses too early here, but he already knew what he wanted—this woman in his arms forever. He was willing to take her any way he could get her, even if that meant having three interfering older half brothers with the package.

He framed her face in his hands, still not quite believing that he had his own Christmas angel right here beside him. "The Daltons will love you almost as much as I do," he said. "How can they not?"

She gave him one of those soft, tender smiles that never failed to take his breath away and then she kissed him back.

Nate thought about life at the ranch before she came, how he and the girls had just been going through the motions, trying to make it from one day to the next. She had done the impossible. With her smile and her quilts and her sugar cookies, she had brought joy and laughter back into their lives.

He held her in his arms as the fire burned low in the grate and the lights of the Christmas tree flickered in the window.

Once more, there was hope at Hope Springs.

* * * * *

YOU HAVE JUST READ A
HARLEQUIN®
SPECIAL EDITION
BOOK.

Discover more heartfelt tales of **family, friendship** and **love** from the Harlequin Special Edition series. Be sure to look for all six Harlequin® Special Edition books every month.

◆ **HARLEQUIN**®

SPECIAL EDITION

HALOHSE1014R

HARLEQUIN®

SPECIAL EDITION

Life, Love and Family

Use this coupon to save

$1.00

on the purchase of any
Harlequin® Special Edition book.

Available wherever books are sold, including
most bookstores, supermarkets, drugstores
and discount stores.

Save $1.00

on the purchase of any Harlequin® Special Edition book.

Coupon valid until February 18, 2015. Redeemable at participating retail outlets
in the U.S. and Canada only. Limit one coupon per customer.

52612129

5 65373 00076 2   (8100)0 11997

Canadian Retailers: Harlequin Enterprises Limited will pay the face value of this coupon plus 10.25¢ if submitted by customer for this product only. Any other use constitutes fraud. Coupon is nonassignable. Void if taxed, prohibited or restricted by law. Consumer must pay any government taxes. Void if copied. Millennium1 Promotional Services ("M1P") customers submit coupons and proof of sales to Harlequin Enterprises Limited, P.O. Box 3000, Saint John, NB E2L 4L3, Canada. Non-M1P retailer—for reimbursement submit coupons and proof of sales directly to Harlequin Enterprises Limited, Retail Marketing Department, 225 Duncan Mill Rd., Don Mills, Ontario M3B 3K9, Canada.

U.S. Retailers: Harlequin Enterprises Limited will pay the face value of this coupon plus 8¢ if submitted by customer for this product only. Any other use constitutes fraud. Coupon is nonassignable. Void if taxed, prohibited or restricted by law. Consumer must pay any government taxes. Void if copied. For reimbursement submit coupons and proof of sales directly to Harlequin Enterprises Limited, P.O. Box 880478, El Paso, TX 88588-0478, U.S.A. Cash value 1/100 cents.

® and TM are trademarks owned and used by the trademark owner and/or its licensee.
© 2014 Harlequin Enterprises Limited

NYTCOUP1214

H HARLEQUIN®

SPECIAL EDITION

Life, Love and Family

New York Times bestselling author
Rachel Lee
brings you the final chapter of
Montana Mavericks: 20 Years in the Saddle!

Don't Miss
A VERY MAVERICK CHRISTMAS

Available now wherever books and ebooks are sold!

Heartfelt tales of **family, friendship** and
love from Harlequin® Special Edition

www.Harlequin.com

HSE65856-2

Jensen Fortune Chesterfield is only in Horseback Hollow, Texas, to see his new niece...not get lassoed by a cowgirl! Amber Rogers isn't the kind of woman Jensen ever imagined falling for. But, as Amber's warm heart and outgoing ways melt his heart, the handsome aristocrat begins to wonder if he might find true love on the range after all...

***

"What...was...that...kiss?" She stopped, her words coming out in raspy little gasps.

"...all about?" he finished for her.

She merely nodded.

"I don't know. It just seemed like an easier thing to do than to talk about it."

Maybe so, but being with Jensen was still pretty clandestine, what with meeting in the shadows, under the cloak of darkness.

The British Royal and the Cowgirl. They might be attracted to each other—and she might be good enough for him to entertain the idea of a few kisses in private or even a brief, heated affair. And maybe she ought to consider the same thing for herself, too.

But it would never last. Especially if the press—or the town gossips—got wind of it.

So she shook it all off—the secretive nature of it all, as well as the sparks and the chemistry, and opened the passenger door. "Good night, Jensen."

"What about dinner?" he asked. "I still owe you, remember?"

Yep, she remembered. Trouble was, she was afraid if she got in any deeper with him, there'd be a lot she'd have a hard time forgetting.

"We'll talk about it later," she said.

"Tomorrow?"

"Sure. Why not?"

"I may have to take my brother and sister to the airport, although I'm not sure when. I'll have to find out. Maybe we can set something up after I get home."

"Maybe so." She wasn't going to count on it, though. Especially when she had the feeling he wouldn't want to be seen out in public with her—where the newshounds or local gossips might spot them.

But as she headed for her car, she wondered if, when he set his mind on something, he might be as persistent as those pesky reporters he tried to avoid.

Well, Amber Rogers was no pushover. And if Jensen Fortune Chesterfield thought he'd met someone different from his usual fare, he didn't know the half of it. Because he'd more than met his match.

***

We hope you enjoyed this sneak peek at
A ROYAL FORTUNE by USA TODAY bestselling
author Judy Duarte, the first book in the brand-new
Harlequin® Special Edition continuity
THE FORTUNES OF TEXAS:
COWBOY COUNTRY!

On sale in January 2015, wherever
Harlequin Special Edition books and ebooks are sold.

Copyright © 2015 by Judy Duarte

HSEEXP1214

REQUEST YOUR FREE BOOKS!

2 FREE NOVELS
FROM THE ROMANCE COLLECTION
PLUS 2 FREE GIFTS!

YES! Please send me 2 FREE novels from the Romance Collection and my 2 FREE gifts (gifts are worth about $10). After receiving them, if I don't wish to receive any more books, I can return the shipping statement marked "cancel." If I don't cancel, I will receive 4 brand-new novels every month and be billed just $6.24 per book in the U.S. or $6.74 per book in Canada. That's a savings of at least 22% off the cover price. It's quite a bargain! Shipping and handling is just 50¢ per book in the U.S. and 75¢ per book in Canada.* I understand that accepting the 2 free books and gifts places me under no obligation to buy anything. I can always return a shipment and cancel at any time. Even if I never buy another book, the two free books and gifts are mine to keep forever.

194/394 MDN F4XY

Name   (PLEASE PRINT)

Address   Apt. #

City   State/Prov.   Zip/Postal Code

Signature (if under 18, a parent or guardian must sign)

Mail to the Harlequin® Reader Service:
IN U.S.A.: P.O. Box 1867, Buffalo, NY 14240-1867
IN CANADA: P.O. Box 609, Fort Erie, Ontario L2A 5X3

Want to try two free books from another line?
Call 1-800-873-8635 or visit www.ReaderService.com.

* Terms and prices subject to change without notice. Prices do not include applicable taxes. Sales tax applicable in N.Y. Canadian residents will be charged applicable taxes. Offer not valid in Quebec. This offer is limited to one order per household. Not valid for current subscribers to the Romance Collection or the Romance/Suspense Collection. All orders subject to credit approval. Credit or debit balances in a customer's account(s) may be offset by any other outstanding balance owed by or to the customer. Please allow 4 to 6 weeks for delivery. Offer available while quantities last.

Your Privacy—The Harlequin® Reader Service is committed to protecting your privacy. Our Privacy Policy is available online at www.ReaderService.com or upon request from the Harlequin Reader Service.

We make a portion of our mailing list available to reputable third parties that offer products we believe may interest you. If you prefer that we not exchange your name with third parties, or if you wish to clarify or modify your communication preferences, please visit us at www.ReaderService.com/consumerchoice or write to us at Harlequin Reader Service Preference Service, P.O. Box 9062, Buffalo, NY 14269. Include your complete name and address.

ROM13R

New York Times **bestselling author**

RAEANNE THAYNE

welcomes you to Haven Point, a small town full of big surprises that are both merry and bright.

NEW YORK TIMES BESTSELLING AUTHOR

RAEANNE THAYNE

SNOW ANGEL COVE

"Thayne has a knack for capturing those emotions that come from the heart." —*RT Book Reviews*

Nothing short of a miracle can restore Eliza Hayward's Christmas cheer. The job she pinned her dreams on has gone up in smoke—literally—and now she's stuck in an unfamiliar, if breathtaking, small town. Precariously close to being destitute, Eliza needs a hero, but she's not expecting one who almost runs her down with his car!

Rescuing Eliza is pure instinct for tech genius Aidan Caine. At first, putting the renovation of his lakeside guest lodge in Eliza's hands assuages his guilt—until he sees how quickly he could fall for her. Having focused solely on his business for years, he never knew what his life was missing before Eliza, but now he's willing to risk his heart on a yuletide romance that could lead to forever.

Available now wherever books are sold.

Be sure to connect with us at:

Harlequin.com/Newsletters
Facebook.com/HarlequinBooks
Twitter.com/HarlequinBooks

HARLEQUIN® HQN™
www.Harlequin.com

PHRAT907

HARLEQUIN®

SPECIAL EDITION

Life, Love and Family

Life, love and **family**! These
contemporary romances will strike a
chord with you as the heroines juggle
life and relationships on their way to
true love. Romance is for life, and
these stories show that every chapter in
a relationship has its **challenges** and
delights and that love can be renewed
with each turn of the page!

**When you're with family,
you're home!**

www.Harlequin.com

HALOHSE1014-2